About the Author

Penny Parkes survived a Convent education largely thanks to a ready supply of inappropriate novels and her passion for writing and languages.

She studied International Management in Bath and Germany, before gaining experience with the BBC. She then set up an independent Film Location Agency and spent many happy years organising shoots for film, television and advertising – thereby ensuring that she was never short of travel opportunities, freelance writing projects or entertaining anecdotes.

Penny now lives in the Cotswolds with her husband, two children and an excitable puppy with a fondness for Post-its. She will often be found plotting epic train journeys through the Alps, baking gluten-free goodies or attempting to reach an elusive state of organisation.

Her novel *Out of Practice*, the first book in the Larkford series, won the RNA Romantic Comedy of the Year Award in 2017.

Follow Penny on Twitter: @CotswoldPenny

Penny Parkes

Practice

makes

Perfect

**SIMON &
SCHUSTER**

London · New York · Sydney · Toronto · New Delhi

A CBS COMPANY

First published in Great Britain by Simon & Schuster UK Ltd, 2017
A CBS COMPANY

1 3 5 7 9 10 8 6 4 2

Simon & Schuster UK Ltd
1st Floor
222 Gray's Inn Road
London WC1X 8HB

www.simonandschuster.co.uk

Simon & Schuster Australia, Sydney
Simon & Schuster India, New Delhi

A CIP catalogue record for this book
is available from the British Library

Paperback ISBN: 978-1-4711-5306-8
eBook ISBN: 978-1-4711-5307-5
eAudio ISBN: 978-1-4711-6608-2

Typeset in the UK by M Rules
Printed and bound by CPI Group (UK) Ltd, Croydon, CR0 4YY

For Willow –
who lay beside me as I wrote

Practice
makes
Perfect

Your mind is the garden
Your thoughts are the seeds
The harvest can either be flowers or weeds

WILLIAM WORDSWORTH

Chapter 1

Holly couldn't help but smile as she stepped out into the glorious sunshine and saw the Market Place of Larkford humming with activity. There was an excitable holiday atmosphere in the valley today and she knew exactly who to blame. Taffy Jones and Dan Carter, her partners at The Practice, stood beside her, blinking in the brightness and running their hands tentatively over their newly shaven heads.

'You look fine,' she reassured them, putting aside her own misgivings that their fund-raising efforts were in grave danger of going too far.

Her young twins were not so tactful.

'You look silly now,' Ben said very seriously.

'I can actually see your brain,' said Tom, wrinkling up his freckled nose in mock disgust.

Taffy just smiled indulgently, taking Holly by the hand and holding her gaze, 'It'll grow back,' he said, leaning in for a kiss. 'If you hate it, I mean.' A rare flash of vulnerability showed in his eyes, as though his confidence might have disappeared, along with his chaotic, tousled mop of chestnut hair.

Lucy, their perky, yet deceptively ferocious receptionist, wandered over to join them, shaking a large plastic bucket with the legend Health in the Community emblazoned on the side. 'They *really* weren't joking about the size of your head, were they, Dr Carter?' she joked. 'Shall we maybe fashion you a hat to make it look bigger? More, you know, normal-sized?'

Dan just laughed, well accustomed to their teasing. 'Or you could get people to pledge even more cash, to make up for my emotional angst?'

'Leave it with me,' she said in a determined voice that made Holly fear for the contents of the residents' wallets, as Lucy's bobbing ponytail disappeared into the thick of the crowd.

It had not been your average afternoon at The Kingsley Arms, but there was no denying that it had all been in a good cause. The four partners at The Practice had been working their socks off to re-launch their Health in the Community programme, with each fund-raising idea becoming more and more extreme. There had simply been too many youngsters through their doors of late with totally avoidable health problems – it really seemed as though the very least they could do was to put aside their personal pride and, in Taffy's words, 'take one for the team'.

Only last month, Holly had screamed the whole way down Larkford church tower, having committed to a sponsored abseil in a brief moment of madness. The photos of her bottom in fluorescent leggings, outlined against the beautiful Cotswold stone backdrop, had been worthy of their own full-colour photo spread in the local paper and Holly still got wolf-whistles whenever she donned those self-same leggings to go jogging. It was rather a dent in her professional pride that her bum was now seemingly more recognisable than her face, no matter how much Taffy and Dan reassured her it was for all the right reasons.

As Holly looked around the vibrant town of Larkford, at the huddles of friends and neighbours, even she could see their point (although she still had plans to buy new leggings at the very next opportunity). There were truly very few places on earth that Holly would rather be and, as the afternoon sunshine illuminated the swathes of woodland sweeping down the hillside around them, she felt instantly calm and at home, even as the boys pulled on her hands excitedly.

Today, the entire Market Place was crammed with beautiful stalls, artfully stacked wooden crates and more bunting than was probably healthy. The pastel buildings that lined the streets were almost friendly with their open frontage, sash windows and sweeping rooftops. It was a picture-postcard scene and Holly wished she had remembered to bring her camera.

The new initiative by the Parish Council to give local producers their own dedicated venue each week was clearly paying off, as half the town and just as many tourists had turned out to stock up on gourmet salamis, seasonal veg and the odd jar of saucy pickle.

'We should have realised sooner that Lucy would be the perfect fund-raiser,' Taffy said, watching as she charmed a donation out of a notoriously tight-fisted farmer.

'Maybe it's the ponytail,' wondered Holly, rather in awe of Lucy's skills in raising money without risking life and limb. Taking no for an answer was apparently not an option, as the petite blonde worked her way through the queue at the bakery stall, gathering donations at every step.

'Or the steely determination,' said Dan. 'Have you ever actually *tried* saying no to her?'

Holly and Taffy briefly caught each other's gaze – Dan was gaining a reputation as a bit of a softie at work, utterly worn out from all the emotional wrangling at home with his girlfriend Julia Channing, the fourth partner at The Practice. Her ambition of late seemed to have eclipsed all other considerations and poor Dan was bearing the brunt of it.

Holly looked around, trying to spot her amongst the crowd. These days it wasn't all that difficult, because wherever Julia went, a small huddle of men followed her, weighed down with television cameras, microphones and, more often than not, a clipboard bearing release slips for signature. It was fair to say that Julia's role in the reality health show *Doctor In The House* had placed them all under a lot of strain.

True to form, Julia was at the quieter end of the Market Place doing a piece to camera and Holly was in no doubt that Taffy and Dan's hairy heroics would have been captured on B-roll for use in the programme – whether they liked it or not.

As Taffy and the boys tried out their usual routine of trying to inveigle as many different samples as possible from each of the stalls, she stopped to buy a few crusty rolls for their traditional weekend bacon butties.

Pru Hartley from the baker's began plying the twins with biscuits and Holly didn't even have to ask to know that Pru would have remembered that Ben was on a strict dairy-free diet. The residents of Larkford had simply absorbed Holly and her boys into their midst and were more nurturing and supportive than any family that Holly had ever known.

She gave Pru a hug in greeting and looked her up and down. 'You're seeming a bit more sprightly there, Madam.'

Pru took a stiff little bow, her recent hip-replacement having put her out of action for longer than she'd anticipated. 'I think we're actually making progress now. The stairs are still a complete pain in the arse, but thank God we've had my niece down to help, or we wouldn't have coped at the bakery. Feisty little madam she is, but she's got us all organised. Shame she's off to Bristol really . . .'

Holly couldn't help but agree. Although she'd yet to meet Pru's niece, Alice, it was clear that she'd worked wonders getting Pru's recovery back on track after a shaky start. Young, dynamic and newly qualified, she was heading down to Bristol to join a GP practice in one of the trickier parts of the city. It was just a shame they didn't have a vacancy here – Alice Walker sounded as though she might be the answer to all Holly's prayers.

In a flash of 'use it or lose it' mentality, their patient roster had almost doubled overnight after their successful Save The Practice campaign last year. If only they had the staffing to keep up with the increased demand, it might almost be considered a triumph.

Pocketing her change and swinging an aromatic bagful of freshly baked rolls over her arm, Holly quickly found herself pulled into conversation.

Holly seemed to bump into so many of her patients at the Farmers' Market, that she'd often wondered whether to simply admit defeat and hang up her shingle amongst the aubergines and goat's cheese. She'd advised on cough mixture dosage, nappy rash and a sore throat by the time she made it to the coffee wagon. It was partly her own fault, she conceded. It felt mean-spirited to deny support to her friends and neighbours just because it was her day off, but sometimes . . .

Her face broke into a smile as one of the worst offenders hove into view. A car park consultation was the closest the Major had ever got to visiting any of the doctors at The Practice, since he'd taken on a bet with an old friend over a rare bottle of whisky. In the entire time since Holly had joined the team, the Major had never once made an appearance in their consulting rooms and defiantly refused to do so before his old friend had surrendered and consulted a physician first. With a bottle of the legendary *Black Bowmore* whisky up for grabs, they were both taking this bet ridiculously seriously.

Still, Holly actually had rather a soft spot for the old boy and she willingly accepted a whiskery kiss on each cheek from the Major and complimented him on his suntan. 'So,' she asked, 'how was the honeymoon?'

The Major's weathered face creased into a grin, 'It was top notch, thank you, Dr Graham. Marion even caught her first salmon and there's no way you could top that. Over the moon, she was. Few more lessons from me and she'll be just grand.'

Holly smiled at the mental picture of the blousy Marion up to her thighs in a Scottish river, rather than lying on the sun-drenched beach she'd been hoping for. Still, it sounded like they'd had a lovely time. The Major and Marion had enjoyed a twilight, whirlwind romance – falling in love whilst falling out over a sausage roll. It may not have been the most auspicious of beginnings for some, but the Major had been pining away for a sparring partner and Marion Gains from the local supermarket had been the unlikely candidate that surprised them all.

'No Marion this afternoon?' Holly asked, looking around. The Major shrugged. 'Not today. She's back on the checkout already. Can't stop her,' he said affectionately. 'Had no idea I'd married a career woman.'

Holly silently applauded Marion's decision to maintain a little independence – where would Larkford be without their local store and Marion's encyclopaedic knowledge of everyone's comings and goings?

The Major blew his nose noisily into an enormous spotty handkerchief, making his little terrier, Grover, jump. 'Think I may have caught a chill on the river bank, you know. Best pop to The Kingsley Arms for a hot toddy, just to be on the safe side, don't you think.'

Holly waved, as he adroitly made his way between the stalls, making a beeline towards Teddy Kingsley's pub and the remnants of the fund-raising party that was now spreading out into the pub gardens.

Taffy and the boys reappeared at her side, each clutching a bag of delicacies from the sweetie stall. She couldn't help noticing that Taffy's bag of sweets was considerably bigger. He really did eat like a teenager, but it seemed to make no dent in his otherwise impressive physique.

'Thought we might have a movie-night, Holls. I've got supplies and big plans for exhausting the nippers with a quick game of rugby. What do you say?'

Cassie Holland, local busybody and self-nominated arbiter of parenting lore, tutted loudly as she sailed past. Whereas Holly had learned to ignore her jibes, Taffy was still new to her judgemental ways. 'Was there something you wanted to say there, Cassie?' he said, his voice dangerously sweet.

She stopped in her tracks, unaccustomed to being challenged and clearly rather thrown. She spluttered for a moment or two, while Taffy stood patiently, one eyebrow raised and clearly awaiting a response. She nervously adjusted her poncho, before giving in to the urge to have her say. She nodded toward the bags of sweets and sighed, 'It's just hardly setting a good example is it, Dr Jones? All that refined sugar?' She gave a mock shudder and, seemingly oblivious to her own son's efforts to demolish the cake stall behind her, carried on, 'Since you're not a father yourself, you probably don't even realise how much processed sugar can affect a child's development.'

Taffy nodded, clearly riled, but trying hard not to laugh, as Cassie lectured on and her darling Tarquin – deprived as he was of anything that didn't seem to involve agave nectar and honey at home – spun in circles and grabbed handfuls of flapjacks from the stall and stuffed them into his mouth, much to the stallholder's disgust and everyone else's amusement.

Cassie however was on a roll. 'It's quite a different thing, Dr Jones, being a role model to a child, rather than just *playing* at being dad, you know.'

It was a step too far and they all knew it. Holly remained silent, not trusting herself to speak but confident that Taffy was more than capable of handling himself. The bloody cheek of the woman!

It was par for the course in such a tight-knit community that there would be occasional disagreements and scuffles, but to be fair, Cassie did seem to cause a disproportionate amount of upset. Holly had learned the hard way to pick her battles with care. It was quite a skill to take the rough with the smooth in Larkford, but one that was infinitely worth fostering and Taffy, to give him his due, could use sympathy to better effect than anyone Holly had ever met.

'Oh Cassie,' he said, tilting his head to one side, an edge

of steel creeping into his voice, 'are you having trouble at home again? You don't need to deflect, you know. You can just say . . .'

She scowled at him in frustration and, abruptly yanking Tarquin's sticky hand away from yet another flapjack, she flounced away between the market stalls, clearly offended.

'Seriously? What *is* her problem?' Taffy muttered furiously, his brow furrowing in unfamiliar irritation.

Her jibe had obviously hit home with him far more than Holly had realised, but then that was Cassie's unique skill. She had an innate ability to find your Achilles heel and hone in like an Exocet missile – never one to miss an opportunity to guilt Holly over the prevalence of un-organic, alcoholic or just plain naughty-but-nice treats in her supermarket shop, or indeed to pinpoint Holly and Taffy's concerns about how to best integrate him into the twins' lives.

Holly took Taffy's hand and they walked home together, the boys weaving around their legs like excitable spaniels, alert to the promise of a throw-about with a rugby ball and already practically fizzing after a handful of sweets. Holly chose not to point out that Cassie may have a point about the sweets' effect on her normally manageable children, but then they'd be running around the garden soon enough, so what did it really matter?

'I don't know how you women put up with Cassie Holland,' Taffy was still grumbling. 'Interfering old . . .'

Holly stopped him with a kiss. 'Don't let her ruin your afternoon. Anyone who's that judgemental probably has issues of her own to deal with. Besides, it comes with the territory: from the minute you get pregnant, everybody starts having their say about how you should be raising your children. You just learn to tune it out.'

He sighed. 'Well, you're ahead of me on that one, Holls. Everybody keeps telling me how to behave around the twins and it's starting to really piss me off.'

Holly pulled back a little, the ever-present protective part of her brain flinching at his tone and slipping, by default, into siege mentality – an unfortunate legacy of her failed marriage to Milo.

Taffy, however, was quick to qualify his statement, 'I mean, I want to build my own relationship with them gradually – on our terms. They've had enough change this past year, haven't they? The last thing they need is me marching in saying, "Just call me Dad"- don't you think?' he added in a voice that was tentative and heart-felt.

Holly smiled, hiding the relief that surged through her and loving that he'd given their feelings so much thought. 'I think, just keep doing what you're doing. The boys still can't quite believe their luck that you'll go outside and throw a ball about with them.'

He shrugged. 'I think that says more about you-know-who's shortcomings on the parenting front than it does about any prowess on my part though, Holly.'

She had to concede he made a valid point – the twins were just in Seventh Heaven having a man in the house who was prepared to put down his newspaper and engage with them, let alone the den-building, ball-throwing, river-swimming, finger-painting gamut that was a weekend with Taffy Jones at the helm.

As they strolled out of the Market Place and into the network of small residential streets that spread out like a cobweb into the valley, they passed Lizzie's Georgian townhouse and stopped on autopilot, as the twins clamoured to collect Eric, the barmy Labradoodle that Holly had on a 'puppy time-share' agreement with her best friend.

Holly paused, undecided.

'Do you think it's safe to go in?' Taffy asked, looking uncertain.

Only this morning, Lizzie had bowed out of attending the Charity Head Shaving on the basis that her house currently resembled a scene from a Ridley Scott movie: Archie had nits, Jack had the trots and little Lily was under close observation for a possible parasite infestation. And of course her husband Will had chosen – chosen, Lizzie had stressed– this particular weekend to be away on business. Holly had already swung by earlier with supplies from the Pharmacy but had chickened out and left them on the doorstep. Anything that wriggled, bit or hatched was way outside her comfort zone, even as a doctor.

As the boys took matters into their own hands and hammered on the door, Taffy and Holly looked at each other aghast, before each grabbing the nearest twin. 'Do *not* go in,' Holly admonished, taking a few steps back.

The glossy front door creaked open an inch and Lizzie's voice echoed through from the hallway, 'Are you mental, woman? Save yourself and run ... Words cannot begin to describe what I've been ... What?' She disappeared from view as she shouted back through to the kitchen, 'Well aim for the bowl then!' Her small, harassed face appeared at the crack of the door again, just as Eric decided that enough was enough and pushed his way out, leather lead dangling in his mouth and a hopeful expression on his tufty blonde face.

'Shall we take him back with us? You look like you've got your hands full,' Holly said, carefully making sure to keep Ben clamped to her legs.

'Could you,' replied Lizzie, 'and if I haven't emerged in a day or two, send in some gin. Sod mother's ruin – at this point it might be the last known means of survival. You did say it had medicinal properties, didn't you, Holls?'

Taffy chuckled. 'Splash of tonic and you'll be sorted on the malaria front anyway … Besides, gin's practically an antibiotic.'

Lizzie just shook her head and went to close the door. 'Just keep an eye on Eric, won't you? He appears to be going through … well … a bit of a phase.' The door clicked shut and Holly was left none the wiser. Eric just sat there, lead now dropped at Holly's feet, doing his best love-me-love-me-love-me face.

'Come on, Tiger,' Taffy said as he bent down to attach the lead. 'You can come and help me wear out these little tykes.'

To be fair to Taffy and Eric, it had taken a lot longer to wear out the twins than either of them had foreseen. Even Holly was struggling to keep her eyes open for the end of the movie and Taffy was dozing beside her, with Eric firmly wedged under his feet.

Even as she felt her eyes drifting closed, the sense of utter contentment only increased as she felt the weight of Taffy's arm settle around her shoulders and pull her in to his side.

'You snore,' Taffy murmured drowsily, affection laced throughout his words as he kissed the top of her head.

'So do you,' Holly retorted lightly, pulling him in closer and snuggling down. At that moment, she didn't care that it was late and there were jobs to be done, she just wanted to stay here, in Taffy's arms feeling loved and appreciated and desirable.

As Taffy's hand circled on her waist with gentle insistence

and his arm tightened around her, she couldn't help but be amazed by her own physical response and how he made her feel. She almost laughed now to think that all her qualms about what gorgeous, athletic Taffy might make of her stretch-marks and C-section scar had almost sabotaged their relationship before it had even begun.

It was fair to say that she needn't have been concerned. Over the last year, Holly and Taffy had managed to forge the kind of loving partnership that some couples spent years of marriage trying to create or emulate. But still, Holly was aware that Taffy sometimes struggled with the constant chaos that was part of the package when four-year-old twins were involved (having conveniently forgotten that she, their loving mother, sometimes did too).

Right now though, his mind was clearly focused on something a little less PG. His hand slid up under her t-shirt and she batted away all other thoughts, letting herself just enjoy the moment. He leaned in and kissed his way along her collarbone and, as she realised just exactly how much she wanted this, her breath became fast and shallow.

She stroked Taffy's head as they kissed, the new soft peach fuzz nestling intimately under her touch.

'I've been wanting to do this all afternoon,' she whispered, as she slowly unbuttoned his shirt.

He smiled wickedly and was on his feet in moments, scooping her up off the sofa. 'Allow me?'

The romantic gesture was a little undermined by tripping over Eric, some Fireman Sam paraphernalia and then clipping Holly's head on the doorframe as they made their way upstairs. By the time they reached the bedroom doorway, all talk of domesticity was forgotten and their kisses had grown increasingly urgent.

Finding two small boys sprawled out on their bed was not really the sight they'd been hoping for. Eric bounding noisily up the stairs behind them with Holly's bra in his mouth was hardly ideal either. But whatever else they'd had in mind, Holly thought, at least they were able to laugh about it together.

Chapter 2

Holly rolled over in bed and sighed, one eye blearily registering the flashing red digits on the clock beside her. Less than
two hours until a waiting room full of patients required her
undivided and professional attention.

She yawned and wondered when it had become so much
harder to get out of bed. She couldn't ignore the fact that it
might just have coincided with Taffy's gradual 'moving in'
programme and that her brand-new king-sized bed was now
somewhere that she actually wanted to linger.

The phone trilled loudly beside her and they exchanged
glances – phone calls at this hour in the morning rarely boded
well with two doctors in the house. Avoiding their regular
game of Rock-Paper-Scissors, Holly leaned over and picked
up the handset, as the twins and Eric burst through the door.

'Elsie!' she exclaimed in delight, as the crackling connection cleared and she could just about make out the
distinguished voice at the other end. 'How's Borneo? Have
you adopted an orang-utan yet?'

'Don't be so utterly ridiculous, darling, I couldn't possibly
keep an orang-utan in Larkford,' Elsie replied, taking her
question completely seriously. 'What's all that noise in the
background?'

Holly pushed back the duvet and walked through to the bathroom – often the only quiet place to take a phone call in the whole house – 'Can you hear me now? It was a bit chaotic in the bedroom ...'

Elsie chuckled, her sense of the double entendre still rather well-developed despite her advancing years. 'Well, I won't keep you long, my darling. I just wanted to tell you I'm heading home.'

'That's wonderful news,' said Holly, who had been missing the indomitable Elsie far more than she'd been letting on. A small smile flitted across her face, thinking how proud Elsie would be to see all the changes she'd wrought in her absence. Of course, they chatted on Skype from time to time, as Elsie's surprise fling with '80s crooner Barry O'Connor seemed to go from strength to strength and they took 'one last turn around the world' together. Cheesy, yes, but also undeniably romantic – assuming you ignored the vaguely gag-inducing thought of what Lizzie referred to as Saggy Sex. 'I'm so pleased.'

'Hmm, well – let's see if you still feel that way when I'm under your feet every day and being generally geriatric.'

Holly paused at Elsie's tone, the undercurrent of negativity so wholly and completely out of character as to raise an enormous red flag. 'Is everything okay?' she asked.

A humming pause crackled along the airwaves and Holly had no way of knowing whether the connection was to blame. 'I'm flying back next week and I've a lovely little man collecting me at Heathrow. We can have a drink and catch up once I'm home. No point clogging up the airwaves.' She stopped for a moment and then ventured, 'I've rather missed you, Holly. Do tell that delectable Taffy that he might need to share your attentions for a while, won't you?' She gave an echoing laugh and Holly was concerned to note an edge of hysteria quavering at the edges.

'I certainly will and . . .'

The phone call ended with a decisive click, Elsie's habit of not bothering to say goodbye on phone calls leaving Holly on the hop as usual. She wandered back into the bedroom to find that Taffy and the boys had dozed off back to sleep again.

As Larkford's resident celebrity and Holly's adopted matri-arch, Elsie Townsend had a lot to answer for around here. Her tenacious drive to encourage any young woman to live to her best potential had spread ripples throughout their little com-munity. She was a phenomenally influential and incredibly generous soul and Holly had missed her terribly.

Elsie's Life Lessons had in fact changed Holly's world beyond measure. She was becoming adept at picking her battles and her moments, and the dreaded *should* was still banished from her lexicon and now also that of her children. It was also, she'd discovered, *so* much easier to ask for what she wanted, now that she'd figured out what that actually was.

Speaking of which, she walked over to the bed and kissed Taffy's newly shorn head gently. 'Wake up, Sleeping Beauty, we're running a bit late. And I think Elsie and Barry might have fallen out – she's coming home.'

Taffy opened one bleary eye. 'Does that mean you're going to get all feisty again?' he asked.

Holly grinned. 'There is every chance.'

He snuggled down into the duvet some more, refusing to admit that it was time to get up, 'Brilliant,' he said sleepily. 'I love feisty Holly.'

The next phase of morning madness swung quickly into action. Having spent ten minutes searching under every bed and cupboard for Ben's mislaid trainers, they were finally unearthed in the laundry basket. 'Because they were dirty, Mummy.' Indisputable logic, to be fair, thought Holly as she reflexively checked her watch.

It was muddly, disordered, wonderful chaos and Holly loved it. Gone were the days of tiptoeing around Milo and his sensitivities. Now there was a genuine feeling of working towards the same goal – even if right now that goal of leaving the house on time with all four of them dressed in an appropriate manner might seem a tad unrealistic.

Tom sat on the bottom stair stubbornly refusing any help as he concentrated incredibly hard on doing up his new 'big boy' laces. Ben was determinedly taking everything out of his backpack in the search for his favourite Transformer and Taffy – well, Taffy seemed to be sporting reading glasses, a cravat and very possibly a beauty spot.

Holly raised an eyebrow. 'Well hello, Handsome, did I miss something?'

Taffy looked bashful for a moment. 'No. It's just a silly . . .'

Holly managed to disguise the relieved smile that threatened to erupt. All this good behaviour for Julia's camera crew had been putting rather a dampener on Dan and Taffy's natural exuberance.

Taffy folded a handkerchief into his jacket pocket, carefully smoothing the silk into a perfect triangle. 'Today's challenge,' he said, nonchalantly, 'will be Face Buckaroo.' He was trying to look casual, but Holly could tell he was secretly loving it. 'Dan's idea – you have to keep adding things to your face during a conversation until somebody notices. Or taking them away. It's scientific research really, on how unobservant we all are.'

'Brilliant,' she said with gusto, 'I do love a bit of science in the morning.'

Taffy leaned in and kissed her firmly, barely even objecting to the fact that one twin was wrapped around his leg and Eric was chewing his shoelaces as he did so. As with everything else, he just took it all in his stride. 'You can join in if you like – I've a fake nose and a wig still up for grabs? Loser cooks supper . . .'

With the twins duly delivered to pre-school, Holly caught her breath as she walked around to The Practice. Even at this hour on a summer's morning, the little town was bustling with energy and the sunlight danced along the River Lark. She smiled, happy to slow down for a moment and let Eric sniff his way along the verges. The Practice looked so welcoming, with its warm Cotswold stone and little red-brick 'eyebrows' over each window and some days, Holly had to pinch herself that she actually got to work there.

'No dramas last night then,' said Grace, their resourceful Practice Manager, as she walked into Holly's consulting room with an armful of paperwork and handed Holly a printed copy of her morning patient list. 'I suppose we should be grateful for small mercies. Although you won't be thanking me when you see your ten o'clock.' She perched on the edge of Holly's desk, enjoying that rare moment of peace before the phones started ringing off the hook and the front door seemed to be in perpetual motion. A cry from the car park rang out suddenly through the stillness and Grace was on the move before Holly's brain even caught up.

Cassie Holland stood outside the main entrance, tears streaking her face, clutching her son Tarquin, as he held out his hand in front of him, as though it might detonate at any moment. Holly swallowed hard; the sight of a ten-inch chisel protruding through the poor boy's hand was enough to turn even the strongest of stomachs. She flicked a glance at Grace, the message clearly communicated without words.

'Well, that looks incredibly uncomfortable there, Tarquin,' said Holly calmly, taking care to keep her tone even and upbeat as she ushered them hastily inside. 'Let's pop you through to my room while Grace is calling an ambulance for you. I think you might even get to hear the sirens today, if you're really lucky.' She looked up at Grace, only to see her shaking her head and mouthing 'twenty minutes'.

'And I think we'll just bandage that poor hand up for you while you wait.' Holly turned to Cassie. 'We need to make sure that the chisel stays in place. It's important, Cassie, because the chisel is actually stemming the worst of the bleeding at the moment.'

Cassie nodded dumbly, sinking down into a chair as they walked through the waiting room, unable to go any further or formulate the slightest reply. Tarquin promptly sat down beside her, white-faced and on the verge of tears. His uncharacteristic quietness actually worried Holly more than anything else. Holly's attempts to convince him out of the chair seemed to be failing and she was only too grateful when Taffy came through to see what all the fuss was about. He beat an immediate retreat and returned moments later with a complete and sterile First Aid tray from the Nurses' Station.

'Crikey, Tarquin,' he said, 'you've been in the wars this morning and it's not even nine o'clock.' Seamlessly, Holly and Taffy worked together to bind the chisel and the wound in a sterile bandage, each of them aware that one false move could trigger more bleeding. They certainly didn't want him moving around until it was stabilised.

'He was working on a woodwork project,' said Cassie abruptly. 'He's home schooled.' She glared at Taffy, even as he diligently taped the dressing in place and Holly held it firm.

'Don't judge me!' she said, her voice cracking. 'I can see you, you know, judging me as a parent ...'

Taffy sat back on his heels and calmly held her gaze. 'Cassie,' he said gently, 'I wouldn't dream of it.'

Her face flooded with colour, her own conscience clearly reminding her that she herself had not been so magnanimous. She abruptly turned her attention to Holly. 'Thank you, Dr Graham.'

'It's my pleasure,' Holly said, as she rose to her feet and signalled through to Grace for an update on the ambulance. Dan ambled in from the car park, ear-buds in place and demolishing his morning croissant. He frowned at the sight that greeted him.

'You've been busy,' he said, ever the master of understatement, taking in the signs of disarray in the waiting room and Grace fidgeting on hold.

'Ten minutes,' she said to nobody in particular. 'They're asking for a sit rep?'

Holly nodded. 'We're looking good. But don't let them de-prioritise this, okay?' She turned to Dan. 'Morning. You've missed all the fun,' she said quietly, pinching a bit of his croissant. 'It was looking a little hairy there for a moment.'

It was the hot metallic smell suddenly flooding her senses that made Holly look down and in that moment, time seemed to expand and contract around her. She took in the aghast expression on Tarquin's face and the chisel that he had clearly seen fit to pull out of his hand.

So much blood ...

Holly ran from the room, as Cassie gaped after her, mouthing mutely in disbelief at her abandonment. But only seconds later Holly was back, deftly inserting a cannula into Tarquin's other arm for a saline drip, even as Taffy and Dan worked quickly together to pack the wound and apply a basic tourniquet. The whole time they were working, Dan was murmuring a small, soothing running commentary to Tarquin and Cassie. He seemed to slip so easily back into his army training and it was apparent that his field skills were still second to none: Holly had never felt more reassured by his presence.

She began feeding figures back to Grace on the telephone – in such a small child, a relatively small blood loss could trigger a hypovolemic shock and Holly was monitoring his pulse and blood pressure as though his life depended on it; she tried not to think about the fact that it probably did. She knew perfectly well that, by the time she registered a drop in BP, it would be a horribly ominous sign.

She barely batted an eyelid as Cassie swayed away from them, the sight of blood from her own child too much for her subconscious to take, as she slid down in the chair. Taffy hollered for support from the gaggle of nurses arriving to start their routine shift and stunned into silence by the scene in front of them.

Jade and Jason quickly swept Cassie into the recovery position and checked her vitals.

'I'm getting rapid breathing here,' called Holly. Taffy knelt back down beside her, oblivious to the blood seeping into his trousers.

'Pale, sweaty, cold hands . . . How long, Grace?' he called.

Even calm, unflappable Grace was on the verge of tears now. 'Eight minutes,' she managed.

There was a blast of cool air on Holly's back as the door opened and closed behind her. She felt, rather than saw, Julia appear at her side.

'Lucy,' Julia said calmly. 'Could you draw the blinds and ask the patients to wait in the foyer?' The morning was proceeding without them, as the four doctors used everything in their arsenal to stabilise this little boy. In that moment, it didn't matter that he was a rude and disrespectful little tyke; it didn't matter that he'd actually pulled the chisel out himself – it was their job, their calling, just to keep him alive. Taffy rigged up another drip – it was time for emergency measures, but the plasma they needed was still speeding towards them down the A36.

'Is the mum a type-match?' asked Julia. 'Does anybody know?' Her efficiency to even consider a real-time donation was true to form. 'Jade? Find out,' she said abruptly. 'It doesn't take two of you to handle a fainter.'

Holly watched as Julia deftly supported Dan in applying pressure to the double-sided wound. She noticed that they didn't even speak, as they manoeuvred around each other in close proximity, and Julia placed minuscule stitches around the sterile wadding to hold Tarquin steady for transport.

'Three minutes!' called Grace, and Taffy instantly began to assemble the team for maximum accessibility. Jason shepherded a blinking Cassie to the side and the double access doors were thrown open. Taffy gently took the receiver from Grace's shaking hand. 'Dr Taffy Jones here, can you patch me through?' He spoke clearly and firmly to the paramedics, even as the echoing sirens could be heard from the Market Place. 'Holly, it's a Blood on Board rig – they've got O-neg. Can you get him prepped?'

'Already on it,' she called.

Dan looked up. 'Tell them I've done a light tourniquet to minimise structural damage and we've been pressuring the puncture site. Ask them if they've an inflatable device?'

Julia shook her head. 'That's military kit, Dan. They're not going to have one in a local ambulance.'

He glared at the offending wound in front of him. 'Well maybe they bloody well should,' he said grimly, as the paramedics dashed in through the doors and the team began the process of handing over their patient: Holly with relief, Julia with a litany of instructions and Dan with obvious reluctance. True to form, it was Taffy who shepherded Cassie into the ambulance beside her son, all personal acrimony forgotten, in his role as their family GP.

Chapter 3

By lunchtime, a sense of unease still spread throughout The Practice. So often the team's interaction with their patients was limited to the mundane and routine, that this shocking and dramatic turn of events had shaken them all. Even Dan, who had no doubt seen so much worse in his army days, was quietly brooding over a cup of tea. Eric, sensing a need for comfort, was curled up on his feet and, for once, Dan made no complaints about the doctors' lounge becoming Lizzie's Doggy Daycare.

He looked up as Julia leaned against the table beside him, careful to keep any hint of dog-hair away from her tailored trousers. 'Any news?'

She shook her head. 'He's still in surgery. Looks like there was quite a lot of nerve damage. Cassie's in pieces apparently.'

Dan sighed. 'Can't help thinking we got lucky, though. All of us here … No film crew recording our every move …' He watched Julia's expression carefully, waiting to see if she would switch into defensive mode, but to his surprise she just nodded.

'I'm trying not to think about what might have been, to be honest. Maybe our film-free Mondays actually *were* a good idea?'

Dan tactfully sipped his tea, choosing not to remind Julia that she'd fought them tooth and nail on that very concept. Of course, if it were up to him, then every day would be film-free, Dan thought.

Holly and Taffy walked into the lounge, chatting easily together and bearing a huge bag of doughnuts from Hartley's Bakery. 'Best cure for shock,' announced Taffy as he tore open the bag on the table and the entire team descended like locusts. Even Jade, of the teeny-tiny uniform, managed to snaffle two before her fellow nurses could stake their claim. Only Julia held back, her lips forming a moue of distaste at the unseemly scrabble for carbs and the ridiculous contest that Holly had immediately instigated, not to lick your lips whilst eating.

Eric, to give him his due, was working his puppy dog charms on everyone and quickly began to look rather sickly at all the titbits heading his way.

'Why is that dog here again, anyway?' asked Julia, as Eric brushed past her immaculate trousers leaving a trail of the doughnut sugar caught in his whiskers. 'Lizzie off on another course to find herself?'

Dan scowled at her dismissal of his cousin's attempts to find her new niche in life since quitting her high-powered job as editor of local glossy *Larkford Life*. It was true, Lizzie had explored a succession of possibilities – a long line of passing fancies – each one begun with utter conviction and an expensive course, only to fade into obscurity as Lizzie continued on her quest for a job that was emotionally rewarding, paid well and meant she could be home in time for the school run. It was no small wonder she was having trouble finding the perfect solution. But then, what did he know? He wasn't a parent and if Julia had her way, then he probably never would be.

Holly, ever the peacekeeper despite all Elsie's efforts, could obviously sense the tension and stepped in. 'You know, Jules, if you're stressed, you could always get Lizzie to rub your feet. She's been on a new reflexology course actually and I'm a rubbish guinea pig because I'm too ticklish,' she suggested.

Dan noticed Taffy give her a slow, easy smile from across the room that implied intimate knowledge of her ticklish spots and brought a pink flush to her cheeks.

Julia just rolled her eyes. 'Enough with the lovey-dovey crap, you two. You don't see me and Dan all over each other like a couple of teenagers, do you?'

'No,' said Taffy, with conviction. 'We certainly do not.'

Dan studiously avoided catching his friend's eye, knowing that Taffy found the constant bickering between them both wearing and bemusing.

Julia raised one eyebrow but beat a tactful retreat. 'Anyway, I thought Lizzie was studying floristry, wasn't she, Dan?'

Dan shrugged, seemingly un-fazed by his cousin's career carousel. 'She was. But with the early starts and the hay fever ...'

'And the crapness,' interrupted Taffy. 'Don't forget the crapness. I've never seen anyone make pink roses look quite so bloody miserable before.'

Holly laughed guiltily, as she snaffled the last of the dough-nuts; Taffy's comment, as always, was particularly astute.

Julia was laughing too, clearly amused by the notion, but there was no affection there. The undercurrents of rivalry between Lizzie and Julia were always just the right side of civil, but everybody knew that they were only really friends for Holly's sake.

But then maybe that was okay, Dan reasoned. You couldn't be best friends with everyone all the time. Even here at work, the petty disagreements could quickly escalate when essentially living and working in the Larkford bubble.

It was obviously challenging at times, and certainly a little unconventional, having the four managing partners at The Practice neatly coupled up, but mostly the four friends worked together extremely well.

Mostly.

Even if Julia's ability to micromanage did drive them all insane from time to time. As if to prove his point, she raised an eyebrow at Taffy's second doughnut, quietly pointing out the fat to sugar ratio in each delicious jammy mouthful.

But then, Dan thought, nobody ever said their plan was perfect.

He watched Julia pause mid-sentence and look at Taffy in confusion. 'Since when do you wear glasses?'

Taffy silently passed a crisp ten-pound note across to Dan, who pocketed it with a nod and a smile. 'Buckaroo,' he said.

His afternoon having passed without incident, trauma or blood loss, Dan was finally starting to relax. He'd followed up with the ICU in Bath, where young Tarquin was now stable and there was every chance he'd retain full use of the damaged hand with some fairly intensive physiotherapy. He couldn't deny that the poor boy had been on his mind pretty much constantly all day, and the relief he felt at hearing that news made him physically sag back in his chair.

His pulse leapt, automatically on high alert, as Taffy burst through the doorway, his laptop balanced precariously in one hand as he shoved the door open with the other. 'You're going to want to see this!' he said.

Dan pushed his paperwork to one side, fully expecting to see some outlandish video of a cat on a surfboard or a

water-skiing piglet. It wasn't until he saw that it was the conference feed from last night's National Healthcare Symposium
that he belatedly registered the lack of humour in Taffy's tone.
If anything, all he heard was concern and confusion.

'Just watch,' Taffy insisted, clicking on the pause button to
unfreeze the video.

'That's Harry Grant,' said Dan, recognising the small
bespectacled man who had been so influential in helping
them save The Practice the year before. He was their go-to
guy in the bureaucracy of the NHS machine and it never hurt
that he had such a soft spot for Holly when it came to calling
in the occasional favour. Even now, a year later, Harry still
referenced her selfless offer to step aside, in order to let The
Practice continue.

Harry was standing on a podium in a large auditorium,
his hair smoothed down and a striped tie making him look
incredibly uncomfortable and buttoned up. The banner across
the bottom of the screen scrolled slowly, forcing Dan to read
aloud in instalments, 'Harry Grant – NHS South West –
The Importance of Evolving and Symbiotic Relationships in
Primary Care.' Dan looked up at his friend. 'Well, what the
hell does *that* mean?'

Taffy shrugged. 'Damned if I know, but here, this is the bit
you need to see ...' He clicked on the little icon to increase
the volume and held up his hand to stay Dan's questions. 'Just
listen.'

'Well, to answer your question, Derek,' Harry Grant said in
his nasal voice, the distortion from the microphone making it
hard to make out his exact words, 'I *do* believe there is a better
way. A hierarchy in General Practice creates division – by
necessity, there have to be leaders and followers. In my experience, some of the best ideas and input don't always come

from CEOs, Senior Partners or indeed the GPs themselves. I would like to encourage a wider forum – a more collaborative style of management.'

The camera panned around to where 'Derek' – whoever he may be – looked flushed and well-fed in an expensive suit that strained to accommodate his bulk. He had senior management written all over him.

'It's all very well speaking in generalities, Harry, but it's just not practical, is it? You'd be letting the lunatics run the asylum. Let's be honest, we applaud your ideals, but realities must weigh in. You can't seriously expect us to fund a research project on a large scale just because you've dreamed up a management concept you "think" might work.' He was patronising in the extreme and Dan, who had never even met the bloke, took an instant dislike to him. He could already see that this was the kind of guy who would loudly endorse cutting costs in community care, whilst happily charging his lobster dinner on expenses.

'Twat!' said Dan with feeling.

'Keep watching,' Taffy cautioned.

As the spotlight returned to Harry Grant, Dan felt a surge of solidarity for the poor bloke on the stage. Obviously he hadn't heard the full paper that Harry Grant had delivered, but his passion and support of his troops on the ground was enough to have Dan on his side whatever was coming next.

'But, Derek,' Harry said, his calmness under fire almost unnerving, 'I can prove to you,' he swept his arm around the room, 'that collaborative management *does* work. In fact I have evidence of it in my own jurisdiction. There's a town called Larkford—'

Dan reached out and hit pause almost instinctively. 'Oh, he didn't?'

Taffy just nodded and set the video to run again.

'Some of you may even have seen it in the press last year. The surgery there was blighted by inefficiencies, an unmanageable hierarchy and escalating costs. One year later, it has better doctor:patient ratios, patient satisfaction levels and higher efficiency ratings than any other practice I oversee.'

Derek butted in from the audience and the camera lagged behind in trying to locate him again, so his voice echoed from off-screen. 'Well you were obviously right not to close it. So what?'

Harry smiled, as though he had Derek on the ropes. 'So, they manage without seniority. There are four equal partners. Each with a vote, each with a say in how their practice is run. In my opinion, The Practice at Larkford is quite literally a model surgery. A model we should all be aspiring to.'

There was a bark of laughter from Derek and several others in the auditorium. 'Well, that's quite a claim to make in a public forum there, Harry. Let's explore that, shall we?' He turned to confer with the gentleman sitting beside him, an identikit bureaucrat in an even pricier suit. 'We'll give you a budget,' he said after a few moments of whispering, as he made a show of standing up and striding on to the stage, 'but there'll be compliance and evaluation. Considerable oversight. Are you sure you're ready to take this on?' He held out his hand as though to shake on a bet. 'No shame in backing down now.'

Dan wasn't even in the room with him, but he could see that this wasn't really the case. The gauntlet had been laid down and Harry Grant really had no choice but to pick it up and run with it.

Harry nodded, standing firm as he shook Derek's hand. 'I'm ready.'

Derek smirked slightly. 'Well, let's just hope the good doctors of Larkford are too.'

Taffy clicked on pause, freezing the image of the two men shaking hands and the first glimmer of doubt on Harry's face.

'Fuck,' said Dan simply, sinking back in his chair.

'My thoughts exactly,' said Taffy.

Dan was frankly relieved to have got through evening surgery without dropping the ball. The sheer effort of concentrating on the job in hand and not having imaginary arguments with Harry Grant was exhausting. Nevertheless, as he waved Emily Frank on her way, clutching a prescription for some mild tranquilisers for panic attacks, he felt hard pushed not to prescribe something similar for himself. He wasn't entirely sure whether it was fear of the impending scrutiny coming their way, or fear of telling Holly and Julia, but finding a calm equilibrium seemed like a good idea either way.

Taffy knocked on his door, this time gently, mindful that Dan might be off his game. 'I've told the girls we need to talk. Come on, I've even bought chocolate Hobnobs.'

He pushed open the door to the doctors' lounge to find Holly and Julia already waiting, bickering – or so it seemed – about biscuits.

'Holly Graham, you evil temptress, get those bloody Hobnobs away from me. You know the camera adds ten pounds and Dan's already been fattening me up on steak and chips. I basically feel like *foie gras* at this point.'

Dan watched as Holly obediently slid the packet to the other end of the table, as she tried not to laugh. It was just the tableau of normality that he needed to find his composure. Julia's protestations were genuine enough – she was becoming paranoid about how she appeared on screen in her new role as TV Doctor. But to Dan's eye at least, Julia looked just as slender, toned and elegant as she always had. If anything, he was worried that her obsession with her on-screen image was getting a little out of control. Hence the steak, and his recent insistence on Hobnobs (her secret vice) at every meeting. Julia, it seemed, could resist everything except temptation and this tiny foible made Dan love her even more, despite how hard it was sometimes to look beyond her prickly exterior.

He only hoped her openness to the media might extend to a little scrutiny from the NHS, at least without somehow finding a way to blame him for it.

'Right,' he said firmly, calling them to order. 'Grab a seat and watch this.' He set up the laptop on the table for them. 'And then we need to have a little chat.'

There was a groaning creak as the door to the lounge was pushed slowly open and Harry Grant's myopic face peered in. He clocked the laptop on the table and stepped inside. 'I had hoped to, ah . . . that is, I was hoping to talk to you before you—'

'Hi, Harry,' said Taffy, stepping forward to shake his hand. 'You're a little late for that, I'm afraid. But since you're here, maybe you can fill Holly and Julia in on your bet.'

Harry looked aghast. 'Is that what you think this is? A bet? Dr Jones, I would never ever play God with your livelihood like that.' He paused, obviously reflecting on the footage online. 'Although, to be fair, I can understand why you might feel that way.'

Julia stood up abruptly. 'I don't mean to be rude, but perhaps you'd like to include us in your conversation?'

Holly had been staring at the paused image on the screen, where the usually scrolling banner flickered unmoving, bearing the title of Harry's presentation. She looked up at Dan and he nodded. Clicking the mouse, Harry's voice echoed around the room on high volume and everyone stood in silence as the video scrolled to the end.

'Sounds like a bet to me,' said Julia coldly.

It took a little while for the hubbub in the room to calm down to the point where Harry could actually address their individual questions, and he shuffled his feet as he composed himself. 'The thing is—' he began.

'The thing is,' cut in Julia, 'you've committed us to something without even consulting us. And I have to be honest, I don't even understand why!' She was clearly baffled as to why anyone would think their chaotic brand of management was something to aspire to. Decisions by committee made Julia incredibly uncomfortable and more than once, Dan had borne the burden of her displeasure once they got home. He only hoped that she went a little easier on Harry, who would be unlikely to view her harsh words through his own filter of being madly in love with her.

Harry cleared his throat uncomfortably. 'Sit down, won't you, and let me explain.' Nervous he may be, but Harry still took his time for them all to settle before speaking again. 'You need to be aware of how incredibly impressive the turn-around here has been. You might not even realise how unprecedented it is, to go from imminent closure to the kind of numbers we're seeing from here.' He held up a hand to fend off another interruption. 'And it's not all about the numbers. The feedback we're getting is that your team management style is contemporary and accessible and that there is a real community vibe here. It's something we'd very much like to analyse and emulate elsewhere. And, of course, it means you have an absolute reprieve from closure,' he paused, 'so that's something.'

'Harry?' Holly said quietly. 'Is this a foregone conclusion? I mean, could we even say no if we wanted to? The reprieve is fabulous, of course and thank you – but can we consider how all this analysis will affect the patients – they are the priority here, after all.' Dan could see that the whole notion of over-sight and scrutiny would basically be Holly's worst nightmare. She was all for putting the patients first and anything that interfered with that would struggle to get her blessing; Julia managing to insert her blasted film crew into their lives had only heightened that perspective.

Harry took off his glasses and polished them with a tea towel. 'Well, technically you *could*, I suppose,' he said. 'But I'm honestly not sure why you would.' He looked confident then, for the first time since entering the room. 'There's a rather healthy budget, you see. For you to spend as you see fit and another to cover the expenses of oversight. You'll need some considerable support on the admin side, of course, but the reality is this. You can afford another GP if you'd like, or to modernise some of your systems and equipment—'

'We could have an in-house physio,' interrupted Taffy, whose support for the scheme seemed to have increased con-siderably with the prospect of a little working capital. 'And you know, this could be just the thing to re-launch the Health in the Community programme properly,' he wondered aloud, as Dan nodded encouragingly.

Julia nodded. 'It might even mean that you two could stop with all the bonkers fund-raising schemes and concentrate on the job in hand?'

Taffy looked pointedly at Dan's shaven scalp. 'The lady does make an excellent point there, Dan – you could even let your hair grow back and then you can have a normal-sized head again.'

Dan had been doing his best to ignore all the one-liners about the fact that he had a teeny-tiny head – in proportion to his gym-honed body anyway – and he tried not to let his irritation show. Trust Julia to be all about the optics, he thought tiredly.

'But, if you think about it,' Julia carried on, 'whilst a Physio would be nice, wouldn't we be better off expanding the nurses' clinics? They've been getting slammed recently, with all the chronic care patients. Our ratios are really skewed in that direction – everybody round here lives too damn long. They could really use the help.'

Dan sat back in his chair, a little ashamed of himself for having doubted her. He knew Julia was difficult. He knew her social skills were a little wide of the mark sometimes and she certainly came with baggage. But he should never have doubted that she also came with a good heart and the best of intentions.

He listened to the debate around the table, each doctor considering a different angle and Harry answering their quick-fire questions with patient attention.

Traditionally, Dan liked to steer well clear of bureaucracy – the regulations always seemed to have a rather loose affiliation with the reality of medicine – but in this case, he couldn't help feel that this nomination might actually be a blessing in disguise.

There remained so much latent tension bubbling quietly under the surface at The Practice about the decision not to nominate a Senior Partner, even if nobody was prepared to admit it. At the time they'd all been so relieved to rescue The Practice from closure that it hadn't seemed like a big deal to any of them. As the months had passed, it had become apparent that Dan was not the only one feeling that their career ambitions had been thwarted and secretly wanting to be in charge. Some days, it felt like a glass ceiling on any progression or promotion.

But now this – endorsement from on high – and it looked as though doing the right thing might not have been the wrong thing after all. For any of them.

Chapter 4

The next morning, as her clinic dragged on, Julia took another calming breath and made sure that her tone belied none of her impatience. 'So, as I was saying last time you came in Mr Phillips, if you have a double espresso and a cigarette before you come in for your blood pressure review, it does make it terribly hard to get a sensible reading.' She dutifully made a note of the terrifying numbers on a piece of paper, but didn't enter them into the computer for fear of triggering an emergency response.

Much as Julia was loath to admit it, Dan Carter had a point when he said that having the TV camera crew following her every move would change how she behaved around her patients. From his perspective, the main concern had been that there would be some error caught on film and therefore The Practice would end up indisputably liable. Or even that Julia's split focus between her patient and how she appeared on film might make her patients feel irrelevant, unheard or simply resentful of having their privacy invaded.

What neither Dan nor Julia could have foreseen is that the patients that opted to be included – and everybody was given the choice – were loving their five minutes of fame, and that Julia's bedside manner had never before been so empathetic, patient or compassionate.

Admittedly, it had been a bit of a shock that first week when she and Quentin, her producer, had watched the rushes together. Catching sight of each sigh, tap of her biro and the occasional look of utter disdain had been a complete eye opener. They'd binned the lot and started again. She wouldn't tell a soul this, of course, but now when the little light on the camera turned red, she would simply ask herself, 'What would Holly say?' and go from there.

Her patients were delighted. Her producer was delighted. Only Dan was getting the short end of the straw, because after a long day of being personable and caring, it was incredibly hard for Julia to go home and not pick a fight with the next person that moved.

It was fair to say that, if being 'nice' was this much effort, then maybe it was time to accept that it wasn't her natural state. Pithy and judgemental made life so much easier to bear, apparently.

'So I think it would be a really good idea if you sat down quietly in the waiting room for a little while and then we'll check those numbers again,' Julia said as she leaned forward in her chair, the epitome of caring compassion. 'I just wouldn't feel right about sending you home, Mr Phillips. Just in case.'

He shook his head, even as he agreed, 'I suppose you're right, Dr Channing. Better safe than sorry, eh?' He pulled himself to his feet and sighed, playing to the camera as he shuffled out of the room in his tweed suit.

It was probably lucky that the camera panned to follow him out and missed the look of utter disbelief on Julia's face. Seriously, how hard could it be to follow the instructions in the letter she now issued as a matter of course?

'Are we nearly done for the morning, then?' asked Quentin from his position tucked behind the camera. 'Only I think we should have a strategy meeting about this Model Surgery business. Could be a little goldmine, that one.'

Julia bristled slightly. Somehow, it was okay for her to think about the commercial implications of the nomination, but it felt prurient and opportunistic when the self-same sentiments came from her erstwhile producer.

She shrugged. 'Let's talk in a couple of days when we've a clearer picture of what's involved. At the moment it's just a concept, really.' A concept she couldn't quite get her head around.

Quentin blinked slowly, his scrutiny of her face making her feel even more uncomfortable than the high definition cameras that emphasised every individual flaw. 'Okay,' he said eventually. 'We'll make an evening of it.'

Julia was never really sure of Quentin's intentions. She knew that Dan had taken an almost instant dislike to him, but she had never been able to pinpoint the source of her boyfriend's unease. Was it simply because he didn't appreciate Quentin and his film crew disrupting life at The Practice, or could Dan see something that Julia herself had missed? Sometimes, when she caught a lascivious glance at her thighs or a lingering kiss on her cheek, she wondered what exactly Quentin's real agenda was. Certainly right now, the notion of an evening out was not something that seemed terribly advisable, given how incredibly attractive he was and how vulnerable she had been feeling of late.

By way of distraction, she clicked on the appointment screen and, without prompting, turned to do a piece to camera.

'So, Mrs Jennings will be here in a moment and she is actually one of our Frequent Fliers,' she smiled charmingly as the little red camera light blinked, having been told by a focus group that they loved it when she was a little humorous. 'She has a condition called Trigeminal Neuralgia, which presents as extreme facial pain and it's been getting gradually worse over the last few months.'

Quentin's slightly pompous voice interrupted her, clearly annoyed by her taking the initiative, 'And will she be getting a referral to a Neurologist, or is she stuck on yet another lengthy waiting list?'

The original idea of the voice off-screen had been for Quentin to guide Julia's pieces, but when he was rattled he would also take the opportunity to pose those questions that he claimed the viewers at home would be dying to ask. Julia felt that it was often a case of being contentious for the sake of it, but was rarely in a position to deflect his line of questioning, for when she did, he simply called 'cut' and started over.

Julia paused for a moment, marshalling her thoughts. 'Mrs Jennings has already been reviewed at the hospital and her scans have all come back NAD. That's the acronym we use for No Abnormality Detected. So really at this point, it's a case of working together with her consultant to manage the pain as best we can.'

'So there's nothing to see? And there's no way of knowing what triggers the pain?' Quentin asked, his voice now laden with faux-concern for this woman he had never met.

'I'm afraid at this point, we'll probably call it Idiopathic Neuropathy, but that doesn't mean that we can't make Mrs Jennings more comfortable with a combination of pain relief and other medication.' She didn't go on to explain that in medical terms, the use of the word idiopathic was roughly the same as throwing up your hands and saying 'fuck knows!'.

Luckily, Quentin didn't pursue it, but his alternative agenda soon had Julia on her toes. 'And aren't you worried that in fact there is no facial pain and that, what was she called? – Mrs Jennings, that's right – might actually be exhibiting drug-seeking behaviour?'

This was nothing short of sensationalising and Julia struggled to keep her face in neutral whilst swallowing the urge to strangle him. Pain was such a slippery beast to deal with: everyone's opinion subjective and often with nothing visual to go on. It could be devastating for her patients and frustrating for her, as their doctor, to try and find them some level of comfort. Ignorant comments like that didn't exactly help.

As the purported drug-seeker inched her way into Julia's consulting room, hunched over a walking stick and looking every one of her eighty-seven years, Julia was pleased to see that Quentin at least had the decency to blush – perhaps not quite the stereotype he had in mind.

Julia took great pleasure in standing up to help Mrs Jennings into her seat, trying not to be irritated by the look of surprise on the old lady's face. She'd surprised herself recently too. It seemed that half her patients came into The Practice with the simple requirement of a willing ear and a sensible, calming opinion. All these years, she'd felt as though they had come to her demanding miracles she could rarely produce. It had been a highly unsatisfactory arrangement, whereby both parties had gone away disappointed. And all she'd had to do to change gear professionally was to put herself in Holly's (slightly dated, rather unfashionable) shoes.

If only it was so easy from a personal perspective, too.

After Mrs Jennings had departed, she could only feel grateful that Quentin had chosen that moment to step outside too, as her mobile phone began to trill. She noted the three missed calls earlier, all from the same number and tried not to let her agitation show. There were no voicemails – all part of the control game that her mother liked to play – 'if you want to know what I called for, you'll have to call me back, or perhaps you'd like to sit on the worry that it was something important?' Of course, it never was, and Julia's mum had become adept at manipulating her daughter into making contact at all hours, against all her better judgement and despite her jam-packed schedule.

She answered the phone with the sick feeling of dread that appeared to have become her default setting whenever her mother's caller ID flashed up on the screen. 'Hi, Mum,' she said, forcing a certain lightness into her voice. 'It's not the best time actually, can I call you back?' She glanced out into the corridor where Quentin and the team were packing up for lunch and quietly pushed the door shut with her foot. The last thing she needed was him nosing around her family situation.

Her mother's sigh echoed down the airwaves. 'Well, that's a lovely way to start a phone call. I should be grateful you answered at all, I suppose. If you're so busy.' She imbued the word with as much doubt and disappointment as she could muster.

Julia determinedly refused to rise. 'Well, I've a waiting room full of patients and the TV crew are here too, so why don't we chat this evening when we've got more time.'

'And you can start the conversation with "I haven't got long" like you always do?' said her mother astutely.

Julia felt the beginnings of the prickling heat on her neck, the one that warned that her tenuous grip on her patented 'cool, calm and collected mode' was in danger of letting go altogether.

'I'll make myself a cup of tea and we can chat for as long as you need,' she said instead, squashing the voice in her head that angrily pointed out that she hardly had time for the bloody cup of tea, let alone seven verses of life's-so-unfair and your-father-doesn't-listen. Credit to Julia's dad though, he seemed to have done nothing *but* listen for the last forty years – the opportunities for getting a word in edgewise around Candace in full flow were few and far between. But nevertheless, as an only child, Julia felt a cloak of obligation on her slight shoulders. There was certainly no point suggesting that Candace chat to her friends about her marriage – she'd managed to alienate almost every single one of them with her drunken bouts of 'honesty' over the years.

'Hmmmm,' said her mother, sounding suspiciously like Marge Simpson. 'Well, make sure you do.' She paused. 'There are *things* we need to discuss.'

Had the way her mother stressed the word 'things' carried an ominous ring to it, Julia wondered yet again, as the conversation still niggled at the back of her mind hours later. She tried to block out the raised voices from along the corridor – let someone else deal with it, she thought, she had enough on her mind – and forced herself to concentrate on the referral letter she was dictating.

Dan pushed the door open abruptly. 'So you *are* in here! Can you not hear what's going on?'

Snippets of conversation filtered through and Julia shook her head. 'Seriously? Not this again? Somebody needs to have a word with the nurses.'

'They do,' agreed Dan. 'And since it's *your* TV programme, it probably should be you.'

Julia scowled. It sounded as though Quentin had managed to rile the nurses for the umpteenth time, with his constant requests for B-roll footage and now apparently Dan had taken umbrage on their behalf.

'Look, Julia,' he said firmly, 'you need to understand that they just don't like it. It's one thing to constantly interrupt their work and do tactless voice-over commentary whilst he's filming them, but Jade in particular is getting very annoyed that he keeps referring to them as B-roll,' he said.

Julia shrugged helplessly. 'But that's what it's called. It's the little bits of film that fill in the gaps — it doesn't make her *B-list* if that's what she's worrying about.'

Dan stepped forward and held out his hand for her to take, almost giving her no option but to stand up and deal with the problem. 'I'm only telling you, because you need to be aware — Quentin's stepping on an awful lot of toes.'

She nodded, knowing full well that Dan's toes were firmly among them. 'I'll talk to him again,' she said tiredly, a small part of her resentful at being repeatedly put on the spot to justify Quentin's behaviour. For all his drive and charisma — and neither were in short supply — he did manage to ruffle an awful lot of feathers. The nurses, the admin team, Holly Graham — none of them succumbed to his charm in the way that he was used to and it only served to make Quentin ratchet everything up a gear. It didn't matter how many times Julia tried to tell him that life in the countryside was very much a 'less is more' proposition. His own insecurities meant that he just pushed harder.

She walked through to the doctors' lounge, where Jade was standing with her hands on her hips, in full-on confrontation with Quentin. 'You could try saying please occasionally, before you barge in on one of my clinics,' she shouted, her eyes flashing in anger and her low-cut uniform barely coping. 'And stop staring at my boobs every chance you get.'

Jason may have been leaning against the table in a more casual stance but his words carried just as much fury, 'And don't think we didn't hear that line about "wannabe doctors" in last week's show. We don't have to put up with this, and if you keep throwing your weight around, then you'll have a chance to see how much we "wannabes" actually do around here!' Jason belatedly noticed Julia's arrival. 'Sorry, Jules, but this arsehole just needs to know his place.'

'I think we can probably have this conversation without the profanities,' Julia said awkwardly, as Jason, Jade and Quentin all glared at her, each expecting her to take their side – there was no winning solution to being the jam in this sandwich. It was one thing to mediate between her parents, quite another to attempt it at work as well; she felt as though she were being pulled every which way, with no respite.

'Look, guys,' she said to Jason and Jade, 'we can work this out, if you can give me and Quentin a few days to look at the filming schedules—'

'I'm not changing my schedules to fit around them,' protested Quentin. 'They're only nurses. The programme is *Doctor In The House*, in case you'd forgotten.'

Julia gaped at him, his ignorance and lack of diplomacy only showing how little he really understood about the dynamics of The Practice. 'Only nurses?' she queried, her voice taut. 'Only nurses? Quentin, you are way out of line. The support staff here are the backbone that holds the rest together!'

'Actually,' interrupted Jason, the self-nominated spokesperson apparently, 'the film crew have upset Maggie, too. That's what started all this.'

Julia looked around to where Maggie was cowering in the corner of the room, unhappy at being made the focal point of the dispute. 'I only wanted them to be a bit more considerate about the amount of dirt and mud they were dragging in, with all their kit bags.'

Jade walked over and stood beside her in solidarity. They were unlikely bedfellows, but this common enemy had obviously brought them together, for now at least. 'And you can stop making fun of how Maggie runs the pharmacy. She likes things to be organised and clean, so what? In case you hadn't noticed, we're quite big on clean around here – what with it being a place of medicine and all!'

Jason pushed himself off the table and stood next to Jade. 'To be fair though, Jade,' he whispered, 'we *all* look at your boobs because they kind of draw the eye in that little dress.'

Jade elbowed him in the ribs. 'I don't mind people I *like* looking at them. Just not him.'

Julia sighed, taking in the angry red faces and acrimonious atmosphere. Dear God, maybe Holly had a point and they really did need a little time to get their ducks in a row before any official oversight began. She daren't think what jowly Derek Landers would make of all this discord; he'd probably be delighted. Her phone rang out in her pocket and she automatically hit Decline, only for it to ring out again, and again.

Dan stepped forward. 'I can hold the fort here if you need to get that?'

Julia shook her head. 'It's just my mother.'

The next moment, Dan's mobile began to ring and he answered immediately. 'Oh, hi, Mrs Channing.'

Julia glared at him, knowing he was about to pass the handset over and shook her head. 'I am *not* here,' she whispered urgently.

'Oh, I'm sure she would love to talk to you, but perhaps she's with a patient right now.' He nodded into the phone. 'Of course I will pass the message along ... Yes, well, I'll leave you two to organise a date ... Yes, of course, I'll look forward to seeing you then.'

He hung up to find all eyes on him. 'What?' he said. 'How difficult would it be to have her here for a weekend? She's obviously lonely.'

The very fact that Dan could make such a naïve statement told Julia everything she needed to know. He'd obviously grasped the intellectual notion of her mother's drinking problem, but having had zero experience of living with an alcoholic, he had no frame of reference for the day-to-day realities. It certainly seemed to her as though he had never actually taken on board just how much her family baggage affected her.

Larkford was Julia's sanctuary, her own little place to be: there was no way she would allow her mother to come barging in and ruin it all – let alone with Quentin's film crew lurking around every corner. Judging by the beady expression on his face, his antennae were already pinging for a story. Besides, she wasn't sure that her rapidly depleting bank account, let alone her own sanity, could cope with Candace Channing's ever-escalating demands.

The atmosphere in the room grew heavier. 'Right,' said Julia, 'it's been a very long day and I don't know about you lot, but I think we'll all be much more diplomatic after a good night's sleep. So, you don't have to go home, but you can't stay here ...' She echoed Teddy Kingsley's favourite end-of-the-night phrase at The Kingsley Arms, aiming for levity, trying to soothe the disgruntled feathers just a little bit. She saw Dan watching her every move. 'And if it's easier to talk to me than to each other, then I'm happy to mediate any issues. How does that sound?' It was an appeasing gesture that cost her nothing, but she saw that Dan's demeanour softened instantly. He was forever harping on about people clearing up their own mess and apparently, this particular mess had Julia written all over it.

As everyone shuffled out of the room, Dan took her arm. 'I can't be arsed to cook, can you? Why don't we grab a quiet supper at The Deli?' His intentions were all in the right place, but for Julia the very idea of listening to chirpy Hattie at The Deli going on and on about her miracle twins was more than she could cope with after a hectic day on parade.

To Dan's eyes, Hattie and Lance were prime examples of how becoming parents had changed their world for the better. Lance's drive to overcome a bleak prognosis of testicular cancer had been phenomenal – his steadfast determination not to miss the arrival of his first-born had defied all statistical odds. His motivation had been further stoked when a later scan had revealed a second heartbeat, lurking in the background and catching them all off-guard. Lance's remarkable recovery and strength of character had amazed them all and even Julia could acknowledge that they really made a lovely little family: Hattie, running the kitchen at The Deli and juggling her offspring, Lance behind the counter as master of his Gaggia and so clearly besotted and amazed by every milestone he was able to witness.

Julia felt the band of tension around her head tighten. She knew she was being unnecessarily defensive with Dan, but how on earth had she managed to fall in love with the only man in the world whose biological clock was ticking down so loudly that a detonation was inevitable?

And she really wasn't in the mood to open *that* can of worms again.

Somehow, in her mind, the whole parenting/parent thing was muddled together. All the efforts she'd made to separate herself from her dysfunctional family were in danger of being undone, simply because she and Dan were now a proper couple. What was it about the road to domesticity that forced you to rekindle the concept of family, she wondered. That alone was reason enough for Julia to reject the whole notion of marriage and children out of hand, even putting aside the dark fear that, should she become a parent herself, there was always the incipient danger of turning into her mother.

She reached out and squeezed Dan's hand. 'I'll cook,' she said, a small but emotive gesture to try and show him that she cared. Julia was not known for her conciliatory nature, but even she could tell that Dan was edging towards the end of his tether with her. The only problem was, she had absolutely no idea what to do about it, short of sacrificing her every belief and conviction.

Chapter 5

Holly shuffled through the paperwork in front of her and felt utterly rattled. She was all for making hay while the sun shone, but the haste with which they were approaching the hiring of new staff was bordering on the ridiculous. She'd barely blinked and a week had flown past, punctuated only by an increasingly large amount of paperwork that seemed to end up, almost exclusively, on her desk. Julia's TV crew had been breathing down all their necks, desperate to capture their reactions to the nomination on film and Holly had been forced to use her Lamaze breathing technique not to shove Quentin's clipboard somewhere medically unsuitable.

Her mobile pinged beside her with a text from Lizzie:

> **Thank you for my bouquet – you nutter – how many wooden spoons could I possibly need though? Seriously? One of them is two foot tall . . .**

Holly grinned – as so often was the case, the point had sailed right over Lizzie's immaculately coiffured head. Based on the amount of meddling Lizzie had been up to of late though, it had seemed the perfect gift:

They're for all the stirring you do! xx

The reply pinged back almost instantly:

Oh ha ha . . . Coffee? Please say yes - I'm sooooo
bored . . .

Holly was thrown for a moment; now Lizzie was a lady of
leisure, it was as though she had forgotten about pesky things
like jobs and commitments. Sometimes, she honestly wondered what her friend thought she did all day, as she tapped
out a quick reply that she had patients to see.

Ple-ease - I miss you came the plaintive response, playing
right into Holly's guilt that she hadn't been there enough for
Lizzie recently, through all the big changes in her life. She
felt for Lizzie, she really did. It was hard to re-invent yourself
career-wise, but a little bit of focus would surely help? And
maybe not using her friends as guinea pigs for every crack-pot
venture. Holly's wardrobe still hadn't recovered from Lizzie's
practice run as a personal stylist – she'd been sneakily buying
her own clothes back from the Cancer Research shop ever
since.

Let's walk Eric together in the morning? she replied, feeling
guilty that it was all she could offer right now, and then
flicked her phone to silent to focus on the job in hand.

Pushing aside the heap of CVs, she took a deep breath and
picked up the phone, hesitating for a second as she dialled
the number that was almost engraved on her brain. How
many times in the last week had she dialled it, only to lose
her nerve and hang up? It felt disloyal, it felt sneaky and she
still wasn't completely convinced it was the right thing to do.
The only thing she was sure of, was that there was no way

she was signing up to this Model Surgery nonsense without a little more information.

'Harry Grant,' answered the disembodied voice at the end of the phone.

'Harry, it's Holly Graham from Larkford. Have you got time for a quick word?'

She'd never taken him up on his regular offers of support or advice before, but somehow knowing he was there in the background watching over Larkford had given her some measure of comfort. And now this! What on earth had Harry Grant been thinking, throwing them into the deep end like that?

'I did wonder if you'd call, Holly,' he said, seemingly unsurprised. 'In fact, I've even been working up some figures for you. Patient care budgets, patient referral targets and – well, am I on the right track?'

'Am I so very predictable, Harry?'

She could almost hear him shrug. 'I'd be almost disappointed if you weren't. Patients first, then plaudits, isn't that the Holly Graham way?'

'And the numbers?' said Holly, refusing to be mollified too easily, although wildly flattered. 'Do they add up? You have to realise, Harry, that this is hardly an ideal situation.'

'I'm so sorry if I've put you all on the spot, Holly. And perhaps I should have been more upfront with you all about Derek Landers' slash-and-burn policy – I've been shouting it down for the last few months, but he does have an awful lot of friends in high places. This is a life-line for The Practice, Holly, make no mistake.'

Holly took a breath, a little winded by this revelation. 'Well, that does rather put things in perspective,' she said.

'I want you to know, Holly, that this isn't a whim or bravado on my part. I've seen what you and the team have achieved and this is no small endorsement. I know the speed is almost improper and the commitments on your side seem a little loosely defined, but I want you to know that I have your back. I wouldn't let The Practice enter into any agreement that I had doubts about – not after all your sterling efforts last year. It's a little unusual, granted, but then so is your set-up in Larkford.'

'So it's *really* not just a bet, then?' Holly ventured, daring to question out loud what she'd been dwelling on for days and unable to hide the concern in her voice.

'It's not a bet at all,' said Harry tersely. 'I know that your Dr Jones saw it that way, but if you could think of it as more of a challenge, I think we'd all be more productive.'

'You know it's the patient care angle that concerns me—' she began, before he interrupted her smoothly.

'And that is our priority too. Having another GP on the payroll, having extended hours for the nursing clinic – these are all measurable attributes and I can configure ...' He stopped with a chuckle. 'Sorry, Holly, slipped into bureaucrat-ese there for a moment. Allow me to be blunt, off the record, of course?'

'Of course.'

'You and your team are really going to earn this extra funding one way or another. But I'm absolutely convinced that the improvements in patient care and patient services will more than offset the increased bureaucracy. If I'm being frank, it's your admin team who will feel the weight of this initially.'

'Poor Grace,' said Holly under her breath.

'Grace Allen?' Harry said, clearly having no issues with his hearing.

'She's our Practice Manager,' Holly reminded him, only to hear him chuckle at the end of the phone.

'Oh, I know who she is, Holly. She's currently making waves over in Bristol on their Medical Administration Diploma.' He paused. 'Leave that one with me – maybe we can sweeten the deal for her, by making all this compliance count towards her coursework?'

'So, hiring a new GP?' Holly ventured.

'Go ahead and get it done, Holly. Spend the money while it's on the table and between you and me, try and make hay with this one while the sun shines. You and your team can do no wrong at HQ at the moment, so before they come knocking on the door for a favour, get your house in order and get yourselves properly staffed. Plus, you know, it's one in the eye for Derek bloody Landers.'

'Thank you, Harry,' said Holly with feeling, appreciating his blunt honesty more than he might realise. She wasn't stupid, though: this nomination may turn out to be a sensible course of action for them professionally, but there was no denying that, on some level, for Harry Grant, this was personal.

As she hung up the phone, she clicked Send & Receive on her e-mail account and automatically scanned her Inbox for Milo's name. It had become an unconscious action now. Every time she sent him an update about the twins, she would be twitchy and on edge for days, waiting to hear back. The fact that she never, ever did, hardly seemed to make any difference.

She jumped guiltily as Taffy pushed open the door. 'Are you hiding away in here?' he asked, his brow furrowing at her reaction.

Holly quickly pushed her mouse to one side, knowing what Taffy's response would be if she explained. She honestly couldn't bear him to patiently and sweetly rationalize for the umpteenth time why she really shouldn't be bothering any more. She couldn't listen to all the reasons why maintaining contact with the twins' father wasn't doing her any favours at all.

She focused instead on the light grazing of stubble on his jaw from where they had 'overslept' that morning and hustled out of the door, late and ruffled and laughing like teenagers. 'Do you need me?' she said, standing up and walking towards him with her folder of CVs, shoving a pen into her ponytail for safe-keeping.

'Always,' he said, sliding a hand around her waist and managing to find the tiny gap between her blouse and her waistband. 'But in this case, actually in the doctors' lounge because Julia has called a meeting.' He pulled an aghast face, which pretty much mirrored Holly's own feelings on that scenario.

Falling into step beside him and dropping her guard, she almost jolted when he spoke quietly to her, 'You don't need to hide your e-mails, Holly. I know you want to keep Milo in the loop about the twins and what they're up to, but it doesn't need to become a thing between us, unless you let it.'

'I wasn't hiding anything, I just—'

Taffy stopped and turned to face her, oblivious to the comings and goings around them. 'You know how you get all defensive when somebody is mean to the boys? Well, imagine a version of that feeling. Imagine watching the person you love set themselves up for pain and disappointment over and over again.' He shrugged. 'Just think about it. I know you want to do the right thing by Milo, but is his radio silence doing the right thing by you, or the boys?'

Holly shook her head, touched and riled in equal measure, but not truly knowing how best to react, 'This isn't about sinking to his level. This is about the fact that, whether we like it or not, he is their father and he needs to know what his children are up to.' Her tone was defensive and she could see Taffy reacting in kind, anger flaring in his eyes.

'But does he respond, interact, appreciate your efforts?' Taffy said abruptly, clearly trying hard not to be more outspoken on this particular topic – realising, as Holly did, that it was the only thing they ever argued about. 'Does he know, do you think, how much it upsets you to write those e-mails? Because I do, Holly,' Taffy said with feeling, 'and I really want you to think about whose welfare comes first in this scenario – yours, or his?' He took a deliberately deep breath and changed tack slightly. 'You need to look at the big picture on this, Holls, and you know that. This is a marathon not a sprint, and if you don't take a proactive approach to managing—'

'What?' Holly challenged, utterly riled. 'The boys' welfare? Doing the right thing? Or perhaps there's some sports psychology theory that covers childhood abandonment issues that I might have missed?' She caught herself before her tone could become more scathing. She knew her anger was misdirected, but Taffy's habit of oversimplifying everything and his tendency to use sporting analogies for every facet of life, wound her up every time. She squeezed his hand. 'Sorry. But honestly, there's no right way to do this, Taff, we just have to find the way that works for *us*. But for me, this isn't applied theory: it's my boys. And their dad. And finding a path that gives them a reasonable shot at getting through a divorce with *some* self-esteem and confidence left over.'

Taffy smiled knowingly. 'You see – big picture . . .You're doing it already.'

And to his credit, he barely flinched when Holly elbowed him firmly in the ribs.

*

Holly still felt jangled by Taffy's comments, irritated that
Milo still managed to cause problems in her life even as an
absentee, annoyed that Taffy weighed in so heavily on this
particular issue every single time it came up. Even with the
best of intentions, it still felt as though he was telling her
what to do and that made Holly's defences spring up on
autopilot.

Pulling her mind back to the job in-hand, she spread out
the CVs on the table for discussion: A-levels, degrees, work
experience all blurring into one amorphous haze. She struggled to quieten the voice in her head that told her not to take
her frustrations out on Julia, whose pinched expression of
disappointment at the 'quality of the candidates' made Holly
want to pass the whole vetting process over to her lock, stock
and barrel.

But, if they were going to find a good fit, then even a
grumpy, irritated Holly could see that wouldn't be the ideal
way forward. She took a breath. 'I really want to talk you
through my choices here, because I think there are a couple
of really good applicants that would have been over-looked if
I'd rigidly stuck to the original Qualification Criteria. And,
I know, we were only going to look at . . .'

'The best of the best!' butted in both Dan and Taffy in their
highly practised Top Gun impression, which made Holly
laugh every time, even when she was annoyed or tired.

'But . . .' she managed, when she'd caught her breath,
'there's a little part of me that says I'd rather work with someone who's a better match with the team, than someone who
has an extra A★ in Geography from way-back-when.'

There were two candidates in particular that stood out
for Holly and neither of them would tick all the Top Gun
boxes; but both had an eloquence and passion in their personal

statement that gave the impression they truly cared about what they did. So what if one of them had to retake their History GCSE a decade ago, he'd still got into Med School and graduated, hadn't he? And so the other girl had a few gaps in her CV, the odd month here and there unaccounted for – was she not allowed to have a life?

'And there's something to be said for availability. If we crack on and get the position filled,' Taffy chimed in, 'we can announce them at the Health in the Community launch. Really reinforce the message that we're investing in our patients.'

Dan laughed and lobbed his KitKat wrapper across the table. 'Have you been secretly swotting up? Holly, be honest, has he been reading marketing books on the loo, so he can pretend that he knows what he's talking about?'

'Nope,' Holly replied, loyal to a fault, her earlier irritation fading into the background. 'He prefers to read the kids' Garfield comic books on the loo.' She didn't feel the need to add that he'd been working his way through *Marketing for Dummies* every time he had a bath for weeks now. 'And, although obviously the PR angle is sound, I'm not keen to rush into making this appointment. Repent at leisure and all that. Let's just find someone who fits, yes?'

Dan flicked through Holly's shortlist in front of him. 'Listen, Holly, the last thing we need around here is someone who's making do. If they want to be in a hospital setting, then tough it up sweetheart and get used to having no sleep. But don't come here and moan about the lack of challenge and variety. We've had that before, remember?'

Holly bristled slightly at his tone: if they were all so opinionated on the topic, then let them do the bloody interviews. And, let's be honest, she thought, it would probably be a good

introduction to the challenging dynamic the new doctor
would be expected to join!

Julia surprised her though, before she could even make
that suggestion. She looked over Dan's shoulder at the CVs
in question and shrugged. 'Holly has a point, though. These
two sound human. Approachable, you know? And I'm led
to believe that's an important skill in General Practice.' Julia
smiled, being self-aware enough to know that her brilliance
and inability to suffer fools gladly could sometimes be classed
as off-putting. Or 'Intimidating as hell', as Taffy tactlessly
reminded her on a regular basis.

Holly felt slightly queasy watching Julia sipping delicately
on a wheatgrass smoothie, the contents undulating with
every sip. She herself nibbled on the last of the KitKats to
take her mind off what might have turned the smoothie
such a luminous green and to quiet her stomach. She had
to applaud Taffy's choice in making the humble KitKat the
new 'Nominated Snack' of all partnership meetings – that
dalliance with toffee Clubs had been a huge mistake, she
thought, and since Julia had laid down the law and banished
the Hobnobs ... well, let's just say that Holly needed more
than a little caffeine to get her through this morning's scheduled activities.

She never thought she'd see the day, but she was actually
missing having time with her patients. Obviously the partners
needed to share out the admin roles here to keep the ship
running smoothly, but Holly was well aware that it was not
her forte. She wanted to be at the coalface, not in the office.

Grace poked her head around the door. 'Can I borrow one
of you? I've got an asthmatic situation out front?'

Holly was on her feet before the others got a look in.
'Who have we got?' she asked, as she willingly abandoned

the meeting and pulled her well-worn stethoscope from her pocket, feeling her mood instantly lift. As Grace updated her efficiently on Geoffrey Larch's symptoms, Holly pushed aside the insidious wave of guilt that swept over her, hot on the heels of the sheer relief at being away from the paperwork and interacting with her patients again. Even as she knelt down beside Geoffrey, checking his vitals and promptly organising a nebuliser, she knew it was hardly a long-term solution.

Harry Grant had made it perfectly clear that they would be expected to sing for their supper – that the gentle increase in paperwork now was probably nothing compared to the deluge yet to come.

Thankfully, she thought, in medicine as in parenting, he who shouts loudest often gets the most attention. And, for now at least, her patients' needs still qualified.

'I don't like using this thing,' gasped Geoffrey, trying to pull the clear plastic mask away from his face. 'It makes me feel panicky!'

'I know,' said Holly, calmly and with sympathy. 'But right now your oxygen levels have me a little worried, so we're just going to sit here for a bit, while we get some of the medication to where we need it, okay?' She took his hand gently, as he squeezed his eyes shut to prevent the tears spilling over. At forty-three and a life-long asthmatic, one might have assumed he'd be used to this by now, but Holly knew only too well of his struggles with claustrophobia and anxiety, neither a winning combination with chronic asthma. She tried to imagine Julia kneeling on the floor and calmly talking nonsense to soothe him and failed. She tried to imagine any one of the 'high-fliers' on her interview short-list thinking this was a worthwhile use of their super-qualified time.

As she began telling Geoffrey about Eric's latest habit of

opening the fridge and helping himself to the salami, making himself a stinky stash behind the sofa, she noted his breathing steady and his pulse rate calm. He even managed a smile.

It was this small victory that flicked the switch in Holly's mind. She'd been lumbered with the interviewing process because the others had flattered her into it – she was the people person, the best judge of character they'd said. She wasn't stupid though, and she knew it was simply because they hated the idea of doing it themselves, all of them – Holly included – feeling incredibly uncomfortable with asking people to essentially brag about themselves, not that some of them needed much encouragement!

As Geoffrey's colour gradually returned to normal and the hustle and bustle outside the door told Holly that afternoon surgery had started, she handed over his care to Jason, with the strict proviso that he fetch her immediately should anything change. Jason gave her a grin. 'You can trust me, Holly. Geoffrey and I will absolutely *not* be listening to the racing from Newmarket on the radio and we *certainly* won't be having a little flutter to take our minds off things, will we, Geoff?'

Holly shook her head. 'Honestly, you two,' she chided, only too familiar with the bets and books that ran out of the back room of The Kingsley Arms. These two together were trouble on legs, but seeing Geoff's whole-hearted response to the idea, she could hardly suggest it was medically inadvisable: engaged and distracted patients tended to panic less and breaking the cycle of hyper-ventilation was a significant factor. 'No accumulators, then,' she said. 'And try and keep the excitement down to a dull roar,' she suggested to Jason as she left.

Moments later she popped her head back around the door,

unable to resist, 'If you were to find yourself having a little bet, could you pop me a fiver each way on Miss Nellie in the 3.40?' It was totally worth it, she reckoned, just to see the shocked expressions on both of their faces.

Chapter 6

It only took two mornings of interviews for Holly to lose the will to live. She began fantasising about premature labours in the waiting room, or perhaps an outbreak of H1N1 requiring all hands on deck. One thing she knew for certain – she was not cut out for a career in Human Resources.

She ducked into the doctors' lounge for a swift caffeine infusion before the final candidates arrived. At this point, she'd volunteer to do the overtime herself, just to make the process stop.

'Latte?' asked Taffy, solicitously, knowing better than most how challenging Holly was finding this task.

'No, just black – can't risk diluting the caffeine today,' she said, as she flopped down into his chair. 'You lot are utter sods lumbering me with this. I've had Braggy McBraggerson who thinks obese patients should be denied medical care until they've lost weight. I've seen the quietest, shyest girl, who could barely be coaxed to share her own name, let alone an opinion – it was like pulling teeth. And my ten o'clock phoned to ask if we could do his interview by Skype because he's at a Médecins Sans Frontières recruitment day and wanted to keep his options open.'

Dan looked sheepish. 'We should probably have saved you a Jammy Dodger then really.'

'Yes, you jolly well should,' said Holly, but unable to keep a straight face. There was a reason she was doing the preliminaries after all – Julia would have punched someone, Taffy would actually have nodded off and Dan would, in all probability, have tried to rescue the little shy-girl by taking her out for a drink.

'What's this?' she asked, pointing to the large brown parcel in the middle of the table.

Taffy pushed it towards her. 'It's for you. From Borneo. Frankly you're very lucky we didn't open it already.' He ripped back the Sellotape to 'help' without waiting for her to start – everyone knew that Taffy loved nothing more than opening parcels.

They rummaged amongst the polystyrene chips and pulled out a fat ugly little statue, just as Julia reached forward and pulled out another one with a simply enormous willy. There was silence for a moment until Holly thought to open the accompanying note and burst out laughing. 'You might want to put that little chap down,' she said to Julia. 'It's a Malaysian fertility icon. Don't say you haven't been warned.'

Julia's face was a picture as she thrust the ill-proportioned little fella away from her with alacrity. 'They're from Elsie, for lovely Katie House apparently. Well, let's see if an enormous bronze penis will succeed where six rounds of IVF have failed.' She patted him on the head and grinned. 'Metaphorically, I mean.'

She downed her coffee with a grimace. 'Wish me luck, be nice to the icons won't you – I'm going back in. It's a shame Elsie didn't send me an icon to bring serenity and patience,' she muttered as she left.

After only five and a half minutes (yes, she was counting) with Rebecca Havant, Holly knew she'd heard enough. This girl was Julia without the charm, the looks or actually the medical skills to pull it off. Undoubtedly qualified on paper, in person she was dominating and terrifying and actually really rather mean.

Having already learned from her earlier mistakes about making snap assumptions about people, Holly gamely persevered for a few more minutes, before realising that sometimes first impressions were exactly on the money. This girl had instantly got Holly's hackles up, she was patronising about women in medicine to the point where Holly wanted to shake her and shout, 'Look in a mirror – have you noticed that *you're* a woman!'

The way Rebecca had repeatedly turned the conversation towards 'media opportunities' had been another red flag for Holly. They wanted a doctor, not a wannabe celebrity.

Although Holly was sure there was a reason that Rebecca had adopted such a confrontational approach, she knew perfectly well it wouldn't work in Larkford. Holly couldn't help but think that, had she been meeting Rebecca as a patient rather than a candidate, she would be advising a lengthy course of Cognitive Behavioural Therapy to deal with the enormous aggressive chip on her shoulder.

Just the mention of the word chip and Holly could almost smell the salt and vinegar, making her mouth water and her stomach rumble. As she thanked Rebecca for her time and pulled open the door, she could understand why.

Sitting on the chair outside was her next interviewee, scoffing from a cone of newspaper-wrapped chips, which she hurriedly and sheepishly bundled away. 'Sorry,' she said. 'Thought I had longer and I was utterly starving.'

Holly blinked hard, trying to marshal her thoughts. Not only was the next candidate incredibly petite, with an elfin crop that made her look about twelve, but there was also a small chocolate-coloured spaniel sitting neatly at her feet. The dog glanced up at Holly and slowly beat its tail against the floor.

Without a word, Holly opened the door and ushered them through, wondering whether there was some particularly salient point she may have missed.

'I really do appreciate you taking the time to interview me, Dr Graham,' Alice Walker said, the faintest Scottish burr softening her vowels. 'My aunt Pru was all about the serendipity of the timing, but to be honest, I was just relieved you weren't put off by Coco here.'

Holly looked up from the CV that she'd been hurriedly re-reading. 'Aunt Pru? Does that mean . . .'

Alice furrowed her porcelain brow and sat back in her chair, her embarrassment obvious. 'Oh Lord, she didn't tell you, did she?'

The little spaniel sat unmoving at Alice's feet and Holly couldn't help but wonder at its self-control. Eric would have been sniffling around for treats and distractions the minute he arrived somewhere new. This little poppet simply watched every movement with his eyes.

'Let's start again?' suggested Holly. 'Why don't you introduce me to this little chap – he's incredibly well-trained.'

The entire expression on Alice's face changed, relaxing from the taut mask of anxiety that had tightened her beautiful face. 'Well, this is Coco and she's five.' Holly noticed the way that Alice hadn't corrected her directly, but rather tactfully carried on talking as though it were the most natural mistake in the world to make. If only people were quite so forgiving when you got the sex of their babies wrong.

'And she's just my life-saver, aren't you, Coco?' continued Alice, reaching down to stroke the dog's ears. 'She's my medical assistance dog, you see, Dr Graham. So she goes everywhere I go. She's incredibly clean and her training is second-to-none, but still . . .' her voice cracked slightly, a quaver hinting at the hurt that her upbeat delivery concealed. 'Well, let's just say that some people don't like having dogs around.'

Holly nodded, only too used to people around here aligning themselves as 'dog people' or 'cat people' as though the two were mutually exclusive. 'And the job in Bristol?' she ventured, her conversation with Pru Hartley at the market coming back to her now.

'Cards on the table, Dr Graham?' Alice looked up with open, trusting eyes, not entirely dissimilar to Coco's beside her. The pain and frustration was clear to see. 'I was only there for a few days before the patients started a petition. Obviously Bristol is a very multi-cultural city, but to be honest, Dr Graham, I might have underestimated how much cultural values would play a part. Lots of the patients seemed to be upset by Coco's presence – they seemed to believe that dogs are dirty, unclean, you know . . . Either way, they didn't want us there and I decided it was better to move on of my own volition rather than kick up a storm. I was probably a bit naïve in thinking that once anybody met her, they'd think differently.' She swallowed hard. 'People were spitting at her in the street, Dr Graham. It was an easy choice to leave in the end.'

Holly was so shocked that she wasn't ready with an appropriate response, but when Alice looked up, she smiled. 'You look how I felt.' She shrugged. 'Coco has saved my life on more than one occasion. I probably am a bit guilty of being biased in her favour.'

As the sun glanced down through the window, tiny dust motes floated above Coco's nose and she followed each one with her eyes. A tiny, almost imperceptible shift of her fluffy front paws showed how much restraint it was taking for her not to chase them around the room. As Alice dropped a hand down to touch her again, the motes were obviously instantly forgotten as Coco placed her nose into Alice's palm and snuffled affectionately. The bond between them was so strong it was almost tangible and it actually made Holly feel a little choked up.

'Would it be okay if I said hello to her?' Holly asked. 'Or is it too distracting while she's working?'

Alice smiled. 'Well, there's immediate Brownie points right there, Dr Graham. Thank you for asking.' At a single, precise flick of her hand, Alice gave Coco the command that obviously meant 'off duty' and Coco bounced on the spot for a moment, before snuffling her way over to Holly.

It was an unlikely way to conduct an interview, but over the next fifteen minutes, Holly learned more about diabetes detection dogs and Alice's medical background than she could possibly have foreseen, all the while sitting on the floor in her best navy skirt with a fluffy little cocker spaniel on her lap.

When she got to the last official question on her list, Holly scratched Coco's tummy as she asked Alice the Big One: 'Can you talk me through the reasons that General Practice appeals to you?'

Hearing about Alice's family and their appalling medical history, it was a wonder that she hadn't been tempted to go into medical research, Holly thought. But obviously, Alice had found that helping on the front line kept her own issues firmly in perspective. 'I'm not the only person with a chronic health condition, but sometimes I am the only doctor who has actually walked in their shoes,' she said. 'And I really believe that first-hand experience is an incredible learning opportunity, don't you? I mean, what the whole family went through after my grandfather lost his leg to diabetes – well, let's say that I can really relate.'

'And please don't think this has any bearing on the decision here, but I am intrigued a little. How does your own health impact on your work?' Holly asked.

Alice shrugged. 'It doesn't really, as long as I take my breaks and eat lunch when I'm supposed to. Not so far anyway.' She looked around for something wooden to touch and murmured under her breath. 'But Coco here gives me an early warning if my blood sugar goes loopy.' She grinned. 'That's a technical term obviously. And she will have to go everywhere with me, so if that would be a problem, I'd much rather you said now. I mean, I'd love this job and I know I could do it really well, but having Coco has changed my life completely and I could never give her up.'

'Of course not,' said Holly, indignant at the very thought. 'And nobody should ever ask you to choose.'

Alice smiled resignedly. 'Ah well, as I mentioned before, some people are just funny about dogs, Dr Graham. This is my sixth interview – nobody ever *says* it's the diabetes or the dog, but I've been passed over for less qualified candidates every single time.' She shrugged. 'It's something you get used to.'

Holly sighed. She had a really strong feeling about this girl and it wasn't obligation. They hadn't really added 'personal & family experience of hideous health conditions' to their search criteria but, speaking to Alice now, hearing her talk with such calm authority and empathy about truly challenging experiences, she couldn't help thinking that this had been a mistake.

Holly was still mulling over her decision that lunchtime, as she sat on the windowsill in the doctors' lounge in the calm before afternoon surgery, hiding out from the film crew who had been on particularly unsubtle and intrusive form all morning. She had a couple of hours left before picking up the twins, but finding a quiet spot to think had eclipsed popping to Tesco on her To Do list.

Feeling over-committed and under-resourced, she reluctantly had to concede that Taffy might have had a valid point that morning, when he'd gently suggested she had a few too many balls in the air. He'd quietly removed the moisturiser tube from her hand and replaced it with toothpaste, before suggesting a take-away supper from The Deli. She clicked distractedly on her phone to check her e-mails without any expectation of a reply from Milo – once again Taffy had been proven correct. No reply, just a week's worth of agitation on the off-chance.

'How did it go?' asked Taffy, as though her thoughts had conjured him, quietly slipping on to the windowsill beside her. 'Did you manage to find anyone who's good enough?'

'I did. And she's perfect,' Holly said quietly but with conviction. 'But I just need to be sure this is a head not heart decision.'

Taffy frowned. 'You've lost me.'

'She comes with a medical dog for her diabetes, you see,' and Holly went on to explain all the issues that young Alice Walker had experienced in trying to find a new position.

'Are you saying that you want to hire her just because you love the dog?' Taffy teased her.

'No!' said Holly vehemently.

Taffy shrugged. 'Although to be fair, I have heard of worse reasons . . .'

'It's not that,' Holly said. 'It's just that the other candidates were so awful, Taff. They wouldn't have fit in and they had all these *opinions* . . .' she shuddered slightly. 'And I know that Alice would just – work.'

'Then I really don't understand the soul-searching.' Taffy admitted defeat.

Holly turned to him and tried to explain, ticking her reasoning off on her fingers. 'There was no basis for comparison, because the others were truly awful. I want to help, because I feel awful about the prejudice she's experienced elsewhere. Her aunt is Pru Hartley and she's lived in Larkford for ever, so there's another potential conflict right away. Plus, I really love the idea of having another female doctor on staff and one that is brimming with compassion and empathy and is just a breath of feisty, Scottish fresh air . . .' She shrugged, running out of steam. 'She's just perfect really.'

'Well, don't go too far,' Taffy said seriously, hamming up his Welsh accent. 'You did say she was Scottish?'

Holly laughed. 'Don't get all Celtic on me, Jones. I just feel like I'm letting my personal bias towards her – and her dog – cloud my judgement.'

Taffy sighed, well accustomed to Holly's ability to overthink every scenario. 'But if you don't hire her, then you'd be doing us all a disservice. She's an excellent clinician and her references are glowing. Just because she's head and shoulders above the other candidates, doesn't mean you've missed something – maybe she's just in the right place at the right time.'

'Serendipity?' Holly said.

'No, Alice What's-her-face,' countered Taffy, deliberately

misunderstanding. 'And if you ask me, even though you haven't, we need to crack on and get this junior position filled – get a bit more structure in place.'

Holly nodded. 'I know. I've been thinking so much about all the scrutiny this Model Surgery business is going to unleash. I mean, if they sat in on our Partners' Meetings ... Well, it wouldn't take long for them to see the reality isn't quite so perfect.'

'But we do have fun,' Taffy said. 'I never thought Dan would finish Julia's vile smoothie this morning, did you? He'll do anything for a dare at the moment. Seriously, I'm having to work very hard not to take advantage of his vulnerable state. I even said no to a wager on our weekend run – hardly fair to just take his money—'

'But if we're already committed ...' Holly continued, almost as though he hadn't even spoken, 'then really it comes down to making the best of it. And that means hiring the best candidate, right? For us?'

Taffy nodded. 'I'd say so. But then I'm still banking on the new doctor to make up a five for poker, so ...'

'And I'm banking on the addition of a junior to remind us to set a good example,' Holly reminded him.

'And Alice will do that?' he asked.

Holly nodded, relaxing into her smile. 'Do you know, I rather think she will. And if not, then I'm sure Coco will corral us into line in no time.'

She looked across the room to where Lucy and Jade were mucking about trying to ascertain who had the biggest 'thigh gap'. They were going through all the magazines, tearing out pictures of celebrities they wanted to look like and pinning them up on the noticeboard for 'thinspiration'.

Of course, the Most Wanted poster of the Major still took

pride of place on The Practice noticeboard and Holly saw that somebody had recently scribbled on a reward of three pounds fifty. She also noticed that the nurses' scavenger hunt trophies had grown in scope lately, with a rather graphic photo of a boil being lanced, alongside one of Cassie Holland's gnome collection, caught in compromising positions doing unspeakable, ungnomely things to one another.

The idea of someone a little more level-headed diluting the gene-pool at The Practice was really rather attractive, no matter how much Holly secretly enjoyed their silliness.

'I knew you were the best person for the interviews,' Taffy said, leaning easily against her. 'You don't realise how freaky it is, how well you can read people. Patients, potential employees . . . I've never known you to get it wrong. Yet.'

She pulled back from him with wide eyes. 'Errm, are we forgetting about Milo in this scenario? I think we can agree that I got that one wrong . . .' She snuggled back into his chest, unwilling to relinquish the comfort of his arms. 'Maybe that's my Super Power? You know – lousy at picking husbands, great at picking colleagues . . .'

'Hey, so you're lousy at picking *first* husbands,' Taffy corrected with a nudge, 'but then, you always throw away the first pancake, right?'

Holly stiffened in his arms but said nothing. Her opinion on this particular topic was never one that Taffy wanted to hear.

Chapter 7

Julia shifted in her seat, crossing her legs until they were no longer pressed intimately against Quentin's; he certainly seemed to have a tenuous relationship with the notion of personal space. She smoothed a hand down the tanned length of her calf, annoyed with herself even for checking that they were as silky smooth as she might like them to be.

She looked up and caught the amused expression on his face that made her wonder if he could actually read her mind. They were clearly spending altogether too much time in each other's company. His eyes flickered appreciatively over her body and she was shocked to feel a brief, answering flash of attraction. This was not good news – this was not welcome news – and she was beginning to think that Dan might have a point about Quentin's private agenda.

She didn't fancy Quentin, of course she didn't. But there was something so beguiling about having the full beam of his focus on her, that it didn't hurt to remind herself of that fact occasionally. He was far too good-looking for his own good and he knew it.

Quentin's undivided attention, when he chose to bestow it, was almost bewitching. In his company, she felt her own moral compass swing wildly from the true north she had been working so hard to find. Quentin's priorities were simple. His show was more important than anything else – friends, colleagues, lovers, children. The rest of his crew were dedicated and slavish in their adoration of him, happy to throw in their lot to be swept up in his media ascendency.

It was almost as though he could sense Julia's hesitancy to completely commit and it only piqued his interest further.

'Since we've a few quiet minutes before the hordes descend,' he pulled a face that said all too clearly what he thought of Larkford's great unwashed, 'I thought we might have a little chat about us.'

Julia flinched a little. 'Us' was a topic with too much scope for conflict and she was already struggling to get a handle on where this conversation was heading. Quentin could be a hard one to read, a real task-master, who could turn on the charm and charisma like a switch when needed. He obviously felt that he needed something now, as his eyes were dancing with flirtation as he leaned against the desk beside her.

'Let me lay my cards on the table: I want you,' he said slowly. 'None of this fitting around schedules and taking the time you have left over. I just want first call.'

'Oh,' she managed eloquently, unable to push aside the images that danced through her mind of the two of them entwined. 'I'm not sure that's a good idea.' Julia wasn't stupid. She knew men like Quentin – had dated men like Quentin – and he was definitely bad news.

'Think about it, though,' he insisted. 'Your own show on prime-time TV. No painful patients to deal with every day. We can pick the agenda and, God knows, we could lead the debate about health care in the UK. Do you really want to pass up the opportunity?'

Julia was utterly thrown and she could see from the smug

expression on Quentin's face that it was exactly the outcome he'd been aiming for. He was toying with her for his own amusement, no doubt, but possibly also to see just how far he could push her before she bit back.

'You seem to have this all planned out,' she hedged, using so much effort to be nonchalant that a small muscle began to twitch in her eyelid.

'It's not a difficult equation,' he countered. 'You leave Larkford, move to London and then we take your career in the direction it deserves. Upwards. I have absolute faith in your abilities, Julia – and I don't mean in treating the sniffles. You have a credibility, a voice that we can use to shape the agenda. I'm in discussions for a nine o'clock slot – an hour, weekly for a twelve week run. I just need my leading lady . . .'

He reached out and laid a soft hand on her shoulder, his fingers lightly caressing the skin at the side of her neck. 'What do you say? Fancy taking things up a notch?'

Julia felt all her composure wobble under his piercing gaze. 'Quinn—' she began, reaching out for clarification. Her mobile phone skittered across the desk in front of her and she glanced down to check the caller ID, tapping the screen to reject the call when her mother's photograph flashed up.

Quentin watched her carefully but pointedly made no comment, even as she switched the phone to silent and it vibrated repeatedly across the desk. He rested his warm hand on hers, as it twitched towards the phone in a Pavlovian response, effortlessly holding her gaze. Julia swallowed hard, as his thumb began to circle her palm insistently. He leaned in towards her, almost as though he were about to kiss her, before whispering in her ear, 'Turn off the phone. I don't like to share.'

She hesitated for a moment before doing as he'd asked, gathering her thoughts and her resolve as she did so.

She pushed back her chair and moved over to the window, hoping the sight of Larkford laid out before her might give her the motivation to make what was undoubtedly the right decision.

'It's an interesting offer,' she said, deliberately avoiding his gaze. 'I'll need to give it some thought.'

'Don't think too long,' he said, walking around the desk to join her. 'I know you think this place is the answer, but to me, it seems as though you're settling for comfort over ambition.' He smoothed a stray lock of hair away from her face, his thumb fleetingly brushing her lips.

Julia batted his hand away, her physical reaction to his touch making her edgy and short-tempered. 'Oh Quinn, don't be tiresome,' she said, knowing full well that her non-chalance was beginning to annoy him and unwilling to admit how hard she was having to work to keep up the façade. 'I have a life here. I can't just up sticks on a whim! Five minutes ago, you were all for milking this Model Practice for all it was worth and now you're abandoning ship?'

'What can I say? The chance at a primetime slot changes everything.' He frowned, as though the thought had just occurred to him. 'On the other hand, we could keep the link with this place going in the new show? A regular segment on our rural cousins?'

'*Your* rural cousins,' Julia retorted. 'I live here.'

He shrugged. 'We'll see. Think about it. And maybe we can head up to London next week – you can sit in on a few of the development meetings. I guarantee this show is going to be a success, so all you have to decide is whether that will be with you, or without you.'

He leaned in and kissed her briefly on the cheek, his hand brushing her waist and lingering just a fraction too long. The intimacy of the gesture was not lost on Julia, but then Quentin had no scruples when it came to getting what he wanted. If only Julia was completely clear on what that actually was.

The sound of a different ringtone broke into her reverie, followed by the sound of Dan in the doorway, pointedly clearing his throat. 'If I'm not interrupting anything, I believe your mother would like a word.' He held out his mobile phone to Julia, the call already activated.

Julia reluctantly took the handset and held it to her ear, unsettled by Quentin's familiarity and angry at being backed into a corner; she was unwilling to have *this* conversation in front of anyone.

'Hello, Mum, it's not the best time actually . . .' she began, before being cut off by a torrent of words from the other end of the line. Her eyes fell to the floor automatically, as her whole body language seemed to slump and she made her way out of the room without saying a word. After all, her input was not always required on these soul-destroying telephone calls that seemed to be happening with increasing regularity.

Julia sat on the wall outside, as a light summer breeze lifted the hair from the back of her neck and she shivered. She held Dan's phone loosely in her lap and mentally replayed her mother's requests – no, demands – for yet more financial support. It occurred to her that she hadn't even asked Quentin what the remuneration for the London job might be. How ironic, if she were forced into her old habits of ambition and self-destruction to fund her parents' retirement. Would that make them proud? she wondered. Nothing else she ever achieved had.

'I thought you might like this.'

Julia turned at the sound of Grace's gentle voice and took the proffered cup of coffee.

'It's not as warm out here as it looks, is it?' Grace continued, sliding up beside Julia onto the wall.

Julia soundlessly sipped at the warm drink, unwilling to admit how chilled she was feeling. 'Thank you,' she said eventually, once the tiresome lump in her throat had subsided.

Grace just nodded. 'It's been a funny few days, hasn't it? The nurses in revolt, this Model Surgery nonsense and I've never sorted out hiring a new GP so quickly in my life! She seems like a good egg, though. I'm sure having another pair of hands around here won't hurt anyway.'

Julia stared across the Market Place, watching the Major and his little dog Grover amble along, stopping every few steps to greet someone and have a brief chat. What had once seemed exhaustingly incestuous and claustrophobic now seemed almost welcoming and familiar – was she really prepared to give all of that up, to return to the anonymity of London?

'You look like you've got the weight of the world on your shoulders,' Grace said quietly. 'And I know you're not one to idly gossip, but I did just want to say – if you fancy coming to my yoga class later, or you ever want to talk . . .' Her words petered out and Julia realised just how difficult she was making it for Grace to offer the hand of friendship in her direction.

She tore her gaze away from the tableau before her and turned to Grace. 'Will it work, do you think? Having a new GP and all the extra admin?'

Grace just shrugged. 'I guess we're going to have to take each day as it comes. Alice is lovely. I can do a lot of the new protocols and admin as part of my coursework apparently. And your producer chappie seems pleased anyway. He told me just now that I can have a bigger screen presence now I scrub up okay.' The laughter was bubbling through Grace's words, so it was clear she hadn't taken offence, but Julia was yet again aghast at Quentin's tactlessness.

'He didn't? Oh, Grace, I'm so sorry.' Not for the first time, Julia found herself shying away from Quentin's insensitive and forthright behaviour – it gave her a tiny taste of how life might be *all* the time, if she chose to jump ship. Having somebody represent you, who chose to represent themselves in such an abrupt manner? It was hardly a recipe for success.

'On the other hand,' Julia said with a genuine smile, 'he may have a point. You are looking particularly lovely today, Grace. It can't just be all the yoga, can it?'

Grace beamed, a compliment from Julia meaning so much more, for being such a rare beast. 'A little bit yoga, a little bit freedom, a little bit shopping.' She tugged at her lengthy plait, which hung neatly over her shoulder. 'I'm thinking that this might have to go, though – it's really getting in the way of my headstands.'

Julia blinked – the very idea of planning one's hairstyle around such practical considerations being virtually alien to her. 'You wouldn't cut off all your beautiful hair just for that?' she clarified.

Grace twiddled the offending plait around her fingers. 'If I hate it short, it'll grow back,' she said calmly. 'And it's not like I need to please anyone else these days. It's actually rather liberating,' she confided. 'With Roy gone and the boys finally off at college, I only have to think about me, myself and

I – and it turns out we're all remarkably easy-going. Nobody telling me not to wear jeans, nobody needing a three-course meal every evening, or insisting I'll look like a boy with short hair . . .'

Julia watched the animation on her face as she spelled out all the little ways in which her marriage had limited her true self, rather than supported and encouraged her. It was the best advert that Julia had heard in a long time for staying single.

'Of course, it's not like that for you, is it?' Grace carried on. 'I can't imagine Dan ever trying to clip your wings. Or bemoaning having breakfast cereal for supper.'

Julia said nothing. She had no idea what to say. Watching the enthusiasm on Grace's face as she talked about rediscovering all her old passions and interests left her feeling lost. Before Dan, there had been work. And her mother. And anxiety. And work.

Being with Dan had given Julia all the liberation she needed. She just couldn't work out why that still didn't seem to be enough.

Sitting side by side with Grace, she let her chatter on about how the nomination was going to affect them all. Only half of her was listening, though; the other half was tentatively exploring the idea of a fresh start in London and her own primetime TV show. It was only when she realised that Dan starred in both scenarios that she realised that, in this case, fantasy and reality were unlikely to overlap and some incredibly difficult choices lay ahead.

Grace slid down off the wall and waited for Julia. 'Come on then, Dr Channing. Let's go back inside and crack on. Your patients will be starting a mutiny in a minute and I've an essay due on the parameters and opportunities for social media in a public healthcare setting.' She pulled a face. 'Of course, it's a load of pretentious twaddle, but if I want my shiny certificate ...'

Julia held back for a moment, unsure whether to ruin the moment by confessing that she had no idea what Grace was going on about. All this talk of coursework and essays had been billowing around The Practice for weeks. It was somewhat galling to Julia to realise that she had never once bothered to ask what it was actually all about.

She looked up to find that Grace was standing in the doorway waiting. 'Not long 'til home time,' she said reassuringly. 'And if you change your mind, we'll be on the river bank from eight. Just wear something comfortable and I'll bring a spare yoga mat just in case.'

'Thank you,' said Julia, not knowing what else to say. Somehow she didn't think sticking her bum in the air al fresco was going to offer any solutions to her problems, no matter how much good it was obviously doing for Grace.

Chapter 8

Early the next morning, Holly blew furiously on the whistle and prayed that, on this occasion, Eric might surrender his squirrel obsession and come back to heel. What had started out as a family joke had now escalated to the point where Eric could not catch even a glimpse of a squirrel without throwing caution to the winds and giving chase. The twins would now scream 'Squizzel!' at the top of their voices upon the merest hint of a bushy tail, for fear of being pulled along at the end of Eric's lead. Again.

Holly sighed and pushed her hands deeper into her pockets. It may technically have been summer, but at this hour of the morning all the dog-walkers in Larkford Park were bundled up against the fresh, crisp chill. It was such a shame that Lizzie had bailed on their plans to walk together; it was probably the only time in the day when they could have an uninterrupted conversation. She blew on the whistle again and briefly considered giving chase, only the thought of making a complete prat of herself in front of everybody else in the park giving her pause. Somehow Lizzie managed to laugh off his appalling behaviour when she was in charge, but Holly found it harder to excuse. She was a play-it-by-the-rules girl at heart and found it excruciating whenever the twins or the dog went rogue, as was increasingly the case.

She checked her watch and waved hello to the lovely couple from the fishmonger's, with their beautiful Lhasa Apso trotting obediently at their heels. There was nothing for it – she was going to have to brave the shrubbery and pull the little tyke out.

'Dr Graham? Holly?' called a voice from behind her. 'Are you looking for this young man?'

Holly turned to see Alice Walker waving at her, her cheeks flushed pink and her hair tucked neatly behind her ears. She looked like a china doll, assuming you ignored the Doc Marten boots and super-skinny jeans, and indeed the rather tatty, oversized Aran jumper.

She carried a ball thrower and Coco's little on-duty jacket was looped over her shoulder. Coco herself was frolicking in an almost puppy-like manner with a very big, very dirty Labradoodle. A Labradoodle that was following her every move with his enormous brown eyes and occasionally bouncing on the spot like Tigger when she got too close. A Labradoodle that looked an awful lot like Eric.

'Alice – you're a life saver,' said Holly with feeling as she jogged over towards her. 'I was just weighing up whether to disown him completely or take to the shrubbery to flush him out.' She smiled. 'His passion for squirrels has taken a turn for the obsessive, I'm afraid,' she said, by way of explanation.

To her utter amazement, as she spoke, a large grey squirrel scampered past the two dogs and straight up an ancient horse chestnut tree, within yards of Eric's quivering nose.

Nothing. Niente.

No reaction.

Holly gaped attractively, before realising that she was look-ing a bit bonkers in front of her new colleague and slowly closed her mouth. 'That,' she said categorically, 'has *never* happened before.'

Taking a moment to watch the two dogs mucking about with Alice's tennis ball, it was easy to see why. Apparently for dogs, tail beat, well, tail every time. Eric's attention was utterly focused on the little chocolate spaniel and when Alice finally blew on the whistle to recall Coco, Eric meekly trotted along beside her, his nose inches from her ears at all times. When Coco sat, so did Eric. When Coco lay down, so did Eric.

Alice turned to Holly in amazement. 'I thought you said he wasn't very well trained?' She clicked her tongue and both dogs were immediately on their feet beside her.

'He isn't,' said Holly. 'He's basically been a stroppy, hor-monal teenager since he turned two.'

Alice grinned. 'Maybe he just needs to find a sense of purpose, like Coco? Maybe squirrel hunting wasn't terribly fulfilling?'

'Or,' countered Holly, 'maybe he just has a huge crush on Miss Coco?'

They turned to look as Eric nudged his nose against her ears and Coco deliberately turned her back. The expression on his face was nothing short of plaintive, like when Taffy ate the crusts off the twins' plates that had previously been destined for Eric's enjoyment.

'Oh dear – unrequited love at this time in the morning,' sighed Alice. 'I'm so sorry.'

'Don't apologise,' said Holly. 'It's actually rather good for him to realise that he can't get everything he wants. To be honest, I think we might all be spoiling him a bit – going back and forth between mine and Lizzie's, he has permanent novelty value.'

Alice nodded. 'It's a bit like a weekend relationship for him. You know, when you never get to the boring, mundane stuff like who unloads the dishwasher or replaces the loo roll.'

Holly raised an eyebrow but said nothing. There was a stillness and confidence in Alice Walker that gave her maturity and gravitas way beyond her years. It was impressive, to be sure, but it was also a little galling to realise that somebody significantly younger than you, might actually have more of their ducks in a row. This one innocent comment allowed Holly to breathe easier; this calm certainty that Alice carried around her, had actually been the one question mark in Holly's mind. It was a delicate balancing act being a GP after all: self-assured enough to inspire confidence, but open enough to invite sharing and take on advice.

There were enough strong personalities at The Practice already that Holly had been wary of inviting another one into their midst, whilst also acknowledging that anybody shy or self-effacing might simply sink without trace.

They fell into step beside one another, heading back towards the centre of town, conversation flowing freely. It was both a blessing and a curse of the dog-walking community in Larkford that it was all too easy to over-share – bundled up in coats and scarves and walking alongside one another. This morning Holly had to keep reminding herself, that however chatty and lovely Alice was, in a little over an hour, Holly would essentially become her boss.

Alice stopped suddenly. 'Holly? Do you mind if I ask you a question – off the record, I mean?' Both dogs sat neatly beside her and Holly began to wonder whether that ship had already sailed.

'You've all been really open about this Model Surgery business and I can understand that it's exciting to get recognition for doing your jobs so well, but . . .' She frowned. 'I guess what I'm trying to ask is why? Why add to your workload with all the extra admin and the extra scrutiny? What could you possibly gain from being under the spotlight, except loads of stress and a three-line press release in the *Larkford Gazette*?'

Holly smiled, a tiny bit relieved that the question hadn't been something more personal. She knew that the coupled-up nature of the partnership would be giving her reason to pause, if she were in Alice's shoes. 'Off the record? You're right. It's a blessing and a curse. We do, as you rightly say, have to jump through some administrative hoops. But on the other hand, there are quite a few perks that we believe will benefit our patients.' Holly was trying to be tactful, but then she hadn't picked the brightest candidate without realising that it would come with its own challenges.

And Alice wasn't prepared to let this one go. She shrugged. 'I don't see it.'

Holly nodded, making the decision that Alice would probably find this out sooner rather than later anyway. 'You, Alice. We get you. And we get funding for an extra three nursing clinics a week. So, in our minds, the trade-off is worth it.'

Alice was silent for a moment, as though her counterargument had been swept away in the breeze. 'Crikey,' she said quietly after a moment. 'No pressure, then.'

Holly stepped a little closer, careful to maintain a certain professional distance. 'We're excited to have someone young, dynamic and switched-on joining our team. We think our patients will love you and quite frankly, we could do with the occasional day off.' She aimed for a light, jokey tone, but could tell that Alice had taken news of this extra responsibility seriously.

'I really hope I can deliver for you, Dr Graham. I'm so excited about this opportunity and I didn't mean to sound like a nay-sayer before – I just wanted to get a clearer idea of the team's motivations.'

Holly grinned. 'You mean, you wanted to know if we were all out for maximum media exposure and glory? I don't blame you. And Alice – you haven't expressed any doubts just now that I haven't already thought a hundred times over.'

'Sorry,' Alice said.

'Don't be. I quite like that you're already getting the lay of the land around here. Patients first, plaudits second. And somewhere in there, a social life if you have the time, the energy or the inclination.'

By the time they reached the Market Place, Holly was more convinced than ever that she had made the right decision, which was just as well really. The alternative didn't bear thinking about, since all the red tape had been neatly marshalled, and in record time, by the wonderful Grace. Talk about fast-tracking an application!

'Good morning, good morning,' called out Marion Waverly, bustling over to say hello. 'I was just about to open up the shop and saw you both chattering away there. You looked like you were having a lovely gossip. I'm Marion. Are you a friend of Holly's?' The woman was an unstoppable barrage of words and Holly could see Alice struggling to keep up.

'Marion, I'd like you to meet Dr Walker. Alice. She's going to be joining us at The Practice, along with the lovely Coco, of course.'

She noticed Marion's eyes flicker down to Coco, who was now re-suited and booted in her assistance jacket. Holly knew that there was no better way of gently disseminating the presence of Coco at The Practice than by telling Marion – the Larkford Oracle. Nevertheless, she was intrigued to see that the wonderfully calm and capable Alice immediately tensed beside her, as though awaiting judgement.

Marion smiled warmly. 'Well, I won't say hello to Coco just now, as I can see the little mite's on duty, but I'll gladly welcome you to the town.' She reached out and shook Alice's hand. 'I'm sure the other doctors will just have to get over the fact that we'll all come and see you now instead, just to visit with your gorgeous little spaniel there.'

Alice's eyes widened, as though this gushing welcome was so very far from what she'd been expecting that she was almost disbelieving. 'We do love Julia Channing, obviously,' blustered Marion, trying belatedly to involve a little tact, 'but she's not really a dog person is she? Shame that. But then with you and Holly here ... well, two out of three ain't bad.'

'Meatloaf?' Holly smiled, trying to place the lyrics out of context.

Marion gave her a strange look. 'Not at this time in the morning, Holly love. I'd rather have one of those croissants the Major likes.' She gave a little shudder. 'Meatloaf? For breakfast? Whatever next?' With a waggle of her fingers, she was on her way, leaving Holly feeling a bit daft.

'Don't worry, Dr Graham. I got the reference,' reassured Alice kindly. 'And how lovely was she about Coco?'

Holly smiled. 'Do you know, Alice, I think you're going to fit in here rather well.'

*

'I just can't see how she's going to fit in here, that's all,' Julia was saying stubbornly, as Holly walked in to Dan's office before morning surgery.

'Well, it's a bit late now,' Dan responded tiredly. 'All the paperwork's been done and her references are spectacular. Stop worrying. We'd have been fools to miss out on having her here.'

Julia sighed heavily as she noted Holly's arrival. Despite having been consulted every step of the way throughout the accelerated interview and hiring process, Julia was clearly rattled and having buyer's remorse. 'How old did you say she was?'

Holly smiled, knowing exactly the train of thought that Julia was following. 'She does look awfully together for twenty-eight, doesn't she?'

'Christ! Is that what twenty-eight looks like these days? I rather wish you'd chosen someone a little more . . . well, that's to say a little less . . .' Her words petered out, as though the effort to find the next one was just too much.

'You're going to have to finish that question you know, if you actually want me to answer it,' Holly teased her.

'Well,' Julia shrugged. 'She makes me tired just listening to her. She's been in the office with Grace since eight o'clock and she's so bloody peppy – I mean, seriously, worse than you were with your bouncy little ponytail when you first arrived. And does she have to sound so completely certain about everything? There's no prevarication, no hesitation – she's just straight in there with a well-considered opinion. Where's her endearing sense of self-doubt?'

'Wearing, that, isn't it?' interrupted Taffy, wandering into the office behind Holly. He grinned as his gentle jibe sailed straight over Julia's head. 'Seems like a winning combination to me actually – all of your conviction, Julia, but tempered with Holly's enthusiasm and general gusto.'

He ducked as Holly swatted him. 'What?'

Julia looked mutinous. 'Well, I think you've all had your heads turned by that little dog. It's well documented you know – lame duck syndrome – you lot are such softies that you just can't resist wanting to help.'

Holly shook her head at Julia's inconsistency – she was clearly just looking to pick a fight this morning. 'Well, I've spent more time with her than any of you and I think she's a find. Trust me – lame duck or no – with the right guidance she'll be a swan in no time.'

'Unless it's another peacock you're after, Jules. There seemed to be plenty of those on the short list – all style no substance.' There was an undertone to Dan's words that made Holly glance at him sharply, but his face was neutral.

'Look, Julia?' Holly interrupted. 'You don't need to worry – she's entirely human. And you're right, she has had a tricky time and, okay, so if she needs to act super-confident when starting a new job – well, hats off to her. Just hold off on the judgement and let her find her feet, okay? Don't go looking for trouble.'

Without waiting for an answer and unwilling to get pulled in to whatever argument Dan and Julia were clearly having, Holly walked back through to her office, to find Alice waiting for her. She lingered in the doorway for a moment and watched, as Alice made sure that her canine companion was looking her best. To a casual observer, it would be easy to mistake the little chocolate spaniel as a well-loved pet. She sat directly beside Alice, one paw resting lightly on her thigh, happily submitting to having her ears smoothed down and nuzzling in to accept the proffered kiss. A closer look, however, would reveal the neat little red jacket that the dog wore, announcing her role as a diabetic assistance dog to all of Alice's patients.

The younger woman wore a neat tailored skirt and a dinky jacket that gave her petite frame structure and poise. It was a far cry from her tomboyish dog-walking attire. All scrubbed up, she was the medical equivalent of Audrey Hepburn, with her gamine crop and wide eyes. Their main problem, Holly considered, might actually be convincing the patients that she was old enough to be a qualified doctor.

Holly lightly cleared her throat before stepping into the room. 'Morning, morning. I gather you've been sorting out the paperwork tsunami with Grace?'

Alice nodded. 'I can't believe how quickly this has all happened.'

Holly couldn't help but agree. For her though, it wasn't so much the speed with which they had interviewed and hired their new junior doctor, it was the fact that not so very long ago, she'd been sitting down the hall as Dan Carter had given her a similar induction into life at The Practice. How times had changed.

'I know, but it's a good thing. No time for nerves. We can just crack on. The basic plan is for you to spend a few days shadowing us. Probably half a day each, something like that and then we'll let you loose on your own. We'd like for you to get a feel for how we do things here – we don't always choose efficiency over empathy, or indeed cost over care.

'But what we do try to provide is a community health programme – that includes prevention as well as treatment. We don't consider health to be an absence of illness. We have a slightly more proactive approach here. And I know Dan's spoken to you about our Health in the Community Scheme and I really want you to play a big role in that. You're young and eloquent and, dare I say it, a little inspirational – so maybe we can use that when we're talking to school children and our more youthful intake.' Holly paused, a little flushed. 'Sorry – I do tend to get on my soapbox about this. Have you got any questions?'

Alice smiled. 'I did just want to clarify – this proactive approach to health – are we talking beardy-weirdy alternative stuff or just the basics?'

'Good question. And, to be honest, without an easy answer. I would have no problem personally suggesting weekly massages for a patient with chronic stress, or indeed kinesiology for suspected food intolerances, but really when we talk about a proactive approach within the confines of The Practice, we're talking about nutrition, hydration, safe sex, healthy relationships, stress prevention . . .' Holly was ticking issues off on her fingertips when Alice interrupted.

'Is that what we're aiming for – prevention being better than cure and all that? Get in ahead of it?' she asked earnestly.

'In a nutshell, I suppose we are,' Holly replied, any annoyance at being interrupted overshadowed by her pleasure at Alice's eagerness. She just hoped that Alice's enthusiasm for the job would remain so blissfully un-jaded after a few days of verrucas, sore throats and non-specific whining by the General Public at large.

'Most importantly,' Holly said, flicking a glance at the clock on the wall, 'remember that there is no such thing as a stupid question. If there's a gap in your knowledge, we need to fill it, but be tactful. In the next few days, our patients need to have faith that you know what you're doing, so save the questions for after the consultations today. Jot them down and never be afraid to tell a patient that you'd like to consult with a senior GP. They may not appreciate coming back for another appointment, but it's definitely better than giving duff advice with potential consequences.'

'Okay then,' said Alice, sitting forward on her seat, with Coco mirroring her every move. 'Where do we start?'

Chapter 9

'Whatever you do, don't agree to look at Arthur Beckett's funny-looking mole,' said Taffy, as he slumped down in the chair beside Dan's desk. He'd just returned from a quick prawn baguette at The Kingsley Arms and was looking decidedly green around the gills.

Dan frowned. 'Nasty one? Should we organise a biopsy?'

Taffy shook his head. 'Nope. Just a rather dead one he'd trapped in his garden.' He swallowed hard. 'Quite a while ago, it seems. He's inexplicably proud of it.'

Dan guffawed at Taffy's unlikely squeamishness. 'Yeah, they can get a bit competitive about stuff like that around here. I remember a few summers back, one of the farmers had a party in the woods to celebrate his enormous ant hill.' Dan paused. 'It would probably have been better if he hadn't tried to pose for a photo on top of it, but I suppose you live and learn.'

He looked up and grinned at Taffy's queasy grimace. 'I thought you were a country boy through and through?'

Taffy shook his head. 'Easy on the rotting stuff. Could happily go my whole life without insects. You should see me and Holly if there's a spider in the bath. We'd be screwed without Eric, to be honest,' he confided sheepishly. Eric's legendary spider-catching abilities had been one of Lizzie's only successful training gambits – a fact that she and Holly both hugely appreciated.

Grace pushed open the door with her hip, balancing a precarious pile of A4 binders in her arms. 'A little help here, boys?'

She plonked them down on Dan's desk with a thud and fixed them both with a steely glare. 'And this, my erstwhile friends, is what "a little extra paperwork" looks like!'

Dan could feel himself blushing as Grace quoted his own words of reassurance back at him. Obviously they all knew that the admin team would carry the load of the procedural documents generated by their nomination. Seeing it in the flesh, so to speak, was quite a different reality. Six vast ring binders formed a sloping tower on his desk and he pulled an apologetic face. 'Do you want me to help hand these round to everyone?' he offered, as an olive branch.

Grace shook her head. 'No need. Besides, these six are just your copies.'

Taffy let rip a snort of laughter that he quickly swallowed when Grace's attention swivelled towards him. 'Oh, no need to feel jealous, Dr Jones, I've popped yours on your desk already.'

'But Grace ...' he protested pathetically. 'You know I'm no good at paperwork.'

'Or insects, arachnids or moles, apparently,' Dan butted in supportively, earning himself a filthy look from his mate.

Grace, on the other hand, was a gentler soul than was probably sensible in her position. She wiggled her bottom up onto the treatment couch and took pity on them. 'Look, just skim-read them and stick a Post-it on the pages you disagree with or don't understand. I'll have to go through them line by line anyway ...'

Taffy scowled at the heap. 'Are you sure we've actually got enough Post-its?' he queried tiredly, as he stood up to leave.

Dan quietly watched Grace from behind his leaning tower of filing, as she sat on the couch with the afternoon sunshine streaming through the sash windows onto her face. She turned to look at him and smiled impishly. 'Don't worry, I'll take pity on him in a minute. I just have to be able to say that each partner has been given a set of the procedural codes for reference.'

He grinned. 'Well, don't let him off the hook too soon, will you? I think he should probably read the first two at least, don't you?'

Grace laughed and leaned back against the wall. 'You, Dan Carter, are a bad influence! Do you think I could persuade him to get some quotes in for the Health in the Community launch party? Or maybe he might enjoy doing my cost:benefit analysis of additional nursing clinics for my coursework, too?'

'Crikey, that sounds a bit dry. Are you sure this course is worth all the hassle, Grace? You've always got a job here, and last time I checked, we weren't insisting you get this diploma to do it.' Dan tried to be reassuring but the filthy look Grace gave him obviously meant he'd put his foot in it again.

'I'm not doing it for you,' she said fiercely, before remembering who she was speaking to and taking a calming breath. 'I'm doing it for me. Because I can and because sometimes it's nice to challenge what you're capable of, don't you think?'

'I guess,' Dan said apologetically. 'I really didn't mean to imply—' He stopped, suddenly realising that he had absolutely no idea what he'd been implying. He'd just been making conversation. He shrugged and leaned forward, suddenly anxious to connect. 'Have we been there for you, Gracie? Enough, I mean?'

She smiled, the sun illuminating the smooth lines of her face and the extraordinary length of her lashes. 'I can't pretend it hasn't been utterly vile at times. But you know, it's getting easier.'

It was just under a year since Grace's husband Roy had taken one too many chances with drink-driving and hit an articulated lorry on the M5. Thankfully nobody else had been injured, but it was an ignominious end for Roy. Grace had simply withdrawn into herself for a few months, before quietly and steadily piecing her life back together. Dan would never say it out loud, but he couldn't help thinking that, without the influence of their lay-about father, her two boys were actually starting to show some resourcefulness and drive. Having abandoned signing on in favour of signing up, Freddie was now doing basic training at the Army College in Harrogate and Luke was doing a college-based apprenticeship in carpentry. It had been a difficult year all round, but the signs that Grace was recovering had been there to see for a while – Dan just couldn't quite believe he hadn't noticed them before.

Where the knee-length skirts and sensible flat shoes used to be, were now gentle sundresses and wedge-heeled sandals. Her yoga mat had taken up permanent residence in the corner of her office and he was quite sure he'd spotted her and some friends only last night, bending themselves around like pretzels on the river bank.

'And this course?' Dan prompted, amused to see her blush rather sweetly.

'Well, that's just a little something I promised myself. I know it's probably too late to go and get a degree, but it's a place to start. Once I get the diploma for Medical Administration, it opens up a whole raft of options.'

'As long as you don't get any ideas about leaving us, Gracie,' Dan said firmly. 'You know we'd be lost without you.'

She slid down off the couch abruptly. 'Don't say that,' she said sharply. The atmosphere in the room had shifted slightly and Dan was at a loss to know what he'd said wrong. But Grace wasn't Julia; she wasn't about to flounce out of the room in a cloud of uncertainty and ill-feeling.

She pulled up a chair to Dan's desk and tried to explain her reaction. 'It's a bit embarrassing actually. But, you know how if you hear something often enough, it becomes famil-iar – even if it's not true? If somebody tells you over and over – whether it's with their words or their actions – that what *you* need isn't important. Well, you start to believe it. Even if you get praise and support elsewhere – it just doesn't ring true because the old dialogue is still playing in the back of your mind?

'Well, it was like that for me with Roy. I wasn't happy. He knew that I wanted more for myself – but he was convinced that if I went out and found it, it wouldn't necessarily include him. So it was easier for him just to keep me doubting.

'Honestly, Dan, grieving someone after they've died is hard – and don't let anybody tell you otherwise – but in some ways it's actually easier than grieving the person you might have been. Every single day.'

Dan reached out and took her hand. 'I was only joking, Grace. I was trying – obviously in a very ham-fisted way – to let you know how much we appreciate you here. Diploma or no diploma.'

She squeezed his hand and then let go. 'I just wonder sometimes what would have happened if I hadn't got preg-nant when I did. I look at you and Holly and it makes me wonder . . . And I guess the whole turning forty thing, it does rather focus the mind on the road less travelled, don't you think?' She stood up and smoothed down her skirt, gathering her papers and her composure.

Dan tried and failed to hide the shocked expression on his face. His own upcoming fortieth had certainly prompted a few gags from his mates, but somehow he'd automatically assumed Grace to be that bit older.

There were no flies on her though, and she shook her head, teasing him, 'I knew it – I knew you'd all got me marked as a fuddy-duddy. Just because I had my boys a bit younger than most . . .'

She shrugged off his protestations. 'I'm the same age as you, you wally. How did you not know that? Just because you had a somewhat closer relationship with contraception at Med School than I did, doesn't make us all that different, you know.'

She left with a smile, but Dan couldn't help but disagree. Becoming a parent so young had clearly changed the course of Grace's life, whereas Dan was still essentially living like a carefree bachelor. And though she'd often mentioned in the past her desire to work in medicine, he had always assumed – sexist plonker that he apparently was – that she meant in a supporting role. The fact that Grace had once had her sights set on becoming a doctor herself had rather blown Dan's mind. The way the tiny strap of her sundress had slipped off her tanned shoulder as she left was frankly just adding to the confusing array of emotions he couldn't begin to process.

Luckily for Dan's sanity, there was never much time for navel-gazing and reflection at The Practice and he'd clearly used up today's share chatting to Grace. He was just getting to grips with dictating some consultant referrals when Lucy launched herself through his doorway like a human tornado. 'He's here! He's actually here!' she cried. Her voice was like a clarion call throughout the building and all the doors along the corridor flew open.

There was no need to scroll through his mental Rolodex of local celebrities, even though the area seemed to have become the newest place to be, for an off-duty celeb these days.

Dan knew differently. There was only one local resident who could elicit such excitement by showing his face at The Practice.

'He doesn't have an appointment,' said Lucy breathlessly, her words running over each other, 'but I think you should just come out and get him before he changes his mind and leaves.'

But Dan was already on his feet, rushing towards Reception with alacrity, gathering followers in his wake as the whispers around them grew to heated debate and his entourage swept through the waiting room.

'Major!' said Dan in delight, hand outstretched to shake. His relief at finding the old boy here under his own steam and seemingly in reasonable health was not to be underestimated. 'Do I take it then, that Andy McLeod has finally succumbed?'

The Major gave him a wicked smile. 'You can indeed. All bets are off. Bronchitis, they reckon, maybe a touch of pneumonia since he left it so long to see anyone.'

'There but for the grace of God, Dr Carter . . .' chimed in Marion, not wishing to be excluded from the festivities.

'Indeed,' Dan replied. He knew only too well about the Major's bonkers bet with his oldest friend – it had been the source of much speculation and debate over the years. Many people could not understand why the Major would commit to a lifetime without any medical care whatsoever, on the strength of winning a bet. A bottle of the legendary Scotch, *Black Bowmore*, was at stake, but Dan firmly believed it was the pride and stubbornness of the two men that had forced the bet into its fortieth year. Indeed, without the local vets and some off-book treatment by Julia from time to time, Dan was rightfully relieved that the outcome had not been more disastrous.

'Where shall we start then?' Taffy interrupted, his excitement getting the better of him. 'Quick MOT and a cholesterol test?'

'Don't spook him,' hissed Dan, trying to keep his demeanour upbeat and non-threatening. 'At least let the poor old bugger get through the door before you start threatening him with needles!'

Thankfully their exchange went unheard as Holly was so busy congratulating Marion for having kept her new husband in such fine fettle and getting him here.

Richard Le Grange, the Major's snooty neighbour poked his head through from the waiting room. 'I'm assuming it won't take all three of you to look after that old buffoon. Only, I've been waiting half an hour already and I'm ten years older than him!'

Their entourage reluctantly departed, despite Taffy's best attempts at getting Dan to 'toss for it'.

Marion bustled along beside her husband looking pleased as punch at all the attention. 'Thank God, Andrew went down when he did, Dr Carter. This one's been clutching at his chest with heartburn for weeks.'

'Well, maybe if you weren't such a nag, I wouldn't be so stressed?' the Major countered, as he did indeed begin to paw at his barrel chest with discomfort. Marion, a force to be reckoned with at the best of times and well accustomed to this state of affairs, simply reached into her voluminous handbag and pulled out a tube of antacids.

As the two of them bickered and bantered away, every word laced with cheerful affection, Dan began to wonder if he would ever get a word in edgewise and Taffy seemed unable to stem the laughter bubbling up, still trailing after them by default, caught up in the excitement.

'Ooh, Peregrine – you're getting a BOGOF,' said Marion happily.

'There's no need for that kind of talk, I'm here, aren't I?' protested the Major breathlessly, as he obligingly chomped on his tablets.

Dan and Taffy struggled not to catch each other's gaze to avoid complete impropriety as they struggled to come to terms with the Major as Peregrine.

'Well then, Peregrine,' said Dan in the end, 'let us at least Carpe Diem and give you a once-over. Or possibly an ECG,' he added, noting that his patient had gone a rather alarming colour. 'Maybe we should be talking about these antacids you seem to be mainlining?'

'He does make a terrible fuss about his heartburn though, Doctor,' began Marion.

'But there's nothing wrong with my hearing though, woman, so perhaps you'd like to pipe down, so we can get this business over and done with?'

It didn't surprise Dan to see that, beneath all the bossiness and bluff exterior, the Major was actually looking a little bit worried. It was only natural, he supposed, to be concerned that something entirely treatable might have taken on life-altering proportions through simple neglect, much as it apparently had with his co-conspirator.

Taffy grudgingly left them to it, at Dan's insistence.

The Major leaned in close to Dan as Marion shuffled around to find a place to sit. 'Just to be clear, Doc, I'm here under sufferance and to get some peace and quiet at home, okay. So no needles, alright?'

Dan smiled and gestured for the Major to take a seat. 'If necessary, I can get young Jade in here to do the honours – always fairly distracting that – but I would suggest we take your blood pressure first, eh?'

The Major harrumphed happily and began to roll up his sleeve. 'I imagine you'll find that I'm fitter than a man half my age,' he said confidently.

'Yes, if he's a smoking, drinking, coal miner with insomnia and a false leg . . .' cut in Marion. 'Don't go easy on him, Dr Carter. He's no spring chicken, but in his head he's thirty and invincible.'

Before the two of them could pick up with the bickering, Dan made an executive decision and banished Marion to the waiting room. 'I'm trying to get his heart rate to go down, Marion, and you do appear to be having the opposite effect!' She silenced him completely by giving him a knowing wink, which he felt he would have been so much happier without, opening up as it did, a whole new train of thought about the pair of them.

'Well,' breathed Dan, as he sat back in his chair and assessed his patient. 'At least we can talk a little privately now. What can I do you for?'

'Mine's a double whisky, if you've any lingering in that drawer of yours,' the Major blustered, obviously uncomfortable.

Dan just shook his head. 'I'll buy you one in the pub later. Now, spill the beans. How bad are the chest pains really? Are we talking, I-ate-too-much-roast-beef heartburn, or

I-can't-actually-breathe-and-my-arm-hurts?' Dan asked gently.

The Major harrumphed again. 'A little of both to be honest.'

Dan tried not to let his eyebrows shoot entirely into his hairline as the numbers on the Major's blood pressure reading steadily climbed higher and higher. 'And how would you say you were feeling right now?' he asked.

'Not too pretty,' the Major said, after much consideration. He leaned forward in his chair. 'The missus and I had a bit of a to-do about coming here on spec, so it got the old ticker racing a bit. Fabulous filly, my Marion, but, dear God, she's got a mouth on her!' He didn't look at all upset about that, thought Dan, in fact pride was the closest emotion that Dan could identify.

'Of course,' said the Major, 'I did have one or two snifters just to celebrate when I got the letter as well . . .'

Dan guided him across to the examination couch where Grace had been sitting earlier, swinging her legs in the after-noon sunshine. He couldn't help but think how much she would have enjoyed hearing the affectionate banter back and forth between Marion and the Major. It wasn't lost on him though, that the only sentiment he attached to Julia in this scenario was whole-hearted relief that she hadn't been the only one on duty when Peregrine Waverly finally plucked up the courage to march through the door.

'Any other medical issues you're aware of?' asked Dan as he gave him a complete once-over; after all, who knew when he might be tempted back?

'Nothing dramatic,' shrugged the Major with a hacking cough. 'I may have gone a bit deaf in one ear, there's a chance one of my toes might be broken – Grover's fault that, tripping me up after the pub the other night – and, now let me see, it hurts like a bastard when I pee and there's a bit of blood in my you-know-what . . .'

'Right,' said Dan faintly, jotting down a few notes beside him. 'Well, at least it's nothing dramatic.'

Chapter 10

Holly was already fuming at being summarily summoned to sit on the tiny chairs at Pinetrees Nursery the next day, while she awaited her latest bollocking from Mrs Harlow – the erst-while Headmistress of Larkford's only pre-school and surely the inspiration for Roald Dahl's infamous Miss Trunchbull. She checked her watch yet again, wondering what Alice might make of all this.

It was one thing for Holly to be excited about becom-ing a mentor for their new GP, it was quite another to give a prime example during her very first week that juggling family and work was no easy feat. Holly tapped out a text to Grace, explaining her delay and stared out of the window, awaiting her fate with resignation. Gales of laughter and chatter billowed around the grassy playground outside, where the children were playing Grandmother's Footsteps at high volume.

Louise, the sweet girl who helped out with the admin from time to time, noted how long she had been kept waiting and took pity on her, leaning in, her voice low, 'Apparently the twins have been giving the other kids special haircuts, Dr Graham. Something about wanting to be like Taffy, I gather.' She was unable to hide the humour in her voice, but

Holly was absolutely aghast and plunged straight into Parental Shame.

'Seriously? But that's awful! What were they thinking?' she managed, thrown completely on to the back foot and no longer feeling quite so incensed at the interruption to her working day.

Louise patted her arm. Having been a staunch supporter of The Practice's fund-raising of late, she knew exactly what the twins had had in mind. 'I don't think they got as far as taking everybody's pocket money for sponsorship, if that's what you're worried about, but I gather a few of the girls did lose their ponytails in the process and Mrs Harlow is rather out for blood. I imagine she's keeping you waiting on purpose. If you'd like me to, I'll go and get her – I know you must be busy at work.'

Louise herself balanced erratic hours at the nursery with a six-month-old baby and had often told Holly how difficult she found the juggling act – and that was with a hands-on granny in town for cost-free childcare. Lovely Louise had also gone on to point out that 'cost-free' did not mean that the help came without a price – she believed you paid for the help one way or another, even if it was just in constantly feeling beholden.

Holly took a deep breath and quietly reminded herself that pride came before a fall and that she was doing the best job she knew how. She'd been so keen to impress Alice and to prove to her that it was possible to manage work and a family, she'd rather ignored the maxim that something, somewhere, would always have to give. Previously it had been her fitness, but these days the twins were older and they had sport-mad Taffy in the house – she hadn't been in such good shape for years. Obviously, the weak point in the equation now was the

twins' worsening behaviour and their increasing naughtiness.
Plus they'd taken to walking everywhere in a pair, like those
creepy little girls from *The Shining*. It was actually a little disturbing, but Holly tried not to show it – if only because she
had absolutely no idea what to do about it. What a cliché she
was becoming, she thought, being a ditsy, distracted working
mum with out-of-control children.

Mrs Harlow's dramatic entrance was somewhat lost on Holly,
so wrapped up was she in her thoughts that she barely registered the woman's presence until she was practically looming
over her.

'Dr Graham? If you'd like to come on through,' said Mrs
Harlow coldly. She was a funny woman to deal with at the
best of times – running a childcare facility but secretly seeming to disapprove of working mothers. The expression on her
face was set to judgemental and furious, so Holly sat down
with her knees practically wedged under her chin, perching
on a teeny-tiny chair to hear all about her shortcomings as
a parent. Obviously Mrs Harlow was unhappy and deserved
to have her say, but with each minute that ticked past, Holly
felt increasingly unprofessional, knowing the chaos that her
absence would be causing to the clinic schedule at work.

Her loyalties torn, she really wanted to address the issue
that concerned her the most: why were her boys acting up?
What were they hoping to achieve with these increasingly
demonstrative displays of rebellion?

She pushed aside the treacherous thought, that if the twins
were persona-non-grata for a while, it might at least free
up the odd weekend, away from the incessant schedule of
play-dates and birthday parties. She tried not to think too
hard about the irate parents that would be advancing on her

later today, with their shorn-headed children, demanding restitution and possibly blood. And she tried not to rise at Mrs Harlow's tactless and ill-judged spiel about family values.

Her head physically throbbed with restraint.

Holly took a deep breath. 'Mrs Harlow, I'm so terribly, terribly sorry. Please let me explain what they were trying to do.' She tried to explain their desire to be swept up in the zeal for sponsorship along with everybody else in Larkford, but Mrs Harlow was not interested in listening.

Obviously her telephone had been running white-hot with furious parents and whilst Holly did genuinely feel that Mrs Harlow should be able to pass on some measure of her anger to the culprits' parent, after a third particularly derisive swipe at working mothers, she was struggling to hold her tongue. Mrs Harlow's flushed and jowly face glared down at her and a vein pulsated in her forehead. Her little piggy eyes bored into Holly.

Apologising had not been enough. Offering to personally write letters to the parents involved had not been enough. It took a moment for Holly to realise that nothing she could say or do would be enough, because Mrs Harlow was actually enjoying taking her down a peg or two.

Holly had never been more grateful for Elsie's voice in her ear, whispering that it was time to stand up for herself. Bullies are cowards deep down, Elsie used to tell her. And whatever the boys had done, this aggressive response really was a step too far.

Holly tried not to think about the monopoly that Pinetrees Nursery enjoyed in Larkford and she could feel her stomach churning at the very thought of the logistics involved in finding somewhere new.

Mrs Harlow, however, decided to make that decision easy

for Holly by continuing her spiteful monologue. 'Of course, Dr Graham, you have to understand that children of this age are very easily influenced. And I'm sure the – er – flexible arrangement you have at home isn't exactly the example one might wish for.' She sniffed lightly. 'I gather that their father is no longer in the picture, so perhaps you'll be formalising things with your new beau soon? For the sake of the children if nothing else.'

Holly was about to correct her when she realised she had no need to. This wasn't pastoral care; this was a witch-hunt that she had no desire to sanction.

Whatever her sons had done, they still deserved unconditional support from their mother. She could, and would, admonish them later, but with balance and an appropriate punishment, rather than disdain and disrespect.

Children would insist on behaving like children at times, after all. And if their idea of an inspirational role model was Taffy Jones, then Holly knew that she must be doing something right, whatever the consequences.

She stood up abruptly, a deliberately calm expression on her face. 'Just one question, Mrs Harlow, before I really do need to get back to my patients. I can understand how one little trim might have escaped your staff's eagle-eyed attention, but the issue that's bothering me is this – nine haircuts, nine children queuing up and two very unsubtle little boys wielding a pair of scissors . . . I can't deny their culpability, they were after all, holding the scissors – but I can't help wondering where your staff were, when all of this was going on?'

Holly managed a hint of a polite smile. 'Just something to think about . . . And, if you'd like one of the working mothers to come and give your staff some tips on multi-tasking, I know we'd be only too pleased to help. In the meantime, rest assured, I shall be dealing with the twins. Appropriately.'

Returning to The Practice, Holly felt utterly winded. Finding her brave had taken far more effort than she'd realised. Finding that Mrs Harlow had inadvertently identified her Achilles heel was an unwelcome revelation that required more thought than Holly had to spare.

She took a deep breath and walked into the office, an apology ripe on her lips and expecting chaos. The calm productivity that confronted her made her pause. 'What have you done with all the patients, Grace?' she asked, trying to keep her voice light.

'All sorted,' replied Grace, swivelling her chair away from the two vast monitors that took up most of her desk. Grace's IT skills were now scarily polished and her insistence at digitising everything was proving to be a Godsend, now they had so many statistics to compile; Holly had lost count of how many times Grace had saved their proverbial arses of late. She stood up and held out a list to Holly. 'Dan and Taffy shared out the tricky ones and we let Alice loose on a couple of easy ones. She's been properly impressive actually.' Grace dropped her voice, 'Even Julia was impressed at how she handled Kieran Friar's acne. She didn't bat an eye and that's no mean feat.'

Holly nodded, rather impressed herself, if young Alice had been confronted by Kieran's reliably gruesome back-ne and not even flinched.

'And Coco?' Holly asked, mentally crossing her fingers for a positive response.

'Good as gold,' replied Grace, her own smile complicit in

their shared affection for the little dog. 'I have to tell you, I think all the patients are a little bit in love with her.'

Holly grinned. 'Alice or Coco?' It was frankly quite easy to see the attraction to either.

'Indeed,' replied Grace, swinging a large straw basket over her shoulder. Holly noticed that, once again, Grace had eschewed her usual office attire of fitted skirt and blouse in favour of a daffodil-yellow sundress that was like a ray of warmth into the office.

'You're looking very summery and gorgeous,' Holly commented. 'Are you off somewhere nice?'

Grace smiled at the compliment. 'Just thought I'd grab a quick swim over lunch. There was even talk of Pimm's at the River Club if you fancy joining us?'

'Liquid lunch, Grace Allen? Sexy sundresses? Whatever next?' Holly was so thrilled to see her friend so much happier. So much free-er, it seemed.

Grace leaned in confidentially. 'If there's time, I'm sneaking off for a haircut later.' The way she said it, almost brimming with exhilaration, made it perfectly clear this was no work-a-day trim.

Holly held her hand at shoulder height, 'A haircut?'

Grace shook her head and lifted Holly's hand to jawline. 'A haircut.' She could barely contain her excitement and the effect was contagious.

'Wow!' said Holly, knowing this was no small decision. Roy had always made such a thing about Grace's hair. 'That'll make life simpler. I can't wait to see it.'

Grace beamed. 'You won't tell anyone, will you? I want it to be a surprise.'

'I shall forget we ever spoke,' promised Holly. 'And, Grace, thank you for covering for me this morning.'

'My absolute pleasure,' said Grace as she left the room with a spring in her step and a twinkle in her eye.

'Blimey,' muttered Holly to herself. 'Maybe we should all be doing a bit of yoga?' She checked the print-out Grace had given her and made her way over to her office, feeling a little discombobulated and like a guest at her own 'party'.

She knocked briefly on the door and went in to find Alice holding her own with Cathy Davis, as she sobbed her way through a box of Kleenex and begged for something to help her sleep. Holly quietly sat down in the corner, noting that although Coco's eyes had flickered in her direction, she hadn't moved a muscle.

'Please don't think me indelicate, after all, I haven't had children, I'm not married and having your mother-in-law move in for a month does sound horrifically stressful,' continued Alice calmly, leaning forward in her chair and taking Cathy's hands, 'but I don't think filling you up with sleeping tablets is the answer. If we can get you just a few nights of uninterrupted sleep, refill the tanks, I think you won't even recognise yourself. Of course, we can talk about sleeping tablets if we really need to, but the other things we discussed – the exercise and diet and mindfulness – I really believe we should focus on that first. Not to mention keeping family visits short in future. Will you think about it?'

Cathy nodded, her eyes red and sore. 'I will, Dr Walker. And thank you. For really listening to me.'

'My pleasure,' said Alice, ushering her towards the door.

As the door swung shut behind Cathy, Alice turned to Holly and pulled a face. 'How did I do? I live in fear of putting my foot in it when it's sensitive family stuff.'

'You did great,' Holly said. 'And as long as we follow up and make sure this really is just a lack of sleep and not a symptom of a bigger depressive interlude then we're on top of things.'

'Dare I ask how your morning went? From a purely selfish point of view, it was really great to do my own clinic on my first week,' Alice said.

Holly smiled. 'I shall pass your thanks along to the twins. In the meantime though, shall we see the rest of the patients?'

'All done,' said Alice, patting a pile of paperwork beside her. 'And I've sorted out an emergency referral to the Cardiology clinic for Mrs Owen because her pacemaker's being a little erratic, she says. That was probably the highlight of the morning's events.' Alice stretched her arms out in front of her to release the tension in her shoulders, her expensively tailored jacket falling instantly back into place. It was almost unfair, thought Holly, for someone so young to have mastered the art of the capsule-working-wardrobe so quickly.

'Is it always like this?' Alice asked. 'There seem to be a lot of people coming in for relatively minor ailments.'

Holly shrugged. 'Be careful what you wish for. Last week we had an anaphylactic shock, a heart attack and an early labour all in one day. You'll learn to love the mundane – trust me.'

Coco sat up again and whined, pawing at Alice's knee. Alice leaned down and dropped a kiss on her head. 'Thank you, Coco.' She deftly unzipped the pouch containing her blood sugar monitor and pricked her finger without even flinching. Holly watched as she noted down the reading and calibrated her medication accordingly. The minute the pouch was out and open, Coco calmed down and resettled at Alice's feet.

'Amazing,' said Holly in awe, this being the first time she'd seen a diabetic assistance dog in action. There was no hustle, no drama, just a calm and considered interaction between Alice and Coco that was clearly borne from years of practice.

'She's my hero,' said Alice simply. 'Catches me early every time.'

Holly nodded, wondering how many unnecessary hypos and hypers had been avoided by Coco's prompt intervention. No heroics; just amazing.

Making their way into the doctors' lounge, they found Taffy filling the kettle already. 'Don't you ever do any work?' Holly teased him, Taffy's almost constant presence in the kitchen area having become somewhat of a standing joke.

He shrugged. 'I was hungry. Besides I've had a difficult morning – a Jaffa, two Tubbies and Percy Lawson.'

Alice looked from Holly to Taffy in confusion. Holly grinned. 'Don't get sucked in to his shorthand, Alice. That way madness lies.'

'Do I even want to know?' Alice asked, rather tentatively.

Taffy pulled down three mugs from the cupboard and clattered about looking for spoons. He managed to make so much noise just making a cuppa that Alice barely caught his translation. 'A Jaffa – you know – seedless? So that's shooting blanks. Tubbies? Well, that's solving the riddle of who ate all the pies and Percy Lawson . . . Holly, how do I explain Percy Lawson?'

Holly passed him the milk from the fridge in a well co-ordinated tea-making routine. She turned to Alice. 'Percy Lawson is our resident adrenalin junkie. He parachutes, he hikes, he surfs . . . Sadly, he's a bit inept . . .'

'He's shit, Holly, stop sugar-coating it. He has all the gear and *no* idea. He's been in traction three times in the last ten years and there's more metal holding him together than a

Meccano set – he's fundamentally a drain on the NHS.' He paused for dramatic effect. 'And now he's gone and bought himself a motorbike!'

'Jesus!' exclaimed Holly, slopping hot tea over her hand in shock. 'You have to be kidding me?'

Taffy shook his head. 'Seriously, Alice, if you see a red BMW motorbike coming towards you at any point, just take to the shrubbery. I suppose the only question is, whether he'll kill himself or someone else first.'

He took a slurp of the tea and then grinned. 'Although when he told me what he'd bought, I did make him fill out the Organ Donor forms, so I might have given him pause for thought. Told him it was a statistical likelihood he'd be needing them and he did go awfully quiet.'

Alice was still for a moment and Holly wondered whether Taffy's cavalier approach to mortality was all a bit much, but it turned out she needn't have worried.

'When I did my surgical rotation and we were hoping for a donor, we used to check the weather forecast first. If it was raining, the odds were always in our favour,' said Alice matter-of-factly.

'I hate motorbikes,' said Taffy. 'Always seems incredibly arrogant to travel at such speed with no real protection. When you read about a father of five dying in a motorcycle crash, my first thought is what a selfish bastard he must have been.'

There was a moment of silence as Holly and Alice took in the flush to his neck and the vehemence of his voice. There was no way that this opinion was based on news headlines alone. Holly laid a hand on his arm and he smiled ruefully, 'My best mate at school lost his dad that way.' He visibly pulled himself together and gave a little shrug, bouncing a little on the balls of his feet, the way he always did when he felt uncomfortable. 'We should probably start a little sweep-stake. A fiver says he crashes it in the first two days.'

'I'm in,' said Alice. 'Twenty pounds says I give it a week.'

There was a sudden commotion as Dan and Julia and the nurses descended into the lounge at the same time, surging towards the kettle.

'So,' interrupted Dan, 'how's your first week panning out so far, Alice? Has Holly been setting a fabulous example?'

'She has, actually,' Alice said, quite firmly. 'I think it's wonderful that there's more female doctors here than men.'

'Are there?' Taffy asked, looking panicked. 'How did we let that one slip through the net?' He grinned at Alice to show that he was kidding. 'In all seriousness though, isn't that the way it should be? Surely it's more uncomfortable for a woman to have a bloke poking about, than the other way round?'

Holly gave him a shove. 'That's not very PC.'

Taffy rolled his eyes and tucked his arm around her waist. 'True, though.' Alice wandered off to have a rummage through the fridge and Taffy dropped his voice. 'So is Mrs Harlow on the warpath?'

Holly nodded. 'And she probably has every right to be.' She filled him in on the boys' exploits with the craft scissors and tried her hardest to keep her bubbling frustrations with Mrs Harlow under control.

'Well, if imitation really is the sincerest form of flattery, then I guess I should be flattered?' Taffy said uncertainly.

'Well, you can be flattered by Mrs Harlow's opinion that the boys are playing up because of the "flexible arrangement" I have at home! She made it sound as though I had a parade of men through my bedroom . . .' Holly sounded properly pissed off at the notion and refused to react to Taffy's eloquently raised eyebrow.

She gratefully took the Hobnob he gave her by way of apology. 'It just seems like everybody wants to have their say, you know?'

'I do,' said Taffy, taking a rare moment to be serious. 'You're not the only one getting flak for our living arrangements. Honestly, you'd think this was 1965 the way some of the people around here carry on.' He leaned in and kissed the soft skin just below her ear. 'But I say, if we're going to live in sin, there should probably be a lot more sin and a bit less washing up.'

She knew he was teasing; she knew he was trying to make light of her concerns, but she'd used up all of her diplomacy on Mrs Harlow. 'Why,' she blurted out, 'is everybody in such a hurry to get me back into a stupid white dress?'

'Er? So you'll match all the other appliances?' interrupted Dan, casually eavesdropping.

'So you can annoy that one special person for the rest of your life?' said Julia with unusual humour on the topic.

'Ooh, how lovely!' exclaimed Alice, completely misreading the situation. 'I didn't know you were getting married! You'll have to tell me what you'd like for a gift. Shopping's kind of, well, my thing.'

Holly sighed. 'Oh Alice, we're not. We're *perfectly* happy just living together.' She gave Taffy an odd look when he stayed resolutely silent and let Holly blather her own excuses.

'Anyone want another cuppa?' interrupted Dan, who thankfully seemed to realise that they had blundered into a private conversation, as he shepherded Alice towards the secret stash of pink wafers kept only for emergencies.

'Taff?' Holly queried. 'You're not saying much.'

He shrugged uncomfortably. 'I knew you didn't want to

get married now, now. I just assumed you might want to at some point. You know, in the future.'

'Oh,' said Holly, somewhat deflated. 'And I suppose it doesn't help that I just don't know? I mean, I did all that once – the till death do us part? For better or worse? Forsaking all others in a big stupid meringue of a dress. And where did it get me?'

Taffy frowned. 'Well, to be fair, Holls, you seemed to do an awful lot more forsaking than Milo did. I suspect it was more that causing the problems than the dress. Although I have seen photos of your wedding dress and you're quite right, it truly was awful . . .'

She elbowed him. 'I was young and easily persuadable!'

'And now you're a little bit older, a little bit wiser and shouldn't be letting silly decisions you made when you were young affect the rest of your life.' There was no fuss, no drama in his words, but for the first time, Holly realised that he really wasn't joking on this front.

He didn't need her to be dashing up the aisle right now – he didn't even need a promise – he just needed hope that it was still a possibility.

Holly kissed him tenderly on the lips. There were no words that she could honestly offer, because her own hope for a happy ever after was apparently still in short supply.

She knew to her own personal cost that the very definition of insanity was doing the same thing over and over again and expecting a different result. Why should this be any different?

Chapter 11

Dan parked his Land Rover and walked along the river bank the next morning, the birdsong building to orchestral levels under the trees. It was a picture-perfect Saturday and for once the weather was being kind for the annual Larkford Duck Race. The sunlight streaked across the water's surface and the gentle breeze made the long grasses and reeds undulate gently. The whole bucolic scene was like something out of a travel magazine. He sighed a little. When this idyll was your everyday reality, it was easy to take it for granted sometimes and forget his good fortune in living here.

It was so easy to dwell on the things that weren't going well that the little moments of absolute perfection were disregarded in favour of stewing. And Dan had recently become an expert in stewing, even to the point of having angry one-sided conversations in the car as he drove along the country lanes this morning. It wasn't the first sign of madness, he knew, it was more like the fourth or the fifth – but then, nobody said that living with Julia would be easy.

He rounded the bend in the river and spotted the huge new banner (sponsored by The Kingsley Arms) announcing the Duck Race, along with the various local food businesses who had decided that today would be an excellent opportunity to ply their wares. As a result, the crowds were forming much earlier than usual and the air was scented with coffee, warm pastries and the occasional waft of bacon that made his mouth water.

Holly caught up with him as they approached the first of the food stands and fell into step beside him. 'You okay?' she asked simply.

He pulled a crumpled fiver from his jeans' pocket and ordered two black coffees. There was no need to double-check Holly's coffee requirements – she seemed to be powered by caffeine and sheer determination most days. 'I'm fine. Just, you know,' Dan said eloquently, for once glad that it was Holly who had asked.

'Yup,' she said easily, and with feeling.

He knew she wouldn't judge or try to provide solutions like most people did. He also knew that Holly and Taffy managed to keep their friends' secrets without the need to share them over pillow talk. It had taken him a while to have faith in that ability, but he now respected their friendships all the more for them being willing to hold a little something back from one another.

'Don't make a thing of it with Taffs, will you?' Dan said, just to be sure.

Holly gave him a look. 'Couldn't if I wanted to. You might need to give me a little more information . . .'

He shook his head. 'Nothing new; just words at home.' He paused, wondering if this was the time to discuss with Holly how much the filming was driving a wedge between him and Julia. He'd be the last one to admit it, but having Holly in Taffy's life had been a blessing and a curse. A curse because he really missed his muck-about mate, whose diary was decidedly less flexible and spontaneous these days. A blessing, because he had gained in Holly that rare and wonderful thing, a female friend. And one who knew when not to push.

'So what's the bet today, then?' Holly asked casually, changing the subject as though reading his mind, as she sipped from her cup, sunglasses propped precariously in her hair. 'Are you aiming for sabotage, cheating or may-the-best-man-win?'

Dan shrugged. 'No bet today. Just, you know, helping out with the organising.' He looked like a forlorn little boy, whose mate had abandoned him for the new kid with the Raleigh Chopper.

Holly leaned in closer. 'Really? Are you sure? Only I heard ... Oh well, never mind. Forget I said anything.' She looked a little shifty, as she plonked her sunglasses down on her nose. 'Thanks for the coffee, though.'

The smile she threw over her shoulder as she left felt more like a challenge and Dan could feel his spirits lift a fraction.

It was one thing being ultra-professional now they were all partners, it had been quite another trying to be on their best behaviour for Julia's camera crew all the time. He knew it was a little childish, but his jokes and bets with Taffy Jones had often sustained him through stressful times, giving him breathing room to let off steam. And it wasn't as though Holly disapproved: she'd mentioned on more than one occasion that she quite missed the silly camaraderie that their jokes brought to The Practice.

And maybe that was part of the problem with their new arrangement, he realised. For their practical jokes to work, there had always been the pretence of playing against management. Whether they liked it or not, in the new Partnership, weren't they all management these days?

He looked along the grassy bank to where Taffy was trying to get things organised for the race, with Holly's twins 'helping' him. Their excitable smiles were infectious and the beginnings of a plan began to take shape in his mind.

He downed the rest of his coffee, happy with his decision and walked over to Taffy, who was trying to count legions of bobbing yellow plastic ducks, which would insist on moving about.

He leaned in. 'Taffy? The Mallard is in play,' he whispered.

'What?' said Taffy, losing count yet again. Then the light slowly dawned in his eyes as he grasped what Dan was saying. 'Do you mean . . . ?'

'Oh yes,' said Dan. 'Fair means or fowl – do you see what I did there? – may the best duck win . . .'

It was honestly the most fun that Dan had had in ages. By the time he had roped in a few more willing participants, he felt he had upped the traditional ante at The Duck Race sufficiently. The new addition to the Auction of Promises guaranteed to be a crowd-pleaser: the winner offering his services to the highest bidder, to do with as they wished. Even the Major and Jason had jumped on board with alacrity. It seemed they were all in need of letting off a little steam.

An hour later, Dan sat back on the warm grass and wondered why they hadn't thought of this before. Simple pleasures, really. The bet was mate against mate, duck against duck, and Dan hadn't felt so contented and relaxed in months. And what more could a professional man really ask for on a sunny morning, than the joy of sabotaging his best friend's rubber duck?

Alice sat down beside him, with Coco at her heels, both quite clearly convinced that the residents of Larkford were all losing the plot. 'Is this a regular thing then? Because you might need to clue me in – I've just seen Jason lugging a helium canister behind the bushes and I'm not sure he was filling party balloons, if you know what I mean!'

Dan grinned. 'There are no rules. May the best duck win.' He paused, kicking himself for not thinking of the helium angle. 'Sabotage is expected, if not strongly encouraged – but not in the Kids' Race,' he clarified, as he clocked the expression on her face.

She shrugged. 'Okay then. So where do we get our duck? And how do we join the bet?'

Dan stood up and pulled her to her feet. 'Ducks we can do, but the bet's a bit more . . .' He struggled to find the words without sounding like a sexist Luddite.

'One for the boys?' she suggested. 'I suppose it is a slightly different proposition to auction off a girl?' Her light easy tone implied no judgement, no feminist ire at being excluded and Dan breathed a sigh of relief.

'Come on, let's get you and Coco a duck each and then I can introduce you to some of your patients.'

'Neighbours,' she corrected him. 'It's Saturday and we're off-duty, right?'

'Oh, Alice,' Dan sighed, clocking the concern on her face, 'I don't know how to break this to you, but in Larkford, you are never off duty.'

'Yes, Boss,' she said cheekily and Dan knew straight away from the grin on her face that she'd been teasing him.

'You laugh now, Walker,' he riposted, 'but let's see how you feel in six months' time . . .'

Before they could start winding each other up further, Holly bounded over, her infectious enthusiasm and obvious delight for the boys' bonkers bet making her seem a little hyper. 'Alice! You're with me, come and grab a duck or two . . .'

Taffy was still wrangling his rubber flock into line and the twins were honestly being more of a hindrance than a help, but Holly had clearly laid down the law: they had a day full of volunteering and good deeds ahead of them, to offset their actions with the craft scissors. Dan watched for a moment, uneasy with the envious thoughts that swept through his mind. Holly and Taffy worked together so seamlessly, apparently anticipating each other's every need, as they numbered, labelled and sold each rubber duck in a perfectly orchestrated routine. As Taffy leaned in and kissed Holly's tanned shoulder and she brushed a hand against his Saturday stubble in wordless reply, Dan stepped away. He didn't fancy Holly; he certainly didn't fancy Taffy. But there was something about their obvious intimacy and affection that he definitely coveted.

He sighed deeply, wondering when his life might find the balance he was looking for. In one of those serendipitous moments – that it's all too easy to give too much credence to – just as Dan was raising his eyes to the sky, looking for answers, Grace stepped into his line of vision.

But not the Grace that he knew and recognised from work. This Grace was wearing soft jersey yoga pants and a slender camisole that showed off her lithe figure. This Grace wore her hair in the neatest of bobs, that swung easily along her jawline as she walked towards him and looked so completely at home in her own skin, that for a moment, Dan began to think he had mistaken her for somebody else. Where was organised, methodical Grace that had always been there, working quietly in the background?

'Morning,' she said happily. 'I gather the Mallard's in play?'

Dan could only nod as his eyes ranged over this virtual stranger in front of him. Suddenly all the little changes that had been manifesting over the last few months fell seamlessly together. Her figure had been just as trim yesterday in that yellow sundress, he realised, her contribution to the running of The Practice growing exponentially with her confidence.

She leaned in towards him, the familiar kindness and affection still obvious in her eyes. 'It's a haircut, Dan. We can't have you popping an aneurism trying to work out what looks different about me today.' She casually laid her hand on his arm and whilst there was nothing flirtatious in her gesture at all, Dan was suddenly aware that he would have rather enjoyed it, if there had been.

He blushed. 'Well, it looks really . . . well, just lovely.' He waved a hand in the air as though to encompass her new look entirely. 'Is it part of the whole yoga thing?'

She shrugged. 'It was getting in the way of my headstands and what with swimming before work . . . This will just be simpler.'

Simpler, in Dan's book, being almost always better. He nodded. 'It's not just the haircut, Gracie. You look so peaceful and serene. And that rather puts you in the minority this morning.' Even as he spoke, several harassed parents chased after their offspring, who were determined to splash about in the shallows.

'Oh, I don't know,' she replied. 'They look like they're having fun.' He could tell that her gaze was fastening on the shrieking toddlers and not the red-faced parents pursuing them, but then that was her talent of late – for Grace could find the silver lining almost anywhere. Grief, he supposed, had a way of focusing the mind like that.

Now, if only there was a way he could get the focus, without the grief, he mused. He looked up and caught Grace's expression, making him feel flustered and on edge, as though she were reading his disrespectful thoughts. 'So, are you officially a yoga bunny now then?' he blurted, cringing at how oafish he sounded.

She frowned in confusion at his change of tone. 'No. It's helped, that's all – recently. I get to just be me for an hour or so, without any other claims on my time or attention. It's quite an addictive feeling. You should try it. I know you rely on your sweaty man-running for some headspace, but we could bend you around like a pretzel too – might give you a little clarity and perspective? It works. For me, anyway. And if you don't mind me saying, Dan, you look like a man in need of a little time-out from your thoughts.' She'd answered him honestly and frankly, but Dan couldn't help but feel she was disappointed in him.

That feeling only intensified as she made her excuses and left, waving to a few of her friends as they arrived and being swept away to join them, their laughter and greetings full of animation and affection. His own attention, by contrast, was pulled towards the edge of the festivities, where Julia was doing a piece to camera and the crew were avidly capturing every moment of the carnival atmosphere. The intensity they generated around them made Dan feel tired just watching.

'Dan!' called Taffy, interrupting him. 'Don't just stand there like a stuffed muppet; come and help with the Kids' Race!'

And so, in moments, Dan found himself running along the river bank with Tom's tiny, sticky hand in his, falling into step beside Taffy, chasing little yellow ducks.

'Run, Uncle Dan!' shouted Tom excitedly. 'I think mine's winning.' So Dan ran, bumping along between all the other dads in Larkford and with such mixed emotions he had to swallow the lump in his throat.

The cheering and shouting reached apocalyptic volume as the finish line hove into view and Dan collapsed gratefully to the grass as all the town's children huddled round to see who had won.

There were children and babies in pushchairs everywhere; some of them sporting rather severe haircuts and shooting wary glances in Holly's direction. Lance and Hattie had pitched up in support with their twins and they waved hello to Dan as they passed. Julia materialised from nowhere and sat down beside him. 'Isn't this wonderful?' she said, surprising him with her sincerity.

'It really is,' he replied, loving how many of the local kids were so utterly entranced by an old-fashioned duck race – not an iPad or smartphone in sight.

'It's going to make some great B-roll footage,' Julia said happily.

'I suppose so,' he said, unwilling to revisit the argument that had erupted over breakfast, 'but I think the kids might be enjoying it too.' His sarcasm sailed straight over her head, he noticed, as she simply tucked herself into his side.

Half his brain was focused on potential means of duck sabotage when his mind caught up with what Julia was saying, casually dropping a bombshell into their conversation.

'I think I missed something there,' he said slowly.

'I said,' Julia repeated impatiently, one of her pet-peeves being when Dan zoned out and didn't listen to her, 'that we need to talk about work for a minute. I've had a job offer.'

Dan took her hand and firmly guided her away from the crowds, annoyed that she had chosen this moment to talk about work. Shoo-ing away Gerald-the-goose, who resolutely believed that this particular stretch of the river bank should be his alone, Dan sat down on the wrought-iron bench and turned to her. 'What does Quentin want now? More hours? More access? Are you honestly telling me that this can't wait until later?' His eyes skittered past hers to the merriment over her shoulder and it should have been obvious to anyone that this was neither the time nor the place to discuss anything controversial.

Julia, however, ran to Julia-time. If she'd been bottling something up to discuss then Dan had learned the hard way that they talked about it when she was ready. Whenever and wherever that might be.

'The job's in London,' Julia said, with the grace to look almost apologetic. 'I've been trying to work out what I want to do . . . but now Quentin's pressing me for an answer.'

'So this isn't something new? You've known about this a while?' Dan said, trying not to bite. 'All the time we've been discussing the Model Surgery implications, in fact?'

She shook her head. 'No, not all the time. It's just – well, I'd decided I wasn't going to take it. But it's such an amazing opportunity – my own prime time show. And you know there *are* trains and motorways. I could easily commute to begin with. Come on, Dan – I have to at least consider the offer.'

'You do,' he said shortly. He wanted to congratulate her. He wanted to be supportive, but she made it just so bloody difficult. He took a moment to marshal his thoughts. 'This sounds like something we need to discuss properly then, since it's obviously going to fundamentally affect both our lives . . .'

'Quentin says he needs an answer today,' she whispered, almost embarrassed.

'Then it would probably have been good to talk about it sooner.' He could feel himself detaching from the stress of the situation. All his mindfulness practice was designed to deal with his flashbacks, not relationship stress, but clearly old habits died hard.

She stood up, clearly annoyed. 'I don't need your permission to consider a job offer, Dan.'

'You don't,' he said, still sitting on the bench, his hands clasped tightly together. 'But it might have been nice if you'd felt you could share the news, or even that you wanted to . . .'

Julia floundered. 'Listen, Dan, it's not a big thing. It's just a job. A really, really good job, that I don't even know if I want.' She fidgeted uncomfortably and Dan could see that she really was torn.

'And it's good to be asked, right?' he suggested. 'Go buy some time. We can talk about it sensibly this evening. But, Julia, think about what *you* really want. Not what I want, or Quentin for that matter . . .'

Even as he watched her walk back along the river bank, even as she yelped as Gerald chased after her, honking, Dan stayed on the bench with a heavy heart. The willow trees beside him cast patterns and shade across the water and the shrieks of laughter from the other side of the weir made everything feel a little surreal.

He scuffed his deck shoes amongst the cut grass and didn't flinch when Gerald returned and stood a few metres away, staring him down.

'Get used to it, mate,' Dan told the furious goose, 'I live here too.'

Julia may not call Larkford her home, he realised, but for Dan, this was it. And right now, he couldn't see how they could possibly have such different priorities and agendas and stay together, no matter how much he loved her.

He stood up and walked back towards the sunlight and to

Taffy waving his arms and mouthing, 'Where the hell have you been?' with a pair of rubber ducks in each hand.

He smiled, reconciling himself to the fact that he might as well enjoy his day, because by the time he'd said his piece, this evening would almost certainly not end well.

Chapter 12

Holly wiped the twins' faces clean of the candy-floss that had been pressed into their hands by the Major, despite his wife's insistence that it was a bad idea. 'Oh, do be quiet, woman,' he'd said, 'and let these youngsters enjoy their childhood before they're old and decrepit like me.'

Holly had been unable to bring herself to say no after that, and when it quickly became clear that the unholy pink confection was just as much for the Major's benefit, she quietly let it go. She knew only too well that getting him to commit to a healthy-eating plan was not going to happen overnight, no matter how hard Marion tried.

It didn't take long for distraction to arrive though, as the final lot of the Auction of Promises was about to be sold and Dan clambered on to the hay bales and took the microphone.

As the lovely waves of laughter and cheering around them died down, Dan cleared his throat, looking uncharacteristically shy. 'Ladies and Gentlemen, just before we get to our main event – the Adults' 200m Duck Sprint, there is just a small matter to attend to. Dr Jones and I have rallied a few friends for our own personal contest today – a surprise addition to the running order. So we now have this final extra lot for your enjoyment. And the lot itself is actually contingent upon the outcome of our race. A little added jeopardy, if you will.'

He waved a hand across the crowd. 'So, if you fancy a punt, many of the gentlemen here have entered our little challenge. The winner of which will give one evening of their time to the lucky bidder of Lot 13. Do with them as you will, ladies!

'Do I hear twenty pounds? Of course, you may get Dr Taffy Jones, or indeed Major Waverly over there with that attractive pink moustache. You may get myself, or actually get lucky and have Teddy Kingsley and his culinary skills at your disposal. Thank you, Madam, do I hear twenty-five?'

Obviously nobody was taking it seriously, but when Dan called all the gentlemen up to the front, there was a swell of oohs and aahs throughout the crowd. The numbers went up and up, along with the volume on the river bank. A couple of the local farmers lowered the tone a bit, with their dodgy beards and muddy wellies, but generally speaking, it was a strong showing and the bidding went up accordingly.

'And remember, ladies, all this lovely money is going straight into your Health in the Community Scheme this year. Apart from £83, I'm told, for Gladys Jones to get a new hearing aid.'

'What? Did somebody say my name?' asked Gladys in confusion from the side-lines. 'I wasn't bidding! Somebody tell him I wasn't bidding!'

Everybody fell about laughing, until Alice crouched down beside Gladys' camping-chair and slowly repeated what had been said.

'Money well spent, I'm sure you'll agree,' said Dan. 'Now, with this veritable feast of testosterone in front of you, do I hear one hundred pounds?'

'Did he say Toblerone?' asked Gladys loudly, still utterly

bemused. 'Tell him I can't eat Toblerone on account of my dentures.'

Dan lost any credibility as a professional auctioneer then, dissolving into laughter and forcing Taffy to take over. As Taffy drummed up more money and one of the farmers slipped out of his Barbour to do a twirl, it was all Holly could do to restrain the twins from joining in.

It was fair to say that, if fund-raising always seemed to be this much fun, she'd be back on the teeny-tiny chairs in no time, as Ben and Tom tried to auction themselves off to their class-mates. As if to rain on their parade before it could even begin, she handed them both a carrier bag. 'Spit spot, you two, litter duty, please.'

Tom's eyes widened in disgust as if about to complain, when sweet little Lara Smith wandered past with her newly wonky pigtails and baleful glance. He silently turned his back and started picking up sticky napkins and half-used cups that had been left lying around. Holly smiled to herself; it was no bad thing for them to see that sometimes doing 'nice things for the community' included, well, doing yucky jobs for the community.

'Right then, let's get our ducks in a row!' said Taffy, with a cheesy grin for the boys as he ambled over, auction complete, and picked up Ben, plonking him on his shoulders to give him a better view.

It did not go unnoticed by Holly. It was nothing short of wonderful to her that, rather than shying away from her awk-ward, difficult little boy, Taffy actually seemed to gravitate towards him. For everyone else, Ben was too demanding of their emotional input and Tom presented the easier, more instantly rewarding option, throwing out smiles and laughter like confetti. You had to work harder to get a smile from Ben, often as not in his own little world, but when they came . . .

Just watching Ben run his little fingers across the peach fuzz on Taffy's scalp, loving the sensation and looking perfectly content, Holly could see all the positive changes in her little boy. And if that meant playing up occasionally? Well –

She tactfully averted her gaze from little Ivy Granger's pixie cut and tried not to think about the foot-long pigtails that had always been her trademark, before stopping dead, and staring hard.

Even as the childish cheers of delight around her grew, Holly's attention was no longer on the Duck Race. Making sure that Dan and Taffy had the boys covered, she broke into a run across the water-meadow, her face breaking into wreaths of smiles as she breathlessly approached the bridge, the reeds and grasses brushing against her bare legs as she ran.

'You're back!' she cried, as the slight and glamorous figure came into focus. Holly threw her arms around Elsie and had to resist the urge to scoop her off her feet and swing her around. Holly planted enormous kisses on Elsie's cheeks, making the old lady flush with delighted embarrassment. She'd obviously been worrying for nothing – if Elsie felt well enough to hop straight from an international flight to the Larkford Duck Race, then there was obviously nothing too awful amiss.

'Now that's a welcome . . . Anyone would think you'd missed me,' Elsie remarked drily, her casual tone rather undermined by the unshed tears shining in her eyes.

Holly released her and looked around. 'No Barry?' she asked tentatively.

Elsie shrugged. 'He was getting a little clingy, to be

honest, so I left him in the jungle. I believe a rather lovely American divorcee should be looking after his every need any day now.'

'He cheated on you?' Holly was stunned at the very thought.

Elsie flapped a hand lightly in her direction. 'God no. But I always know when enough's enough and if you can distract them with a shiny new bauble, they tend to get less emotional when you dump them. Men like to think they have options you see, my darling, and we both know that they're inherently lazy little buggers . . . Oh, don't look so shocked. At least this way we're both happy.

'Now do stop gaping like a salmon, poppet, and we can both head home for a stiff drink. I'm parched and I want to hear all the details about what's been happening here while I was away.' She wobbled slightly and casually leaned her hand against the shiny Mercedes that had delivered her here, complete with uniformed chauffeur, who appeared to be patiently awaiting his next instructions.

'Are you okay?' Holly asked, thrown a little by Elsie's sudden fragility and noticing for the first time her birdlike frame.

'Yes, yes, don't fuss so – but even First Class travel can be wearing for the soul at my age. Now, do we need a little glamour on the river bank to upgrade proceedings, or can we just go?' Elsie had a habit of forgetting that not everything on the planet revolved around her, and that, occasionally, Holly might have other commitments.

'Let's get you back in the car, anyway,' said Holly firmly, as Elsie's colour seemed to fade by the moment. She looked over at the river bank where Ben and Tom were cheering like crazy as Taffy was hoisted into the air and paraded along the bank as the ultimate Duck Race champion.

Holly felt completely torn and Elsie, to her credit, adapted instantly. 'Phil? Can you drive me around to the River Club? I think there's a trophy that needs presenting.' She gestured imperiously at the rather muddy slipway down to the river and Phil, to his credit, only glanced briefly at his beautiful, shiny car in hesitation.

'No problem, Ms Townsend,' he said deferentially, as he held open the door and ushered them both into the cool, refined interior.

Holly lifted her legs slightly, trying not to let them stick to the leather upholstery. 'Oh Elsie!' she said, as she noticed the perfectly equipped mini-bar between the seats and the half-empty bottle of champagne chilling on ice.

'What?' said Elsie, a picture of innocence. 'I was thirsty after the flight!' She leaned back into the upholstery with a vague smile. 'A girl has to have a little fun, darling, and I've always found laughter and fizz to be the best medicine for everything, Holly, you know that.' She paused reflectively. 'Well, except for impotence ... Then it's just counter-productive frankly.'

It really was a proper homecoming and Holly half wondered whether Elsie had in fact timed her arrival deliberately. Sweeping down the slipway towards the boathouse in the hi-spec Mercedes, having Phil – who was decidedly easy on the eye in that uniform – step out and open the door for her ... It really was perfect.

The local photographer for the *Larkford Gazette* snapped away as she made her entrance, despite Elsie 'pish-tosh'-ing him every step of the way.

She graciously took the trophy – a large ceramic duck of unspeakably ugly proportions – from Chief Inspector Grant and presented it to Taffy with absolute panache. She willingly succumbed to the kisses and greetings and was almost in danger of being knocked to the ground when Ben and Tom threw their arms around her in welcome.

'Speech!' called Dan from the crowd. 'Speech!'

Taffy cleared his throat and held the duck aloft. 'Well, obviously this is an enormous honour and I couldn't possibly have done it without—'

'Not you! Elsie!' cat-called Dan, bouncing a rubber duck off Taffy's head with perfect aim.

Holly, lightning-sharp reactions at the ready, managed to catch hold of the twins' hands before they could pelt him with more. She was beginning to see that the role-models she'd found for her boys also came with a few bad habits best avoided around impressionable minds.

'Oh well, if I must . . .' Elsie prevaricated. Chief Inspector Grant handed her the microphone and offered a steadying arm. 'I'd like to start by saying that there's no place like home. And although obviously it is rather wonderful to extend one's horizons, this horizon here –' she waved her hand at the vista around them, 'is my favourite of them all.'

Holly wasn't quite sure what tipped her off – was it the unusual brevity of Elsie's speech, the way her hand lay rather limply on the Chief Inspector's arm, or simply the fact that her words were so very studied and carefully enunciated. She stepped back for a moment and quietly sought out Phil in the crowd, who wasn't suffering from a shortage of over-zealous female attention and actually looked a little relieved.

'Phil, is it? May I ask you a question?'

'Of course,' he replied, retrieving his hat from a gangly teenaged girl with serious flirtation on her mind.

Holly frowned, she didn't know quite how to put this.

'When you collected Ms Townsend from the airport, was she fit and well?'

Phil blushed deeply. 'I'm not sure I'm supposed to say, ma'am.'

Holly gave him a look she normally reserved for the twins, 'Ma'am? Seriously? And of course you can say. I'm her doctor.'

'Oh right, sorry, I didn't want to put my foot in it.' He dropped his voice. 'She didn't want everybody here to know, but if you're her doctor, then you'll need to anyway, won't you?'

Holly didn't like to disillusion him of any of these assumptions, so remained quiet, her suspicions niggling at the back of her mind as she watched Elsie talking to Dan.

'Well, obviously her travel insurance people organised a medical transfer to begin with, since she was being sent home for treatment, but I gather she kicked up quite the fuss. So she had the ambulance take her to the aeroplane from the hospital in Malaysia and then I met her at the gate at Heathrow with a wheelchair.' He looked worried. 'She does seem to know her own mind that one, stroke or not, but to be honest, I really think I should be getting her home now.'

Holly nodded. 'Do you know, Phil, I rather think we should.'

Phil walked over to the car and opened the door, as Holly gently inserted herself beside Elsie in the crowd. Close up, she could see that the old lady was only holding it together by a thread.

'Home time for you, I think,' said Holly quietly. There was little point getting angry or frustrated at Elsie's stubborn approach to everything, including apparently, her health.

The fact that Elsie instantly acquiesced frankly worried Holly more than anything else. With Taffy's help, and with him prepared to scoop up the twins, Holly slipped along the back seat beside her.

'So, a stroke?' she said gently, making sure that Elsie was strapped in safely as they pulled away up the slope.

'Just a teensy-weensy one,' Elsie replied. 'All such a fuss. It was a moment, that's all. A funny slurry, dizzy moment. Had no idea Barry was such a worry-wart.'

Holly nodded, taking it all in and unable to help the automatic appraisal she began making of Elsie's every movement. It obviously hadn't been the post-flight champagne that had made her speech a little slurred then.

Elsie gently took Holly's hand in her own. 'Now don't you start worrying too.' She hoiked up her trousers to reveal startling white surgical stockings. 'I'm being very sensible. But to be fair, if I'd known they were going to pump me full of rat-poison to thin my blood, I probably wouldn't have held out on the bloody Botox for all these years!'

Chapter 13

Holly already felt as though the week was running away from her. First there had been the excitement of Elsie's return, followed quickly by the heart-wrenching moment of panic when she'd decided to sleep off her jet-lag for twenty-four hours straight without letting anyone know, and they'd been forced to break into her house just to check she was still alive.

Julia's TV-crew had sunk to a whole new low in Holly's opinion, when they had cajoled old Gladys Jones into having her ears syringed on camera and then zooming in with horrific magnification on Gladys' expression when she saw the resulting fallout. It had taken some rather forceful negotiations on Holly's part to get Quentin to agree to edit out the old lady's distress.

She had to confess that haggling with Quentin had not brought out her best self and watching him manipulate Julia had been an eye-opener. And although Julia clearly seemed to rate him as an individual – calling him Quinn and not even missing a beat when he smoothed a stray lock of hair away from her face – Holly found his faux intimacy tiresome in the extreme.

Thankfully Alice and Coco had slotted into the routine at

The Practice as though they had always been there. Alice's dry and observant sense of humour was exactly what the team needed, Holly thought. She'd had Holly in stitches yesterday going on about her 'Sherlock Holmes diagnosis' theory – when you eliminate the impossible, whatever remains, however improbable, must be the truth. Even Alice had been forced to admit its limitations though, when by that token, Mr King from the greengrocer's should be hitting menopause any day now.

It was taking a little restraint on Holly's part not to interfere and to let the young doctor find her own path, but everything she had seen to date made her think she had made the right call. Plus it was really very sweet having a wagging tail in the doctors' lounge at break time. Even if the addition of Alice to their team was the only benefit of this Model Surgery nonsense, thought Holly, then it would still count as an unqualified success. Based on the twenty-three-page questionnaire on management practices and seminar proposals waiting on her desk though, Holly was beginning to think that the team would be earning every single penny of their new funding. Very possibly in blood, sweat and tears. Or more realistically, in paracetamol, gin and paper-cuts.

Alice's ability to hit the ground running could not have been more welcome. Divvying up their patient lists for the day, Holly had to work hard not to take advantage of Alice's eagerness to make a good impression. She'd even had a quiet word with Dan and Taffy, once she'd realised they were already offloading their Moaning Myrtles in her direction, citing her boundless compassion and patience. Her total indifference to Quentin was yet another bonus point as far as Holly was concerned.

If only her judgement was so reliable on the home-front: the twins had been up to their usual devilment at pre-school, hiding individual shoes, so that not one child had the full complement come home time. Seeing their woebegone faces as she'd yet again had to withdraw television and snack privileges though, had begun to make her wonder if she was misreading the situation. There was something about their pranks that spoke of exuberant high-spirits, rather than disruption – was it possible that the boys were actually so relaxed and happy now that the tension had left their home, that they were finally able to let off steam? Rather than constantly having The Talk and then punishing them, might she be better served to find them an outlet for their energy and enthusiasm?

They'd certainly been unimpressed by a week of puzzles, tests and quizzes at nursery, dismissing the whole thing as 'boring and stupid'. Holly didn't hold out high hopes for the results, despite her personal opinion that key-stage testing for pre-schoolers was an unproductive farce. If the two boys could tackle the Sudoku in the back of the local newspaper without breaking a sweat, she didn't foresee any massive issues with standardised colouring-in.

On the other hand, their social skills were clearly in need of a little tactful guidance – since they'd also managed to invoke Cassie Holland's ire, by insisting to Tarquin that he was in fact a *lonely* child, not an only child, as the poor lad had previously understood it. Cassie on the war-path was yet another issue that Holly could do without.

She stared at the e-mail update she'd drafted to send to Milo. A photograph of the boys falling about laughing on the river bank at the weekend was open in a different window, having been attached and removed several times already. How many times did she have to go through this stressful charade, she wondered. He never replied. He opened her e-mails, but never replied. So, maybe Taffy had a point – what exactly was she hoping to achieve, and was it really worth the stress? Besides, she could hardly ask for his opinion on this, after the cross words they'd exchanged last time. And since Taffy now insisted on disappearing for a run every time they tried to discuss anything to do with Milo or the divorce, it was only really his lap times that were making progress. At this rate, he'd be marathon fit in no time and they'd be no further forward.

She deleted the attachment again and sent the e-mail back to her drafts folder, resolving to add it to her List of Things To Think About, along with Elsie's erratic attitude towards her health, Eric's hormonal behaviour and of course, in the back of her mind, the impending trip to Wales to meet Taffy's parents. The timing couldn't really be worse, but as Taffy had pointed out, they couldn't really rearrange his parents' Golden Wedding Anniversary to fit around Larkford's ever-demanding populace.

It was actually lucky, thought Holly, that they had been so run off their feet – any time to dwell on the prospect of meeting his parents and his brothers would have sent her thoughts spiralling. Her relationship with Milo's mother had been a few degrees cooler than liquid nitrogen and she couldn't bear the thought of going through all that again. Knowing how close Taffy was to his sprawling clan only put more pressure on her to make a good impression. As a mother of boys herself, she didn't actually know how she would react if one of the twins came home with a divorcee on his arm and a couple of kids to boot.

*

Thankfully her morning clinic was chock-a-block and she didn't have much time left to ruminate. She tried to tell herself that this was a good thing, but somehow, she had just ended up feeling distracted and tetchy.

'I've got a spot of gout,' said the earnest young man in front of her. The fact that he was holding a print-out from the internet in his hand did not bode well for the next seven minutes of Holly's morning. Just seven minutes was all they had allocated for each patient these days and normally that thought alone would make Holly cross. Looking at the intense expression on this hipster's face though, for once she felt grateful that their conversation would, by necessity, be finite.

Gregory Dance – that couldn't be his real name could it? – was young, slim and clearly athletic, but nevertheless his foot was propped gingerly on the floor and he'd come in with his own (very fine) cane.

She took a deep breath and reminded herself to be sympathetic – the excruciating agony of a true case of gout was not to be underestimated.

Careful not to cause any unnecessary vibrations as she pushed her chair back, Holly gestured to the treatment bed. 'Hop up on there and we'll have a proper look.' She slipped on a pair of gloves and gave Gregory time to remove his own sock without rushing him. Privately, she was thinking, that if he had managed to get a sock on, then his internet search may well have led him in the wrong direction. Imagine that, she thought, immediately chastising herself for letting her mood influence her patient care.

To be fair to him, his big toe was indeed red, swollen and almost visibly throbbing with pain, in a Tom & Jerry style caricature. As much as she hated, properly detested it, when patients came in with their own diagnosis already pre-formed and just with a hand out for a prescription, Holly began to wonder if he might be right.

His words echoed her own thoughts, as he began to read aloud from his print out, 'Although once the preserve of over-indulged port-drinking old men, the reoccurrence of gout in recent times has even seen young healthy women affected.' He paused and tried not to flinch as Holly gently palpated the area, making sure to include his ankle and other joints. 'Did you know, Dr Graham, that nearly one per cent of the population will suffer from gout at some point in their lives?'

'I did know that, yes,' said Holly, trying not to shake her head. It was honestly as though her patients never gave any thought to the years of training that their GPs had undergone. 'But I also know that it's mostly as a result of lifestyle choices. Let's talk about yours for a minute and when this toe started flaring up?'

Gregory furrowed his brow. 'Well, me and the boys had quite a Big One a couple of nights ago – a real all-nighter, old school – and then, when I woke up the next morning, there he was. All big and shiny and red and hurting like hell. So my housemate suggested a hair of the dog, but I knew you see, Dr Graham, about the uric acid building up in my joints, so I drank lots of water and went for the most excruciating jog and, to be honest, it seems to have got much worse.'

Holly took off her gloves and tried not to judge. 'Gregory,' she said tiredly, 'on this big night out of yours, were there any incidents? Falling over, football with a brick?'

'What?' asked Gregory bluntly. 'I don't mean to be disre-spectful, Dr Graham, but I don't think falling over is going to trigger a gout attack.'

'No,' she replied patiently, 'but falling over drunk, or kicking something hard, can very easily trigger a broken toe attack.' She gestured at his toe. 'I can check your bloods if it would make you happier, but in my opinion, what you have there is a toe that is broken in at least two places and which, after the jogging-it-off solution, may well require a small surgery to realign the bones. I'm afraid I need to refer you to the RUH in Bath.'

She sat on the bed beside him. It was clear to her that this boy had thought that having 'a spot of gout' was almost an endorsement of his coolness and party lifestyle. 'Next time you're in agony, Gregory, please don't rely on the internet. This was probably a really clean break before, but it's a right mess now. Let me see if I can get someone to transfer you to Bath – I don't think driving yourself is the best idea.'

'But I was so sure I'd got gout,' he said plaintively. 'My mate had gout last year and it looked just like this.' He looked at her, as if she might be persuaded to change her mind. He stood up and hobbled towards the waiting room so Holly could make a few calls. 'You're the doctor, I suppose,' he said resignedly as he left.

Holly hung up the phone from sorting out a referral for Gregory Dance – seriously? – and finally exhaled. There was a small chance she might actually finish on time. She had no desire to inflict on Taffy the singular joy of being stuck in a car on the M4 in rush hour with two excitable passengers in the back.

Taffy had so far proven himself adept at getting things organised for their Welsh excursion and to be fair, he had thought of almost everything – kids, dog, food, cover at work – with one exception, Elsie.

Elsie, who was so far refusing a referral to the stroke unit in Bath. Elsie, who seemed to be more interested in catching up on gossip and scandal than taking care of her health. To give her credit, Holly had been giving her a check-up every morning before work and she was showing no lasting effects from the TIA she had suffered in Borneo. If indeed that's what it had been.

Feeling guilty but justified, Holly had put through the referral anyway. By the time the appointment came around, who knew how Elsie might be feeling.

She looked up as Grace popped her head around the door. 'I've squeezed in a few walk-ins on the end of your clinic. Hope that's okay?'

Holly nodded. 'Just give me a minute, I want to log in with Elsie again.' She picked up her mobile and pressed 'Favourites'. Knowing that she wouldn't be able to pop in every day and keep an eye on her niggled at Holly's conscience – after everything that Elsie had done for her, Holly thought of her as family. Not the obligated kind, but the kind that made you feel supported by their unconditional love.

Grace, as always, was one step ahead of her. 'Listen, I don't know if it helps, but when I knew that Elsie was coming back and that Taffy had booked the time off for you both, I made sure my diary was free and clear. I can visit her just as much as you do and, to be honest, I'd rather enjoy it. I've been longing to do a bit of travelling and if I have to live vicariously through Elsie's photographs, then that's fine by me.'

'Would you really?' Holly said, touched beyond measure.

Grace leaned in then, merriment dancing in her eyes. 'Of course! I actually quite fancy having an evening with Elsie. I'm sure that she has a few tales to tell . . .'

'Oh, she does,' Holly laughed. 'Just make sure she doesn't lead you astray. She'll take one look at that new haircut and start playing dress-up with you if you're not careful.'

Grace smiled. 'I can think of worse ways to spend an evening. And frankly, it'll make a change from staring at my coursework until the wee small hours.'

'Just think, though,' said Holly, standing up to follow her through to the waiting room, 'what a sense of achievement when you get your certification. I hope there's a graduation ceremony? I can't think of a better excuse for a party.'

Well, fifty years of marriage probably qualified too, she thought, as she mentally tallied up a list of things she would need to pack when she got home later, which seemed to consist of everything the boys owned in terms of weather options – it may be summer, but it was also Wales and wellies came as standard. She only hoped it hadn't been a mistake to let Taffy take the twins shopping to choose his parents' anniversary present!

Her heart sank a little at that point. It was the curse of the mother, that every holiday required so much hassle and organisation, that if she hadn't been in need of a break beforehand, she certainly would be by the time she'd got them all out of the door. And let's be honest, she thought to herself, it hardly counts as a holiday if you're going against your will.

Her last patient of the day came as a bit of a surprise. 'Lizzie!' said Holly, as her friend appeared, limping, in the doorway, Eric walking sedately beside her on his lead.

'If anyone asks, he's an assistance dog, okay? I gather that's A Thing here now,' Lizzie grinned. 'And his overnight bag is in reception with Grace. I've given him a very stern talking to about table manners and snoring, and he reckons he's good to go.' She kissed the top of his head and he looked at her adoringly. 'Although he's never been on holiday before, so he's feeling a little bit nervous about being away from home.'

'Is it possible that actually *you* are a little bit nervous about him being away from home?' asked Holly gently.

'There is that small possibility; I won't deny it. But I know he's in safe hands, it's just that, well, I'm not really sure how strong a swimmer he is and with being by the sea ...'

Holly nodded, completely understanding; Eric was just a big baby really. 'I'll be super careful, I promise.'

Lizzie visibly pulled herself together and changed tack. 'Anywaaaaay,' she said, 'I'm here about my back actually. Played tennis last night. Can't stand up straight this morning. Feels like the whole bloody thing's in spasm.'

'Crikey,' said Holly. 'I knew exercise was bad for us really. Let's have a little look. What painkillers did you take?'

'Oh, I didn't take any painkillers,' said Lizzie in disgust. 'If I disguise the pain, how can I tell if it's getting better?'

Holly shook her head in frustration. 'But you managed to get into the car okay, to get here? Or did that make it worse?'

'Oh no, I didn't get Will to drive me. He's flat out busy at work, so I just walked over here with Eric as my guide dog.'

Holly settled back on the edge of her desk. 'Lizzie, you know I love you, but you're talking crap. If you had debilitating back pain, you wouldn't be able to get off the floor, let alone go for a quiet stroll through Larkford and poo-poo the idea of painkillers! What's going on? Really?'

Lizzie looked petulant for a moment. 'Well, my back really does hurt and you're not being terribly sympathetic.'

'Granted,' said Holly, realising that Lizzie had a valid point. 'But what's the real problem? The one you couldn't have asked me about at the kitchen table later?' she asked gently.

Lizzie scowled. 'I feel weird,' she said petulantly.

'Well, I suppose it's natural, I am your mate after all. But Julia's in this afternoon, if you'd rather see her ... I guess that might be a bit weird too though?' Holly tugged absent-mindedly at her hair. 'Maybe it's just as well we've got Alice now, to give patients like you a bit of distance ...'

'Are you done?' interrupted Lizzie with a sigh. 'I didn't mean I felt weird talking to you about it. That's why I'm here. I'm here because I feel weird.'

'Oh,' said Holly succinctly.

'Oh indeed,' replied Lizzie. 'But can we not forget the back-ache in all of this? I know I'm just a statistic now – eighty per cent of people will suffer back pain at some point in their lives ...' she parroted off.

'Stay away from the bloody internet,' said Holly, exasperated. 'Come on, Lizzie, you know better. Now tell me all about this weird and when it actually started.'

So Lizzie did and, as she spoke, Holly became increasingly aware that she had let her friend down. Dismissing Lizzie's indecision and puddle jumping from one career to another, as the hallmark of a woman with too much choice and not enough financial pressures, she hadn't seen it for what it really was: the desperate searching for calm from a woman who was riddled with anxiety.

'So once my heart starts racing really quickly, I get odd things going on with my vision and I feel nauseous and then I kind of, well, I have to sit down before I fall down.' She looked studiously at Eric, as she asked the question she had clearly come to ask, 'Am I going mad, then? Is it off to the funny farm, with a nice white linen jacket with wrap-around sleeves?'

'At least you haven't lost your sense of humour, anyway,' said Holly. 'And no, you're not going mad.'

'N'yeah,' replied Lizzie disparagingly, as though she had already made up her mind that she was. 'It's like Schrödinger's Cat this – if your friend has a nervous break-down and there's nobody there to hear it, will it make a sound?' She sniffed, still trying to lighten the mood. 'Do I need a week at The Priory to treat me for "exhaustion"?' she asked, semi-hopefully.

'Are you exhausted?' asked Holly drily.

Lizzie shrugged. 'Probably no more than the next poor sod. Am I to be put on the funny pills then?'

'Nope,' said Holly. 'We're going to talk some more over the next week or so – you get preferential treatment, you know. And then I'm thinking that a course of CBT would be a good place to start – Cognitive Behavioural Therapy. Let's find out what's really going on, rather than doping you up to the eyeballs. It's a tricky beast, anxiety. We can just stick on a Band-Aid, of course, but I'd rather work out *why* it's happening, wouldn't you?'

Lizzie nodded. 'Makes sense. Anything to do in the meantime?'

Holly smiled. 'That one's easy.' She scribbled intently on her green prescription pad and ripped off the page.

Her beautifully swirly handwriting was the exception that proved the rule among doctors' usual unintelligible scrawl:

Be kind to yourself – if in doubt, treat yourself like you'd treat me in the same situation xxx

Holly leaned forward and took Lizzie's hands in hers. 'Elsie is always telling me that real compassion means being kind to yourself first and then others. You can't pour from an empty cup. So cut yourself some slack – if we talked to our friends like we talk to ourselves, we wouldn't have any friends left. Promise me, follow the amazing advice you're forever throwing my way and take it easy on yourself. And when I get back from Wales in a few days, we are going to get you sorted, okay?'

Lizzie nodded again, a single tear escaping the others that were welling in her eyes. 'I can't believe I'm crying at the fricking doctor's – I'm such a cliché.'

'Nah – everybody cries at the doctor's. You're just normal.'

'Oh dear God,' said Lizzie in shock. 'Now you're just making it worse!'

Holly stood up and gave her a proper hug. 'And take some ibuprofen for your back, have a hot bath and accept that you're not twenty-one anymore,' she said with a smile, as she shepherded her through to the waiting room, giving her one last bear hug as she was leaving.

Old Mr Jarley rubbed his hands together with glee and gave a filthy cackle. It was entirely in keeping with his reputation as the town's lecherous old git. 'Now why do I never get to see *that* doctor, eh? I could use a bit of her medicine, if you know what I mean?'

'I know exactly what you mean, you dirty old man,' exploded Lizzie. 'And to be clear, we all know it's you that's been scaring all the joggers in the park, in your disgusting old mac. So back off, lay off and fuck off, or I'll have to flatten you. Okay?' said Lizzie with such forceful conviction that Holly wondered whether Lizzie might actually have succeeded where all the police cautions had failed.

She turned to Holly apologetically, 'Oh yeah, did I forget to mention the sudden rage at inappropriate times?'

Holly just shrugged, relieved to see that, on some levels at least, her friend was still fully functional. 'Don't know what you're talking about. Seems entirely appropriate to me.'

Chapter 14

Julia pushed open the door of the Gatehouse and immediately the familiar and soothing aroma of vanilla and jasmine made her breathe more easily. She kicked off her mules and noted with a mild wave of irritation that their nude suede finish had not fared too well on the river bank at the weekend. She pulled a can of Diet Coke from the fridge, and tried to ignore the hectoring voice in her head that rattled on about the perils of artificial sweeteners. Surely, she might be allowed to have just one vice in peace, she thought.

She'd been working late in the edit suite with Quinn for the last few days and she and Dan had been subtly avoiding each other at work in a well-choreographed dance that they had perfected when they had broken up last year. It still hurt though, when his eyes repeatedly slipped past hers without making contact. She only hoped this wouldn't be a case of history repeating itself.

With every day that passed and every opportunity they missed to really talk, the elephant in the room grew bigger. Hence this evening. A part of her was irritated that they needed to diarise a time to have a decent conversation, the other part was just relieved they weren't one of those couples that booked in their sex life too.

Julia knew she'd bungled their conversation on the river bank. Since saying the words out loud, she'd even wondered whether she actually wanted the London job, or whether she'd just wanted to cast a fly over the waters, wanted Dan to realise that it was a huge honour – what Holly's boys would call 'A Big Deal' – to have even been *considered* to present a primetime health and lifestyle programme. Maybe, she conceded, a little part of her mind had just wanted him to be proud of her for that alone.

Leaving Larkford was an argument she couldn't bring herself to lose, but couldn't quite muster the energy to win.

She sipped at her vile fizzy drink and realised that nothing had really changed: she was still subconsciously seeking acknowledgement and approval – the needy child inside her still apparently wanted reassurance that she was doing okay.

She hovered in front of the fridge, wondering whether a nice home-cooked supper might be enough to build a few bridges between them. Enough, anyway, to allow them to discuss this new job offer openly without it having cataclysmic overtones for their relationship.

She heard his key in the lock and stiffened slightly. 'I thought I might cook those steaks,' she called through to the hallway, careful to keep her tone light and breezy.

'Good idea,' he replied. The tension in his shoulders made him look hunched and unhappy, his hands rammed deeply into his pockets as though he were gearing up all his energy to cope with the conversation ahead.

The awkwardness between them made even the shortest exchange feel arduous. She placed the bundle of bloody greaseproof paper on the worktop and tried not to feel sick. Red meat was the quickest way to Dan's heart and right now, she would do almost anything to clear the air between them.

'I'm so sorry,' she blurted out, catching him as he began to say the same.

They laughed awkwardly. 'So, I guess we're both sorry,' he said, leaning against the worktop and taking her hand gently in his. 'I know I didn't react very well when you told me about—'

'God, Dan, I just dropped it like a bombshell because I didn't know how—'

'I love you,' he interrupted her gruffly. 'You *do* know that, don't you?'

She nodded. 'Me too. But somehow – have you noticed? We don't seem to be making each other very happy.' She swallowed the tears that rose unbidden into her throat. 'I just don't think I can be the person you want me to be, that's all.'

He pulled her into his arms, enveloping her slight frame as he kissed the top of her hair. 'I don't want to be the reason you give up on your ambitions, though. I can't be the only reason you stay here. I need you to stay here because *you* want to.'

She nodded into his chest. It seemed the easiest answer. Nodding because she agreed with his statement though, rather than anything else.

'Maybe it will feel better if we talk it all through?' he suggested. 'If nothing else, there are boring practicalities to consider at work if you really are thinking of leaving – this Model Surgery business for one thing and the Health in the Community launch for another.'

Julia shrugged in his arms, barely trusting herself to speak. This was one of those rare times where she truly had no idea what to do for the best. 'Would you think I was mad if I made a list?' she mumbled into his chest, the smooth and cool linen of his shirt soft against her cheek. Held tightly there, in that moment, there was no job in the world that could compete.

Dan's laugh echoed in his chest against her face. 'I wouldn't expect anything less.' He stepped back and reached for a pen, casting around for a piece of paper.

Julia sat down at the kitchen table, banging her ankle as she always did, as they tried to manoeuvre around this tiny kitchen. She really hadn't been joking when she'd suggested they find somewhere slightly bigger than this very beautiful, but completely impractical dolls' house. Maybe living quite so on top of each other hadn't been the cleverest idea after all, no matter how romantic it had seemed at first.

'Quinn says I have to choose,' Julia said, so quietly it was almost a whisper.

Dan scooped up the post from the mat beside the front door. 'And I imagine Quinn isn't just talking about the job, is he?'

Julia shrugged. 'I still don't see why I can't commute. It's not a million miles away . . .' She deliberately didn't address the issue that Dan had raised.

Dan placed the pen in her hand and pushed over the pile of envelopes for her to scribble on. 'I might be wrong, but if you have to think this hard about it, then staying with me in Larkford can't be quite the happy ending you're hoping for.' He paused, clearly waiting for Julia to interrupt and contradict him, but she said nothing.

His shoulders dropped and he leaned back against the worktop. Had Julia looked up, she would have seen the utter despondency on his face, his beautiful eyes hollow with disappointment.

But she couldn't.

Her own gaze was riveted to the transparent window of the envelope in her hand. 'Dan?' she managed eventually, her voice cracking with the strain.

He looked down and saw the official looking sticker from the Royal Mail, even before his brain could register what it truly meant.

'Redirection?'

Julia stood up suddenly, yanking open the sash windows with such force that they rattled in their ancient frames and drawing the fresh evening air into her lungs as though she were drowning.

'I guess it's one way to let me know,' she said, the brittle edge of hysteria making her words waver. She turned and roughly spread the rest of the mail across the table. Three other letters bore the same sticker: Candace Channing – Redirection.

'Did I mention that my mother's moving in?' Julia said with a slightly hysterical sob, blinking away the heavy tears that threatened to spill down her face.

They stared at each other in muted dismay. Pros and cons forgotten. The Talk? Clearly postponed.

'If you want to leave now, I wouldn't blame you,' Julia managed eventually. 'It's not as though we didn't know that was a possibility anyway.'

Dan shook his head, ever the gentleman. 'Now you're just being daft. If – and I do mean if – we decide to call it a day, it certainly won't be because your mother is coming to stay. Maybe it's a blessing in disguise anyway – we can take our time to think things through and not rush into anything. And I get to meet your mum properly.' He paused awkwardly. 'Which is nice.'

Julia took the two small paces necessary to cross the kitchen and wrapped her arms around him, kissing him deeply. 'I love you. For your optimism. For your patience . . .'

'Stop talking,' murmured Dan, pushing his hands into her hair and savouring the kiss. He wrapped his arms around her and lifted her on to her tiptoes, all talk of if and when and endings forgotten. At least this aspect of their relationship seemed to weather the test of time and reality.

The phone rang out into the empty kitchen behind them as they slowly made their way through the Gatehouse to the bedroom. Taffy's voice echoed out around them. 'Er, guys? Pick up if you're in?' His voice became muffled as he spoke to whoever was with him. 'Listen, I'm coming over. I've got Julia's mum with me. She's a bit, well, erm . . . Look, we'll be there in a mo, okay?'

There could be no quicker way of smothering any nascent flickers of passion than the prospect of Candace Channing arriving on their doorstep.

Dan may have looked a bit bemused, Julia thought, but she knew perfectly well what Taffy's awkward message translated to. She stepped out of Dan's embrace, her whole demeanour suddenly detached and emotionless. 'Put the kettle on, Dan,' she managed.

'Right, sure, yes, tea,' he replied, tucking in his shirt and smoothing back his non-existent hair automatically. Julia watched him go through the motions of a nice boy, from a nice family, preparing to meet his girlfriend's mother.

'Dan,' she said gently, 'make it coffee. Strong and black.' She had to look away as the penny dropped for fear she might make it worse by being a bitch. Because God knows, that's what she felt like being right then: an angry, unforgiving, shouty bitch. His hand seeking hers for mutual reassurance was somehow enough to stop the transformation, but the seed was already sown and Julia could only envisage the end.

Because now Dan would get to meet the Julia that her mother knew.

And, for all his patience and optimism, there was no way he would ever look at her the same way again.

'My darling girl,' cried Candace, as Julia opened the door. 'What a gem of a house – no wonder I couldn't find it, my angel! Blink and you'd miss it.' She clutched tightly at Taffy's bicep as though it were the only thing holding her up. Julia knew from bitter experience that it probably was.

'Mum, what a nice surprise,' Julia said, stepping aside to welcome her in. It would no more have occurred to Julia to hug or kiss her mother than it would have to Candace.

Dan on the other hand had clearly not been briefed. 'Mrs Channing. What a pleasure to meet you, I'm Dan.' He kissed her on both cheeks and was clearly not prepared for the tenaciousness of her grasp or the intensity of her inspection.

'So you're the boyfriend,' she said, her tone so completely ambiguous that Julia could see the confusion flit across Dan's face. She caught Taffy's gaze and mouthed her thanks. He nodded and to his absolute credit, made no comment about her mother's inebriated state or her lack of shoes. The silk dress she was wearing and the remains of some glamorous nail extensions at least proved that she'd made the effort to look respectable when she'd left home. Obviously none of those good intentions had survived the drinks trolley on the train.

Julia experienced a sudden flush of panic. 'Mum, you didn't drive here, did you?'

Taffy spoke up quickly. 'She was outside the train station. Don't worry. I checked.' He leaned in and kissed her fleetingly on the cheek, an unusual display of affection between the two of them that seemed to be the only way to communicate his support and concern. 'We're leaving first thing tomorrow now – bit of an early start planned, if I can actually persuade Holly out of bed, but if you need anything just drop me a text tonight, okay?'

'Thank you,' mouthed Julia again, as Taffy made his excuses and left.

Watching him walk away down the lane, back to Holly and the twins and some semblance of normality, Julia felt as though, yet again, she were waving goodbye to her chance at ever having that simple domesticity in her life. In that moment, of course, she had chosen to ignore the fact that the tableau of domesticity she was now apparently mourning was everything Dan was offering her.

Chapter 15

With Elsie's words of 'pish tosh, stop worrying about me — bugger off and have a lovely time' still ringing in her ears, Holly stared out of the car window as they barrelled along the M4. Apparently Grace was now planning on a sleepover at Elsie's and Holly half-wondered whether she knew what she was letting herself in for. Grace, it seemed, had 'Project' virtually stamped on her forehead and Elsie was practically chomping at the bit to get started. There had been talk of designing a 'blog', the content of which was being treated as a hotly guarded secret, and Holly could only hope that Elsie's Wi-Fi had a cut-out switch for after the second Martini.

Holly tried to quash the tiny flicker of resentment that Grace got to spend the evening with Elsie, while she got to play 'Happy Family' with her not-even-in-laws.

As the CD changer clicked over and the Best of C-Beebies started to play at full volume, Holly burst out laughing. Without missing a beat, Taffy and the twins were singing along with Gigglebiz and Holly couldn't help but notice that all three were word perfect.

To give Taffy his due, he hadn't batted an eye-lid at the vast quantity of teddy bears stuffed into the back seat, or at the emergency vomit-stop on the hard-shoulder. He had however looked a little perplexed at the fourth wee break, completely failing to grasp Ben's fascination with the motorway services and Tom's obsession with tins of travel sweets. But all in all, he was doing extremely well on his maiden family voyage.

'What?' he said suddenly, turning his head briefly to look in her direction. 'Stop staring at me, Graham. I mean, I know it's tricky being in a confined space with all this charisma, but you're making me feel objectified.'

She laughed. 'You're doing alright at this road trip business, you know.'

He gave her a long appraising stare. 'Then do me a favour and stop looking for problems, will you. I've never heard anyone get so flustered about mucking up the directions. Besides,' he said, 'as road trips go, we haven't even started yet. We've got travel games and popcorn in reserve.'

'And these games you speak of?' Holly asked. 'Are these for the twins' benefit or yours?' She couldn't resist teasing him; he looked so proud of himself for the little bag of 'in-flight entertainment' he'd put together.

He grinned. 'Well, I have to confess that there is something rather lovely about having two eager and willing participants. Dan gets really bored with Twenty Questions on long journeys. I think it's just because he's rubbish at it, myself.'

'Try me,' suggested Holly.

'Ok-ay,' said Taffy, 'but let's make this interesting. You see, it's probably a good time to mention that we're not actually going straight to my parents' house. I thought we could have a little pit-stop somewhere lovely for a night on the way: we get to chill just the four of us and then it's only the one night of professional Twenty Questions for you.'

Holly swallowed hard, a little blind-sided by his thought-fulness. 'Well, that sounds really rather lovely. And also explains the need for directions – I did think it was a bit weird that you didn't know the way.' She threaded her fingers through the long fur on Eric's ears as he sat happily by her feet; there had certainly been no space for him in the boot once umpteen wet weather supplies and crabbing nets had been wedged into place.

Taffy grinned. 'It's basically a bribe. And you don't know where we're going yet . . . So, over to you, Twenty Questions, yes or no only. Go . . .'

'Erm . . . Have I been there before?'

'Yes.'

'Really?' she clarified, sounding surprised, as she could only think of one or two occasions in her life when she'd crossed the border into Wales.

'Yes. And that's two questions down.'

'No, that's not fair! I didn't know we were taking things that seriously.'

He shrugged. 'Don't mess with the rules of Twenty Questions, Graham. It's basically tradition in my house. I'm only getting you warmed up for when you meet my broth-ers – they're virtually Ninjas at this.'

'Can you be a Ninja at Twenty Questions?' queried Holly, momentarily confused.

'Yes. And that's three.'

Holly spluttered, indignantly, 'I'm seeing a whole new side to you today.'

He shrugged unapologetically. 'Well, you'd best get used to it. Like I said, I'm the warm-up act.' He pressed stop on the CD and called through to the boys in the back, 'Right, you two, we're coming up to the border. Are you ready?'

They nodded enthusiastically. 'I've never been to a whole
other country before,' announced Tom in wonderment. Holly
just tried not to laugh at his earnest anticipation. She hoped
he wouldn't feel too let down when a few miles along the
road, everything looked pretty much the same . . . For a little
while at least.

'Three. Two. One,' said Taffy and the three boys burst into
song. How Taffy had found time to teach them the Welsh
national anthem, Holly did not know. How he'd managed to
get them to sing, not just in tune, but in harmony, was beyond
her. As the car rattled along and the boys sang lustily behind
her, she felt really rather choked up. She reached across and
squeezed Taffy's knee.

'I love you,' she whispered.

'I bloody hope so,' he whispered back. 'I'd hate to feel
like I was in this on my own.' He looked worried for a
moment. 'Let's just hope you still feel the same on the way
back.'

As Taffy manoeuvred the fully-laden car into a tiny space on
the sea-front, Holly couldn't help but be impressed: firstly, by
his expertise with the parallel-parking and secondly, by his
choice of 'somewhere lovely'.

She slipped out of the car and looked out across
Saundersfoot Bay, the gulls circling and cawing above her
head. Taffy was quite right: she had been here before – for
the bonkers tradition of swimming in the sea on New Year's
Day – whatever the weather. It was strange to realise how
rarely she thought of that special day with her dad, yet it had
been one of their most treasured times together. Yet another
act of self-preservation, she assumed. But actually being there,
breathing the same air and smelling that heady aroma of

chips with salt and vinegar ... She probed the memory, like an aching tooth, seeing how far she could go before the pain began and she realised that she could finally think about that day without sadness. It felt like a gift.

'I thought that, since we were having a meet-the-family weekend, you could show the boys where their grandpa used to bring you,' said Taffy, coming to stand beside her, as the twins carried on sleeping in the back of car, worn out by the fifteen or so renditions of 'Land of My Fathers' they had performed with gusto as they'd barrelled along the motorway, the scenery changing with each passing mile.

'We'll be needing to have fish and chips for lunch, you know,' she said.

Taffy turned her shoulders until she was looking in the other direction at her beloved top-notch chippie, The Mermaid on the Strand. 'Dairy-free and all booked in,' he said, so chuffed with himself he looked as though he might burst. 'But that will have to wait, I'm afraid, because there are sandcastles to be built and moats to be filled. There's probably some decorating with sea shells, if you fancy it?'

She walloped him playfully on the arm. 'Bog off. None of that stereotyping, thank you. I shall have you know that I was once the Saundersfoot Sand Castle Champion.'

'When you were, like, nine ...' he countered. 'Are you prepared to put your money where your mouth is, that's the question. Loser buys lunch, mate.'

Holly must have looked as bemused as she felt as Taffy immediately reined himself in. 'Sorry,' he muttered. 'Got a bit carried away. You see Dan likes to ...'

'I'm *not* Dan,' she reminded him.

'Indeed you aren't,' he said, thoroughly kissing her until a little hand banging on the window disturbed them.

'I'm awake now!' announced Ben unnecessarily. 'Can we play in the sea?'

Several hours later and after a mammoth helping of fish and chips for lunch, their sandcastle had reached epic proportions. There were tunnels and moats and bridges and crenellations. It was also interesting to note that Holly's skills in moulding a sturdy turret had won her praise and awe from not just the twins, but also – slightly begrudgingly – from Taffy.

They cracked open the flask of hot chocolate and some biscuits, determined to stay on the beach for every last moment, even if it was starting to feel a bit chilly.

Eric whined pitifully on the end of his lead, casting accusatory glances at Holly every time she looked his way. He couldn't understand why he wasn't allowed to frolic in the waves or leap all over the lovely castle they had built. To give him his dues, Eric certainly knew how to work those big brown eyes of his and managed to make Holly feel ridiculously guilty, to the point that she kept apologising to him. At which he would turn his back on her and sulk.

'Dear God, he's like a hormonal teenager,' said Taffy. 'What happened to his adorable puppy years?'

'He grew,' said Holly. 'My main concern at the moment is when he's going to *stop* growing. Well, that and the fact that eating a meal with him watching every mouthful is a bit like being back at school.'

Taffy tossed Eric a small chunk of his biscuit and earned himself a filthy look from Holly for his troubles. 'Back at school?' he asked, by way of distracting her from the inevitable puppy training talk that was brewing.

'What? Oh, you know, when the girls got all competitive about who could eat the least and then would watch every single mouthful you dared take from plate to mouth like a pack of judgemental but hungry vultures? "Are you going to eat that *whole* apple? You are brave, the way you don't care what anybody thinks . . ."' Her words petered out, as she saw the look of complete and utter confusion on Taffy's face.

'Girls are weird,' he said simply. 'Boys are easy. Eat. Run. Fight. Eat again. We're very simple souls really.'

Holly nodded. Living with three of the male species (four when Eric was with them) had been quite the eye-opener. Milo had always been rather metro-sexual around the house; true, his piles of laundry and squalor were a sight to behold, but he had been otherwise meticulous about his personal hygiene and there were never any bags of sweaty sports kit hanging around. Milo hadn't gone for team sports. He ran. Alone. It was kind of symbolic in a way. Whereas Taffy's every pursuit was a raggle-taggle bunch of mates just getting on with it and having fun, even if his sporting paraphernalia did seem to be slowly colonising her utility room.

'In fact,' Taffy continued, 'my mum is a big believer in raising boys like you raise your dog. Lots of fresh air, exercise and food. And hugs obviously. And she kind of has a point. Look at the twins . . .'

Holly looked over to where two exhausted small boys were snuggled together under a picnic blanket: tired, contented, with little pink cheeks and fighting the urge to doze. They'd demolished every meal that had been put in front of them, run circles around and around on the beach and matched Taffy trip for trip with bucketfuls of water for the moat of their castle. It had been a perfect day.

Holly's gaze skittered across to Eric, who looked similarly healthy but definitely up for more. He had stationed himself firmly across Holly's legs now, so that every time she moved he could stare at her longingly to let him off the lead.

Taffy reached over and scruffed his ears. 'You're a big soft nutter, aren't you?' Eric responded by licking his hand enthusiastically.

'Takes one to know one,' Holly teased him, pinching the last biscuit from under Taffy's nose.

He tried, but utterly failed, to look affronted. 'Listen here, Graham. I happen to be an excellent advert for the Spaniel Approach to Raising Boys. Me and my brothers used to disappear off to the woods with a picnic and be gone all day. We came home knackered and happy. Completely filthy, obviously, but that's why we're all so bloody healthy. Lots of mud. Probiotics in every gloop.'

Holly listened, entranced as always by tales of a childhood that was totally alien to a city-dwelling only child. Taffy always spoke with such affection about his band of brothers; he made them seem invincible, a team to be reckoned with. His childhood of fields and woodland, tree-houses and dens, penknives and catapults sounded like something from a novel.

To be totally fair, as much as she wanted her boys to have the perfect childhood, she wasn't sure that she had it in her to untie the apron strings so completely. She wasn't convinced that her personality was compatible with the risks and stresses of such free-range parenting, but then she reasoned, if you were a free-range parent, you probably weren't the type to dwell on the threat of death and injury on an hourly basis.

Having boys had certainly forced Holly to take a more relaxed view towards life, cleanliness and Health & Safety. She just wasn't sure yet quite where the line between relaxed and negligent lay.

Taffy casually peeled an orange in one perfect swirl with his penknife. 'It occurs to me though, there are one or two things you should probably know about my family before they all drop me in it tomorrow. Fair warning and all that,' he said seriously, into the momentary stillness. He laid the orange peel spiral down on the sand with a flourish, instantly earning both Holly and Eric's undivided attention, albeit for different reasons.

Holly looked up, his abrupt change of tone alone enough to set her warning bells jangling. She couldn't stop the hint of suspicion that crept into her voice, old habits still apparently dying hard. 'Was this whole day just to soften me up then, before you drop some big bombshell?'

He shook his head. 'No!' he said vehemently, realising his mistake. 'And don't go leaping to the very worst eventuality all the time – I just meant, that you seem to have built up this idyllic picture of my childhood, all puppies and lambs and band of brothers romping around the farm ... I don't want you to be disappointed by the reality.'

'No puppies? No lambs?' she clarified, more bothered than she would admit by her instinctive overreaction.

'Oh no, there probably will be,' he replied. 'And my brothers will be there, with their wives and all their kids and it will be utter chaos and they'll be taking the piss and ... I just – well, to be honest, Holly, it's making me nervous. And it's no big deal, but I wanted to say– I wanted to say that ... Oh shit, I'm getting this all wrong.' He looked frustrated and forlorn – without humour to fall back on, his discomfort was obvious. 'Oh dammit, Holly, I love the way you see me, okay? And I don't want that to change once you've looked at me through their eyes. To them I'm just the squirt, the tagger-along, the baby brother. If you're not used to it, they can seem a little …' He held up his hands as though words failed him. 'You know?'

Holly frowned. She could honestly say she was none the wiser. Whenever Taffy spoke about his family it was with love and affection. Whenever she had expressed concerns about meeting them, he had reassured her that they would love her, simply because he did.

And now this.

Whatever *this* was.

She could cheerfully strangle him for casting a shadow over their perfect day – the day that *he* had organised.

'No,' she said softly. 'I really don't know. I never had brothers, or sisters for that matter. So you're the youngest, I get that. I know that. But you're all adults now. What difference can that possibly make?'

Taffy tossed the remains of his mangled orange to Eric who swallowed it in one bite. 'All the difference in the world.' he said quietly.

Holly sipped at her drink as Taffy tried to explain about the reality of life with three much older brothers and with every anecdote, she got a slightly clearer picture of what made Taffy tick, of how the man she loved had evolved. Even as he described waking up as a teenager, to a bed filled with frogs, his love for his brothers was obvious and absolute – even if, to Holly at least, some of their pranks just seemed rather mean.

Taffy paused. 'Just give them a chance, Holly. Because whatever they might say or do, if you ever need them – no question, they're there.'

Holly sighed, wondering what it would feel like to have three big brothers on speed-dial and whether that might explain why Taffy slept so soundly at night. He knew for certain that there were three pairs of hands to pick up the pieces if he fell. Apparently even if those self-same hands were the ones to have pushed him over in the first place!

'I didn't mean to worry you,' he said apologetically. 'But forewarned is better, I think. Just go in with an open mind. And relax, the whole family will love you.'

Holly shrugged, unable to articulate the fear that they might not. The only times Holly had spoken to Taffy's mother on the phone, she had been short and to the point. Taffy had said that she just wasn't a 'phone person', but Holly wasn't convinced that was even a thing. 'I'm not sure they want to meet me, though,' she mumbled.

'Look, maybe I shouldn't have said anything.' Taffy backtracked. 'Mum's a real sweetie and she'll love having another girl in her life. Four sons, can you imagine what the poor woman has been through. And yes, she might be a bit protective to begin with ... I mean, you're the single parent taking advantage of her baby boy, aren't you?' He grinned, attempting to lighten the mood and so obviously winding her up, but still.

Holly couldn't arrange her face into anything other than the shocked horror of someone saying one of your very worst fears out loud. This day was quickly going downhill and her growing frustration with Taffy's clumsy explanations was making her irritable. Not everything was a joke, whatever he might say. 'Is that what people really think?'

Taffy stopped dead, suddenly appreciating how badly his flippant remark had hit home. 'Oh Holly. Of course that's not what they think. If they think anything at all, it's that we're incredibly lucky to have each other. They probably think the boys are okay too ...' His humour still falling wide of the mark, Taffy took both Holly's hands in his. 'They will love you for two reasons, Holly Graham. One: because I love you and you're amazing. And two: they'll see how happy you're making me ... You and the boys and Eric and living in our bonkers town. I'm home. I'm happy.' He leaned in and kissed her thoroughly. 'I'm pretty low maintenance really. I've got everything I want from life. All in one place. Stop doubting me, Graham. You think I don't notice, but I do. Have a little faith in me.'

'I do,' she protested, but he kissed her again.

'Most of the time, granted, but it's bloody annoying when you don't.'

'Then stop making jokes that aren't funny – it's too real to be funny.'

He kissed her again. 'Okay. No more jokes.'

'Are you going to hug in a special way now?' interrupted a small voice. Tom elbowed his way between them and on to Holly's lap.

Taffy tried to stifle the shocked laughter that caught him on the hop and began packing together their belongings, leaving Holly mouthing mutely.

'It happens,' said Tom earnestly, 'when a man and a woman love each other very much.'

'Good to know,' said Holly, totally unprepared to handle this conversation already. Oh, to have a precocious child.

'Eric wants to hug Coco,' he continued sagely, referring to Eric's epic crush on Alice's assistance dog.

'He does,' agreed Holly. 'He loves her very much, doesn't he?'

Tom nodded, distracted for a moment by a rogue corner of biscuit that had escaped Taffy's attention. 'Eric loves Winnie the Pooh too.'

'Sorry?' asked Holly, wondering if they were wandering off on some random non sequitur like normal.

'It's true. He hugs my biggest Winnie bear in a special way. A lot.' He shook his head crossly. 'Mummy, I don't think Winnie likes it very much.'

Holly's shocked reaction was totally obscured by the explosive laughter from Taffy. He clasped at his sides as the tears rolled down his cheeks. 'Poor Winnie . . .' he managed, as Tom fixed him with a confused stare, before turning his back in disgust. If nothing else, Tom took the wellbeing of his teddy bears extremely seriously.

'Sorry,' said Taffy, before dissolving once more, until Holly joined in and the pair of them laughed until they cried.

Chapter 16

Holly had never considered herself a terribly religious person, but she did feel, as they barrelled down the increasingly narrow country lanes towards Taffy's parents' house the next morning, that a certain amount of faith might serve her very well right now. The fronds of cow parsley hung into the lanes and swiped the windscreen as they passed, leaving trails of dew to trace their path behind them.

She stared out of the window as Taffy gave the twins a running commentary. 'And that over there? That's the field where Rhys and I dammed the stream and caused a big flood. And that tree on the horizon – I got stuck up there once for six hours . . . You see that ditch by the road? I fell into that on my new mountain bike when I was showing off.' He pointed to the tiny silver scar on his forehead. 'Five stitches,' he said, almost proudly.

Holly shook her head at him. 'Don't give them ideas.'

He shrugged. 'Boys will be boys, Holly. In fact, the more you restrict them, the more they'll act up when they're given a little independence later on. My mate Rhys? His mum was so anti-army the whole time we were growing up, she'd go on and on about it. So, what's the first thing he did after school? Only went and signed up, didn't he?'

Holly reached across and laid her hand on his thigh as he drove, watching the clouds scudding across the sky that perfectly mirrored the expression on his face.

They turned off the lane onto a mud track, where the lush rolling fields either side were dotted with sheep grazing in the sunshine. 'Nearly there!' he said to the boys in the back.

Holly slowly exhaled, trying out the mantra she'd been working on. 'I am not taking advantage of your son and lumbering him with my offspring. I am not taking . . .' Too wordy, perhaps? She swallowed hard, suddenly realising how terrified she was of walking into their home, of meeting his brothers and trying to make a good first impression. Tiredness aside, even she could acknowledge that she was only this worried because of how much she cared.

'Right,' said Taffy in a low voice, as though he had anticipated this last-minute wobble. 'This is an anniversary party. People will be talking about weddings and marriage.' He glanced at her sideways to make sure she could see he was smiling. 'This does not mean that you have to get all twitchy. Even if there's a pop-up vicar and a bridal bouquet with your name on it! It's just talk, not pressure, okay?'

Holly nodded. 'Got it. Smile. Be nice. No twitching. Marriage a good thing.'

He shook his head. 'Don't be such a cynic, Graham. Fifty years is quite some record. We, on the other hand, are going to take our own sweet time. And it's *our* decision when and if it happens, deal?'

'Deal,' she said.

They pulled up outside a ramshackle farmhouse that seemed to epitomise everything she knew about Taffy: it was scruffy, yet cared for – welcoming and familiar. The front door burst open and six or seven dogs came bursting out as the welcoming committee. Holly could see two spaniels, a black lab and several others whose breeding was possibly a bit more eclectic.

The twins happily piled out, completely unfazed by the canine attention they received. Tom said firmly, 'Sit!' when one of the dogs got a little too licky and, to everyone's amazement, every single dog sat beautifully still. Tom's face lit up as though he had won the lottery. 'I am the Alpha Dog!' he proclaimed delightedly, patting his leg to see if they would fall into line beside him. When they did, Holly couldn't help but be impressed.

Mrs Jones – call me Patty – came out of a different door, wearing a vast floral apron and wiping her hands on a teatowel. 'You made good time, Meirion.'

Holly turned to look at Taffy, inappropriate laughter threatening to burst. 'Meirion?' she whispered, her eyes dancing at this nugget of information. How had she never stopped to think about what his real name was?

He just shrugged, completely unfazed. 'Only Mum calls me that and even then it's mostly Merry instead.' He scowled for a moment, as though assessing her reliability to keep this particular secret. 'Of course, if you tell anyone at home, I shall have to kill you.'

Holly nodded, desperately trying to keep a straight face and wondering what other little secrets she might discover on this flying visit.

'You're just in time for breakfast, so don't dawdle about,' Patty called.

Holly was about to say that they'd already eaten when Taffy laid his hand on her arm warningly and fractionally shook his head. 'Never turn down food or a dog-walk,' he murmured under his breath. 'Sorry, something else I should have said.'

Holly stepped forward to say hello and found herself crushed into an enormous bear hug from Patty. A genuine affectionate squeeze – not even of the checking-for-back-fat variety that Milo's mother liked to inflict.

'Let's have a look at you now,' said Patty, holding Holly at arm's length and looking into her eyes. 'So this is the lovely lady who's stolen my Merry's heart, eh?'

Holly felt herself stiffen as though she'd been lulled into a false sense of security. When Patty's face broke into an enormous grin and let forth a deep gutsy roll of laughter, Holly dared to breathe again.

'Well, hasn't he found himself a corker?' said Patty, with such a strong Welsh lilt to her words that Holly's brain took a moment to translate. 'Now come and introduce me to these lads of yours, Holly, if we can tear them away from their dog training. We can take them for a yomp over the hills later on if you like; buy ourselves some peace and quiet.'

A few minutes later, Holly found herself being swept into the kitchen on a tide of chatter and spaniels. Taffy's father and brothers had been put to work on a batch of bacon sandwiches and Holly was beginning to wonder how to tell them all apart. All of them tall, dark and athletic, Taffy really did look like the baby of the family and it was evident in their affectionate teasing and greetings that they all still viewed him as such.

Aldwyn, Dylan and Bobi all greeted her with hugs and kisses, Mr Jones only offering a 'How-do' from beside the Aga where he had been put on bacon rotation duty. The twinkle in his eye at watching Taffy trying to persuade Tom and Ben to wash their hands told Holly everything she needed to know: he may be an old-school farmer but he was a softie at heart.

'Right then,' said Patty. 'Boys, do you want a little biscuit and a drink while you're waiting?' Obviously the five minutes until the bacon would be ready was deemed too long for a small lad to wait for sustenance. 'You must be starving after your drive.'

Holly was about to leap in to intervene and to make sure that Ben didn't eat anything he shouldn't, but Patty was there before her. She leaned across to Holly and quietly said, 'Now I made these myself and there's not a scrap of dairy gone anywhere near them, so you mustn't worry, poppet. And there's no nuts either, because I didn't want to risk it.'

Holly inexplicably felt the tears well up in the back of her throat and could only manage a strangled thank you. Patty gave her shoulders a rub. 'Seems to me that Taffy was right and what you need, my darling, is a little more kindness in your life. Now sit yourself down and let my boys wear your gorgeous twins out while we have a coffee.' She leaned across the table. 'Dylan. Bobi. Aldwyn.' She hadn't raised her voice but she had their instant attention. 'Take Ben and Tom out to feed the chickens and see if there's any eggs this morning, would you? I don't know about you, Ben, but I like a fried egg in my bacon butty.'

The easy camaraderie in the room was unlike anything Holly had ever experienced before. She took in all the scribbled pictures stuck to the fridge and the array of framed photographs on the vast windowsills, featuring a parade of ballet dancing grand-daughters and a selection of slightly faded childhood snaps of the four brothers as teenagers. In these, the age gap was more obvious than it was now; the three older boys already tall and lanky, as a younger Taffy – sorry, Merry – followed their every move. It certainly explained why the whole family was so protective of him. And possibly his competitive drive to keep up at all costs.

Patty watched Holly with interest, trying to get the measure of this tousled-headed woman who had appeared in her kitchen with a pair of adorable boys at her heels and her youngest son clearly smitten.

'I speak as I find, Holly, and you should know that when Meirion told me he had fallen in love with a single mother, an older lady to boot, I did have my concerns.'

Holly looked up, eyes wide, wary of what Patty was going to say next. It was as though Patty had read her mind and her worst fears were now being discussed over milky coffee with a geriatric spaniel propped against her leg. Patty smiled then, leaning forward to take Holly's slender hand in her own. 'But it seems to me that it's actually what he's been waiting for and you've finally made him look at his priorities. It was all very well and good him wanting to be a locum and foot-loose and fancy-free, but now look ... I haven't seen him come home so proud of his achievements in a very long time.'

'Well,' said Holly slowly, 'I'd love to take the credit, but it's all down to Taffy really. He's so passionate about Larkford, that he ...'

'Well, he is *now*,' said Patty with an effusive chuckle. 'He calls it home now.' She picked up a vast mug and took a sip. 'He never did before.'

Holly realised that Patty was right; when she first met him, Taffy would always refer to his parents' house as 'home' and now, that was how he referred to the house they lived in together. True, in an ideal world, they would find somewhere new together – somewhere that didn't have uncomfortable echoes of Milo lurking in the shadows – but Holly now suspected that 'home' for Taffy might have more to do with the people he lived with, than bricks and mortar.

'And I have to say,' Patty continued, still watching Holly very closely, 'it's lovely to have young lads in the house again – as much as I adore my grand-daughters, it's a very different pace of life. They're all at ballet this morning, but they'll be here later and you'll see what I mean. I always think that boys are like dogs, you know,' she confided, little knowing that Holly had already been briefed. 'Physically demanding it is, looking after little boys; but then that's nothing to how emotionally demanding it is with these little girls.'

'So girls are like cats, then?' Holly ventured and earned herself a grin.

'Do you know, I think you might be right. You'll get to meet Shona when they come, Aldwyn's wife. Now there's a lass who knows her own mind – terrifies me, she does,' Patty confided.

Holly nodded, quietly unable to believe that anyone could intimidate Patty, with her maternal certainty and calm control. Holly could sense that this kitchen was very much her domain, and as the only woman in the family for many years, she wondered how Patty coped with her daughters-in-law and their cat-like offspring.

Her questions were answered, as a flurry of barking outside announced the arrival of several cars and chaos ensued. It was nothing short of a miracle that, within five minutes, the entire extended family was packed around the kitchen table, tutus jammed inwards and muddy wellies swinging under the table. The bacon and tea was flowing as freely as the conversation and Holly simply allowed herself to be swept up.

This was how she had imagined that some families celebrated Christmas – it hadn't occurred to her that it could happen over a bacon sandwich, simply because they all took so much pleasure in each other's company. She listened in as Bella, the youngest of the ballerinas at five, proudly lectured Ben and Tom on who was related to whom and how. 'You can be my cousin now if you like,' she said, casually, as though it were an honour she lightly bestowed, but Holly could see a longing in the way that Bella leaned forward to hear their response.

'Alright,' said Tom, also nonchalant but looking up at Holly with big eyes. 'Mummy, can Bella be my cousin?' he asked.

There was an awkward silence amongst the grown-ups at the possible implications of this question. Patty chuckled and gave Holly a wink. 'Out of the mouths of babes ...'

'One big happy family here, aren't we, Bella?' hedged Taffy easily. 'And go on, admit it, it's quite cool to have a couple of boys to play with?' Taffy leaned across to Holly. 'Our Bella here is a bit of a tomboy. Deeply resents the ballet, don't you, Bill? She'd rather be up a tree in her jeans, but as the youngest, she just has to fall in line really.'

Holly looked around the table and could see what Taffy meant; Bella's big sisters were most definitely girly-girls and Shona was a rather stunning, if overly made-up, beautician. The opportunities for mud-pies and snails were clearly only possible at her grandparents' house.

'Taffy calls me Bill, because he knows I'd rather be a boy,' proclaimed Bella firmly, daring Tom or Ben to comment.

Ben just nodded. 'Cool.'

Where Patty had let the idea dangle, Taffy's brothers weren't quite so tactful. It would appear that when it came to the pecking order of the siblings, nothing had really changed and Taffy would always be the baby brother being forced to play catch-up.

'Probably about time you two got hitched,' butted in Aldwyn. 'Me and Shona had been married for a decade by the time we were your age. And Big Picture – neither of you are getting any younger.' He laid it down like a challenge and waited for his little brother to pick up the gauntlet.

Bobi played interference, offering Holly an apologetic glance for his brother's gaucheness. 'Yeah, but then you had knocked her up, so it's no basis for comparison really.'

Taffy mouthed 'Fuck off' at Aldwyn, nodded his thanks at Bobi and they all carried on eating as though nobody had spoken. Only Taffy's leg fidgeting beside her showed that the comment had bothered him on any level. Holly looked around the table, a little wrong-footed.

Aldwyn reached across and soundlessly pinched the last rasher of bacon off Taffy's plate. Taffy didn't even miss a beat.

'So then, Squirt,' Aldwyn pushed, apparently annoyed to be deprived of a reaction, 'how's life as a country GP? Snotty noses and bunions keeping you enthralled?'

'It's good,' Taffy said simply, piling homemade plum jam out of a Kilner jar on to his toast.

'Surprised you sold out so soon, actually. After all that talk of sports clinics and "making a difference" . . .' Aldwyn let the jibe dangle, deniable, but nevertheless diminishing.

'This way, I get to do both,' Taffy said evenly, flashing a glance at Holly to gauge her reaction.

'Hmmm. Still seems like a soft option to me,' chimed in Dylan with a grin.

Holly looked around the table, expecting to see disgruntled faces and stopped short as she realised that all the other little conversations carried on around them as though this were nothing. Nothing new, anyway.

'Oh, Taffy,' cut in his mother, 'since you're talking shop, I was going to ask you a favour actually. Can you phone someone at the hospital and ask about my blood pressure tablets. They keep changing the dosage and I've got a little bit muddled what I'm supposed to be taking and when?'

'I can take a look,' said Taffy easily, taking a huge bite from his doorstep slice of toast.

'Oh no, it's the consultant we need to ask . . .'

'I can check the dosages, Mum, it's fine. We don't need to call the consultant.'

'Oh, oh well, if you're sure? It seems pretty complicated.' Patty looked flustered at the very thought and Holly found her heart sinking a little. Did they really know so little about Taffy's competency as a doctor, or his ambitions, or what they were achieving at The Practice? Did he not tell them, she wondered, or did they not hear him?

As Patty leaned over and refilled Taffy's glass, automatically moving it away from the edge of the table, she began to get a clearer idea of what he'd been trying to tell her on the beach. When she looked at him, she saw a man, a doctor, a competent and vivacious companion – when his family looked at him, did they ever look past the little boy playing catch-up with his much older siblings?

The enormous pine dresser caught her eye, laden with baby photographs, proudly framed and displayed. Generations of Joneses in their romper suits, with gappy smiles. 'If you're looking for young Merry,' Mr Jones said quietly, 'he won't be up there. We rather dropped the ball on the baby photo front after Dylan was born. There's a few from when he started playing rugby though, if you want me to dig them out?

Otherwise,' he looked along the table, 'it's a bit of a touchy subject, I'm afraid.'

Holly nodded and immediately looked away, but not before Aldwyn had clocked the direction of her gaze. 'Oh, you won't find any photos of Taffy as a baby, Holly. Too ugly, weren't you, Squirt?' He grinned. 'Didn't want to risk breaking the camera!'

Taffy, to his credit, laughed along with the rest of the table. Holly, however, found it easier just to fill her mouth with succulent bacon, and hope that the angry flush to her chest could be blamed on the heat from the Aga.

Bobi reached across her to grab a basket of bread rolls for his girls, who seemed to have the appetites of Olympic rowers. 'Just ignore Aldwyn. He takes great pleasure in riling people up. Taffy mostly. He can get a bit competitive.' He flushed. 'We all can actually – drives Mum crazy. And what with *you* being a doctor too – ' He stopped dead. 'I didn't mean . . .'

'Don't worry about it,' Holly interrupted, uncomfortably watching him dig himself a deeper hole.

Bobi leaned back in. 'If you let it go over your head, after twenty years or so, it stops being quite so annoying and if you can't out-run him, you learn to outwit him fairly quickly. But you'll be grand. Although, I will warn you, Mum's planning a toast over lunch, welcoming you to the family, so if you scare easy, you might want to work on your game face.'

He turned away, as one of his daughters tugged on his sleeve for attention and he found himself refereeing in a heated debate about whose tooth was the wobbliest.

Holly quietly excused herself from the chaos as the meal drew to a close and slipped along the corridor to the downstairs loo.

She leaned her forehead against the coolness of the tile above the sink and slowly breathed out.

There was a gentle tap at the door and Taffy's insistent whisper, 'Are you hiding out in there? And if so, do you need coffee? Shall we make a break for it?'

She opened the door and pulled him inside. 'I just needed a minute.'

He smiled in relief. 'So the trick is, with Aldwyn, if you just ignore him—'

'For twenty years or so?' she interrupted.

'Exactly. Besides, I don't remember him being quite so thrilled about his shotgun wedding as he's making out . . .'

'You were right, you know,' Holly interrupted, unable to hold her tongue a minute longer. 'I really don't get it. Why do you let them talk to you like that?' she asked in frustration.

He shrugged. 'They're only mucking around and they're pretty set in their ways. And it's not like I take it to heart and sob into my Corn Flakes, now, is it? By the time we get home, it will all be water under the bridge. Besides, have you ever tried to get a word in edgewise with that lot? Not as easy as it seems . . .'

His nonchalant words were one thing, but the sudden flash of fragility in his eyes made Holly back off immediately. How many times, she wondered, had he tried to speak up and never felt heard? As confusing to her as it was, this weird sibling dynamic had been in place for three decades longer than she'd even known him. And what did she know about families anyway?

She leaned in and kissed him with an unspoken intensity, offering acceptance and admiration for the man he had grown into. She could see him so clearly; it was just such a shame that she seemed to be in the minority.

There was no shortage of love in this house. Every single one of them clearly adored him, but it was as though he were some kind of exotic species that had dropped by to visit. In a world of sheep shearing, jam-making and crop rotations, they clearly found his chosen career an uncomfortable subject.

Whether that was because they didn't understand it, or didn't support it, was hard to say. Whether their affection was hampered by expectation, judgement or, possibly in Aldwyn's case, outright envy, was an even harder call.

His mum was so proud of her boy; Holly had noticed Patty could barely resist reaching out a hand to touch his arm, his shoulder, his face, every opportunity she got. The love shone out of her eyes with every word he spoke to her, until she had to think of him as anything more than her baby. Watching Taffy explain her medication to her had been a lesson in self-restraint, as Patty simply nodded along. Holly would lay a tenner on the table right now that Patty would be on the phone to that consultant before the week was out.

What she couldn't work out though was Taffy's reaction – or lack of it – to all the joshing and teasing. He simply seemed reconciled to his role, his only concern being what she might make of it. But then, she realised, they weren't her family. It wasn't her call.

Seeing him here confused her.

Never before had Holly felt so ill-equipped; as an only child, she didn't have the first clue about family politics. So, she had a choice to make – lean in on faith, or step back and watch.

Holly was surprised to find that it was actually an easy decision.

'Your mum called me poppet,' she said, apropos of nothing,

'And she baked Ben special cookies. They're really very sweet, Taffy,' she said, surprised to find she meant it.

'Except Aldwyn.'

'Obviously except Aldwyn,' she echoed with a smile. 'Well, to be honest, I just hadn't really realised what it would feel like to be sitting around that big table ...' She didn't need to remind Taffy that the latter years of her own childhood had been supper for two on their laps in front of *Tomorrow's World*.

Taffy folded her into a big hug. 'You daft muppet,' he said affectionately. 'I told you it's not always like the Waltons, though. Like the time Shona pierced Bobi's daughter's ears without asking. Or when Aldwyn and Dylan start bickering over crop subsidies. Or when they get on their soapbox about me not living in Wales. Or even,' he grinned, 'the time that Dad fell asleep and let the Christmas turkey burn while Mum was at church ...'

Holly managed a smile. She could see what he was doing – trying to cheer her up and put things in perspective – but the tableau he painted of the ups and downs of a loving family life were almost making it worse. Family life here, being a little like a marriage – for better or worse – they were a team.

How many of Taffy's little foibles, she wondered – the ones she loved and despaired of in equal measure, could all be traced to his place at this kitchen table, or on these hillsides or in this family? It was a sobering thought when the same principles were applied to her own boys.

It was certainly something to think about, though. Was that what they needed too?

She was nowhere near ready to make any big decisions yet, she conceded. God knows, she wasn't even formally divorced!

But for the first time, she began to wonder whether maybe, just maybe – one day – she too could sit down with Dylan and debate crop subsidies – just as soon as she found out what they actually were, of course.

Chapter 17

Grace sipped at the remarkably strong mojito that Elsie had pressed into her hand the moment she walked through the door. She breathed out a little to let the flames of the rum flicker and cool in her throat. 'Crikey, Elsie, you don't mess about with small measures, do you?'

Elsie shrugged coquettishly. 'I'm not sure anything in life is better in small measures.' She looked up at Grace and there was sheer devilry on her face.

Grace couldn't help but grin. 'Well—' she began, before the reality of her day smothered any chance of cheeky banter. She frowned, cutting Elsie's double entendre off at the pass. 'If we're keeping this entre-nous, maybe Julia Channing? I could definitely cope with smaller measures of *Doctor In The House.*'

Elsie topped up her drink, deftly allowing the perfect amount to pour from her silver cocktail shaker, before cutting off the flow with a twist of her wrist. 'And, tell me, are you the only one who feels that way, or is she making everybody's life hell?'

Grace thought for a moment, the rum gradually loosening her tongue and her usual reserve falling away. 'I don't know,' she admitted. 'I think it might just be me, to be honest. She just manages to put me on a slow simmer with every sideways look.'

Elsie twiddled a twist of lime onto a cocktail stick and plopped it into the delicate martini glass that Grace was gingerly holding, for fear of snapping its fragile stem. 'And how much of that has to do with Dan, do you think?' Elsie asked, her tone casual but her perceptive gaze missing nothing, including the rosy hue that suddenly coloured Grace's neck.

'I can't imagine what this has to do with Dan,' she said, sipping at the potent drink with a slight shudder. 'I think it's more likely that Julia just doesn't like the idea of oversight.'

Elsie frowned. 'You mean she's been making mistakes?'

'No – at least I hope not! Oversight, as in somebody keeping an eye on how things work. It's been quite illuminating on my course actually; I could become quite the boffin given the time and the opportunity. Obviously, I'm no doctor, but learning how things are supposed to work in theory and then watching how they actually work in practice . . . Well,' she laughed nervously, 'there's quite a gap! And with this wonderful nomination to be a model surgery – it can only really highlight that.'

'I can imagine,' said Elsie. 'But what about you, Gracie? Do you like the idea of being their over-see-er? If that's even a thing?'

Grace pushed open the French windows into Elsie's garden, allowing the slight evening breeze to dilute the heaviness in the air. 'Can I fob you off with a maybe?' she asked hopefully. 'Because, if I throw myself into this Management course completely, I know it's going to rock the boat at The Practice and that's the last thing I want to do – except it's also the very thing I want to do most . . . To create a role for myself that makes a real difference and actually has a little impact. Maybe even make things better, or at least running more smoothly. Does that make any sense at all?'

She paused as though finding her way through the thoughts before she voiced them. 'It's as though I have to make a choice, Elsie. Do I want to be this ultra-efficient, highly-qualified Practice Manager, who doesn't care about upsetting the status quo and ruffling feathers? Or do I want to be their friend and team-mate? Because by the time I've finished telling them all the things that aren't running to protocol, I'm not sure anybody there is going to like me very much.'

Elsie tilted her head to one side as though appraising Grace like a challenging piece of modern art. 'Then from where I'm sitting, you have a decision to make. Do you want your colleagues to like you, or do you want *you* to like you? After all, that's why you're doing this course, isn't it? To regain a sense of who *you* are in the grand scheme of things?'

Grace fidgeted slightly, uncomfortable under the intensity of Elsie's gaze. 'Shall I make us something to eat? These mojitos are really quite strong.' Without waiting for an answer, she began rooting around for provisions, amused as always to find that Elsie's idea of a well-stocked fridge focused mainly on mixers, make-up and melon balls.

Elsie materialised silently at her shoulder and quietly pushed the fridge door closed. 'It's okay to feel a bit guilty, Grace. Selfishness takes a bit of getting used to, but it also has the potential to be incredibly rewarding,' she said gently.

'I'm not selfish!' Grace blurted out, her expression mirroring how shocked she was by this accusation. 'How could you say that? I've spent years looking after Roy, looking after the boys, looking after everyone at The Practice. How can that be selfish?' She pressed her hand to her throat as though the very idea of such a notion was choking her.

Elsie leaned in and gave her a papery kiss on the cheek, a cloud of Chanel No5 around her as always. 'And now it's your turn. So yes, my darling, your Roy is gone and your boys are all grown. You get to *choose* to be selfish. And I, for one, don't think that's always such a bad thing. You're not being mean or insensitive or cruel – you're just taking a little time to pursue your own ambitions.'

Grace shook her head. 'But I'm not ambitious, Elsie. Julia Channing – *that's* what ambition looks like.'

'Utter bollocks,' said Elsie bluntly. 'That's what a woman in pain and searching for validation looks like. Ambition isn't a dirty word either – what are they teaching you girls these days? You've been a mother and a wife and you put your dreams on hold to do that – but who else do you need to please now, except yourself? Go do this, Grace – go and get this amazing qualification and watch how the world opens up for you. Stay here, leave here. Be bold and opinionated, because I know you, Grace, and there's no way you would ever steamroller anyone with your opinions; I can't actually think of a more tactful person in the whole of Larkford. So use your God-given brains and make the most of this time in your life.'

'But—' began Grace quietly.

'No! No buts. No guilt. It's the guilt that's holding you back and it's misplaced. If you asked Holly or Dan or Taffy if they want The Practice to be the best it can be, what do you think they'd say? Hmm?'

'Yes?' ventured Grace.

'Of course, they'd say yes!' exploded Elsie, infuriated. 'You're all singing from the same song-sheet. Will they like it when you point out their flaws? Of course not. But are they astute enough to realise that sometimes a little objectivity goes a very long way? Well, one would certainly hope so.'

Grace nodded, brow furrowed, as she attempted to digest Elsie's impassioned pronouncements.

'It's like my second – no wait, third – husband used to say: the truth will set you free, but first it will piss you off.' Elsie said firmly, as though drawing a line under the conversation, leaving Grace unsure at that point whether Elsie meant Grace herself, or the partners at The Practice.

Either. Both. Or maybe all of us, Grace wondered.

'Come on, Delilah, stop dithering around looking for sustenance. You'll find nothing in there. Let's pop out and get supplies.' Elsie attempted to wrangle the sleeves of her linen jacket into submission, looking strangely uncoordinated. 'I want to pretend I'm in Capri so we'll need some Prosecco and a Caprese – do you think Marion will stretch to some buffalo mozzarella at this time of night?'

Grace found herself compelled to go out on a provisions mission, mooching through the twilight streets of Larkford, with Elsie's arm tucked companionably into her own. By the time they'd crossed the Market Place, Grace had a better idea of what the Fabulous Fifties had entailed for Elsie – if her stories about having a blast on a Riva off the island of Capri were anything to go by. Elsie clearly was deriving a certain pleasure from seeing the shocked expression on Grace's face, but in the end she relented. 'Look, Grace – the thing you're missing is this: we were young, we had money and we were alive. It seemed almost indecent not to squeeze the fun out of every moment we had. Not to mention the fact that I had a rather classy chassis back then – would have been rude not to take it for a spin occasionally.' She gave an irreverent wiggle of her bottom to make it clear she was not talking about cars and laughed in delight as Grace just shook her head in amazement. No wonder a simple tomato and mozzarella salad had the power to bring back such happy memories.

They were brought up short in their merriment by the sight of Candace Channing weaving through the Market Place, barely missing an erratically driven red motorbike, which bunny-hopped to a halt and then lurched away without even stopping.

'Bloody Percy Lawson,' growled Grace under her breath, carefully easing her arm away from Elsie, ushering her into the supermarket ahead of her. Elsie may not yet know who the sad-looking woman was, but the likeness to Julia was uncanny and Taffy had discreetly updated her on the situation before he left. And there was something about the disconnected look in Candace's eyes that made Grace instinctively nervous.

'Candace?' she said gently. 'Are you okay? Do you want me to call Julia?' Her hand was already reaching for her mobile when Candace swung around erratically.

'Don't you dare,' she hissed. 'Just because that stupid busybody in there wouldn't sell me what I wanted, there's no need to summon the fun police.' She laughed abruptly. 'Don't pretend you don't know what I mean. My Julia can rain on any parade at a moment's notice.' She narrowed her eyes and looked Grace up and down. 'Unless you're one of her acolytes too?'

Before Grace could reply, the clanging rattle of Dan's beloved Land Rover echoed through the Market Place. He pulled to a halt beside them and swung his legs effortlessly to the pavement. Grace noticed the frayed rip in his ancient jeans and attempted to tell herself that the warm rush of feeling that overwhelmed her had everything to do with relief at his arrival and nothing to do with the sudden overwhelming urge to touch her boss's tanned thigh.

'There you two are, painting the town red,' said Dan easily, no trace in his tone of the concern that had been writ large on his face as he'd driven up towards them. 'I know I'm cutting your evening short, Candace, but I thought we'd head back? I've a couple of steaks on a promise and we can put the world to rights.' He made it sound, thought Grace, as though an evening with his girlfriend's mother was the perfect end to his busy day and Candace was clearly flattered.

'You don't have to cook for me,' she purred, taking Dan's outstretched hand as he helped her into the Land Rover. He shut the door firmly and turned to Grace.

'Thank you,' he said with feeling. 'Julia's filming and I've been driving around for ages looking for her.'

Grace shrugged. 'I can't take any of the credit, I'm afraid. I just happened to be here with Elsie getting mozzarella supplies.'

He smiled. 'Ha – Caprese! Then you're in for a treat. Get her to tell you about the time she pushed Brigitte Bardot out of the boat.' He leaned in and kissed her cheek. 'Thank you, Gracie. I know Holly wouldn't have gone to Wales if you hadn't stepped in and, between you and me, I think those two needed some time together.' He stuffed his hands into his jeans pockets and hesitated. 'They deserve to be happy, don't you think, after everything they've been through.'

Grace nodded her agreement and then felt a swell of bravery prompt her forward. 'I think we all do, actually.'

He looked up, caught unawares by the honesty in her voice, snagging his bottom lip in his teeth. 'Do you miss Roy terribly?' he asked. 'Is it hard being alone after so long?'

Grace took a moment, wanting to be as sincere as his quietly heartfelt question deserved. 'It catches up with me sometimes, but I wasn't happy. Before. With Roy. I didn't ever feel like I could just be myself, you know. I always had to be what he needed. So now . . . now, it's easier in some ways.'

He took her hand and squeezed it. 'Now you get to be you.' There was a twinkle in his eye as he spoke. 'God help us all.'

Grace couldn't help but notice that Dan was still holding her hand, lightly, gently, but with a warmth that she couldn't have foreseen.

Candace broke the spell by hammering on the window of the Land Rover. 'Are we going or not?'

'I guess we're going,' Dan said, turning to leave. 'For the record, we're all so proud of you doing this course. It's lovely to see you flourishing, even if it does mean you're going to be a complete pain in the arse at work!'

Grace watched them pull away and couldn't help but smile. Dan had made it sound as though the choices she'd been worrying about might not be quite so challenging after all.

Half an hour later, Elsie was unsettled and fidgety as she perched on the bar stool at the kitchen counter and Grace prepared supper to her exacting instructions: tearing – not cutting – the basil leaves to Elsie's specifications and inhaling the pungent aroma of aniseed and summer as she did so. She handled the warm ripeness of the large red tomatoes with care, as she pulled them from the crinkled brown paper bag to slice, a trace of a smile still lighting her face as she thought of Dan's expression.

Elsie sniffed. 'Good to see Marion was listening the other day – if you want to sell organic produce, there's no point murdering it in a sweaty plastic bag. If only everyone in Larkford was quite so biddable.'

She carried on muttering and every now and then Grace would look up, thrown by an unexpected edge or tone to

Elsie's grumbles. 'Shall we set up camp in the dining room and I can bring everything through in a moment?' she offered.

Elsie gave her a stern look that brooked no argument. 'Is there something you wish to share with the group? Are you concerned your Caprese will be found wanting or are you just reluctant to indulge in a little speculation about this Candace Channing?'

Grace walked around the kitchen island and held out her hand. 'Firstly, madam, it's gossip, not speculation and secondly, you're looking a little pale and fragile to be wobbling about on these spindly bar stools. You may be a petite and delicate flower, Elsie Townsend, but there's no way I can scrape you off the floor by myself.' The two women stood for a moment, the height of the stool giving Elsie a little boost that meant they were almost eye to eye.

'I can't believe I missed Dan,' said Elsie petulantly changing the subject. 'He's such a tonic to the soul, that one. *He* always makes me forget that I'm verging on the geriatric, or maybe he's so evolved that it's just irrelevant to him?' She looked at Grace, the message clear. 'Dan always manages to look past all that and sees the real me, you know?'

'And if he were here, then he could absolutely scoop you up in his arms, but he's busy being somebody else's knight tonight, so you'll have to make do with me,' said Grace firmly, as she helped Elsie down from the precarious bar stool and over to the sofa in the corner of the kitchen, catching her arm as she stumbled slightly. Not the destination of Grace's choosing, but Elsie's will was indomitable and she seemed determined to score a victory of wills, even as she was conceding defeat.

'I've a little project on the go next door, so we'll just stay in here. Pop some music on, would you, darling?' said Elsie, waving an arm loosely towards a complicated stereo system beside her. 'Something summery and sexy should do the trick.'

Grace flicked through the CDs in a stack, noting the prevalence of Barry O'Connor albums and not wishing to be tactless. Her hesitation, of course, was not missed by Elsie's eagle eye. 'You can sling those in the bin while you're there. I think we can do a little better than that.' The words held such vehemence, such intensity, that Grace was frozen for a moment. Both women knew they weren't talking about his soulful melodies and catchy lyrics.

'Are we ever going to talk about what happened in Borneo?' Grace said gently, wiping her hands on the tea towel she had slung nonchalantly over her shoulder. 'It's all very well you fixing all of our little conundrums, but who's there to help with yours?'

Elsie said nothing, but there was something in her demeanour that gave off a prickly warning that Grace had overstepped the mark. After a moment Elsie turned and took her hand. 'You know, the last few months have been such a tiny part of my life when you take a step back – that's what I've been doing, taking a step back and a moment to indulge myself with a few happier memories. So Borneo wasn't great – but it was just a blip on my timeline. When we've had a little bite to eat, I can show you. I've been having a little sort out since I got back . . .'

Elsie blinked suddenly, as though a dart of pain had thrown her off topic. She dabbed her fingers to her lips and a whisper of a gasp escaped them.

Grace missed nothing. 'Are you okay? We didn't have to talk about this, you know. I just wanted you to know that I'm here if you need me.'

Chapter 18

'You're awfully quiet,' said Taffy the next morning.

Holly managed a smile. She couldn't help feeling a tiny bit grateful for Taffy's decision to limit their stay to one night. As lovable and welcoming as the Jones family were, they were also what Elsie would call 'a bit much'. There was no respite from the banter and the questions and the teasing – when one brother tired, another would tag in and Patty would sit through it all with a beatific look on her face at having her whole brood safely ensconced around her mammoth kitchen table. She had practically force-fed them all roast lamb last night, until the twins had admitted defeat and been unable to manage any pudding – a rare and unusual occurrence in itself.

Holly certainly felt as though her own life had been under the spotlight, which would have felt more intrusive if they hadn't also peppered Taffy (or should she say Merry?) with volley after volley of questions. His parents certainly seemed relieved that he had given up his preoccupation with always being a locum and had finally committed to The Practice and by extension to Larkford – even if that meant that he wouldn't be heading back to Wales to set up shop any time soon.

She yawned and stretched. 'Just enjoying the peace.' Ben and Tom had been out of the door at sparrow's fart, questing

Elsie nodded slowly, looking slightly bewildered and disorientated. 'You're a very sweet girl, but I get to be the one with the answers around here. I thought we'd agreed that.' She enunciated the words slowly, with great care and a little red flag started waving somewhere in Grace's peripheral vision.

'Elsie? When you were poorly in Borneo – the funny turn you mentioned – what actually happened?'

Elsie didn't reply for a moment but steadfastly stared at the slow puddle of mojito that was spreading across her skirt, where her left hand lay wilted in her lap. Grace knelt down in front of her, dialling her mobile as she did so. 'Looks like a spontaneous road trip for you and me this evening,' Grace said calmly, her voice soothing and even. 'A little late night outing to Bath.'

'S'not exactly Capri . . .' scowled Elsie, even as the flickers of fear shadowed her gaze.

'No, but it'll do for now. Capri will have to wait.'

Elsie stuck out her tongue in disgust and it was all Grace needed to see. 'Ambulance please,' she said as the phone line connected, 'I have a patient with left-sided weakness, tongue deviation and possible history of TIA.'

for eggs and bottle-feeding lambs with Taffy's dad. Holly snuggled down deeper under the layers of vintage floral eiderdowns that Taffy had unearthed last night as the temperature dropped and Patty's answer for the shivers had been the suggestion to 'throw another dog on the bed'.

Taffy looked relieved. 'So you don't hate it here? My family aren't driving you nuts?'

'God no, and well, yes, a little bit actually, in that order. It *is* quite full-on though, isn't it?' she smiled. Patty charging in with barely a knock to deposit two huge mugs of milky tea had been rather a surprise, particularly since they had been 'making the most' of a child-free bedroom. The fact that Patty had then sat down on the end of the bed for a chat, while Holly tugged the duvet tighter around her naked body had been another!

Taffy sat on the bed to pull on his socks and casually removed a small plastic dinosaur from under his leg without missing a beat. 'I know my lot can be a bit full on when you meet them all at once, but I needed to see that you knew what you were getting in to. This isn't a "meet up twice a year for awkward conversations and canapés" kind of a family.'

For the first time, Holly didn't bristle when he talked about what she might be 'getting in to'. There was no rush. Elsie was right, they could take their time and work out what suited them – both of them. And after all, a marriage certificate was really only a piece of paper and for Holly, that didn't mean half as much as the fact that right now, they woke up together each day and consciously chose to be together.

Patty appeared in the doorway, the house phone outstretched in her hand and looking worried. 'There's a call for you from work. I think it's urgent – Dan says he's been trying to get hold of you all night.'

Taffy took the cordless phone, as Holly automatically checked her mobile and realised that she had no signal at all. Taffy's earnest expression and his tone of voice only confirmed the urgency.

Holly switched on to auto-pilot the moment she heard the news; Elsie had been admitted into hospital overnight. She was stable, he'd said, but asking for Holly. Grace was with her and poor Dan had spent quite some time phoning every Jones in the phonebook trying to track them down.

Even as Taffy filled her in, Holly started tossing a variety of random and unrelated things into her enormous handbag, unsure of what she would need.

'How quickly can we be there?' she asked.

Taffy carefully lifted the porcelain figurine from the dressing table out of her bag and passed her Ben's teddy bear instead. 'I'll get the twins and Eric together and meet you by the car, okay? We'll go straight to the hospital,' he said. 'I'll just stay with the twins and act as chauffeur, if nothing else . . .'

'No, no, no. It's fine. Let's go via home and I'll get my car. I can manage.'

Taffy just nodded. 'Okay then. But I will just say that they're digging up the car park at the hospital, so the parking might be a little bit tight . . .' He let that one dangle for a moment, knowing exactly how to persuade Holly that she didn't need to be brave and do everything by herself. Holly's parking phobia had become a standing joke in the area, as she was often spotted parking miles away from her destination, simply to gain access to the privileged and wide-spaced world of Parent & Child Parking at the supermarket. Holly claimed she did it to keep fit, walking. Her insurance company were frankly grateful, along with any other car owners in the area.

'Actually, Taffy,' she conceded after a moment, 'maybe a little company would be nice after all.'

By the time Holly arrived at the hospital, she'd run through every scenario she could think of and had been dodging morbid thoughts all the way there, oblivious to the beauty of the drive, winding down towards Bath from Larkford, with all the trees donning their glossy summer foliage and a hint of warm hay in the air.

Walking onto the ward in the hospital and watching Elsie hold court was enough to make her stumble in sheer relief. How she could go from an emergency admission to bossing around the nurses in a few short hours was nothing short of a miracle, or indeed a battle of mind over matter.

Elsie was sitting propped up in bed, her cashmere dressing gown swathed around her and her pearl earrings catching the morning sun. It stood to reason that she would have somehow wangled the window bay. She was moaning to the sweet, terribly young-looking nurse about the flickering overhead strip lighting and how terribly ageing it was.

'Honestly, darling, you have no idea how crucial lighting is – do you want all the relatives coming in here, thinking that their loved ones are at death's door, when a simple soft-focus bulb change would make everyone look so much healthier ...'

'Well,' mumbled the sweet nurse, who was clearly over-awed, 'the thing is that most of the patients in here *are* at death's door. Jollying them up with fancy lighting might make things confusing, don't you think?'

'I do hope you're not implying, young lady, that *I'm* on

my way out too. Perhaps you've got me in the wrong ward? There's nothing wrong with me that a stiff gin and a good . . .'

'Elsie!' said Holly, hurriedly interrupting. 'How on earth did you bag the window slot? Morning, gorgeous,' she continued, barely pausing for breath before leaning down and kissing Elsie firmly on her cheek. The nurse took the opportunity to scuttle away, reaching for her phone automatically as she did so. Holly could only hope that she was calling a friend with the news of a Celebrity in her care, rather than going on Twitter or calling the papers.

'Did you have a lovely time in Wales?' Elsie asked, as though they were sitting in her conservatory drinking coffee. 'Young Taffy was so nervous about introducing you to his folks – must be quite the smitten kitten. But, I told him he didn't need to worry about a thing. I bet his mam adored you, didn't she? I mean why wouldn't she? But still . . .'

Holly blinked hard. In the car, in the long strip-lit corridors, she'd been running all sorts of horrendous scenarios, most of which ended with her arriving too late. Now here was Elsie, talking nineteen to the dozen, without a care in the world. She didn't know whether to laugh or cry.

She settled in the end, for taking Elsie's papery hand in her own, pulling up the visitor's chair as close as she possibly could and letting her friend chat on. Rather than exhausting her, every new line of conversation seemed to bring a little more colour to her cheeks and a little more spark to the trademark twinkle in her eye. Holly slowly breathed out. Elsie was going to be fine. It was just another scare and that happened to people in their eighties.

She looked up, suddenly aware that Elsie had stopped talking and was looking at her, waiting for a response.

'I'm sorry I scared you, Holly,' Elsie whispered, a flash of fear tightening her face for a moment. 'There just wasn't much I could do about it.'

Holly smiled. Typical Elsie. Nobody else she knew would apologise for collapsing despite their best efforts.

'But you're okay now? What did the doctor say this morning?'

Elsie waved her hand dismissively. 'Pfft! Something along the lines of "you're old, shit happens, get used to it". He wasn't exactly inspiring, let's put it that way. But honestly, I feel fine now and there must be somebody more in need of this bed than me.'

She went to take a sip of her tea and winced as the hot liquid dribbled slightly on one side of her mouth. It was fractional, but Holly realised there was a definite droop to one side of her face and obviously her lips weren't quite under control – not that they ever really had been.

'So it happened again?' Holly said, concerned.

'They're all over-reacting! Honestly, you spill one little cocktail . . .'

But this time there was no fobbing Holly off and the notion that Elsie's disquiet since her return had been about the whereabouts of the errant Barry O'Connor suddenly seemed very foolish.

Maybe it *was* the unforgiving hospital lighting that illuminated the very signs that Elsie had taken such pains to disguise: the ring hanging loosely on her increasingly slender fingers, the limpness to her arm and hand, and the way she was concentrating so hard to form her words. And of course, the very fact that she had asked for help.

'I'm so glad Grace was there,' Holly said gently. 'I'm so sorry I wasn't.' The guilt laced into her words made Elsie frown.

'What are you going to do now, baby-sit me every minute

of every day? Buy me one of those foul red buttons to dangle around my neck?'

Holly didn't say anything, but Elsie was obviously still astute enough to know that was exactly what Holly had been considering. 'When Cartier make one, I'll wear it,' Elsie said firmly, as if that settled the matter.

'Elsie—' Holly began, before pulling herself up short, clearly deciding that they could talk about this later. 'Where is Grace anyway? I wanted to thank her . . .'

'She's gone to get some coffee and you wanted to *quiz* her,' Elsie retorted. 'Find out all the nitty gritty about which bit of me broke this time. I've been away for months, Holly. I had rather hoped we could have a few weeks of lovely chats about Life, Loves and the Universe, before we started on the mundane.'

Normally, such chastisement from Elsie would have had Holly profusely apologising and rushing to mollify her, but Holly's new-found backbone was firmly in place these days. Even when it came to Elsie. 'Well, we could do, and I could pretend that two mini-strokes in as many weeks wasn't a wake-up call. Or we could actually be honest with one another and talk about the elephant in the room.'

'I don't think you should call me an elephant,' protested Elsie, making one last attempt at humour, before admitting defeat and sinking back into her pillows. She seemed to shrink and wizen before Holly's very eyes. It only went to show how much of Elsie's physical presence was driven by her forceful personality.

'Oh, stop hovering there looking all terrified,' Elsie said grumpily. 'I've said I'm sorry about all this and I'm clearly fine. Go and get that bloody chart before your head explodes and then you'll see what I mean. Big fuss about nothing.'

Holly did exactly as she was told, not just because Elsie quite intimidated her when she got stroppy, but because it was what she'd been wanting to do from the moment she arrived.

She flicked through the admissions forms, trying to disguise her concern at what she was reading. Mini-strokes were like the little tremors before the big earthquakes and not something to be ignored or belittled. It was one of the reasons she insisted on calling them that. A TIA – a transischaemic attack – didn't have quite the associations of severity that the word 'stroke' instilled. And to be fair, Elsie's stats on admission had Holly worried, even if her patient was now seemingly back on her usual acerbic form, albeit with a slightly more painstaking delivery.

Elsie epitomised the very opposite of most of her patients – the Worried Well wanted to have constant reassurance and as many tests as possible, dithering and catastrophising. Elsie belonged to a different tribe: the Stalwarts, Holly called them. They'd lived through World Wars, rationing, losing friends, losing lovers, losing children. They knew exactly how mortal they were, but had no desire to be thinking about it every day, playing out the worst case scenario. Living every day to the full was their creed; Elsie could well have been their leader.

Holly flicked through the pages of notes, thinking through the best way to approach the next few moments. There was a lot of information in here that was news to her. The previous attack in Borneo had been more severe than Elsie had led her to believe. Holly kicked herself for not reading the signs. The very fact that Elsie had even been prepared to take the anticoagulants, when she was a self-proclaimed non-believer in medication's efficacy, preferring gin and an early night.

'Did they run any scans in Borneo?' Holly asked Elsie, flicking through the file.

At this, Elsie's patience wore out. 'Of course I wasn't going to go for scans. It was the middle of the fucking jungle, darling! Why do you think I came home, hmm? Why do you think I left Barry to play footsie with that ghastly American? I'm old, sweetheart. Things hurt when you get to this age, all the time. It's the price of staying alive. Now, don't bullshit me. If we're going to be having this tiresome conversation, let's at least have it without the sugar coating, shall we? What does it say on your little clipboard there?'

Holly sat back, a little blown away by the outburst. She'd known Elsie long enough to realise that this anger wasn't directed at her. If anything, it was Elsie's way of dealing with The Fear. And, had she needed further proof of that, Elsie reached out and clasped Holly's hand tightly.

'I came home to see *you*, Holly. Now, stop looking all Bambi-eyed and tell me what's going on.'

They spent the next few moments in silence, as Holly gave her a thorough once-over herself. It probably wasn't hospital protocol, but for once Holly didn't care. Her touch was gentle and she left nothing to chance, double-checking everything all over again before she spoke. When she did, it took all her strength to remember that hers was the professional voice of reason that Elsie had flown so many miles to hear.

'There's noticeable weakness on your left side, but you can feel that. There doesn't appear to be any loss of vision and you've clearly still got your marbles – that's a technical term.' She attempted a smile. 'I'm a bit worried about your speech, but you seem to have reasonable control. But obviously we both saw what happened when you tried to have a drink. If you want my honest opinion, you should stay here and get all your tests done, all at once, and then when we get you home, we'll organise some live-in help – just temporarily – and a little speech therapy.' Holly frowned. 'So, there you have it, my professional opinion.'

'I did wonder,' said Elsie calmly, as though none of this was news.

'From a personal point of view, however, I'm just so glad you came home . . .' Holly threw her arms around Elsie and hugged her. 'Now, please let us look after you. Properly. No bullshit.'

'Oh darling,' protested Elsie. 'The bullshit is what makes everything so much fun!'

'Are you having fun now?' asked Holly sternly.

'Not so as you'd notice . . .' muttered Elsie, as though it were Holly's bossing that was putting a dampener on things. She smoothed the sheet with her hands and suddenly looked every one of her eighty-four years.

Holly kissed her forehead softly. 'Get some sleep. I'm going to find a doctor and get a few wheels in motion.' She tried to keep her voice even, with no outward sign of how distressed she was feeling. This had been another close call, but Holly refused to believe that life could be so cruel as to let her find Elsie, to make her part of their makeshift topsy-turvy family, and then snatch her away again so cruelly? The notion of soul-mates had always seemed a little bizarre to Holly, but her sense of contentment around Elsie had given her pause – the connection between them was almost tangible in its strength and Holly felt shattered at the very notion of life without her.

For once, Elsie did not complain, did not bluster, didn't even try to tell Holly she was doing things wrong; she simply sat back and let Holly take control of the situation, almost as though it was exactly what she'd been hoping for.

Chapter 19

Holly sat at her desk the next day, scrolling her mouse through all the latest research she could lay her hands on. It was the waiting that was so drainingly difficult, she thought, and then immediately chastised herself. Depending on what the scans showed, the waiting might yet be the easy part. Thank God she'd had the day booked off already yesterday – she felt bad enough about not being there when Elsie had collapsed; at least holding her hand as she got wheeled around from department to department had assuaged some of the guilt, even if they had been forced to sedate Elsie just to stop her talking in the CT-scanner.

She checked her e-mails again, hoping that the consultant in Bath had found time to review the images. Her latest e-mail to Milo was still sitting in her drafts folder, she noticed, unsent and forgotten. She only paused for a moment before sending it straight to the trash. If she was going to make an effort to move on, this kind of emotional drain was only going to hold her back. She was surprised at the tiny wave of release that she felt. It was only a virtual trash can, but sending all that toxic junk there still felt pretty good.

Applying the same strategy to the open pages on her internet browser, she closed down The British Medical Journal, she closed down The Lancet and she closed down a Google search for TIA research programmes. All of this research was premature, until they knew exactly what Elsie was dealing with. They would stagger over that particular bridge when they got to it, knowing Elsie, wearing fabulous shoes and with a strong Pimm's to hand.

With a waiting room full of patients and a splitting head-ache, she knew that playing out scenarios wasn't helping. She cradled her head in her hands, elbows wedged on the desk and tried to take a moment, before the madness of the working day began, just to be.

A small snuffling sensation against her leg brought her out of herself and she looked down to see Coco sitting beside her, brown eyes wide and one fluffy paw resting on her leg. Coco blinked twice and her eyes truly seemed to be a window to the little dog's soul, as she somehow managed to make Holly feel as though this small spaniel completely understood her sadness.

And of course, wherever Coco went, there was Alice not two paces away. Holly was pretty sure it was supposed to be the other way around, but to be honest, she wasn't convinced that it wasn't Coco who was running the show sometimes.

Holly reached down, after getting the nod from Alice that it was okay to give Coco a little attention.

'How're you doing this morning?' Alice asked, her gentle Scottish burr reminding Holly of the matron at her school and imbuing her with an immediate sense of being cared for. 'I gather you had a tricky day yesterday.'

Holly nodded. 'Waiting on some results this morning, so I guess we'll know soon enough.'

It was to Alice's credit, thought Holly, that she didn't rush to smother Holly with empty platitudes, but in the way of those who had experienced this rollercoaster first hand, she simply offered her support, by way of actually being there.

Coco was in her element, having a little break before her own working day recommenced and she rolled around on her back with her tummy in the air. 'It's just as well your Eric isn't here,' said Alice with a grin. 'I think he's harbouring quite the unrequited crush. I bumped into him with Lizzie in the park this morning and he made a complete spectacle of himself. He kept bringing her sticks and following her around.'

Holly laughed at the very notion of brash, exuberant Eric surrendering his cool quite so willingly for a silky pair of ears. As Alice filled her in on their morning walk and all the latest news from the dog-walking community, Holly could feel herself relaxing. Apparently Dishy Dad – the local lothario amongst the yummy mummies – had received fairly short-shrift from Alice when he'd attempted to chat her up. 'I mean honestly,' said Alice, 'who would fall for such a bullshit come-on. Credit us with some common-sense! Men!'

Credit indeed, where credit was due, it took another few minutes for Holly to realise what Alice had so easily and expertly achieved: she hadn't been dwelling on Elsie for their entire conversation. It was becoming increasingly clear that Alice wasn't just a pretty face, but was in fact the wonderfully skilled and compassionate team member that Holly had been hoping for. Well, that and the fact that she came with a side-order of scrumptious spaniel.

'And how is Coco finding it, with all the comings and goings here?' Holly asked intrigued as Alice refitted the little red jacket that signified to everyone – Coco included – that she was back on duty.

Alice flushed a little – the one and only time Holly had ever seen her vaguely off kilter at work. 'Well, to be honest,

I think she's finding it harder than I expected. I was prepared for it to take some adjustments – new place, new smells, new people – but she's being a little bit, well, tricky.' Alice looked utterly mortified at making this confession, as though she were somehow betraying Coco's trust in her. 'Bless her though, she's been perfectly vigilant when it comes to my blood sugar, but every now and again, with certain patients, she's just been really unsettled.'

Holly watched how the two of them interacted together, like dancers who can predict the movement of their partners from years borne of experience. She thought for a moment. 'Just out of interest and because frankly I'll do anything for a distraction today, why don't you jot down the names of the people she's funny around and we can take a look over coffee – maybe they're all smokers, or have dogs of their own. I'm presuming that poor Coco's sense of smell is so sensitive that if we get Curry-Loving-Larry in, it would basically be torture.'

'You joke, Holly,' replied Alice earnestly, 'but if Coco gets so much as a whiff of garlic bread it can really make her sneeze.'

Holly frowned. 'Did you just cover her ears when you said "garlic bread"?'

Coco ears shot up and she immediately lay down and put her paws over her nose. It was a Disney-worthy performance and it actually made Holly feel a little choked up. 'Oh, you dear little dog . . .'

'You see . . .' Alice said. 'Acting bonkers.' She stood up. 'Oh, and Holly, will you please have a chat with Maggie. I thought to begin with, that she was just super-hygiene conscious because of the pharmacy and Lucy mentioned, well, Lucy mentioned she has quite a fondness for hand-sanitisers

in general. But then I found out she's been taking anti-
histamines every day because she has a mild dog allergy and
I feel just awful.'

Holly stood up and they walked out into the hallway
together, Holly delighting in the gentle *thwack*, *thwack* of
Coco's tail against her calf as they walked. 'Do you know,'
Holly said, 'I would just let it lie. I'll discreetly find out what
we're dealing with, but if Maggie has made the choice to
quietly deal with this to give you a welcoming start at The
Practice, then, to be honest, I wouldn't want to spoil that.
Trust me, if Maggie ever has an issue with you, she will tell
you to your face.'

Alice nodded. 'Okay. I'll follow your lead. I mean, I hate to
think of her feeling unwell but then there's also the fact that
I'm so incredibly touched that I don't want to seem ungrateful. It's such a contrast from where I was before, I can't begin
to tell you.'

When Alice talked of contrasts, Holly tried to see it
through her eyes. She'd gone from people spitting at Coco
in the street, to constantly fobbing off all the local children
who came into The Practice and immediately wanted to play
with her. They had been forced to develop a 'greeting routine'
whereby every patient was introduced to Coco and then she
was left alone throughout the consultation to concentrate on
her own, very important, job.

Holly half wondered whether it might be this alone that
had thrown Coco off her game. 'Is there somebody you can
call for advice about Coco's training?' Holly wondered aloud.

Alice nodded. 'I'm already on the case. They sometimes
send a regional trainer out to people when they move house
anyway, just in case there are adjustments to be made, but
because I'd been staying with Aunty Pru, I didn't bother to

register the move. My mistake, I'm afraid. But somebody called and said the Bath regional trainer is a sweetheart and he's got me on his list now . . .' She held up her hand, fingers tightly entwined. 'Maybe it's something as simple as readjusting?' Alice didn't look convinced.

Holly smiled. 'You have had a baptism of fire rather, haven't you? In at the deep end and all that.'

Alice didn't deny it. 'Well, it makes sense now anyway, why you need four partners here. You're never all here at the same time, what with film crews and emergencies and—'

'Life?' Holly interrupted, loving that Alice felt comfortable enough to say these things, but knowing that she herself hadn't yet reached that point in hearing them.

'Exactly. Life. But then, it's all about balance, isn't it? I love that you all still have a life outside medicine. My parents are convinced medicine is the fast-track to spinsterhood,' she scowled. 'I'm the black sheep of the family, you see. I should be squeezing out mini-McWalkers by now and making game pie. I'm not sure my mum will ever recover from the shame of having a daughter with a career . . . Still, at least it gives me an excuse not to settle down with the nearest available Laird.'

Holly nodded, thinking that it sounded like an excellent plan, until her attention was distracted by old Gladys Jones in the corridor outside the pharmacy hatch, tackling a large bottle of pills as though her life depended on it. Holly walked over to offer assistance only to see Gladys finally wrench the bottle open and knock back two of the rather large capsules dry.

'Gladys,' she said gently, 'you do know that those are supposed to be taken four hours apart, don't you?'

Gladys scrunched up her face to listen hard to each word – clearly the new hearing aid had yet to arrive. 'Oh, don't you worry yourself about that, Dr Graham. It takes me a few hours to get the sodding child-proof lid off!' As was her habit, she was talking incredibly loudly, presumably so she could hear herself think. Holly heard a volley of laughter from inside the pharmacy and Maggie poked her head out.

'Come here, Gladys, we'll put them in a nice pill sorter for you,' Maggie enunciated clearly.

'There's no need to shout, dear,' shouted Gladys. 'I'm not deaf, you know.'

Holly got through to lunchtime by the skin of her teeth. It was Sod's Law, or possibly mere statistics, but more than half of her patients this morning had come in to talk about strokes, high blood pressure or heart disease in its various stages and guises. And of course it made her think of Elsie and wonder how her morning was going. She kept watching the clock and wondering how soon she could reasonably start pestering the consultant for answers.

She'd managed to keep a straight face when young Jo O'Leary had appeared on her morning list, having swallowed a small magnet. As the hyperactive and – it had to be said – incredibly rude young child had ricocheted around the room, Holly had used all of her restraint not to make jokes about sticking him to the fridge for some peace and quiet.

She'd been less successful at hiding her sense of the absurd when Meredith Lowe had come in with a new and fabulous idea for weight loss. She'd been ferreting through some old women's magazines in the attic and come across an advert for a tapeworm egg. 'It sounds very straightforward, Dr Graham,' she'd insisted. 'You just send off for the egg and then down the hatch – the tapeworm does the rest.'

'I see,' Holly had replied. 'And what do we do with the

little chap when he's done his work, I wonder?' she'd asked as she typed 'adult tapeworm images' into Google and showed her patient the result. It was amazing how quickly Meredith had abandoned the notion after that. Still, Holly wouldn't take a bet on how long it would be before the next 'quick and easy' plan was suggested. Apparently Meredith simply refused to believe that something so simple as eating less and moving more might be the answer.

Holly finished typing up her notes and was beginning to fantasise about a bacon sandwich — all those images of tapeworms having rather put her off the Tupperware pot of noodle soup that was waiting in the fridge.

Julia tapped on her door. 'Have you got a minute?'

'Sure,' said Holly, pushing back her chair, and swallowing the momentary flutter of irritation that she wouldn't have a chance to phone Lizzie now. 'If you don't mind coming to The Deli; I have a need for bacon.'

Julia nodded, clearly unfamiliar with this particular need. 'I wanted to talk to you about this meeting with the Model Surgery people? It all seems so last minute — almost deliberately so. And I just don't feel as though we're prepared. We don't want to look unprofessional.'

'Well,' Holly said. 'They did only give us a few days' notice, so I'm not sure how much preparation is required. But, if you wear that outfit again, you'll certainly be looking the part anyway.'

Julia grunted. 'Barbie does journalism?'

Holly just looked blank.

'Dan,' she explained, 'said I looked aloof and unapproachable, and could I try and be more accessible to the patients.' She looked incredibly pissed off.

Holly stepped back and gave Julia a proper look. To be fair, she did look so impossibly polished as to make mere mortals feel unworthy to gaze upon her. Holly shrugged. 'Just pop on a cardy and ruffle your fringe a bit?' she offered.

Julia shook her head. 'No. The patients will have to lump it. I've already had two media interviews and my mother to contend with today. I need all the protection I can get – hence the Chanel.'

'Chanel?' croaked Holly. 'Crikey, that's brave around here – I hope it's washable?'

Julia leaned against the doorframe. 'Sod the dry cleaning bill – I'm more worried about this meeting. And honestly, I'm not sure why nobody else is.'

Holly opened her wallet, scavenging for a stray fiver to fund her bacon habit, any excuse to avoid looking Julia in the eye and confessing that, with all the goings-on outside of work, she genuinely hadn't given it that much thought.

'They should be thrilled with us really – we're doing a great job and the patients are reporting increased satisfaction across the board.' Julia was clearly using this fact to reassure herself, and Holly didn't like to mention that the 'increased satisfaction' may have more to do with their patients' sheer relief at not having to drive into Bath or Framley every time they needed to see a doctor, as had been threatened. It seemed unlikely that their new democratic style of management had made a visible impact on the 'consumer side', however many changes they had initiated behind the scenes. In the back of Holly's mind, it was only a matter of time before they were rumbled as being anything but aspirational.

'You finished for the morning?' Taffy interrupted, poking his head around the door. 'Don't forget to phone the hospital, will you?' he reminded her.

As if she would forget that, thought Holly shrugging off

her annoyance. She'd been watching the clock all morning, waiting for the right time to call.

She tried not to automatically run through the numbers that had ingrained themselves on her brain from her research. She knew full well that the likelihood of Elsie having another, more devastating stroke could be predicted from this CT scan. The levels of ischemia – damaged brain tissue from poor blood circulation – and microangiopathy – small blood vessel damage – would certainly give them an idea of what lay in store.

Julia stepped back, waving away Holly's apologies. 'I know you've got a lot on, but can you give it some thought? I hate the idea of walking in without a plan.' She stopped. 'And give my best to Elsie, won't you? When you speak to her?' she said as an after-thought, proving to Holly that not only did Julia listen to her, but on occasion, she also remembered the little things that made all the difference. It was just a shame you had to break through Aloof to get to Attentive every time. Taffy had taken to calling her *The Armadillo* of late: crunchy on the outside ... No, wait, wasn't that a Dime bar advert?

'Thanks, Jules, I will. We're just waiting on results of her CT scan. But she said she had a headache when we spoke earlier, so ...'

'Sometimes a headache is just a headache.' Julia reminded her gently, 'It might be nothing.'

The two doctors shared a look that was loaded with meaning. They knew only too well all the hideously horrible things that could go wrong with the human body. Sometimes Holly envied those around her, living in blissful ignorance. The ones who could see a rash and not think meningitis, the people who could break a leg and still be thinking 'this'll mend', rather than worrying about leaking bone marrow and fat embolisms. And headaches after TIAs weren't exactly promising.

'Shall we?' Holly said, holding up her phone, as Taffy pushed the door closed and stood beside her. She pressed redial to Dr Field's office and held her breath as the phone rang out on speakerphone so that they could both listen.

'I have good news,' said Dr Field straight off the bat, knowing exactly what Holly's first question would be. 'There's a minimal amount of damage visible on the scan – hardly any scarring from the previous attack, some mild indications of blood vessel damage, but it's localised and to be honest, I'm reasonably optimistic. It's only really the fact that she's had two attacks so close together that's still worrying me.'

'Do you think it might be best if she stays with you for a bit longer?'

'Let me see what I can do. If I can swing her a side room, I'd say yes, but to be honest, Holly, it's noisy on the ward and she won't get her privacy. We'll speak later, okay, when the blood work's back? And don't worry – I'll look after her. You just concentrate on your day.'

Holly got off the phone and thought that chance would be a fine thing. She turned and buried her face in Taffy's chest. Reasonably optimistic. She'd known Dr Field a long time and he never pulled any punches.

She'd take that as a starting point.

Holly felt as though she could breathe properly for the first time in days. 'Right,' she said, trying to marshal her thoughts. 'Shall we go and prep for this bloody meeting then.'

'We could,' agreed Taffy. 'Or you could stop running on empty, and I could buy you a bacon sandwich?'

Chapter 20

Later that evening Julia placed her hand over the mouthpiece of her phone. 'Quinn! How long until we're done? I really need to head home.'

He scowled. 'Tell Danny Boy you've got a job to do and he'll have to wait his turn.' He turned his attention back to the editing suite and Julia could have sworn there was a look of satisfaction on his face, almost as though he enjoyed being the spanner in the works of her relationship.

She flicked through the pages of voice-overs that they still needed to record and went back to her call. 'Look, Mum, I'll be back as soon as I can, but we only have the edit suite for a short time each week and—' She broke off as her mother talked straight over the top of her. 'But you see I need to—' She turned her back to the rest of the room. 'Well then, ask Teddy to call you a taxi!'

Quentin's attention noticeably piqued, Julia dropped her voice still lower, 'Well, if you'd stayed at home like you promised, then you wouldn't be in the pub at all now, would you?' Her frustration and resentment were evident to every-one, except seemingly her mother at the other end of the line.

Julia quietly pressed 'end' without another word. It wasn't necessary to say goodbye because Candace had already angrily hung up on her. Again. She ran her hands tiredly through her hair. She really didn't have time for this: voice-overs tonight, filming tomorrow and then the Interrogation Squad from the NHS turning up the next day . . . All she wanted was some peace to think. Not just about her job prospects, but about Dan and her mother and Larkford. For the first time, Julia thought longingly of her old flat with its minimalist décor and not a soul in sight.

She flinched slightly as Quentin slid his arm around her waist. 'Come on, Jules, let's get these last few done before Mummy dearest goes on the rampage.' His tone was teasing and intimate. Julia didn't even have the energy to shove him away, struggling to see the funny side in any of this.

She took a moment to compose herself and returned to the studio, slipping on her headphones and her professional persona as the light above the microphone turned green. 'Every week, we hold a support group at The Practice for our patients with dementia and their carers . . .'

Quentin pressed a button to cut her off. 'Darling, do try not to sound so fucking suicidal. After all, *you* haven't got dementia.'

It took two hours longer than scheduled to call it a wrap, simply because Julia had lost all focus and kept losing her train of thought or making silly mistakes. And the more short-tempered Quentin became, the worse it got.

Julia packed her belongings together as the crew hustled out the door, embarrassed to have ruined their evening's plans and shown herself up to be such a rookie.

Quentin leaned back against the desk beside her and in the sudden silence, she became aware very quickly of just how close he was.

'Happens to all of us, sometimes. Don't stress this, will

you?' he said, his sudden empathy in complete contrast to the sweary frustration he had been exhibiting for the past hour and a half. 'You've obviously got a lot on your mind at the moment.' He moved just a fraction until his hand was grazing her bare arm. Deniable. Innocent.

'Quinn,' she cautioned.

'Don't rush home. Come for a drink. We can talk about this life-changing job you seem so reluctant to accept.' He picked up her jacket from the back of the chair and held it out for her to slip into, knowing that Julia was never averse to a little chivalry, despite her vocal feminism. 'Do you realise, Dr Channing, you are the only girl I know, who prefers me to help them *into* their clothes,' he sighed. 'And I'm not really convinced that Carter deserves you.'

'Don't be tedious,' Julia said. 'I'm taking some time to think about whether *I* actually want your job. It's got nothing to do with Dan, so you don't need to be all competitive. And stop calling me Dr Channing. It's weird.'

'Oh, I don't know, I rather like it.' Plausible deniability had clearly gone right out of the window, as he lifted her hair free from her collar, lingering far too long with his touch. 'Makes me think we should just give in and play doctors and nurses?'

She picked up her bag and deliberately held it in front of her, just in case the swirling emotions got the better of her and she were persuaded to give in to temptation. She took a step back. 'Well, I suppose I could find a hospital trolley and leave you waiting all night . . .'

'I won't give up, you know. You're perfect for this job and I intend to use every inducement at my disposal to convince you.' He somehow managed to make this sound like an utterly filthy proposition and Julia could feel the blush stain-ing her chest in response. 'Commute to begin with, if you must, but we both know you have to choose. You won't have time to play house in Larkford if you get this gig – you'll be too busy being fabulously successful. With me.'

He was a professional at getting his own way, she realised, as he backed away. He was simultaneously playing to her ambitions and to her weaknesses. And he clearly knew exactly when to stop: just as she began to soften, leaving her wanting more.

In a world of contrasts, Julia stood in the middle of their minute kitchen the next morning and looked around at the scene of devastation. The life of luxury that Quentin kept alluding to suddenly looked rather appealing. Dan was still asleep, having come in late from rugby training, but having lived together for nearly a year, she knew that this was not of his doing. There were empty bottles and packets strewn across the kitchen table, sticky puddles of Christ-knows-what on the worktop and the remains of a crusty omelette in a pan on the draining board. Julia did a double-take, her stomach swooping with anxiety as she registered the tiny blue flames still flickering on the gas stove. She turned them out and forced herself to breathe away the moment of panic and relief that had swamped her.

This wasn't the first time and it certainly wouldn't be the last that her mother's drinking had nearly had appalling consequences. She thought of Dan deeply asleep upstairs, the kitchen being the only exit route and sat down heavily. How far did Candace really have to sink before she found her rock bottom, she wondered?

Half of her was tempted to leave the scene exactly as she'd found it – let Dan see what she was really dealing with.

Half of her was utterly mortified.

Of course, Julia being Julia, old habits died hard and she pulled on her beloved Marigolds and began to clean. Even as the clock ticked round and her appointed time to meet the film crew passed, she had slipped down the rabbit hole and was scrubbing at stains that were barely even visible any more. The problem was, in Julia's mind, like a modern-day Lady Macbeth, she could still see them all too clearly.

'You have to be kidding me?' stormed Dan later that day, as he stepped in to her office and slammed the door behind him. One only had to look at the dishevelled and angry look on his face to know that whatever was going on this time had pushed him too far. 'It's not okay to cancel an entire pre-natal clinic with an hour's notice, Julia!'

It was hard to tell whether it was the fact it was a pre-natal clinic that had tipped him over the edge, or whether he'd been witness to Quentin making her behave like a performing seal in the dispensary earlier, making her do take after take to satisfy some ridiculously demanding standard that he seemed to have arbitrarily settled on overnight. It was almost as though he were testing her. Or possibly punishing her for refusing that drink last night – there was certainly none of the chemistry burning between them this morning. Unless you counted anger, in which case they had it in spades.

'And,' Dan carried on, slapping a folder down on the desk in front of her, 'what the hell have you been doing with the budget for the launch?'

Julia pulled at her lip with her teeth, as she always did when she was trying to stop herself blurting out something unpalatable. How could she say to Dan that, by the time she'd cleaned up at home and checked on her mother, the whole day was out of sync. So she'd bumped a few blood pressure readings and urine dips until tomorrow – it wasn't as though the yummy mummies-to-be of Larkford had much else on, she thought. And as for the budget, well that she really did need to address.

'Look,' she said, standing up so he was no longer towering over her, 'I put a hold on the budget because it seemed like it was getting a little out of control.'

'Right,' said Dan tightly, as always trying to refrain from judgement until all the facts were in. 'How?'

She picked up the folder and started talking him through the highlighted areas on her spread-sheet. Yes, that's right, she thought, MY spread-sheet. Because most of Dan and Taffy's plans were the ones scribbled on napkins or Post-its, or in one case, a particularly lurid poster of Mr Tumble.

'We're raising money to promote Health in the Community and then spending a proportion of it on a party. That seems like nonsense to me. It's not as though there's any real PR value in any of this. We get the van kitted out and we do a few school visits, but that's where it will end . . .'

'I see,' said Dan. 'So what you're basically saying is that you don't believe in the scheme, you don't think it's worth promoting and it's probably a flash in the pan that will be forgotten about overnight.' His face was a mask and Julia quailed suddenly.

She'd hit the nail on the head herself only the other day – this project was Dan's baby – and she'd just called it ugly.

'Listen,' he said, a muscle in his jaw working hard, 'I know you've a busy day, but you and I need to find a time to talk. It's all very well you considering this other job, but you have to stay committed to the life you've chosen here – at least until you choose something different.'

He didn't even try to hide the subtext in his words – The

Practice, Dan, Larkford. He obviously felt that she already had one foot out of the door and judging by the expression on his face, it was only a matter of time before he made the decision for her.

'Dan,' she said, hating the supplicating tone in her voice, 'that's not what I meant at all, it's just that—'

'It's just that there's always something, Jules. Always. Let's at least grab a sandwich and talk over lunch?'

Her eyes flickered down to the entry she'd only written in her diary minutes before. 'I'd love to. I would. But I have plans over lunch and to be honest, I really need to keep them.'

He stopped, wrong-footed by her apologetic tone and obvious discomfort. 'Are you okay? You're not – unwell?' It was a reasonable question. The last time Julia had been so cagey about her diary was because she'd thought she was pregnant and had quietly taken herself to see an Ob/Gyn on the other side of Bristol. A false alarm, but when Dan had found out the lengths she had gone to keep it quiet, he had jumped to the logical conclusion of what she had been considering.

'I'm fine,' she said, knowing exactly what he was thinking. She crossed the room and took his hands. 'I would love to have lunch and I am categorically not sneaking off anywhere.' Even as she said the words out loud, she knew they were only partly true. She reached back for her diary and placed it in Dan's hands.

The entry was easy to read: Al-Anon counsellor 1 p.m.

'Al-anon?' Dan said, the penny dropping. 'Oh God, Jules, of course you must go.' He knew only too well from some of their patients, how beneficial a support group could be for children and spouses of alcoholics. 'Do you want me to come with you?' His voice was tender and caring, apologetic even, for jumping to conclusions.

She shook her head. 'I want to do this on my own.' She sighed at the very thought. 'But thank you.'

It was the politeness between them that killed her, the distance that seemed to be growing, despite all her best efforts. Short of pulling out of filming, turning down the job and ovulating on command, Julia honestly didn't know what else might work in crossing the divide.

She reached out a hand and he clasped hers briefly. 'I love you,' she said.

'You know where I am if you change your mind,' he answered.

It wasn't until he'd left the room, that Julia even realised he might not have been talking about lunch.

Chapter 21

Dan tried hard to put all thoughts of Julia, her mother and Quentin-the-Twat aside and focus on his patients. His argument with her earlier was preying on his mind and he hated the guilt that had prickled him since they spoke.

He washed his hands for the third time since looking after Mary Darnley, but he did wonder if they would ever feel clean again. He was beginning to regret throwing down the gauntlet as to who would get to deal with Mary's infected fat flaps earlier, having forgotten Taffy's undeniable luck with Rock-Paper-Scissors. Perhaps he and Taffy might need to find a better way of divvying up their patients – at least until Taffy's winning streak ended and there was a little more parity in the arrangement?

Still, Dan sighed, sometimes it was worth the gamble just for a little light relief. Just because they were doctors and supposedly beyond reproach, didn't mean they weren't human. Some stuff was just plain gross, even with a professional hat on.

He dried his hands and ushered in his next patient, trying not to look shocked at the young lad's appearance.

He considered the emaciated teenager in front of him and checked his file. Everybody knew about girls and the risk of anorexia, but nobody talked about the growing incidence amongst teenaged boys, especially athletes and perfectionist high-achievers. It was a fair assumption that Henry Holt was both, thought Dan. He sat in the chair by Dan's desk, chewing gum like a reflective cow, and looking shocking.

Needless to say, he hadn't made this appointment to discuss his tragically low BMI or his flaking, malnourished skin. 'I need some antibiotics, Doc, please. My throat is so sore and it's been like it for weeks.'

'Let's have a little look then,' said Dan, half wondering whether he would see the tell-tale signs of acid regurgitation and he should change his preliminary diagnosis to bulimia. He picked up a tongue depressor and his little flashlight and swivelled round until he was facing Henry head-on.

'I did everything the poster said first,' Henry said. 'Over the counter stuff, you know, but it's been weeks . . .'

'That's great, Henry, well done. I wish half my patients were as sensible as you.' It was true. Since every appointment at The Practice cost the NHS around fifty quid, the number of slots that tallied up each week that were, bluntly, a waste of his time, was ridiculous. Hayfever, sore throats, mild tummy upsets . . . there was no need for otherwise healthy patients to be taking up slots that others might genuinely need.

There was a huge traffic light poster in the waiting room now: green for pharmacy, amber for your GP and red for A&E. At least Henry Holt seemed to have read it, but he was one of the few.

As expected, the throat was red and inflamed, but there was no sign of infection or acid erosion and Dan genuinely didn't want to throw him some antibiotics, when he suspected deep down that there was an easier way to fix the problem. Easier for him; not necessarily easier for Henry.

He leaned forward, elbows on knees. 'How's the athletics training going?' he asked, catching Henry off guard.

'Good, yeah, I mean, okay ... My coach's been getting a bit frustrated with my times this season, but otherwise ...' There was a stilted silence.

'Henry, I'm going to be blunt with you, okay, because I know how much your sport means to you and I can probably look at things in a more objective way. I know you want to be lean and fit, but when you take it too far, your body has no fuel to run off. Do you know what happens then?'

Henry looked incredibly awkward, avoiding all eye contact. 'You get tired and ill?'

'You do indeed, but more than that, your body has to run on something, so it starts eating away at your muscle. So you might be lighter, but you're losing muscle-tone, so ultimately you'll be slower. Do you see? And when you get into this vicious circle, your body has to prioritise the systems it needs most – your breathing for example – so your immunity to bugs gets depleted ...'

Henry looked up. 'I know everything you're saying, Dr Carter. I do. I study biology. I read the websites. But the problem is, I just can't stop.' He blurted out that last sentence as if ripping off a Band-Aid. He was a sensible lad and he knew that this wasn't right, but his condition had clearly got out of his control.

Now pleased that Henry had wangled the slot before his afternoon break, Dan ignored the clock ticking beside him and got that strange buzz he sometimes felt when his job became rewarding again. He stood up and grabbed a tissue from the box on the side, holding it out to Henry. 'Spit that vile gum out in there and we can talk properly. If we're going to be open and honest about this, then let's talk about the gum as well.' Dan had clocked the practically empty Jumbo Pack in Henry's top pocket as soon as he entered.

'I want to take some bloods to check your electrolytes, Henry. I'm guessing you chew that gum pretty much constantly?'

Henry shrugged. 'Stops me eating.'

'I can imagine. But it also depletes your calcium, your magnesium and your potassium. Now these are really important, Henry, they keep all the major functions in the body running smoothly. Without them, you would actually die. Now, I don't want to scare you, but I'm guessing you've been getting some cracking headaches lately, no?'

Henry nodded. 'Bad ones, yeah. Just thought it was being hungry. Am I, I mean, does that mean . . .?'

'It means that you're here and we can help, before anything too disastrous happens.'

Henry nodded. 'That thing about eating muscle – isn't your heart a muscle?'

'It is, Henry, yes and quite an important one, so shall we be scientific about this and get you on the path to recovery and then I think we should look at the emotional reasons behind where this all started. We won't fix you in a day and it's going to take some effort, maybe some counselling, but you are an incredibly bright boy, Henry. This sore throat may yet turn out to be the best thing that ever happened to you.'

Henry looked pensive for a moment. 'I'm not like the girls, Dr Carter, this isn't about fitting in, or wearing tight clothes. I knew I needed to drop a few pounds to get my times down – I'm a sport scholar at my school – if I lose my scholarship . . .'

Dan poured him a glass of water and gave Henry a moment to compose himself, the conversation reminding him of all the reasons he had chosen General Practice in the first place.

This was his forté – looking further than the obvious to meet his patients' needs. This was the one area of his life that made him feel fulfilled and truly present. 'Quite a lot of pressure then, I'm guessing,' Dan said.

'You could say that,' said Henry in a strangled sob. 'My parents would freak if I got kicked out and I love my school, it's just . . . Sometimes, I feel like a fraud. I've got this scholarship and I'm not the best. Everyone's talking about Nationals and I know I'm not the best.'

'Have you ever heard the expression fake-it-till-you-make-it, Henry? Well, that's what everybody else is doing and nine times out of ten, the ones who brag the most are the ones who are riddled with insecurities. I think you should have a chat with my colleague, you've met him before I think – Taffy Jones? He's got a cracking approach to Sports Psychology that might really help you.'

Henry looked relieved. 'So, when you said counselling, you didn't mean sitting around with all the Lollipop Girls from school, talking calories and weight-shakes?'

Dan shook his head. 'We'll take a different approach with you, young man. But I will remind you of this – those "Lollipop Girls"? Their battles are just as real and just as painful for them as yours is to you. It's only the motivation that varies. So maybe, you could cut them some slack as well, yeah?'

Henry looked mortified and Dan took pity on him. 'Hey look, we all have our demons. Sometimes people choose to share their private battles and then you might understand, but a little empathy goes a very long way.'

Even as he ushered Henry into reception, to make appointments with Taffy and the Nurse Dietician, Dan's own words were echoing in his head.

He thought about Julia with anger and frustration; he thought about her with pity, but even as an adult, it hadn't occurred to him to think about her with empathy. It was an illuminating but disappointing revelation.

Dan set up camp in the doctors' lounge, with every intention of taking his afternoon break to double check the finer details of the impending Health in the Community launch party – budget or no budget. And of course, he wanted to write the best speech he could – persuade others that this wasn't the flash in the pan that Julia was predicting.

The lift he'd felt just now from helping Henry, had reminded him what he loved about this job. It was just so easy to lose sight of that when confronted with all the other aspects of General Practice. Even his excitement about the Model Surgery nomination seemed to have died down a little lately in the face of all everyone's concerns – was it really going to benefit their patients, or was it just another drain on their time and resources? It was only the addition of Alice to their team that was making it feel like a worthwhile proposition at the moment.

Taffy came in looking pale and tired and slumped down beside him. 'Jesus, I need a holiday to get over my holiday.'

Dan looked up. 'You do look like shit actually,' he said supportively. 'Any news from the hospital?'

Taffy shrugged. 'Scans looked good, but she's not out of the woods yet. More tests, I reckon. Poor Elsie.'

'Not the best end to your holiday. How did it go? Meeting the folks?' Dan asked.

Taffy grinned. 'Great actually. They just seemed to fit, you know. I mean, obviously Aldwyn had to be a total dickhead, but that's par for the course. And to be fair, it was kind of full-on, but Holly was a trouper. There's even a small chance that she actually enjoyed it. And I know my mum was in seventh heaven having the twins around.' Taffy flicked quickly through the e-mails on his phone, avoiding eye contact. 'But to be honest, it was probably a horrible mistake to go, because all I'm hearing from Mum now is how wonderful Holly is and how I'd be a fool to let her go. As if I didn't know that,' he said with feeling. 'And I'm bloody starving,' he groaned.

Dan screwed up the first draft of his speech for the launch and tossed it expertly across the room into the bin: if this was to be his convincing proposition to the town, then he'd need to do a better job of it than that.

'Well, if you're on the scrounge for food, there's a lemon tart going begging,' Dan volunteered. 'Mrs Bowe brought it in as a thank you for lancing that horrific boil, but I can't quite bring myself to eat it . . . It's a bit too reminiscent of her procedure, to be honest.'

Taffy scowled. 'Odd choice, I'll agree. Could I overcome my squeamishness for a bit of tarte au boil? Yeah, go on then. I'll have it. What are you working on there?'

'Thought I'd better get started on my speech for the Health in the Community launch – God knows what else we'll be juggling over the next few days. I have to be honest, though – this speech isn't exactly coming together.'

Taffy grinned. 'I'll have a look if you like.'

Dan gave him a sideways look. 'Nah, I've got it. I think you've got enough on your plate. But I did find a few adverts for second-hand vans to convert, if you fancy having a look later?'

'Can we call her Big Bertha?' asked Taffy hopefully. 'I've always wanted a big van called Bertha. Odd ambition, I know. I blame the insomnia.'

Dan gave up on any hope of concentrating and muddled through the coffee table in front of him, digging out a quiz to keep his mind busy – the women's magazines from the waiting room having a strangely addictive quality that neither man could resist. They sat in comfortable silence for a while, flicking through the pages and letting their minds wander.

Dan sighed and tapped the pages of the magazine. 'Are you happy, Taff?' he asked.

Taffy yawned and stretched. 'Well, I'm a bit peckish, but otherwise—'

'No. I mean, with your life choices – are you happy?' Dan attempted to look casual by leaning back into the sofa, but it was obvious that this was a question that required an answer.

Taffy thought for a moment then began ticking points off on his fingers. 'Gorgeous girlfriend, great mates, good job . . . Holly's lads are kind of fun. The rugby team's looking pretty good this season . . .' He stopped to check he hadn't missed anything. 'Yup. If you and Channing stopped scrapping and you handed over that lemon tart, I reckon life would be pretty darned perfect really.' He looked a little reflective for a second and his cheeks coloured slightly. 'Course, it would be nice if Elsie was okay and my girlfriend wasn't actually still married to somebody else, but you can't have everything, right?' He paused, looking anything but happy. 'Don't tell Holly I said that, okay?'

Dan stopped flicking through the pages. 'Okay. But if you talk about it with her, you'll have to do it without your ears turning red, because that's a dead give-away when you're flustered. Maybe wear a hat?'

Taffy lobbed *The People's Friend* at him and Dan ducked without flinching. 'I don't think she's worked that out yet.'

Dan grinned. 'Ooh the power ... Although, you know Taffs, it is pretty obvious and Holly's nothing if not observant.'

Watching his friend's ears turn an even brighter shade of scarlet, Dan began to wonder how observant he himself had actually been of late. Taffy seemed to be moving on, making big life choices and decisions. In contrast, Dan felt as though he were playing musical chairs, waiting for everybody else to pick their seats when the music stopped, so he could choose from what was left.

Stumped by the unusual tumult of emotions, Dan tried his age-old technique to settle himself: he picked up his magazine quiz again and grabbed a biro. 'Okay then, let's put this idyllic happiness to the test, you big girl. Three Steps To Perfect Happiness. One: do you own the perfect pair of jeans?'

Taffy nodded, completely at ease with the abrupt change of pace. 'I believe I do.'

Dan ticked a box and continued to read. 'Do you own a well-fitting bra that makes you feel beautiful and supported?'

Taffy hesitated just long enough to make Dan look up and laugh.

'Sadly, I do not. But then, I feel beautiful and supported most days, even without structural engineering. So, I'll call it a yes, shall I?'

Dan shook his head, the laughter lightening his features and his mood. 'Okay then, last question to ascertain whether you are, as you claim, perfectly happy ... Do you consider yourself to have confidence in your body, your relationships and your achievements?'

Taffy shrugged, actually giving the question proper consideration. 'I would have to say, on balance, that I do.'

Dan tossed the magazine down on the sofa beside him. 'Well then, it's official.'

Taffy picked up the quiz and tried to work out Dan' scribbles in the margin. 'What did you score then?'

Dan sighed. 'One out of three. It's not bad I suppose.'

'Which one?' Taffy challenged, squinting at the page.

'Ah, now that would be telling . . .'

Taffy grinned. 'If it's the bra one, we should probably have a little chat . . .'

'Jesus! I might have known I'd find you two arsing about in here!' Grace's outburst was uncharacteristically blunt. She walked across the otherwise empty lounge and held up a sheaf of papers. Her eyes flashed with an intensity that wavered part way between anger and panic. 'So they've e-mailed through the agenda for tomorrow's meeting. Any ideas? Any thoughts?' She thrust a copy towards each of them and sank down into an armchair opposite.

Dan pulled his attention away from the glimpse of thigh, as Grace's skirt rode up when she sat down and quickly skim-read the document. 'Where are the girls?' he asked.

Grace sighed. 'Julia's gone AWOL and Holly's taken the boys with her to pick up Elsie.' She managed a smile. 'Apparently Elsie needs their youth to off-set the average age on the geriatric ward. So basically, it's you and me, boys.'

Taffy groaned. 'How the hell can we get all of this prepared in time? All these stupid questions about ratios and costings? Do we actually know any of this?' He looked almost plaintive.

Grace shook her head. 'We do. Well, *I* do. But that doesn't change the fact that it is now officially time to sing for our supper.'

Dan read the section headings again. 'I bet that walrus Derek Landers is behind all this. He's deliberately setting us up to fail, you know that? Julia was right. She said they'd be coming in with a list of Asks, but Harry Grant said it was just a preliminary chat! Bastard!'

Grace frowned at him. 'Dan! He's just doing his job.'

'And we've been doing ours – being doctors!' Taffy grumbled.

'We've made the wrong decision, haven't we?' said Dan quietly. 'This was never going to be all sunshine and roses and lovely new funding.'

'If that's what you really thought,' said Grace firmly, 'then you're an idiot.'

His head shot up at this outburst, surprise etched on his face.

'Well, really,' she countered. 'Did you honestly think they were going to give you a blank cheque and ask for nothing in return?'

'But all our data to be publicly published? There's no way we can get this together in time.' Taffy interrupted, administration never having been his strong point in the first place.

'Not all of it, no,' Grace said. 'But I can deal with patient protocols, all the stats and a decent wedge of the accounting queries – I've probably done half of it already, as case studies for my course.'

Dan looked up, still slightly abashed at being chastised. 'Did I ever tell you, Gracie, that this course of yours is a wonderful idea?'

'Hmmm,' she said, softening slightly. 'Maybe once or twice. But you certainly didn't mention the pay rise you'll be allocating to your Practice Manager for all this extra administration.'

He tried to frown at her, but it came out as a smile. 'And will this pay rise be detailed in the projected figures for the meeting, by any chance?'

'It might be.'

Taffy sat on the end of the sofa, never the quickest of read-
ers, as he reached the end of the agenda. 'Well, this raises the
stakes a bit then.'

Dan picked up the biro from the magazine quiz, embarrassed to see Grace clock exactly how they'd been wasting
their time, while she was single-handedly running the show,
apparently. 'Let's allocate tasks and make a start. If nothing
else, we can show willing and arrange a follow-up meeting?'

Grace paused for a moment. 'Tell me again what you want
out of this nomination?'

Dan shrugged. 'Well, since we never actually knew it
existed until it was offered ... I guess, security for The
Practice, funding for the extra clinics and Alice – beyond
that, I have to confess ...'

'Humour me then,' said Grace. 'If we could use this? I
mean, to our advantage? Make sure all our protocols and
accounting practices were completely updated and they were
funding it?'

'That would be amazing, but it's not going to happen overnight!' Taffy interrupted, earning himself a stern glance from
this newly forthright and knowledgeable Grace.

Dan couldn't help but wonder what they were teaching her
on this course. Whatever it was, he had to admit the timing
couldn't be better.

'Appoint me,' Grace suggested. 'If this is how the whole
process is going to be – appoint me as your liaison. You said
it just now – your job is with the patients, not with the paperwork. Let me run interference, sort all the protocols and you
four can be the public face of the nomination. And also keep
your patients happy. What do you think?'

Dan looked at Taffy, wondering if his instinctive reaction

to grab Grace with both hands and say 'yes please' was his professional-self talking.

'Sounds bloody brilliant to me,' said Taffy, his Welshness becoming more evident as always when he was emotional.

'I'd love to do this,' Grace said. 'Please think about it. You all get to make a difference every day, but I need a new challenge here –'

Dan nodded. 'Let's work on this tonight and once we've got everything together and Holly and Julia on side, you can take the meeting.' He reached out for a moment but let his hand stop short of taking hers. 'Are you sure you want this, Grace? It's going to be a hell of a responsibility, with frankly very little reward. And there's a certain amount of accountability . . .'

She smiled her reassurance. 'I know. But I can do this and I can do it well. It would actually make me happy to prove that to myself. And to you, of course.'

Dan knew she meant 'you' as in the plural. 'You' as in the four senior partners. He nodded, unwilling to admit how touched he had been for the split-second before he realised that. 'Okay then, let's get ourselves organised and we can throw you to the lions in the morning!'

They all stood up; magazines, quizzes and speeches abandoned. Taffy had none of Dan's reservations and gave Grace an enormous hug. 'So, as our Gladiator, what shall we have as our working supper? Chinese? Pizza? Both?'

Grace leaned her head affectionately back against his shoulder. 'An army marches on its stomach, right? Let's phone The Deli and see if they can drop round a massive lasagne and we can set up camp in here. We can finalise the plans for the launch at the same time – you could even finish that speech you've been dodging. Time's ticking.'

Dan watched as she corralled them seamlessly into line. No raised voices, just calm and competent reassurance. If Grace was to be representing them, then he for one, could not be happier to place his faith in her.

Chapter 22

As Holly packed together Elsie's meagre belongings from her bedside locker, Elsie suddenly went quiet, reflective, almost to the point of removed.

'Well, isn't this bundles of fun?' Elsie managed eventually. 'But I suppose something has to get all of us in the end. Just seems a shame, that's all. I'd rather hoped for something a little more dramatic than a nasty little blood clot. Hang-gliding always looked promising . . .'

Holly had looked up instantly, the waiver of uncertainty in Elsie's tone shocking her more than anything else. The Elsie she knew was a fighter and in all honesty, Holly had rather been banking on that fact over the last few days.

Elsie shrugged, as if she too had recognised the change. 'I know, I know. Nothing's a certainty. Things turn out the best for the people who make the best of how things turn out. Blah, blah, blah. I should follow my own advice.'

Holly plonked Elsie's Mulberry overnight bag on the bed, now fully packed with Chanel and Dior toiletries and pyjamas. She wrapped Elsie's frail body in her arms and gave her a hug that said more than any number of platitudes ever could. 'You should write a book,' she said, teasingly. 'Elsie

Townsend's Lessons in Living.' She kissed her powdery cheek
and offered a supportive arm.

'Funny you should say that . . .' mused Elsie under her
breath, as Holly busied herself extricating the boys from the
mechanical bed, which was now firmly locked in a right-
angle. Perhaps it hadn't been the best idea to bring them
with her?

As Holly pushed the glossy door of Elsie's Georgian townhouse closed, she realised she'd been holding her breath.
The twins needed no instructions, powering away upstairs
to 'their room' – the guest room they had adopted whenever
they stayed over, because they adored the huge four-
poster bed and the clouds painted across the high ceilings.
'Night night!' they called, pre-empting any suggestion of
home-time.

Holly gave Elsie another enormous hug and resisted the
temptation to squeeze her too tightly. 'I'm so glad you're
home,' she whispered.

'I could say the same about you, young lady, scooting off
to Wales and deserting me the moment I get home – I'm not
sure you really missed me at all!' Elsie replied, attempting to
be haughty, but failing miserably because of the enormous
smile that threatened to spill over from her dancing eyes.

It would never make it as far as her lips, because Elsie's face
was still not completely under her control.

She noticed Holly looking, now highlighted by the crystal
chandelier that refracted light back and forth, illuminating
the hallway. She shrugged. 'And to think that all these years,
I could have been having nice little facelifts and holding on
to my youthful beauty,' she said with annoyance. 'Instead, it
now appears that we're simply trying to preserve me.'

Holly guided her through to the kitchen and pulled open the fridge, filled with tasty morsels only that morning in an attempt to persuade Elsie to eat when she came home. She might have gone a little overboard, Holly realised, as she surveyed a month's worth of groceries.

Elsie looked over her shoulder. 'How very optimistic of you, darling. I've obviously got a few weeks left,' she said drily, batting away Holly's remonstrations. 'Does that hideous hospital smell *ever* go away?'

She picked up a vast bottle of Chanel No5 and spritzed herself liberally.

Holly plopped some ice cubes into a glass and added some bottled water. 'Now,' she said, 'point me in the direction of this caviar you're craving, you weirdo.' Holly gave a theatrical shudder at the very thought of a mouthful of salty fish eggs.

Elsie waved at the larder rather unhelpfully, as Holly attempted to make everything to her exacting requirements and put together a tray of child-friendly snacks for the twins. 'You'll feel so much better for some proper food and a night in your own bed,' she said.

Elsie gave her a stern look. 'Stop blowing smoke up my arse and talking to me like one of your bloody patients. I want *all* the details of your trip to meet *les parents* . . .'

'Elsie!' said Holly, shocked as always by the way the profanities tripped off Elsie's tongue as if butter wouldn't melt. 'You're very feisty this evening. And I can do one better than telling you . . .' She pulled Taffy's iPad out of her handbag with a flourish. 'I have photos . . .'

Elsie frowned. 'If you start telling me that A Picture Is Worth A Thousand Words guff, I shall have to request that you make me a Bloody Mary. No one should have to see holiday photos without an alcoholic beverage to hand.'

Holly frowned at her, trying to get the measure of Elsie's mood this evening and unable to tell if she was still teasing. Maybe coming home hadn't been the best idea, until they'd got the full measure of any lasting effects. Holly tried not to dwell on the notion of 'personality changes' too much, but couldn't pretend that sometimes, they were actually the most distressing legacy of a stroke to deal with. 'You can't have any alcohol, anyway,' she said gently. 'Doctor's orders, remember?'

Elsie gave a dismissive flick of her wrist that was so flawlessly executed that Holly suspected she'd been working on it for a decade or five. 'Am I right in thinking that the hospital use alcohol as antiseptic? Hmmm? Slightly hypocritical, no? Come on, Holly, don't be a prude and make me a drinkie, darling. Just a little one?'

Holly shook her head and put the iPad aside. She'd only brought it as a prop in case there was an awkward gap in conversation to fill in the hospital. She was quietly dreading the moment when Elsie asked her the one question she really didn't want to answer – her prognosis.

Luckily for Holly, the prospect of flicking through 323 snapshots of the twins and Taffy seemed to have popped a lid on the quest for intimate details about their trip too. She was therefore a little bit blind-sided when Elsie pulled herself to her feet and gestured Holly to follow.

'Don't take offence, my darling, but life's too short to spend hours telling you that the twins are cute and Taffy's a wonderful man, because you know that already. And don't think you can use me as an excuse not to deal with your commitment issues, either. I'm old, not stupid and I can see you are wobbling.'

'But I—' started Holly, unsure of where her sentence was

heading even as she started it. She quailed under Elsie's stare. 'Okay, so I'm wobbling. But wobbling is better than running a mile. I shall have you know, Mrs Bossy Pants, that wobbling is actually progress.' Holly filled Elsie in on their trip to Wales and the completely unexpected reaction she'd had to the mad family gathering.

Elsie took her hand. 'I know Milo did a real number on you, darling, but don't let him dictate your future too, will you. I thoroughly enjoyed my second marriage – although not as much as my third, to be fair … Just promise me you won't rule anything out.' She frowned. 'Now, I'm too curmudgeonly to goo over your glossy youthful frolics any more – I'm sure you understand. But, if it's photos you're after, then come and see my new project. I started it while you were away. Before the whole hospital debacle. I rather think you'll approve.'

Elsie pushed open the double doors into the dining room with a flourish. Holly had never set foot inside before, but it was every bit as grand as she had always expected. The high Georgian ceilings and sash windows gave the room a light, airy feel, while the brocade curtains and warm Wedgwood blue on the walls provided the perfect backdrop to the mahogany and crystal that furnished the room.

The table itself was at least twenty feet long, but right now, Holly could barely see a square inch of its surface, covered as it was with photographs and albums and letters and news clippings.

'If we're going to look at photos,' said Elsie, clearly chuffed to bits at the amazement on Holly's face, 'let's make them scandalous photos, at the very least.'

Even from just a brief scan of the dining table, Holly had spotted more famous faces than an average Oscar ceremony – quite a few were partying hard, others in bikinis on yachts, or swanning around in kaftans. There were several which could only be described as boudoir shots and Holly had to stifle a gasp when she realised who they were.

'Elsie,' she managed, 'where on earth did you find all these? They're fantastic!' She gave a little squeak of recognition before trying to remember to look cool and unfazed.

Elsie gave an innocent shrug. 'They're just my little mementos, darling. It's entirely Grace's fault actually. We got to talking a while back and then, while you were off swanning around the countryside with your beau, I made a decision.' She paused for effect, savouring having Holly's undivided attention. 'Sod waiting until I'm dead – I won't be around to see everyone's reactions then, will I?'

'Er, no?' Holly managed, when it became clear that a response was expected from her.

'Quite. So I'm going to go ahead and compile my memoirs now, while I've still got all my faculties and can get some enjoyment out of it. Plus, I can make sure that all the juicy bits stay and they get the context right.' She waved a hand around the room imperiously. 'I don't know what I was thinking leaving it this long. Some random journo wouldn't know where to start with this lot.'

Elsie was on a roll now and she walked around the table, her hand trailing from chair to chair – partly for effect and partly for support. Holly watched her carefully, noting that there was a certain level of hysteria to Elsie's voice, as though she had to get all her words out now for fear of forgetting them.

Holly was only partly right.

Elsie ground to a halt at the far end of the table and she looked down the massive expanse of memorabilia towards

Holly. 'And it's even more important that I do this now, Holly, don't you see? While I still have my voice.'

For a moment, Holly thought that she was speaking metaphorically, worried about being dismissed as old and elastic with the truth.

The fear in Elsie's eyes was suddenly visible even from a distance and Holly realised that she already knew. It wasn't so much the prospect of dying ahead of schedule that was frightening Elsie Townsend; it was the prospect of quite literally losing her voice.

In ten strides Holly was at her side, drawing the fragile, resisting body into her arms. 'Just because you've had these two funny turns, does not categorically mean you're going to have a huge stroke, Elsie. The scans were good. The odds are most definitely in your favour.'

She could feel Elsie shaking her head against her. 'The consultant was very clear,' she said, mumbling against the wool of Holly's jumper. 'I'm a high risk, he said. And I'm already slurring a bit – I can hear myself. And sometimes it's just so hard to find the word I'm reaching for and I come out with utter nonsense.' Holly could feel Elsie's smile against her. 'Don't you dare say it!'

'That you've been talking nonsense for as long as I've known you? I wouldn't be brave enough!'

They stood together for a while, Holly gently stroking Elsie's hair, just as she did for the twins when they were upset. All the while, her mind was running on.

She knew, of course, that it was quite common for patients to filter what they're being told, sometimes fixating on the very worst case scenario, sometimes deep in denial and focusing on the one-in-a-hundred chance. It made no difference how educated or intelligent you were, the very word

'Stroke' sent the human brain into a spasm of survival mode. Whatever Elsie believed right now, it was her truth, and there was very little point trying to reason with her, without at least some concrete facts to support her position.

And then the little voice in Holly's head spoke up – the little voice that hadn't been to medical school and was just as frightened as Elsie – what if the consultant was right and her beloved Elsie, with her wonderful pearls of wisdom and the best perspective on life that Holly had ever heard, was heading for a massive stroke? If that was really the case, then the prospect of losing her beautiful melodic voice might be the least of her worries.

She bent her knees so that they were eye-to-eye. 'We're going to make sure that doesn't happen,' she promised rashly. 'There are steps we can take to get you back on fighting form. But you have to help yourself a little too. I'm going to be on your case about your diet and your recovery programme. And I'm going to find you somebody wonderful to move in for a bit and help, okay?'

They held hands for a moment, digesting the agreement between them. 'She'll need to play poker,' said Elsie. 'Don't lumber me with a house guest that can't.'

Holly smiled. If Elsie needed to think of her home-help as a house guest, that was fine with her.

Holly settled the boys for the night, unwilling to leave Elsie alone and more than happy to stay over until they could organise something more official. They were over the moon at the prospect and Holly felt easier just knowing she was on hand. Taffy, it seemed, was pulling an all-nighter with Dan and Grace but had been happy to reassure her that she was in the right place and they could manage without her.

Holly hung up the phone on the noise and kerfuffle on the other end of the line and sighed, registering for the first time how exhausted she felt and wondering whether a night without Taffy's incessant snoring might prove to be an added benefit. She loved the man, she truly did, but she still felt the urge to smother him with his pillow at roughly 3 a.m. every night.

Elsie was still pottering around the dining table when Holly came back downstairs yawning.

'All this scandal isn't going to organise itself, you know. I'm going to need Post-its, some coloured pens and a large roll of wallpaper. Oh, and a publisher. But let's start with the stationery. I imagine that might be simpler.'

Holly allowed herself to get swept along in Elsie's enthusiasm and it was over an hour later when Holly looked at her watch. They'd decided to sort the photos into chronological order and Holly had been immediately sucked in. Fascinated by the earlier life of this amazing woman, Holly felt as though she were looking at the plot of a daytime movie. This was Brigitte Bardot and Marilyn Monroe, with a hint of Audrey Hepburn for class and good measure. This was properly sensational stuff.

The photos carried a beautiful antique lustre that only added to their credibility. Movie stars, rock stars, Studio 54 – it was all there. St Tropez before it became a tourist mecca. The Hollywood sign when it was still shiny and new. And so many bloody yachts it actually prompted Holly to exclaim, 'Who *are* these people?'

Elsie just laughed, her redolent laugh so perfectly in keeping with the time they were poring over. She held up a fading snapshot of herself in an impossibly glamorous kaftan, bare painted toes and shapely legs just visible below its hem. 'I'm guessing these didn't exactly help,' she said.

It took Holly a moment to see the long, fragile cigarette holder in her elegant fingers. It didn't jar, the way a photograph of a beautiful actress with a fag in her mouth did these days. It was just a part of the image, the time, the zeitgeist. 'Shouldn't have been so incredibly vain, should I? Never even liked the taste – gave me a filthy headache every time – but boy, did it keep me slim.' She tossed another photograph on top, this time of a young Elsie in a Bond-style bikini, her body as beautiful as any supermodel, albeit in scaled down form.

Holly paused for a moment. She had all the evidence in front of her of a life well lived. Even as a doctor, knowing everything they knew now, was it right to be analysing choices they could do nothing to change? 'If I had a choice between living well and living long, Elsie, and looking at everything you have done in your life ... well, I'd be hard pressed to advise you to do anything differently.'

Elsie tried to smile, but never quite made it. Heads together, as they pored over the pictures and diaries from Elsie's Hollywood years, the whole tone of the evening changed, Holly soon weeping with laughter over the caustic, dry comments of a youthful Elsie. It was clear that this lady had always known her own worth and didn't suffer fools gladly. Holly felt almost honoured to be included in this part of her life.

This story had everything – multiple marriages, triumph and tragedy, not to mention enough salacious rumours to keep tongues wagging across the Atlantic for the foreseeable future. She was beginning to think that Elsie might be wrong; getting a publisher might actually prove to be easier than schlepping into Bath to buy Post-its.

Chapter 23

Holly hung up the phone and ripped her list into shreds. 'God give me strength,' she murmured under her breath. It was not the best start to the day. The Happy Helpers Home Help Agency were apparently running short on anyone who might reasonably be described as either happy or helpful – or come to that, available. Knowing that Elsie was home alone made her feel incredibly uncomfortable, but she had no wish to impose anybody on Elsie who would make her feel patronised or demeaned. The one and only great hope of the morning had turned out to be a rather saccharine lady called Marjory, who insisted on referring to her clients as 'old dears' – Holly didn't dare think that the poor woman would escape alive from Elsie's clutches!

Alice poked her head around the door. 'Are you busy? Grace is *still* stuck in her meeting with the Primary Care Trust, can you believe it? She looked amazing, by the way – all polished and efficient. And they seemed pretty happy that we had organised a Liaison Manager; apparently it's a sign of our overall efficiency.' She grinned. 'Which brings me around to my next question. Lucy's in a bit of a tizz about the launch tonight and wants to know if we can help?'

Holly pushed back her chair. 'Right, well let's go and see

how many other balls we've dropped this week. Because unless I can find somebody to look after Elsie at home, it looks like I'm going to be dropping an awful lot more.'

Alice hastened along beside her, Coco at her heels. 'Do you need somebody with particular nursing qualifications, or just somebody level-headed and lovely? Only, my aunt's neigh-bour is a travel writer who's looking for some part-time work between projects? She's mad as a bag of frogs, but I'd trust her with anything and I know she has a first aid qualification. Do you want me to call her?'

Level-headed and lovely suddenly sounded incredibly appealing to Holly and, as Alice described how Sarah had stepped in to support her Aunt Pru when Alice herself had started working at The Practice, Holly felt a weight lift off her shoulders. Happy Helpers be damned, she thought, with no doubt in her mind that this kind of arrangement might be so much more acceptable to Elsie than Marjory in her pink tabard with her endless supply of custard creams, nos-talgia and condescension. Just so long as they didn't cook up another round-the-world extravaganza together, it seemed like a win:win situation.

With the question of Elsie's care no longer taking up space in her brain, Holly took a breath and addressed the next crisis on her radar. They had mere hours until the Health in the Community launch party, where hopefully members of the press and local business owners might be persuaded to help them further their cause, be it with column inches or cash. The only hiccup being that with all the fuss over the Model Surgery Nomination, Holly was concerned that they had rather let things slide on the organisation front.

Lucy the receptionist swung her legs from side to side on the new ergonomic office chair that she had somehow managed to order without any senior say-so, her blonde ponytail swinging like a metronome. 'Well, I thought you guys had things under control.' She said it accusingly. 'But now Grace is running late and nobody gave me a job list,' she grumbled, waving a hand at the spiral bound notebook on her desk, its pages stuffed with tasks to be done. Holly had even spotted Lucy writing something she had just completed on to that very list, simply to get that hit of satisfaction from immediately crossing it off.

And therein lay the problem, thought Holly – they may have set down their marker to become the absolute antithesis to the usual NHS bureaucracy, but, as it turned out, if there were too many visionaries and nobody actually setting any deadlines, nothing really got done. She could only be thankful that it was only a social event that had slipped through the cracks, rather than something more medical. She could only be grateful that Grace had gone into her meeting with a clear head and not worrying about balloons, banners and beverages.

Lucy looked a little petulant. 'It's not my fault, you know, I asked Dan only last week whether we were supposed to be doing anything and he said he had it covered.'

Holly's heart sank still further into her boots. Did Dan think that just because the four of them had discussed a plan of action in the pub, these things just magically came together?

As Lucy chivvied arriving patients into the waiting room with less than her usual joie de vivre, bluntly suggesting to old Mr Jacobs that he should 'sit down before you fall down,' Holly and Alice couldn't help but laugh.

'So, the first step in our plan to promote ourselves within the local community, is to make sure that we are far ruder and less sympathetic than normal? Oh, the irony,' said Holly, struggling to keep a straight face. 'But seriously, are we ever going to be ready?'

'Of course we are,' said Lucy with more blind confidence than was probably realistic.

Alice just shrugged. 'We can always say that less is more and we didn't want to fritter away their donations on a fancy party?'

Holly nodded. 'And actually, that would make Julia happy too ...'

'Score one for total inefficiency,' said Lucy happily.

'I should bloody well hope not,' said Grace firmly from the doorway, making them all jump. Her ease and artlessness took Holly by surprise for a moment, so pleased to see that there was just a smudge of eyeliner to accentuate her eyes, rather than a faceful of make-up. She hadn't so much transformed her appearance, as embraced her own authenticity.

'Well, if your spread-sheets didn't wow them in there, Gracie, then that dress will certainly have done the job!' said Holly.

Grace looked cross. 'Oh, Holly,' she said. 'I hardly think that a bunch of suits from the NHS are going to be swayed by what I'm wearing! I'll let Julia and Alice be the clothes horses around here, thank you very much – although how you manage it, Alice, on what we pay you ... I've never even seen you wear the same thing twice!' Grace paused and almost visibly pulled herself back on topic. 'Besides, it's been *all* about the numbers this morning.' She tossed her files on to her desk and Holly noticed for the first time how tired Grace was looking. A few freckles and a suntan could only hide so much after all.

'How did it actually go?' Holly asked tentatively.

Grace shook her head. 'Better than the Spanish Inquisition,

worse than I'd imagined. That Derek Landers is a smarmy bugger though, and he seemed positively disappointed that we had handled all the compliance at such short notice. We're going to have to watch our backs with him around. I think we'll be okay though, as long as we stay on top of their requests for statistical interpretation and validation.'

Alice breathed out heavily, her fringe fluttering against her forehead, looking incredibly uncomfortable at this conversational turn. 'It's just as well you're in charge of this, Grace. You lost me at compliance . . .'

'You are a star, Grace,' Holly agreed. 'I know you actually wanted to take this on – you nutter – but you have no idea how much it's helping.' Her smile and gratitude lightened the atmosphere considerably. 'We should make you a special badge.'

Grace blushed. 'It's quite sad, isn't it, but I'd actually quite like that!'

Lucy whooped in delight and delved straight into the stationery cupboard before Holly set her straight. 'Launch party first, craft projects later, okay?'

Grace stretched her arms out in front of her to loosen her shoulders. 'Quite right, too. Lucy, grab The Big Red Folder.' You could almost hear the capital letters in how she spoke, but Lucy just looked blank. 'Oh, for goodness' sake,' said Grace impatiently. 'If you want something doing around here, do it yourself.' She reached across to the shelf and pulled down an enormous lever arch file with *Health In The Community Launch Party* printed in huge letters on the front. She flipped it open on the desk and Holly could see numerous sections and tabs dividing the paperwork neatly. 'Right,' Grace continued, running her finger down the annotated list on the front page, 'the only thing left is to collect the cheese from The Deli before they close. Drinks, decorations, fliers and nibbles all sorted.' She yawned. 'Roll on wine o'clock, I'd say.'

'I'll get the cheese,' Holly said, delighted to have her suspicions proven wrong. Under Grace's auspices the party would no doubt be fabulous. 'Alice, you cover the afternoon walk-ins. Gracie, put your feet up. We've all earned a lovely evening.' As she walked past Grace, she gently gave her shoulder a squeeze. 'Some of us more than most.'

Several hours later, with the beautiful Missoni scarf Elsie had once given her wrapped around her to cover Ben's sticky handprints in the silk of her dress, Holly was feeling a little more prepared. The last-minute hustle had clearly been worth every effort.

Lucy and Grace had been working tirelessly for hours to make everywhere look celebratory and were still tying up bundles of balloons even as the guests began to arrive. Maggie, their germ-phobic pharmacist, was busy making sure that all refreshments were beautifully and hygienically arranged. Julia was deep in conversation with a bearded chap with an enormous Nikon slung around his neck whom Holly recognised as one of the *Larkford Life* photographers. Since he was also a stringer for some of the Nationals, Holly could understand why Julia had made a beeline for him, despite his questionable fashion and grooming choices. Socks, sandals and a bright orange windcheater were hardly the Smart/ Casual that the invitations had suggested.

Even that one line had been a compromise, though. Julia had wanted Casual/Sophisticated and nobody else knew what that meant. The boys had wanted no dress code at all, but Holly knew from past experience that all the local farmers would pitch up after work in their smelly boots and overalls, with the expectation of cider on tap. It was a rural stereotype, she knew, but it also happened to be true. The compromise was apparently working though as the reception area began to gradually swell with local residents who had made the effort to come out for an evening of celebrations.

The whole Health in the Community initiative had started out as Dan's brainchild years before. He had wanted to introduce responsibility for health into the local schools' curriculum, rightly supposing that parents who had no knowledge of healthy choices were unable to pass on a wholesome understanding to their children. Indeed, the number of smokers in the Under 25 category in Larkford was at an all-time low, whilst the parents of that same subset were still sneaking the occasional fag and pretending that it didn't make a difference.

She wondered if Elsie really did have any regrets now, knowing the consequences of her hedonistic youth. She hoped not. Eighty-four was a cracking innings by anyone's measure.

Holly fussed around, making sure that the twins were on their best behaviour with the 'Children's Entertainer' that Lucy had found at short notice when it became apparent that half their guests had no intention of shelling out for a babysitter. A little posse of under-tens were huddled together in delight as Sparky the (slightly dodgy-looking) Clown began to make some alarmingly phallic balloon animals. Holly looked back into the main room, only to see that Dan and Taffy were making preparations for the launch speeches. She dithered for a moment, uncertain about leaving the twins until Lizzie appeared beside her. 'I've bribed Lucy twenty quid to sit in here and keep an eye on Spanky McClown, so come and get a drink and tell me all your news. You're so sweet with the supportive texts by the way – but where are you getting them all? The Little Book of Mindful Bollocks?'

Holly laughed. 'You're welcome, by the way.'

'Just as long as you're sending these to Elsie too – then we can be moral support for one another – to survive all your moral support!' Lizzie stopped for a moment and her eyes widened in surprise. 'Although obviously Elsie's not running short in the peppy department!'

Holly swivelled around to look over her shoulder and gasped. There in the doorway was Elsie. For sure, she was looking a little fragile, but it was hard to notice that when one's eye was immediately drawn to the black full-length, full-skirted ball gown, replete with sequinned bodice and long white satin gloves. 'Bloody hell,' whispered Holly, in shock. 'Has she been at the gin?'

Elsie sauntered over towards them and gave a little twirl – wobbly, yes, but undeniably glamorous. 'Don't *you* look amazing?' said Holly, with a lump in her throat.

Elsie gave her a wicked grin. 'It's a Balmain, darling. Vintage. Thought it might deserve a little outing.'

Holly didn't know whether to laugh or cry. Elsie's voice was defiantly, determinedly upbeat. For all her own concerns about whether Elsie was well enough to be there, Holly couldn't bring herself to rain on her parade. 'It's fabulous. You're fabulous.'

'Tsh, now don't go getting all soppy on me. I thought I could bring a little glamour to the proceedings: I need vital input, Holly, and I need you to point me in the right direction. I thought I might do a little networking tonight, you see, find some tech-savvy youngster to help me with my blog. I've been thinking I could work my way through my wardrobe and make sure all my favourites get an outing before I pop off. I could chart each outfit and its history and when I'm dead, you can auction them all off and use the money for this wonderful project. What do you think?'

What did she think? Holly was having trouble remembering her name right now, let alone able to form a coherent response. She was still reeling from the incredibly matter-of-fact way that Elsie had thrown the whole 'when I'm dead' bombshell into their conversation.

'You're not to get maudlin on me, Holly,' said Elsie almost under her breath, her voice stern and no-nonsense. 'There's only one way I can cope with all of this, so you're going to have to follow my lead, okay? Stroke – schmoke . . . I shall dance in a lightning storm if I so choose. So, we're agreed, you can be all soppy on your own time, but then jump on board, would you, darling? I rather need your strength to get through all this.'

Holly nodded. 'I'm in.' She couldn't help but smile as a thought came into her mind. 'It's a good job you helped me find my backbone, Elsie, or where would we be? And now I get to help you . . .'

Elsie shrugged. 'I didn't do it for the karma, darling. I just fancied being your fairy godmother.' They both turned to look at Taffy, who was as usual being mobbed by the yummy mummy brigade, but taking it all in his stride. Every few seconds, his eyes would check in on Holly, making sure she was coping and Holly felt incredibly cherished that he would do so without even thinking about it. For the last few years, that had been her role – always with one eye on the twins and constantly alert. Nobody had ever been looking out for her. Until Taffy.

She smiled at him and turned back to Elsie. 'Well, with a dress like that, you'll be needing a drink and someone

scintillating to talk to.' She pressed a glass of chilled elder-
flower into Elsie's hand and looked around.

Elsie gave a filthy laugh. 'This is Larkford, not the Oscars,
Holly. Do let's try not to over-reach.'

Chapter 24

Julia looked around the room: there was no denying that there was a touch of the country bumpkin about tonight's proceedings and, whilst she should be grateful that they weren't holding the event in The Kingsley Arms, as suggested by Dan and Taffy, she couldn't help but see the room through her viewers' eyes. Would they think it was endearing and welcoming, or would they be a little more discerning and feel only a subtle distaste for the shabby chic look that was somewhat lacking on the chic front?

She checked her watch again and wondered when her mother might deign to make an appearance. Candace Channing was not a woman to be dictated to and Julia felt her palms go sweaty at the very thought of her mother mingling amongst her friends and colleagues, let alone the press. To be fair though, her mother was very good at putting on a show, skilled as she was in the arts of deception and subterfuge.

'Your mum not here yet?' queried Dan, strolling over with a teetering pile of cheese and biscuits in one hand and a glass of red wine in the other.

Julia took one of Dan's cheesy crackers and bit into it, earning herself a shocked look from Dan. 'Christ, you must be stressed if you're eating carbs! Look, she'll be fine – she'll hunker down with the bridge club and they'll be talking chrysanthemums and HRT in no time.'

Julia gave him a scathing look – how little did he know of their conversations? The only time Julia had overheard one of their heated debates, it had mainly concerned the quality of their orgasms post-menopause and the ups and downs – as it were – of Viagra! She gave a delicate shudder at the memory and tried to push it from her mind; she wasn't a prude, she just didn't want to hear her own mother's opinion on that particular topic ever again.

Dan misinterpreted her reaction. 'Don't worry so. She'll be fine. And people will be a lot more understanding than you think, if . . .'

'If what?' asked Julia sharply. 'If she makes a spectacle of herself in front of the film crew and everyone we know?'

Dan looked awkward for a moment, his face flooding with relief as Taffy hove into view, munching on a vast chunk of cheddar. 'Good grub,' he mumbled, offering the cheese forward to Julia.

She recoiled slightly. 'This isn't a Tom & Jerry cartoon – there's journalists everywhere . . .'

Taffy shrugged. 'I think they can cope with the sight of me eating cheese, Julia. Is your mum coming tonight? I'm dying for a few childhood anecdotes . . . No? Really?' He grinned at her and kissed her lightly on the cheek, taking her by surprise. 'We're all on your side, Jules. You can relax.'

Dan checked his watch. 'Well, let's not relax too much until we've done the speechy part, okay. And then, do let's enjoy the party – we never seem to have any fun anymore . . .' He looked a little nervous, thought Julia, as he thumbed through the beautifully written file cards that contained his much-practised speech.

Even as she watched, Taffy plucked them from his hands as though to check something and then began to shuffle them. Dan's reflexes were clearly on delay, as by the time he'd grabbed them back, they were utterly muddled.

'What the . . . ?' Dan managed.

'I thought you said you wanted more fun and spontaneity in your life?' Taffy grinned mischievously, chomping on his cheddar.

Julia shook her head in disbelief, even as Dan mouthed wordlessly. What kind of a tin-pot organisation were they going to look like now?

Taffy leaned in beside her. 'Have a little faith, Jules. He'll be better without his notes. Trust me.'

Julia scowled at him. 'He spent ages writing that speech.'

'Exactly,' countered Taffy. 'Which is why he would have sounded wooden and rehearsed, whereas this way, he can sound passionate and inspired.'

As Dan moved over to tap on the microphone, his hand noticeably shaking, Julia had to concede that Taffy made a valid point.

'Well, wasn't your Daniel, *wonderful*, darling?' said Candace Channing as she swept across the room to clasp Julia's hand, having staged her arrival for maximum effect during the speeches and earned herself a filthy look from Elsie in the process. There was clearly only room for one diva in Larkford and Elsie seemingly had no plans to surrender that easily.

Julia had to confess that Dan's impassioned and instinctive appeal for support had been really rather magnificent and, to her delight, the local media seemed to be lapping it up. And obviously, it looked like the Health in the Community Scheme was not going to be short of support or funding, which was quite important too, she reminded herself.

She gave her mum an awkward squeeze, unused to such public displays of affection and wondering whether her mum had already been at the bottle. But no, it seemed as though Candace was merely playing the role of supportive mother this evening. She was all dressed up in a retro, Dynasty-style suit and was happily introducing herself to everyone she met as 'Julia's Mummy'. Okay, so it was a little cringe-inducing, but it was so much better than any of the scenarios Julia had beta-tested in her mind.

She was so distracted that she didn't notice Alice coming up to say hello, until little Coco was basically sitting on her foot.

'That went well,' said Alice, beaming. 'You must be delighted. Holly told me how much the whole team were invested in this scheme.'

Julia nodded, wishing that Alice had thought to qualify that the 'investment' had purely been emotional and that the currency had been their time. Her mother's head had shot up like a meerkat out of a hole at the very mention of the word and Julia knew she'd be getting the third degree later, having only recently pleaded poverty when being tapped for yet another loan to her parents.

'How interesting,' cut in Candace, 'and look at your darling little dog.'

Coco shifted impatiently amongst the legs of the crowd. 'Should you maybe pick her up?' Julia suggested, not really sure of doggy etiquette.

Alice shook her head. 'Only if it gets really crowded. She's normally fine around lots of people, but she's been really off her game the last few days.' Alice's face conveyed the worry that the statement glossed over and even Julia was sensitive enough to know that it must be bothering her.

'Maybe she's just avoiding Eric's painful crush?' suggested Julia, eyeing up Alice's Gucci pendant with envy.

Alice laughed and reached down to stroke Coco's ears. 'I wouldn't blame her. He's become her morning stalker in the park – even ignores the squirrels now and just lopes along twenty feet behind her.'

'Aw – throw him a bone, Coco. Tell him you can just be friends,' interrupted Holly as she wandered over with Elsie on her arm. Elsie pointedly turned her back on Candace and started talking to Alice intently, all but forcing a divide in the conversational group, but Candace wasn't swayed so easily. She pushed forward until she was pressed tightly against Alice, her thirst for information about Julia's 'investment' almost comical.

Coco immediately began yapping and circling around their legs, pushing so hard against Candace that she wobbled for a moment.

'I'm so, so sorry,' began Alice, crouching down to pull the little spaniel into her arms. 'She did this the other day with Malcolm Granger and again this morning with Rebecca Mountley.'

Holly stroked Coco's ears and soothed her instinctively, making Julia wonder why that thought had never even occurred to her. 'Is it not your blood sugar alert then?' Julia asked, intrigued despite herself.

Alice shook her head. 'Thank goodness the regional trainer is coming down to see us. I think maybe the move has been more upsetting for her than I realised.'

Julia was distracted by the expression on Elsie's face as Candace talked down to her like a special needs patient and

silently applauded Elsie's ability to look extremely regal in
her ball gown, even when holding a plastic cup of elder-
flower cordial. Julia was almost sure that her 'accidental' spill
on Candace's suit was just an unfortunate coincidence and
had nothing whatsoever to do with the caustic comments
Candace had been making about over-gilding the lily. She
sighed, only too aware that she had surrendered control of the
evening the moment Candace had announced her intention
to attend. She hated the rather petulant feelings that were
overwhelming her, a touch of the teenager rearing its ugly
head.

Julia looked around the room, automatically registering
the location of every journalist and camera. She could see
Quentin circulating with his team, trying to record some vox
pops with their guests. Perhaps, if she was really careful, she
could make sure that one of those interviews might *not* be
Mummy dearest. Sober or not, Candace was now ricocheting
around the room like a loose cannon. For Julia, it was not so
much a case of enjoying the party, as limiting the damage that
her darling mother might inflict on her career.

Half an hour later, Julia was wishing the whole thing would
just wind up and she could go home. Her mood had plum-
meted with every passing minute, as it became increasingly
clear how fragile the whole proceedings might become.

'Are you nearly done for the night?' she asked Quentin,
hating the coquettish tilt to her head, but knowing it was
the only way to get him on board. 'It'll be all downhill from
here. Once they start talking about crop rotation and milk
yields, that's it for the night!' She laughed gaily, knowing that
Quentin hated two things in life: being bored and feeling
that he was missing out on something. It was incredible to

Julia how often he was prepared to endure the first, on the off-chance of avoiding the second.

He looked at her sharply. 'And are we just saying that because you want to go home, or because Daniel Dearest has had enough?' His gaze was steady and calculating and Julia flustered for a moment, in itself a sign that all was not well in her world. 'Choices, choices, Dr Channing. The clock is ticking on your little party in Bumpkin Land.' He leaned in and kissed her cheek. 'Just a few more little interviews – maybe a little glamour in the proceedings? Calm down – I'll be tactful ...' He sidled away through the crowd, making a beeline for her mother and she felt physically sick. She also knew Quentin well enough to be aware that the more fuss she made, the more determined he would be.

Her gaze flicked distractedly across the room to where Holly was now chatting amiably with the journalist from *The Sunday Times*. It was all very well Holly bringing her own brand of relaxed camaraderie to the proceedings, she thought, but for Julia this was a professional opportunity that she was missing. Dan appeared at her shoulder. 'We need to talk about your film crew,' he said firmly.

With hindsight, she supposed it hadn't been the best idea to have her film crew from *Doctor In The House* on a completely free rein here tonight. It certainly hadn't been a well-considered move to have the camera man standing so close to Dan during the speeches that all the other guests had seen was the back of the cameraman's head. But Dan didn't want to hear the reasoning, wasn't interested in learning that upfront camera angles made the speaker appear more statesman-like and authoritative. No, he was more worried about whether Mrs Dawes from the newsagent's had been able to see properly.

'Are you even listening to me?' Dan demanded when he'd finished outlining his grievances and Julia fought the urge to stick her lip out petulantly.

'Are you even listening to *me*?' she countered, with the party in full flow around them and oblivious to the odd looks they were getting. 'Opportunities like this are gold dust, from a PR perspective, and you're happy to let Holly-Go-Lightly over there be the main point of contact. I know you're angry with me, Dan, but surely it can wait, because this can't.'

Dan looked at her in disbelief and Julia felt herself shrivel under his scrutiny. 'I thought you liked Holly?'

'I do, of course I do, but surely you can see that . . .'

'That she almost single-handedly came up with the campaign to save The Practice and put it into action? That she handles whatever this job throws at her with dignity and without the need for constant validation? That she, somehow, manages to do all of that whilst raising two small children and building a new relationship?' He shook his head. 'What *is* it you're looking for, Julia? Because, honestly, this obsession with being in the limelight is getting a little old. If your friends and colleagues and patients think highly of you, isn't that enough? If we're in this together, building a life, isn't that enough?'

Julia reached out for his hand, but whether deliberately or not, Dan moved to run his hand over his stubbled scalp instead. 'I understand the need for PR. I do. But you knew how important this evening was to me, Jules. You knew I didn't want it turned into a media circus.' He waved his hand around the room and Julia swallowed hard.

Seeing the world through Dan's eyes was always a humbling experience. Now she looked closer, she could see how many of the locals were shying away from the camera and sound boom that marauded through the room like sharks.

They huddled in small groups, resentfully editing their con-versations as the TV crew passed by and looking anything but relaxed. There were, of course, always a few chatterboxes, delighted to have their moment in the spotlight, but invari-ably they weren't especially eloquent or interesting. The real gems, the locals with lots of insights to share? Well, they were the ones staying firmly out of shot.

'I think they've probably got enough for tonight,' said Julia slowly, as close to an apology as she was likely to get on this topic. There was nothing else she could really say, since Dan gave her a scathing look and she scowled back. 'Look, let's just call it a day, okay?'

She blinked hard at the expression on Dan's face, shocked to see his emotions bubbling so close to the surface.

He took her by the hand and led her wordlessly out through the side door to the car park, making sure they stayed tucked out of sight. A free-range doctor in the car park at The Practice was sometimes akin to a cheetah on a safari – in moments, the patients would cluster around, with just one more question they'd forgotten to ask during their appoint-ment, or with another little ailment they 'hadn't wanted to bother you with'.

He continued to hold her hand tightly, even as they pressed into the shadows out of sight. The light spilled from the waiting room windows and the sounds of laughter and conversation billowed through the summer evening air. Julia couldn't help but notice the levity and excitement in the atmosphere, in complete contrast to the intensity that pulsed between them.

'Is that what you want, then? You've made a decision?' Dan said in a low voice. 'And that's how you tell me you want to call it a day?'

'What—? But, I—' Julia managed, completely thrown.

'Well, I can't say I'm surprised. Quentin told me you'd already decided to take the job, anyway, so it's not exactly news.' Dan's voice was a monotone and he seemed to be fixated on something over her shoulder, unable to meet her eye.

'What? No, that's rubbish! Look, if this is one of those bloke things and you want me to do the dumping then just say, because this is making no sense. I thought we'd decided to wait . . . And, no, for the record, I haven't accepted the job offer. And when I said call it a day, I meant the interviews.'

'Oh,' said Dan quietly.

'Oh indeed,' Julia replied.

'This isn't good, is it?' said Dan after a moment.

She attempted a smile. 'Well, we're not exactly love's young dream, are we?'

He pulled her abruptly into his arms and kissed the top of her head. 'Please don't hate me, Jules, but I just don't think I can do this anymore. I can't cope with the uncertainty and the drama and all the while knowing that, deep down, we both want such different things . . .'

'Do we, though?' she asked, only the tiny tremor in her voice belying her feelings.

He held her shoulders gently and his eyes searched her face for answers that neither of them could provide. 'Do you want to stay in Larkford and start a family with me?' he said gently.

Wordlessly she shook her head, folding herself into his arms for the comfort that she at once craved and feared.

'We could still be friends, though,' she offered, mumbling into his shirt, stunned to find the fabric damp from tears she wasn't even aware of shedding.

'Friends?' he said, his voice cracking. 'Well, I suppose

friends is something.' He rubbed her back gently, the warm evening suddenly feeling chilly and uncertain.

And to think, Julia realised, she'd been worried it would be her mother who might put a damper on the evening's proceedings. She couldn't believe their loving, passionate relationship could end with such a pathetic fizzle. She wanted to fight for them, to fight to save them, or at least go out with a bang, but she couldn't deny the truth of the matter: it didn't matter how much they loved each other, it simply wasn't enough. She untangled herself from Dan's embrace, never once letting go of his hand. She gestured towards the doorway back into the party and all their nearest and dearest. She took a deep breath. 'Shall we?'

Chapter 25

Holly yawned and stretched her arms up over her head until she felt a satisfying pop. Late nights, early starts and boisterous boys demanding breakfast were not a winning combination and she was having a little trouble getting started the next morning.

Holly had counted 27 Wph (*Why?*s-per-hour) over breakfast alone, and her reserves were running low. At this rate, she thought tiredly, Taffy might end up being the better parent. True, he didn't come to the party with four years of sleep deprivation and a wonky pelvic floor under his belt, but nevertheless his enthusiasm for Lego bricks and bacon sandwiches had scored him more points than was actually reasonable where the twins were concerned. Although, she reminded herself, he also had the built-in male advantage of tuning out anything that didn't directly concern him.

She scrolled down the online coverage of last night's launch party and was gratified to see the odd photograph of herself looking reasonably presentable and with her eyes open for a change. She smiled at the 'team photo' of the GPs, which Elsie had insisted on monopolising – lying horizontally across their arms, yet somehow still looking glamorous and dignified.

The launch had been a huge success and Dan and Taffy were riding on a fund-raising high – that is to say, they were pushing through their hangovers and plotting how to allocate all their new pledges of financial support. Whilst the altruistic part of Holly's brain was delighted at the local backing they'd been promised, a little part of her couldn't quite reconcile 'Health – brought to you by Hartley's Bakery!' with their earlier vision.

Julia poked her head around the door and Holly had to force herself not to double take. Her usually immaculate chignon and tailoring had surrendered defeat and her make-up was virtually non-existent. 'Might I ask a favour?'

'Of course,' said Holly, pushing back her chair and walking around the desk. 'Are you – I mean, okay?'

Julia hesitated and Holly tried not to smile – Julia's view of illness as a weakness was well known. Holly was half-convinced that, confronted with a broken leg, Julia would be telling herself to man-up and get over it.

'There's a few nasty bugs doing the rounds, so if you need to head home I can cover your patients?' Holly suggested, thoughtfully giving Julia an out.

'I'm not ill,' Julia protested, before slumping back against the doorframe, 'but I would love to swap shifts, if you felt you'd be okay? It's a child-heavy list this morning ... I just don't think I have the emotional reserves!'

As Julia left the room, her usual poise and posture replaced by an exhausted shuffle, Holly wondered whether she should have given her a proper check-up before she left. She didn't look exactly unwell, more as though someone had taken her batteries out and she was lurching along on basic power only. Still, if it was babies and toddlers a-go-go this morning, it was probably for the best either way. The kids themselves were often oblivious to Julia's curt tone, but Holly knew how exacting the Larkford mummies could be.

And Larkford seemed to have its own sub-strata of parenting styles – all of which required tactful handling: The Helicopter Mums who hovered over their offspring constantly; The Snowplough Mums who barged through any opposition to their little cherubs achieving their goals; and of course, the local favourite – The Curling Mums, who always made sure that they were one step ahead of their darlings, frantically smoothing their way through life for the easiest ride.

Holly needn't have worried though, as her first patients of the day were guaranteed to make her smile. As Hattie and Lance from The Deli manhandled a vast pram that made Holly's Beast look like a pretender, their ten-month-old twins slept on oblivious. Of course it had been a shock for everyone, seeing that sneaky second heartbeat on a later scan and it had certainly thrown all their careful planning into disarray, but Hattie and Lance had taken everything in their stride and Holly had never seen them looking happier. In fact, as she took in their ecstatic smiles and tightly clasped hands the penny dropped.

Holly leapt to her feet, all other thoughts driven from her head. She'd quietly logged away that Lance's review with Oncology was sometime this month, but to be honest, with all the other stuff going on in her life, it had slightly slipped off the radar.

'And?' she said, her hand over her mouth in anticipation, even though the sheer delight on their faces said it all.

Hattie rushed forward, her words tumbling over each other in her rush to share their news, 'He did it! His scan was officially clear. Isn't that the best news you've ever heard?'

Despite herself, Holly felt her eyes fill with tears. Even the sight of Lance beside the pram had been more than they had ever dared hope for. Every test and every scan had suggested that he might never live to see his children arrive into the world – and yet here they were now. 'That's bloody brilliant,' she exclaimed, her professional demeanour flying out the window, as two of her loveliest neighbours got the happy ending they so truly deserved.

Yes, they were going to be a bit strapped for cash for a while and yes, their business had taken a hit as Hattie had juggled new-born twins and a husband with testicular cancer, but it was a small price to pay really. The bags from Poundland hanging on the back of the pram spoke volumes, as did the bags under their eyes, but in light of today's news – totally worth it.

'We must celebrate,' she said. 'Have you told Dan yet?'

Hattie shook her head. 'We wanted to tell you first. Honestly Holly, you've all been so amazing. I reckon Taffy's motivational rugby bollocks helped Lance more than any of the counselling he got at the hospital.'

Lance leaned against the wall with a grin. 'And obviously the odd bonkers tip about raising twins was kind of useful too . . .' He laughed at Hattie's aghast expression.

'Lance! Shut up and be nice, or Holly will stop being my Yoda. If it wasn't for the fact that I know you've done twin babies and survived, I swear I'd have lost the plot at times.'

Lance was about to chip in with his two-pence worth when Hattie glared at him. 'Anyone around here implying otherwise will not be getting a lie-in tomorrow.' He immediately closed his mouth and looked adorably innocent.

'Make the most of your lie-ins now,' said Holly. 'As Taffy will tell you, once they can work the remote and climb into your bed, you may never sleep again.'

Hattie kissed him adoringly on the cheek. 'Well, it seems to be working out so far. Let's review in a decade or so, when they're talking back and being rebellious.'

Holly frowned. 'You won't have to wait a decade for that, I'm afraid. I seem to spend most of my spare time on teeny-tiny chairs getting told off at Pinetrees.'

Hattie looked surprised. 'But your boys are always so lovely and angelic.'

'At home, yes. But not at nursery, apparently.' She shook her head. 'It's astounding that they seem to have developed completely different personas at pre-school. Some of the things they've apparently done . . .' She sighed. 'But enough of that – today is for celebrating. Do you fancy a scruffy supper at ours?'

Hattie flushed pink. 'It's a lovely thought, Holly, and we'd love to come another time, but we have plans for this evening.' She looked as though she might burst with excitement. 'We have a babysitter! We're actually going out. For a meal. And maybe a movie too.' Each little announcement came in a staccato burst of anticipation that showed what a rare and special treat this simple evening would be.

'Good for you,' said Holly, secretly thinking that their evening sounded rather fun. She crouched down in front of the pram and gazed at the twins as they slept. Their long dark eyelashes brushed against the plump pinkness of their cheeks. No longer tiny and fragile from their premature arrival into the world, they were pictures of miniature perfection – petite in a way that her sturdy little boys never had been. 'I can't get over how much they've grown. Let me have a look when I get home – there's bound to be some clobber that the boys have grown out of. Even if it's just wellies and raincoats for later.' She stood back up, but her eyes were still focused on the tiny little fists clutching at beloved teddy bears.

She put the all-consuming wave of emotion down to sheer relief at Lance's results; she pushed the image of those plump little fists from her mind. She had enough trouble dealing with the two she had at home, the mere notion of adding to the set was sheer folly. Nevertheless, Holly stood in the doorway, waving them off with a lump in her throat and an almost visceral pull in her stomach.

As she worked her way down Julia's morning clinic list, Holly could only be grateful that she'd stepped in – it was like an A–Z of childhood ailments this morning and it was certainly enough to quell any notions of broodiness that Hattie's twins might have provoked. Signing a prescription for antibiotic ointment for some 'wet eczema', Holly settled herself back at her desk and opened the next patient file on her computer. It was hard to say who would be more mortified at the scheduling change, Holly or Mrs Harlow from Pinetrees Nursery. Holly scowled. Seeping rashes she could cope with; her children's controlling headmistress was another prospect altogether.

The last time they had seen one another was when Holly had been perched on the tiny, demoralising chairs being roundly chastised for her sons' behaviour. Mrs Harlow's well-known distaste for 'professional mothers' hopefully didn't extend as far as her healthcare professionals.

Never one to let her personal opinion cloud her working demeanour, Holly was determined to take the higher path and be the best damn doctor she could possibly manage on four hours' sleep and with indelible doodles on her lower leg from Tom's impromptu tattoo session at breakfast time.

'What can I do for you this morning, Mrs Harlow?' Holly asked brightly a few minutes later, as she quickly scanned the file and crossed her ankles covertly under her desk. 'I gather you normally like to see Dr Channing?'

'I do, actually,' said Mrs Harlow. 'But your Practice Manager called me and said that when it came to—' she stumbled and flushed bright pink, 'reproductive issues, you were the person I needed to speak to.'

'Okay then,' said Holly, squashing the voice in her head that suggested finding a brave and willing participant was not something she could offer on the NHS. 'Why don't you fill me in on the history a little bit – I see you have a double appointment – and we can make a plan from there?'

Mrs Harlow continued to stare at a point several inches above Holly's head as she reeled off the blood tests and scans that she'd already undergone. 'I think my husband and I both feel that unexplained infertility isn't a very helpful label . . .'

'You're married?' blurted out Holly, the judgemental surprise evident in her voice. Way to be professional Holly, she thought crossly.

'Well, y-es,' said Mrs Harlow slowly, as though speaking to a three-year-old. 'Hence the Mrs?'

'Of course, of course,' Holly blustered, 'I just thought that was something they always did with headmistresses, you know?'

There was an awkward silence, during which time Mrs Harlow shifted uncomfortably in her seat, clearly loathing every moment of this conversation. Sharing her private concerns was one thing; sharing them with someone she clearly resented and disliked was a step too far.

Holly returned to the notes on screen and began to run through her usual questions: How long had they been trying?

Had they managed to stick to the advice about diet, lifestyle and baggy pants? Were they having effective sex?

'I'm sorry? What do you mean by effective sex?'

'Well, chiefly, at the right time of your cycle, frequently enough, orgasms can be helpful, likewise lying down rather than standing up …' Holly reeled off matter-of-factly. 'Sounds a bit old-wives' tales some of it, but to be honest, if things aren't happening naturally then every little helps, doesn't it?'

Now she was back in her medical comfort zone, Holly felt much more in control. None of this biological stuff fazed her in the slightest and she often found that when her patients heard her being so matter of fact, they tended to relax a bit and follow suit.

For all her hoity-toity ways, Mrs Harlow was no exception. She went from mortified and avoiding eye contact to engaged and interested. By the time Holly had pulled up a list of fertility specialists, their waiting times and her options, Mrs Harlow was in danger of behaving like a human being.

She stood up and scooped her handbag over one shoulder, fixing Holly with an indecipherable look. 'Now, Dr Graham, I presume I can count on you for complete doctor/patient confidentiality? I don't want to hear all the details of my private life being bandied around at the school gates.'

Aw, Mrs Harlow, and you were doing so well, thought Holly to herself, her hackles rising again. Did she have any idea how offensive her suggestion of Holly's indiscretion was?

Holly smiled sweetly. 'Well, Mrs Harlow, you have no worries at all on that score. We take doctor/patient confidentiality very seriously here at The Practice. We are professionals, after all, and it is *so* much more enforceable than say teacher/parent confidentiality might be.'

Mrs Harlow's face flooded scarlet – she knew when she'd
been caught out. It may not have been a high point of her
career, having half her class with military haircuts, but
that didn't mean it was appropriate to be overheard in The
Kingsley Arms slagging off both Holly and her, what was it
now, 'pestilential offspring', did it? Holly smiled graciously
and held open the door.

'Still, hopefully one day soon you'll be able to experience
the joys of parenthood first hand,' she said as she waved Mrs
Harlow on her way, clutching a repeat prescription for pre-
natal vitamins and a referral to the fertility assessment unit.

Holly felt a squirm of unease. It was all very well picking
one's battles, but being feisty at work still didn't come naturally. Holly was prepared to let a lot of things slide, but when
it came to her boys, she felt like a lioness protecting her cubs.
But then maybe, that was actually no bad thing?

By the time Taffy got home after Evening Surgery, the sitting
room of their tiny cottage was a scene of devastation. Tom
and Ben were surrounded by heaps of tiny t-shirts, miniature jumpers and more pairs of shoes than the stock room at
Clarks. Holly had always bemoaned the fact that the twins'
feet seemed to grow exponentially and never in the same
direction twice. Two sets of shoes, on a bimonthly basis –
nobody dared do the maths.

Looking at the body of evidence laid out before him,
Taffy had to swallow pretty hard before he spoke. 'It probably wasn't the best idea to organise a nice bottle of fizz at
the restaurant for Hattie and Lance then – since we're clearly
clothing and shoeing a Third World country here. Whatever
happened to hand-me-downs?'

Holly emerged from sorting through a box of trousers,

many of which seemed to no longer have any knees, or backsides, or both. The twins had gone through (were actually still in) a phase where they didn't so much grow out of their clothes as wear them into oblivion. She sat back on her heels and grinned. 'Oh God, you're sweet – they'll love that,' she said, folding a pair of jeans that had somehow survived unscathed and adding them to a heap on the sofa. 'Was it, you know, Very Nice Fizz?' she asked tentatively, knowing in the back of her mind that the boys needed new trainers, new wellies and two new sets of pyjamas. Each.

Taffy ran a hand over his head, where the downy fuzz was now covering his scalp and making it incredibly tactile. 'Nope.'

He plonked himself down on the floor and surrendered to the excitable hugs of two little boys in shrunken PJs. 'I just got Prosecco in the end. Partly because I didn't want to embarrass Lance by being too flash but mainly because, every time I open my wallet, there's a photo of these two little monkeys where my money used to be.' He flashed his eyes at Tom and tickled his tummy until he squealed. Ben got a gentler squeeze that still had his little legs kicking with glee and the noise levels seemingly exceeding that of a Heathrow flyby.

Holly was overcome by an unfamiliar sensation. This. Now. Watching Taffy mucking about with the boys as she folded tiny little socks into pairs and the odd little onesie that brought their baby years flooding back. The thought was in her mind before her rational brain could begin to edit.

I want another baby, she thought. I want to have a baby with Taffy and this time round, it will be different.

He already did so much for her boys, not even blinking at mucking in with bath-time or school-runs or even the

Midnight Monster Mission to seek out and destroy any monsters foolish enough to hide under Ben's bed. He would be a wonderful father, she thought, before promptly correcting herself: he *is* being a wonderful father. But the word 'figure' hung unacknowledged on the end of her thought.

'Oi, Graham,' Taffy called, and clearly not for the first time. 'Earth to Holly! Do you want a glass of wine or will that just make you more broody and emotional?' His tone was teasing, but his gaze missed nothing.

'Would that be the end of the world?' she ventured quietly as the twins hurtled around the sofa and collapsed boisterously into the cushions together, playing sweetly (if loudly and energetically) like the cherubic angels that had been notably missing at nursery. Again.

Taffy shrugged. 'I might be persuaded,' he answered with a comedy waggle of his eyebrows. 'It might be something we should practise for, just in case.' He leaned in and began to kiss his way along her collarbone in a way that confirmed to Holly what she already knew – they really didn't need the practice, but it would almost certainly be fun.

He pulled away to deal with the twins' increasingly vocal snack requests. 'Come on, you two, don't just sit there – let's get some supplies and take them outside. Can't have us all prowling around in here driving your mum crazy. Ben, grab the balls. Tom, we need drinks. Come on you two, go, go, go!'

It didn't escape Holly's notice that this nightly kick-about seemed to be just as much for Taffy's benefit, as for the boys. But at least it meant a moment in peace where she didn't need to deal with him trying to analyse her every motivation. Taffy's growing interest in Sports Psychology and its 'everyday applications' was starting to drive her a little crazy.

Sometimes, she thought, she just wanted to make a decision without questioning the rationale behind it. Like her decision to relocate all the Sports Psychology books to the back of the bookshelf, just for a little respite.

The baby-thing was, of course, an entirely mental suggestion. If they could barely cope with two boys and two careers, plus a part-time puppy that did insist on growing, how on earth could they add another member to this fragile equilibrium? Not to mention the fact that Taffy would almost certainly want to do the right thing and put a ring on her finger ... The thought that another baby was even a consideration flagged up just how deeply she had fallen in love with him; the very thought of the vulnerability that signified, utterly terrified her.

She shook her head in confusion – how could she feel so certain of their relationship and yet so utterly unwilling to commit?

Holly sipped at the glass of soft Merlot that Taffy had pressed into her hand, as he fashioned sailing boats from apple quarters and strips of gouda and the boys gobbled them as fast as he could make them. They seemed to be recreating an horrific storm in The America's Cup, with a fair number of gruesome casualties that were certainly not PG.

She sighed contentedly, a quiet family evening the perfect end to another chaotic day. She wondered how Hattie and Lance were enjoying their romantic date and her phone buzzed in her jeans pocket even as the thought crossed her mind – she pulled the phone out, expecting a silly thank you text from Hattie for the fizz. She froze, staring at the glowing screen as her stomach swooped ominously, her fingers shaking as she opened the message and her fears were confirmed.

You certainly didn't waste any time . . .

She may not have recognised the number, but there was no doubt in her mind who had sent the text in her hand. She obviously hadn't been the only one reading the online editions this morning and Milo's obsession with Google Alerts was still apparently going strong. The phone vibrated once again and a second message followed on, jarring into her comfortable reality with intrusive precision. Seemingly unable to stop herself, she clicked on the screen to scroll down.

> So it seems you've been busy at work *and* at home –
> not sure I like that – perhaps it's time to visit my boys?
> I'll be in touch.

The cold shiver of dread and nausea that the text had triggered might be seen as an over-reaction to some, but not to Holly. It was the targeted hit that had so shaken her, she realised. She knew Milo's bullying ways; she knew too that he must have been reading every one of the e-mails she'd sent him. But for Milo, power was his fuel and in a way, a text out of the blue, into the security of her evening, was much more his style than simply hitting 'reply'. His passive aggressive way of reminding her who called all the shots in their relationship.

There wasn't even an obvious threat, just a casual allusion to a visit.

That was all.

But it was enough.

She sat back heavily and closed her eyes. Only an arrogant narcissist like Milo, who believed he was the centre of the known universe, could talk about 'his' boys after abandoning them quite so comprehensively for months on end.

Was it any wonder she was so reluctant to consider marriage again, when being happily un-married with Taffy was the best relationship she had ever had?

Chapter 26

Dan tapped the final figures into the calculator on his phone and a slow smile spread across his face. In the few days since the launch, numerous pledges had added to the ever-growing funding for the Health in the Community scheme. He wasn't sure of the logistics of how Grace had managed to pull together the updated website in such a short time, or the clever link to the Just Donate account, but the numbers spoke for themselves. He looked across the desk at her glowing face and knew that she was chuffed to bits with their achievement.

'Thank you, Grace,' Dan said with feeling. 'It's one thing suggesting that people donate, but I'm convinced that they're more comfortable doing it online than putting cash in a bucket these days.'

Grace nodded. 'Look – there's a hundred quid from Waves the Fishmongers. They wouldn't do that with cash.' She paused. 'You don't think they're hoping the whole eat-more-oily-fish message will be good for sales, do you?'

Dan laughed. 'Do you know, I rather think they might be and just this once, I'm happy to oblige. We'll be fair though.' He dropped his voice until it sounded like the voice-over in the financial advertisements, 'Other purveyors of seafood are available locally.'

They were distracted from the screenful of figures by the sound of muted crying. Grace was on her feet before he'd even hit save and they both hustled out into the hallway. They stopped, confronted by Alice sobbing into the shoulder of possibly the tallest, most handsome figure of a man that Dan had ever encountered. He felt like a stumpy goblin beside him and that was not a feeling Dan was used to. With both Grace and Alice beside him, this guy looked like an old-school Olympian.

'Dan, this is Jamie,' Alice managed. 'He's come about Coco.' She took the tissue that Grace offered and sniffed, obviously mortified to be baring her emotions at work.

Dan looked down automatically, noticing straight away what was missing in this tableau. He swallowed hard, shocked by how overcome he felt. 'Oh Alice, no. Poor Coco! What's happened?' He couldn't help but assume that only the very worst could have separated Coco from Alice's side.

Jamie held out his hand to shake Dan's. 'Don't worry, mate. The little dog's okay, if that's what you're thinking. She's just a bit off her game at the moment.'

'Then ... why the ... I mean ...' Dan was trying to find the most tactful way to ask what the hell Alice was crying about, when Jamie stepped in.

'Alice has just found out that if Coco can't fulfil her role properly, then she may need to have a different dog that can,' Jamie said gently.

Even hearing the news again was enough to make Alice bury her head in his chest and sob. Jamie didn't miss a beat, he just allowed Alice to cry. 'It's not an unusual reaction,' he said to Grace and Dan. 'The bond with an assistance dog is an incredibly intimate one. It's perfectly natural to be grief-stricken at the very thought of losing her.'

As Alice rootled around in her pockets for a handkerchief, Dan saw the crest on Jamie's waistcoat. So this was the much-vaunted dog trainer that Holly had been talking about. As one of the partners, he couldn't pretend it was ideal that the new addition to The Practice was having so much trouble settling in. And he didn't mean Alice. When they had taken the decision to hire Alice, Coco was part of the package and as such, she was one of their team now. When the regional visit had been suggested, Dan had simply assumed ...

Well, what had he assumed? Coco wasn't a machine. They couldn't call in IT support and reboot her to factory settings. The human angle in all of this had somehow passed him by, namely that Alice viewed Coco as her lifeline – her entrée back into the world of work and a huge factor in her having the confidence to move here and live alone. God only knew how she would cope without Coco. It was shocking to see her stripped of her composure.

Jamie leaned back against the wall, one leg bent at the knee, with his foot on the wall behind him. It was a pose that suggested he was completely at ease with all this emotion flowing around him. Dan only wished he could say the same; just the sight of Alice's tear-stained face was enough to make him feel out of his depth.

Once Alice had regained a little control, Jamie gently went on to explain his plan. 'Look, Alice, we're not there yet, so don't get ahead of yourself. Obviously Coco has a job to do, keeping an eye on you and your blood sugar, and at the moment she's still doing that. It's the question of her distraction that's bothering me. Are there simply too many people coming and going, too many new smells? Will she settle down once she's realised that this is your new routine now?

'I'm going to spend the next few days here, if I may,' said Jamie, 'watching Coco in her work environment and assessing her home situation. If there's something bothering the little tyke, I'll find out what it is.'

Right now the thing that seemed to be bothering Coco was being separated from Alice, as her plaintive whines could be heard from the other side of the door. 'I didn't want her to see me upset,' clarified Alice. 'I suspect she knows what I'm thinking half the time.'

'I have no doubt of it,' Jamie said with a smile. 'You two have a pretty tight bond. We'll do everything we can to keep you two together, okay . . .' Even the implication of the alternative was enough for Alice's eyes to fill with tears again.

Grace opened Alice's door and a little brown bundle of fur hurtled herself into Alice's arms. 'She's a dog with remarkable hearing. She could tell you were upset from a hundred yards away.'

Dan gave a small wave and edged back into his office; he wasn't sure how much more of the heightened emotions he could take. After all, his verbal filters were clearly switched to 'off' today and he didn't think it was wise to tempt fate any further. As he switched on his computer to get ready for his clinic, he noticed three missed calls from Julia's mum, who clearly hadn't got the memo about their break-up either. He sighed, unwilling to get pulled into yet more drama and quietly typed out a text to Julia. Keeping a secret in Larkford was never easy, but in their close-knit working world, it was well-nigh impossible. The only thing worse than breaking up with her though, would be stealing her news-cycle by letting it slip. Giving her the opportunity to break the news was the only honourable thing to do.

*

Dan's day seemed destined to be populated with the over-wrought and emotionally incontinent. He held Jake Norman's hand as he cried about losing his sight, Kerry Langley had a panic attack right there in his office and Percy Lawson had predictably come off his motorbike and given himself one hell of a scare.

Dan pulled open his desk drawer and checked the office sweepstake form – he himself had lost out on the jackpot when Percy had managed to avoid a motorbike accident for the first two days. Holly and Taffy likewise at two weeks. Obviously Lucy, their receptionist, had been a lot more opti-mistic about his chances and had scooped the prize out from under them all.

He sighed as he saw the next name on his patient roster: Lindy Grey.

Dan clicked on the computer screen to pull up the relevant file and his heart thudded hard in his chest. Today was not the best day for him to run into Lindy. Tiny Lycra shorts and per-fect body or not, Lindy was definitely best kept at arm's length. After their ill-advised series of hook-ups last year, she had been distant at first, shying away from the commitment that Dan actually wanted. Friends with Benefits was her preferred scenario and one that she continued to suggest, even once it was clear that he and Julia were back together. Seeing her now, while his break-up with Julia was so fresh and sore, not to men-tion apparently secret, was less than ideal. The only way he'd managed to shrug off her advances without causing offence over the last few months had been the slightly nauseating glow of infatuation that followed him and Julia everywhere.

Today, he was looking tired and pissed off, not to men-tion questioning the wisdom of ever having reconciled with Julia in the first place. Breaking up once, they'd survived.

Wondering how this latest schism would affect their working relationship was making his brain hurt and was not best followed by Lindy Grey in a lacy ensemble, he thought. He really did not need any beautifully tanned, lithe and lean thighs to examine this morning. Still, he consoled himself, maybe she'd come in with some hideous facial warts, or putrid discharge and just happened to have come straight from the gym.

'Hello, Dr Carter,' Lindy said as she walked into the room, settling neatly on the edge of the chair. 'I know you're running late, so we'll have to catch up over lunch one day. But in the meantime, I seem to have a touch of asthma.' Without a moment's hesitation, she peeled off her t-shirt and calmly waited for Dan to locate his stethoscope.

She ran a hand over her chest, where the gauzy bra she was wearing was barely doing its job. 'Do you need to listen to my chest? It just keeps getting really tight and constricted when I run.'

Slowly and professionally Dan listened to her chest, front and back. 'And the wheezing and tightness only comes on with exercise?' he queried, before running through their standard presenting-with-shortness-of-breath questions. Dan managed to keep their conversation to the strictly professional but Lindy wasn't making it easy for him, sitting there in her underwear, leaning forward every time she spoke and repeatedly laying a hand on his forearm suggestively. Dan wasn't blind to Lindy's intentions and the air in the room was thick with unspoken thoughts, as she skirted around making a blatant proposition.

By the time she held a prescription for a new inhaler in her hand and the promise to return if there was no improvement had been elicited, Lindy was looking thoroughly sulky.

Dan heaved a sigh of relief as she left, pleased to have held a certain sang-froid together, knowing he wouldn't have been human not to feel a small flicker of temptation. He was only too aware how simple things with Lindy had been – she was the ultimate no-strings hook-up. But then, he also reminded himself, their 'relationship' had left him feeling vulnerable, disconcerted and wanting more – not marriage and babies per se, just maybe a movie and a meal … Even a conversation occasionally would have been nice.

Besides, he told himself, it was all irrelevant now; amongst all the drama and flirtation, Lindy and Julia were cut from the same cloth. Besides, Lindy had become his patient. Even if she was clearly giving him the come-on, which she so obviously had been, it was the golden rule of medicine – don't flirt with the patients.

Not for the first time this morning his thoughts turned to Grace and her quiet but steady transformation: no bells, no whistles, just an incredibly kind, dedicated member of their team getting her life back on track. Nobody would ever claim that kindness or thoughtfulness were sexy, thought Dan, but right now the notion of a warm, supportive partner like Grace felt like the Holy Grail. He sat back in his chair, a little thrown by where his thoughts were heading. Had he really just wondered what it would be like if Grace were in his life? Grace? The very antithesis to Julia in every sense?

He picked up his phone. It may only be lunchtime but there really was only one thing to do.

'Taffy?' he said. 'Pub?'

Chapter 27

A few days later, as the sun beat down on the banks of the River Lark, and children's laughter could be heard echoing around the Market Place, Holly was at work, sympathetically listening to Molly Giles' recount of her trip to the supermarket. She was overwhelmed with compassion for this poor woman's plight but felt utterly impotent as to how best to help her. This was yet another one of those times when the funding fell short.

'And so then one of the shop assistants said, "Just ignore her, she's probably drunk" and they left me there,' said Molly, the anger and frustration so clear on her face. 'And I tried to tell them, Dr Graham, like we talked about. I tried to say I had Parkinson's but the words came out all slurry and they just laughed and told me to lay off the sauce!' She twitched and her left arm flailed for a moment against the arm of the chair. 'It's bad enough that my new boss keeps calling me Sourpuss . . .'

Holly couldn't actually begin to imagine anyone being that insensitive, but it seemed to be a pattern with these invisible disabilities: people seemed to believe that they could say what they liked, without consequence, as though Molly had stopped having human emotions on the day of her diagnosis.

It was hard enough for this woman already: her children, thank God, were already settled at university, but her husband of twenty years had found the notion of early-onset Parkinson's just too much to deal with and left. Just another statistic, where the women stood by their men if they became ill and at least half the husbands bailed. It fed into every one of Holly's insecurities about abandonment and she reached out and took Molly's hand.

'Would you like me to write to your new boss? I could explain the situation from a medical point of view if you think it would help?'

Molly shrugged and a muscle began ticking above her eye. 'I told him about the muscles in my face going slack – that I can't smile any more – but he just said it wasn't the only thing that was slack about my performance at work these days.' Her eyes looked thunderous and filled with pain, but her face was strangely immobile – and therein lay the problem.

Molly didn't look ill; she didn't look disabled. Most of the time she just looked like everybody else – tired and a bit grumpy. Holly had been aghast to hear that one of the local pensioners had even had a go at her for using her Blue Badge for parking. She wondered how often in a day Molly heard those crucifying words, 'But you don't *look* ill . . .'

She knew from her last appointment with Molly, that she was struggling not to slide into depression. 'When you start being jealous of the people with cancer, Dr Graham, you know something's not right. I mean, they get Macmillan, pink ribbons and moon walks – they get support and acknowledgement of what they're dealing with. What do I get? Abuse for being lazy . . .'

For Molly, the old adage about not knowing what goes on behind closed doors rang only too true – none of these thoughtless people would ever get to witness her daily struggles or appreciate her strength and determination.

Holly knew that they had to limit the remit of their Health in the Community Scheme somewhere, but she couldn't help wondering whether there was something they could do, even if it was just to counteract the ignorance surrounding invisible disabilities. Surely Molly should be allowed to park her car or use the disabled loo at the supermarket without having to defend herself and share her private medical issues?

In the meantime, all she could offer was her own support and an open door. She'd already sorted out the best consultants she could access, and with a bit of luck they could delay the onset of the more debilitating symptoms, but when it came to Parkinson's, you couldn't put the rabbit back in the hat. For Molly Giles it was all downhill from here.

Holly slipped out of the side door on her break. She couldn't quite face the doctors' lounge this morning. To be more accurate, she couldn't quite face Julia trying to pin her down for a day's filming with Quentin when it sounded like Holly's idea of hell. She'd even tried to barter covering Julia's pre-natal clinic to avoid a day with Quentin's crew charting her every move, but it was some measure of Julia's persistence that she'd turned that suggestion down. True, she had wavered slightly, but ultimately she was on a mission for a date in the diary and Holly sensed that Quentin was the one pulling the strings.

Julia's brittle mood since the party had been preying on Holly's mind, but every time she tried to talk to her about it, they got caught up in this farce around the camera crew. Shying away from a lens in her face, meant that Holly was essentially shying away from her friend, but sometimes the friendship felt more like work than a pleasure. It was not something she was particularly proud of.

She made a mental note to follow up with Lizzie about how her CBT was progressing – again, tiptoeing around the issue, because since starting therapy, Lizzie had decided that she didn't want to talk about it, but nevertheless became easily offended if Holly forgot to log in for a day or two. It was a difficult balance to strike. Holly sighed – God knows, she loved her friends and wanted to be there for them, but sometimes she honestly wondered whether she had anything left to give at the end of a long day.

Picking up a speedy take-away coffee from The Deli, Holly nipped through the Market Place, sunglasses on to discourage conversation and wound up, as always, in her favourite spot behind the church. She was shocked to see somebody already sitting on *her* bench, having become so accustomed to being the only one who came here.

'You hiding out too?' she asked Dan gently, as she sat down beside him.

'Is it that obvious?' he asked, running his hand over his head in what had become a new tell of discomfort since the charity head shave. Even though his hair was now nearly back to its usual glossy self, the self-conscious habit remained. 'I think I might be losing the plot,' he said.

'Flashbacks again?' Holly asked, immediately.

'No, thank God,' said Dan vehemently. 'Just life in general.' He smiled tiredly. 'You know how it is . . .'

'I do,' said Holly with feeling. 'This week in particular, I really bloody do.'

They sat content in each other's company for a few minutes, neither wanting to sully the peaceful respite with conversation. The heat of the day was building and a plump thrush was cycling through his various calls in the graveyard like a broken car alarm, switching melody and rhythm every few bars, just to keep them on their toes. The steady buzzing from the bees on the lavender bushes lining the path was soothing and reassuring.

'Taffy's out running. Again,' Holly offered, trying to resist the urge to moan about their disjointed and truncated conversation earlier. The whole idea of an impending visit from Milo had thrown a miniature grenade into their week and, predictably, the waiting to see what happened next was proving the hardest part.

Dan nodded, unsurprised. 'Well, it's how he's coping, isn't it? With this whole Milo business . . .'

Holly sighed. Part of her was actually a little bit jealous that Taffy had found a way to deal with the pressure better than she had; the other part was simply annoyed that every time they hit a stumbling block anywhere in their lives, Taffy's go-to reaction was to pull on his trainers and leave her standing.

'I think it's the unknown that's bothering us both. It might still be nothing . . .' Holly paused, unconvincing even to her own ears. 'Did he talk to you about it?'

Dan shook his head. 'Only in passing.'

'And I just have no idea how to talk to him about this,' Holly confessed. 'He seems so withdrawn suddenly . . . Distant, you know?'

Dan looked sideways at her. 'I'm not surprised. He can't really win, can he? But I can promise you he has an opinion on this, even if he knows it's not what you want to hear.' He paused. 'Hence the running, I imagine.'

Holly nodded. Taffy was in an untenable situation – his own personal feelings about how to handle Milo tempered by the knowledge that, like it or not, he was part of their lives. 'I keep saying we should decide on a plan together, but he just steps back, says he'll follow my lead . . .' She sighed helplessly.

'Your kids, your ex-husband,' Dan said bluntly. 'Is he actually pulling back and being unsupportive, or giving you space to make your own decision? Biting his tongue so he doesn't say something he'll regret?'

Holly frowned and sipped her coffee. He made a valid point and that in itself was incredibly annoying this morning. Her expression said it all and Dan held up his hands in mock surrender.

'Look, just ignore me today. I'm being grumpy and rude with everyone. And what do I know about relationships?' He paused and looked uncomfortable. 'Did Julia tell you she'd been offered a job in London?' he said eventually, as though dipping his toe in the water to test her reaction.

'What?' Holly tipped her face back in the sunshine, frowning. 'She won't take it though, will she? She's got too much invested here.' She turned to look at Dan for reassurance and was stunned by the expression on his face. 'Will she?'

He shrugged. 'I'm beginning to think I've made an awful mistake.' He didn't elaborate and Holly felt the first stirrings of frustration. It was one thing to co-opt her thinking bench, it was quite another to add to her mental gymnastics with yet another problem.

If Julia absconded, where would it leave them? Had all the upheaval to accommodate Julia's blasted film crew and her ambitions in that direction been for nothing? So much for loyalty and working as a team!

'Well? Is she going to take it?' Holly demanded, feeling properly riled now and taking her frustration out on Dan. 'Can't you talk her around?'

She stopped then, Dan's entire demeanour shouting out

that her anger was misplaced here. She could be as annoyed with Julia as she liked, but Dan wasn't the one at fault. She leaned her shoulder against his. 'What's actually going on, Dan? And don't forget, what's said on the bench, stays on the bench, so don't feel you have to filter.' She saw a flicker of a smile as she wildly misquoted their Rugby Club Tour slogan and was pleased to see the tension in his face soften a fraction.

'I don't know about the job, to be honest. She'll take it or she won't, but either way, she and I have called it quits.'

Holly jolted in astonishment. Somehow, they had all become so accustomed to the bickery side of that relationship, that it had ceased to be an issue and Holly had assumed it was a dynamic that worked for them – even if it would have driven her personally insane.

'Oh, Dan, was it awful? Have you two been yelling at each other for days?'

He shook his head. 'We couldn't even muster an argument in the end. Just a quiet conversation in the car park during the launch party. Just a few tired words and that's that.' He looked utterly dejected. 'I'm beginning to think we should have had a bloody good row to clear the air though, because the polite respectful route just means neither of us are admitting it's over. It's been days and she hasn't told a soul.'

'Well, you've told me now; how does that feel? If nobody else knows, at least you have a window of opportunity to get back together. Do you want that?'

He shrugged. 'I keep thinking that Julia might, though – why else is she keeping it a secret?'

Holly drained her coffee cup and expertly lobbed it into the bin a few metres away.

'Nice!' said Dan automatically. 'Taffy's a lucky bloke, you know.'

Holly blushed. 'Actually, I think I might be the lucky one in our relationship. He does put up with an awful lot to be with me.'

'Yeah, but he's not the easiest of souls to live with either. I do realise that, Holly. All that boundless energy for one thing. All that perpetual motion and positivity.' He grinned. 'It has to be wearing.'

She paused. 'Maybe we should schedule in a bloody great argument to clear the air too?'

'Nah. Taffy doesn't do drama.' Dan dismissed the very suggestion. 'You'll have to take him as you find him I'm afraid. But he does do loyal and loving and slightly bonkers – and to be fair, he does it very well . . . If you really want to help him let off steam, buy him some water balloons – he does love a water balloon,' Dan said fondly. Holly couldn't help but notice there was more love, respect and affection in Dan's voice when he talked about his best mate than there ever had been when he talked about his girlfriend. Or should she say ex-girlfriend?

'On the other hand,' Dan continued, 'maybe all four of us need to clear the air? Relationships aside, there's so much going on at The Practice and I can't help feeling that we're building to breaking point.'

'About the Model Surgery?' said Holly, just as Dan said –

'About the staffing levels.'

'Ah,' said Dan. 'Not just me then? Worrying about our doctor to patient ratios has become my new hobby. If we didn't have the lovely Alice Walker to pick up the strain, I think I'd have had an aneurysm by now.'

Holly took a deep breath and plunged right in, fuelled by a need to share her own concerns and make sure Dan's focus was actually where it needed to be. 'Listen, it's probably not the best time, but I actually think our ratios might be the least of our problems. I have to tell you that this Model Surgery business is still making me feel incredibly uncomfortable. We already have so much exposure through Julia's TV show, but I can't help feeling this is different: we're basically standing up and saying this is how a practice *should* be run. And you know how I feel about the "shoulds" these days. Can we at least discuss how we're going to be presented to the world at large, because, well, look at us ... we're making it up as we go along and we are *no* role model.'

Dan sat forward on the bench. 'Since we're being frank about this then, tell me where all this is coming from? I thought you'd be pleased about the nomination, the funding, the reprieve? For God's sake, Holly, you chose Alice!'

Holly shrugged. 'Of course I'm pleased about the funding and the lifeline and Alice, but make no mistake here, Dan – Harry Grant was right. And we are going to pay for this one way or another.'

'Is this because of Milo?' Dan frowned.

Holly blinked. 'How do you mean?'

'Well, last time the press were around for the Save The Practice campaign, you had to pay rather a high price, if I recall. And Taffy's off calling that solicitor-mate of his suddenly ... Are you worried that all the press attention will bring more problems out of the woodwork?'

Holly didn't like to say that that ship had already sailed off the back of the launch party. She wanted him to focus on the very real and valid professional concerns she had. 'Think about it for a minute. Think about how we do things here, with tasks slipping through the cracks because we're all management and nobody is actioning any of our plans. We survive here because we have the most amazing support staff. Without a hierarchy, we're only a few days away from anarchy – God knows what would happen if Grace went on holiday! She's basically the glue holding all this together and we can't afford to take advantage of that.'

Dan listened intently, and Holly could only hope that he was taking her concerns seriously.

'What if they use our business model elsewhere and they don't have a Grace? What if somebody's health is put in jeopardy because we decided that a communal management style was easier than making a tough decision about who should be Senior Partner?' Holly took a deep breath and the momentum of her emotional outburst carried her forward. 'I know there might be a few hurt feelings and it might cause a few ripples in our private lives, but if we're going to be the grown-ups, shouldn't we be able to act like it too? And don't think that Derek Landers won't be out to catch every slip-up we make. Whatever Harry Grant might say, this is no level playing field and that horrible, sweaty man does *not* like us very much.'

Dan sighed. 'Why didn't we talk about all this before?'

But Holly and Dan already knew the answer. It had been easier not to rock the boat – and the very nature of this four-man partnership had meant that their domestic insecurities had encroached on their business decisions.

'Do you think we could formalise something more struc-tured before the NHS team descends?' Dan asked in the end. 'We don't have a choice now about the lack of hierarchy – if we lose that, we lose Alice and the new nursing hours. But is there a way, do you think, that we can keep both?'

'You're asking me?' Holly said, who still considered Dan her senior whatever their job titles may state. She laughed, tiredly. 'Listen, I'm still trying to adjust to the fact that my own children have decreed Taffy a better doctor than me, because he's a man!'

'What?' said Dan.

'Well, they came home and asked for Taffy to represent them on "What Do Mummy and Daddy Do At Work Day" – I can't work out whether to be chuffed to bits that they've so eagerly accepted him or worried stiff in case he decides . . .' Her voice cracked a little and she was about to change the subject when Dan intervened.

'In case he decides what, Holly?'

She shook her head. 'Nothing. Ignore me. I'm just tired too.'

'Oh Holly, give the bloke a little credit to begin with,' said Dan gently. 'Do you honestly think Taffy would have moved in and taken on such a huge role in the boys' lives, in your life, if he wasn't in it for the long haul? Seriously? I can see why you might be worried, but if there was ever a bloke pining for a family it's Taffy Jones. And you, you daft eejit, are the only girl I have ever known him to fall for this hard. This is not a passing fancy for him. Throw the poor bloke a bone – so you don't want the big I Do – who cares? Book a holiday for next year, buy a cat, just do *something* to prove to him that you're in it for the long haul too!'

'Oh,' said Holly quietly, a little taken aback by Dan's vociferous defence of his mate. 'So you don't think . . .'

'That he's a better doctor than you? No,' said Dan with a grin. 'But I do think the boys might be quite proud to have a "daddy" to take into school for once. Had you thought about that?'

Holly silently digested everything Dan had said for a moment. When the boys had said 'better' she had assumed instantly, defensively, that they meant professionally. Of course they must be excited to show off Taffy as the new man in their lives — after all, hadn't she been doing more or less the same thing for the last few months?

'For somebody who hasn't had kids, you're really very good at all this,' Holly said in the end.

'Uncle Dan has his uses,' he replied drily. 'But I really have to stop sticking my nose in — trying to play happy families with Julia has blown up in my face, hasn't it? I should have realised that impressing Julia's mum wouldn't actually win me any credit with Julia. And I'm not even sure she actually wants this London job, you know — but she definitely doesn't want to settle down in Larkford. And I do. I just keep wondering how I'm ever going to get to that place where you are.'

'Riddled with self-doubt and insecurity? I think you can aim a little higher than that, Dan,' Holly teased softly.

He gave her a nudge, realising that they were both emotionally fragile today. 'I just want that feeling that, to somebody, I'm their priority. And you have that, Holly, three times over, whether you choose to see it or not. Me? I'm just part of the window dressing for Julia's big picture and when she uses the word family, it sounds like an insult.'

'The F-word,' supplied Holly. 'I've heard her say it. And maybe when it comes to her childhood, that's how she genuinely feels. But when you two are together, maybe your word is "team" — same meaning, a world of different connotations.'

'Good Lord, haven't you two got patients to be seeing?' interrupted the Major, as he marched up to them in the graveyard, his terrier Grover bounding ahead to pinch the remains of Dan's bacon butty. 'Or is this the unofficial splinter group of the Larkford WI?'

He plonked a bunch of tulips down on his first wife Verity's grave without much ceremony and came and stood before them. 'If you've nothing better to do, perhaps one of you could take a look at my big toe. Hurts like a bastard.'

Holly couldn't help but laugh at the Major's bluff delivery. 'You can come into The Practice now, remember, Major?'

He blustered a little. 'Well, yes, I could . . . But old habits et cetera, et cetera and this is so much more convenient – I don't have to sit around all those *ill* people . . .'

'Come on,' said Dan, clearly welcoming some relief from the intensity of their conversation. 'Taffy keeps telling me about his random acts of kindness – you can be mine for the day. Sit down here and whip your sock off.'

'Oh, Major!' cried Holly, when the offending toe was revealed in all its glory. 'You're such a trend-setter: you've only gone and got the gout!'

Chapter 28

'I have come to the conclusion,' said Elsie in a gravelly voice the next morning, 'that nostalgia just isn't what it used to be.' Holly hesitated on the doorstep, unsure how to respond to such a pronouncement before her first cup of coffee on a Saturday.

'I just wanted to look in and say hello,' she said in the end. She held up a punnet of strawberries and a melon. 'Fruit medley for breakfast?'

Elsie gave her a querulous glare. 'And would that be to replace my lovely flakey croissants, by any chance? You and that bloody carer woman have been conspiring against me enjoying my food – no salt, no butter, no fun ... I tell you this, Holly Graham, I may live longer, but dear God, will it feel longer too!' She paused, an unusual flicker of guilt flitting across her features. 'By the way, Sarah is wonderful and fabulous and I don't think I actually said thank you for organising all that.'

Holly just smiled, it didn't bother her that technically the thank you was still outstanding – as long as Elsie was comfortable and happy, it was one less thing for Holly to worry about.

Somehow every hour this week had brought yet more new challenges and commitments, until her dreams had become filled with images of herself spinning plates on tall sticks, running madly between them. She didn't know what it meant that the plates in question were the hideously patterned ones from Milo's mother, or that there were one or two that never seemed to stay up, no matter how vigilant she was.

In her quieter moments, which were few and far between, she did wonder whether her subconscious was trying to tell her something – maybe she couldn't keep *all* the plates spinning, *all* of the time. Did she need to follow Elsie's advice and pick her battles a little more selectively?

Elsie plonked the proffered fruit onto the sideboard in the hall and wordlessly shepherded Holly through to the dining room where the volume of photographs, newspaper clippings and memorabilia had increased by a factor of ten.

'Where have you been hiding all this stuff?' gasped Holly, looking around her. Elsie's house had always been the epitome of streamlined elegance. Not for her, the cardboard boxes of photographs stacked on top of the piano, or the random collection of trinkets and special memories lying dusty and ignored on the windowsill.

Elsie gave a very Gallic shrug. 'I have my special cupboard. It's all been quietly rotting in there for the last few decades. I'm not even convinced that bringing it out into the light of day was my best idea. But I have to get some bits together for my meeting.' She looked cross. 'It's a lot more work than I'd realised.'

She plonked herself down into the carver chair at the head of the table and it was obvious to Holly, at least, that Elsie had been ignoring all the advice to rest and recover, preferring to gather her proverbial rosebuds while she may.

She graciously 'allowed' Holly to hustle around making her a warm drink, something she would never have permitted

even a few short weeks ago. For Elsie, being the hostess meant
being the most important person in the room, the star of her
own little mini-drama. The fact that Elsie was content just to
sit back and allow Holly free range of the kitchen cupboards
did not bode too well. Clearly, thought Holly, a morale boost
was called for.

'Did you find the magazine spread for your Oscar win?'
Holly asked as she cleared space on a side table for Elsie's
ginger infusion – another compromise, as Elsie's beloved
espresso had been consigned to the bin.

'I did. Although, to be honest, I don't look half as wonderful as I'd remembered,' Elsie grumbled, indicating a beautiful
vintage copy of *Vogue*, whose muted colours and tones were
so archetypal of its age that Holly could barely believe it was
real. Her own love of 'vintage-style' led to her kitchen being
filled with reproduction biscuit tins and postcards. But this –
this was the real deal.

Holly delicately flicked through the pages, where photographs were interspersed with line drawings and top tips for
housewives. 'Do take a moment to refresh yourself – your
husband relies upon you to be delightful and entertaining
when he gets home from work. Put a ribbon in your hair
and greet him with a smile and a drink. He's had a long day,'
Holly read aloud with a grin. 'It's like a different world. Can
you imagine the look on Taffy's face if I did that? He'd think
I was having a stroke.' She clapped a hand over her mouth
in appalled silence at her faux pas, eyes wide with shocked
disbelief at her tactlessness.

Elsie let out a volley of laughter that must have echoed
through to the third floor. She clutched at her sides as the
tears rolled down her face. 'Well, thank God for that,' she
managed eventually. 'You can stop talking to me like I'm

breakable and be real with me. I know I'm not supposed to be having any fun, but fun is my raison d'être, Holly – don't take that away from me in a tidal wave of low fat yoghurt and boredom! If it makes you feel more constructive, just give me one of those placebo thingummies – I gather they can be terribly effective.' she said drily.

'But I just . . .'

'I just, I just, I just,' mocked Elsie, the twinkle back in her eye for the first time in weeks. 'Would you listen to yourself qualifying every statement? Even your e-mails apologise for themselves. Stop subordinating every request you make!' She paused for a moment. 'I bet Julia doesn't,' she taunted, knowing exactly how to push Holly's buttons.

'No, she doesn't, but then she's also rude and abrasive and irritates everyone she works with!'

'Is she, though?' asked Elsie pointedly. 'If Dan phoned up and asked for some figures without chit-chat, wouldn't you assume he was busy and efficient? Why is it so different for Julia? Or you?'

'That's not fair,' countered Holly, 'I just like to make sure that . . . what?'

'Just?' Elsie asked.

'May I remind you, madam, that I came over here bearing fruit and a hug. You can't start bossing me around without caffeine in the house.'

'Your decision, not mine – I'd be sipping a lovely espresso with a *pain au chocolat* if it was up to me!'

Holly scowled. 'I don't apologise for myself all the time. That's not true!'

Elsie pulled her enormous iPhone out of her pocket, its screen almost as big as a paperback book. She tapped on her e-mails and began to paraphrase. 'I was just wondering if you'd had chance to look at the diet sheet . . . Just logging in to check . . . I just thought it might be nice . . .'

She put her phone down and shrugged. 'We can call it post-grad level if you like, but the *just* simply has to go . . .'

Holly paused, remembering every one of the e-mails that Elsie had quoted. 'And what if I *just* wanted to soften my request? Or ask you to do something I knew you wouldn't want to do? Am I supposed to be giving up on manners too?'

Elsie grinned like a Cheshire cat. 'Oh, Holly darling, just look at the progress you're making!' She waved her hand in the air to dismiss her own use of the word. 'This time last year, you would have accepted my advice as gospel and not even questioned it – now you're really thinking . . . But I promise you this, for the next few days, you'll be thinking about the *justs* as well . . .'

'I just might,' teased Holly in reply. 'Now, are you going to show me this Oscar picture of you in all this chaos or do I have to dig in and find it myself?' She smiled to herself as they flicked through the news cuttings in front of them, thrilled beyond measure that Elsie felt up to bossing her around. And there was even a small chance that she might *just* be right, Holly conceded.

The photograph of Elsie at the Oscars was in the Style and Entertainment section when they found it and it took up half the page. Dressed in swathes of jade silk, she was languorously draped over the arm of some chiselled-jawed, Brylcreemed hunk of a man, whose name was synonymous with early Hollywood.

'Didn't he turn out to be gay?' Holly asked, genuinely intrigued.

'Well, darling, he had to start batting for the other team eventually; he'd already shagged his way through every starlet in a ten-mile radius of the Studio. There was simply no one else left,' Elsie said drily. 'Of course, what the poor chap lacked in passion, he certainly made up for with physiology, if you catch my drift.'

Holly laughed at Elsie's attempts to be coy. She never had got the hang of a euphemism and tended to be oblique to the point of confusion or blunt to the point of offence. It was actually one of the things that Holly found so endearing about her. For all her polish and sophistication, deep down she could be a bit of a klutz and, for Holly, it gave her hope that her own clumsy ways need not be the end of the world.

'So, you mentioned a meeting?' Holly prompted, pleased to see that bossing Holly around and reliving her lost youth had brought some colour to Elsie's cheeks. 'Are you planning a reunion of dishy movie-stars, because I could pop home and get my camera . . .'

'Pish!' dismissed Elsie. 'I have no desire to see any of that lot again, thank you very much, especially with me looking half-dead and sounding like a lush. Actually, I have a commissioning editor from Heathergate Lorde coming to court me – well, my photographs probably – but either way, it's a step in the right direction, don't you think?'

Holly felt caught. She had no idea who Heathergate Lorde were, but it was clearly a big deal to Elsie and was at least taking her mind off next week's trip to the Stroke Unit; she hadn't mentioned it once since Holly had arrived and that was progress.

'Oooh, which editor?' she said in the end, hoping that Elsie would fill in the blanks, without the need to expose her own ignorance.

'Jeremy Farnsworth. You know, the one who published all those amazing coffee table books last year – they were everywhere. Beautiful hardbacks with the most amazing collections of ... Holly, darling, you've got that blank look on your face that you get when you're pretending you understand. Am I going too quickly for you?' Elsie's voice may not have been as distinct as before, but she still managed a hint of amusement as she teased her guest.

Reaching across the heaps of papers, Elsie uncovered a stunning slab of a book that had been published last year to enormous acclaim and equally enormous pre-orders. 'Imagine, little old me as part of *this* series.' She reeled off a list of names that sounded like the equivalent of Debrett's for Celebrities – only the timeless and legendary need apply, apparently.

'Wow. I mean, that's really ... Crikey,' said Holly.

'Eloquence indeed,' said Elsie, obviously enjoying her reaction. 'Maybe I won't hold you to being my Ghost Writer after all. But you will stay, won't you?'

Holly looked at her watch and hesitated. There was so much to do. Taffy would be at mini-rugby with the boys until lunch, but there was still groceries and laundry ...

'Holly Graham, do not say that you're considering missing this fabulous meeting for some pointlessly mundane job-list that will still be there tomorrow?'

Holly looked sheepish. 'I'm afraid that's exactly what I'm doing. I promised Taffy we could have a proper family Sunday tomorrow – a real day off. And I wanted to pop in on Lizzie too ... So really, that means the mundane stuff has to be done today.'

'I won't accept no for an answer, you do realise that?' Elsie said firmly and a little sulkily.

Holly laughed. 'I thought you were training me up to stop being a doormat and to say no more often?'

Elsie stamped her foot in frustration. 'I am. But not to me! You don't say no to me, Holly.'

Thankfully, even Elsie could see the funny side of their exchange, as Holly was unable to hold herself together any longer and dissolved into laughter.

'We could get Sarah to pop round to yours with a hoover and stock up the fridge while you're here,' wheedled Elsie, unwilling to admit defeat.

Holly fixed her with a very stern look. 'Elsie, your carer is here to help you. Poor Sarah already has her hands full, no doubt – you cannot use her as currency so that I'll drop everything when you want me to.'

'I pay her wages,' said Elsie. 'And I'm sure she wouldn't mind. Probably fed up of dealing with old farts like me. And please don't take offence, Holly, but I've been to your house recently, it's not as though the bar is set terribly high, is it, darling?' She grinned suddenly, in that unnerving way she often did when she knew she'd overstepped the mark.

Holding up her hands in defeat, she made a counter offer. 'Stay here for a bit, Holly, and help me cherry-pick the good bits and work out what to wear at least. I don't know how many times I'll get to meet this chap, but I'm pathetically keen to make a good impression. Without my voice on top form, I feel a bit like Superman without his powers.'

Elsie did make a valid point, Holly conceded. Yes, Elsie was beautiful and her eyes were indeed hypnotic, but it was the suggestive tones in her voice that had always been most persuasive. She had a knack for cajoling people into doing things they would never normally consider. It wasn't even flirtation, more a gradual seduction into her way of thinking that both sexes were powerless to avoid.

The very fact that Holly hadn't instantly rolled over and

agreed to stay was a case in point. Normally it would have been a moot argument the moment Elsie set her heart on what she wanted.

'No problem,' Holly agreed, mentally running through the contents of the freezer and wondering whether Taffy would find it amusing to play Ready Steady Cook with whatever ingredients she could muster. If she skipped the supermarket and concentrated on the laundry, she could still keep on track.

The tempting prospect of Sarah – the new behind-the-scenes superwoman of this household – whipping her life into shape was distracting for a moment before Holly's moral fibre reasserted itself.

'Let's have a look at these diaries, then,' she said. 'Am I going to need therapy after reading them, or are they mainly PG?'

Elsie thought for a moment. 'If you're feeling delicate, my darling girl, I'd give 1974 a miss. And '76 too. Maybe actually the whole of the '70s, to be fair. We'll read those another time, with wine,' she said firmly.

The hours flew by and in no time, the chaos that documented Elsie's life, loves and career was beautifully sorted and catalogued. Holly had nipped to the study and come back armed with box files, Post-its and a huge sheet of A3. Elsie may not have been terribly confident about meeting Jeremy Farnsworth, but at least now she was well prepared. She also had the most wonderful timeline scattered with salacious gems and nuggets that would surely be enough to seal the deal.

Holly sat on the end of the bed upstairs as Elsie changed into the second outfit she'd selected. 'Honestly, Elsie, the first one was lovely. Do please save some energy for the meeting.

He's not coming here to see what you look like, is he? He's coming to have a lively conversation. No point looking gorgeous if you've all the charisma of a dishrag.'

Elsie scowled. 'Dear girl, have I taught you nothing? Of course he's coming here to see what I look like. They're hardly going to want some saggy old granny promoting their Next Big Thing, are they? Dead or gorgeous, Holly, those are the only two options for a woman of my age. And before you start having a go, no, I haven't told them about the stroke. None of their bloody business.'

Holly looked unconvinced as she stepped forward to zip Elsie into a vintage Dior dress that probably cost more than Holly's annual wages.

'Tsk, when did you become such a doubting Desmond?' Elsie chided.

'Well, let's see – today's Saturday, so give or take, I'd say about three years now.' Holly shrugged. 'I'm getting better at recognising when I'm doing it though, so that's progress, isn't it?'

Elsie shook her head. 'Honestly Holly, I do wish you'd try and move on a little faster. Not everyone you lose from your life is a loss, you know. Milo's old news. And obviously, you'll be utterly devastated when I go – but that will be rather different. Because, well, I'm fabulous and he was rather a shit frankly.'

Holly gaped attractively as Elsie ran on with her train of thought, with little sensitivity or regard for Holly's reaction.

'On the bright side,' Elsie said, as if the thought had just occurred to her, 'if I *do* drop dead suddenly, they can always call it a commemorative edition.' The humour in that last comment was brittle and tight, clearly taking all of Elsie's considerable strength.

Holly impulsively drew her fragile frame into an enormous hug, just as she would one of her boys, when they were being wide-eyed and brave, a trembly bottom-lip being their Tell.

'Don't mess with the dress,' Elsie mumbled into Holly's shoulder and she reluctantly let go.

'Then don't joke about you going anywhere,' Holly managed.

'You can't even say it, can you?' Elsie said, desperate to reassert her upper hand. 'We all die sometime, Holly. I just would quite like a little more time, you know?'

'I know,' said Holly. 'But you are okay, Elsie,' she added quietly. 'You've had a bit of a scare, but with medication and diet, we can do so much these days . . . Please don't go frightening yourself unnecessarily.'

'Hmmm,' Elsie said, her face a mask. 'I'm not immortal, Holly. And I know what you're going to say – surely she saw this coming – but honestly, darling, I kept thinking old age wouldn't happen to me. So, let's just take these mini-stroke-thingies as a warning shot, shall we, and get a wriggle on and publish this bloody book?

'And,' Elsie continued, 'I'd genuinely rather go out early with a bang than live without my independence. Without my voice . . . Well,' she made an obvious effort to pull herself together, 'that's why I need this book deal. It will do more for my health than any amount of rat poison and low sodium what-not. It's my last chance, do you see, Holly? My last chance to have my say.'

It was Elsie who folded herself into Holly's arms then, apparently no longer worried about messing with the dress. 'What would I do without your wonderful advice though, Elsie? I mean, who else can get me into as much trouble as you have?' She was aiming for light teasing, but the fear was present in every word.

'Ah!' said Elsie, rallying herself. 'The perfect intro . . .' She bustled over to her desk and pulled out the most beautiful notebook. It was bound in the softest brown leather, a shoe-lace wrapping it closed, and the smell was pure Italy. 'I was going to leave this to you, but I think you should have it now. There's a few pages left – with a little luck maybe we'll have time to fill them?'

She handed Holly the notebook and left the room straight away, muttering about eyeliner and rouge. Holly slowly unwound the leather lace and the pages fell open from use.

Across each page, Elsie's beautiful, yet erratic handwriting wove a web of their conversations. All those pep talks, all those pointers, all those life lessons and pearls of wisdom: every one of them had been immortalised on paper. She slowly turned each page and realised that the book was not, as she'd first suspected, a diary or a draft of her book, but it was written just for Holly. Every page, every line, was written with Holly in mind, even her name thrown casually into the mix as though they were still chatting over a glass of Pimm's.

She turned to the flyleaf at the front of the book and smiled as she saw what Elsie had written:

In life, as in love, practice makes perfect
Ex

She pulled a tissue from her pocket and was about to reward herself with a bloody good cry, when Elsie came back in the room. 'Now don't go getting all soppy on me, you daft angel. Read it later, when you need a little pep talk.' She stopped for a second and hesitated before holding up a beautiful Diane von Furstenberg wrap dress that could only have been a vintage original. 'Now dry your eyes and put this and some slap on, would you? Jeremy Twonkington-Whatnot will be here any minute and I need you on form.'

'But, Elsie,' Holly protested, looking at her watch yet again, 'I told you I couldn't stay.'

Elsie shrugged. 'And I told you that I needed you today. I've already called Taffy and Sarah's nearly finished mucking out your house by now, I'm sure.'

'You sent Sarah anyway?' Holly asked, dumbfounded by Elsie's brazen lack of remorse, yet wondering why this actually surprised her. She hoped that Taffy and the boys were having fun. He'd said that he wanted Quality Time with them, after all – she could only hope that the quality didn't decrease in inverse proportion to the quantity.

Elsie sighed and shook her head. 'Of course I did, Holly. Honestly, darling,' she said, tossing the dress onto the bed and leaving the room with a laugh, 'I sometimes wonder whether you know me at all.'

Holly held the notebook tightly in her hand and thought of the thousands of photos downstairs, all of Elsie's secrets laid bare in her diaries. 'Well, if I don't now, I guess I will do by the time this book gets published,' she muttered, ambivalently admitting defeat and pulling off her jumper.

Chapter 29

Dan stood at the edge of the Market Place the following evening, his eyes watering and his sneezing reaching philharmonic proportions. His hay-fever was out of control, but serving a rather useful purpose – nobody questioned his red eyes, or his ever-present hanky. Perhaps this is what he should advise his patients, Dan wondered: if you're going to have a nervous breakdown, then do it during the hay-fever season and nobody will bat an eye-lid.

Of course, he reminded himself, he wasn't actually having a nervous breakdown, he was having a communications breakdown, off the back of a relationship breakdown. It was all very well Julia hesitating to make a decision about this London job and refusing to tell anyone about their break-up, but it threw Dan into an incredibly awkward position.

From a personal perspective, he knew the logic: if you love someone, set them free ... And there was no question in his mind that he had loved Julia, but the past tense was so revealing that he didn't need to stop and question his decision, only the fall-out.

From a work perspective, it was possibly harder – the brief from the Primary Care Trust had come through, outlining all the seminars and 'symbiotic learning opportunities' the team would be expected to offer as part of their Model Surgery status. So, if Julia did decide to stay, they had better find a common ground at work if nothing else.

'Oi, Wanker,' said Taffy affectionately as he ambled up alongside him and interrupted his train of thought. 'Shouldn't you be heading home rather than lurking about like a perv?'

Dan punched him on the shoulder in greeting, a little harder than normal, just to make up for the perv comment. Taffy rubbed his shoulder and frowned. 'What the hell are they trying to do to that goose?'

He pulled himself up onto the Cotswold-stone wall that Dan had co-opted as his vantage point and surveyed the chaos around them as Rupert, the local vet, and his team attempted to corral Gerald, the errant goose, out of the road and back down to the river bank.

'This is so much better than Netflix,' Dan said, tearing off some of his sausage roll for Taffy. 'Poor Gerald hasn't been the same since the duck race. He's been all defensive and grumpy.'

'Perhaps he's just defending his territory?' Taffy suggested. 'I feel a bit like that at our house sometimes.'

'Maybe he's henpecked and driven to distraction?' Dan countered revealingly. 'It would certainly account for his anger issues.'

Poor Gerald had been so named by the local school children, once his presence in the Market Place had become a daily event. He was frankly turning into a bit of a menace, terrorising anyone who walked along the river-side of the road and raising his enormous wing span as he hissed his displeasure.

They watched as Gerald bore down on Rupert, corralling him away from the river and Mrs Gerald's nest. Rupert, to his credit, turned tail and ran. He ended up hanging over the wall beside them, red-faced and panting. 'Bastard goose!' he spluttered. 'I'm going to have to shoot the little fucker if he doesn't relent.'

'Aw, don't be so hard on him,' Taffy countered. 'He's clearly having domestic issues. Besides, isn't that treason?'

'What?' said Dan, utterly confused.

'That's swans, Taffy,' said Rupert tiredly. 'They all belong to the Queen, so if you kill one, it's basically treason,' he clarified for Dan.

'Maybe that's why he's annoyed,' Taffy said with a straight face. 'He's out for equal billing . . .' He laughed at his own joke. 'See what I did there?'

Rupert and Dan caught each other's eye and, as one, made to push Taffy backwards off the wall. 'Enough with the puns already,' Rupert said, as he let Taffy go, just before he fell.

'Is a goose not basically the same as a swan, though?' Taffy asked. 'Not as a species, I mean, but when it comes to catching one?'

Dan stopped eating his sausage roll and stared at him. 'Have you been mucking about with the opiates?'

Taffy laughed. 'No, but don't let's pretend we haven't both been tempted this week. I mean, isn't there a swan wrangler or something on the Avon police team?'

Rupert nodded. 'There is, yeah. But it seems a bit crap that I can't get the job done without calling in reinforcements.'

'Alright,' said Taffy, 'you've persuaded me. Come on, Dan. You can help too – I mean, how hard can it possibly be?'

Incredibly hard, as it turned out. After an hour of approach and retreat, the three men were sweating in the evening sun and their good humour was in danger of evaporating. Gerald, as it turned out, was a high IQ kind of goose and seemed, according to Dan, to have received some sort of military training in the defensive arts.

Dan stood with his hands on his hips, chest heaving and his t-shirt soaked with sweat. The audience that had gathered in the garden of The Kingsley Arms to watch their attempts weren't really helping, insisting on cheering loudly at Taffy when he'd pulled his shirt off and laughing when Dan slipped in the inevitable goose-poo and landed on his backside.

Rupert caught up with them as they took a much-needed breather and the Major shouted them all a pint of cider. 'Taff, I don't mean to be personal, but what the hell is on your back?'

Taffy shrugged. 'I don't know, mud, sweat?' He craned over his shoulder to take a look, but Rupert simply snapped a photo on his phone and held up the screen: 'Cheer if you think I'm pretty' was highlighted in milky white letters against Taffy's golden tan.

Well that certainly explained the cheers he'd been getting this evening – and at home, for that matter … But how?

Dan quietly took a step back and prepared to make a run for it, a stupid grin on his face – this evening's lightness and stupidity being exactly what the doctor ordered. Of course, when he'd written the message in Factor 60 last week, as Taffy lay sunbathing, he'd never imagined it would show up so well. The fact that Taffy tanned so easily and deeply had been an added bonus. He stood poised, waiting for the penny to drop and then legging it out of the pub garden as Taffy gave chase, a pint of cider slopping in his hand.

Bizarrely the sight of two grown men haring through the Market Place, shouting rude names at each other and doubling over with stitches and laughter, succeeded where everyone else had failed. With one look of disdain over his shoulder, Gerald admitted defeat and took flight for the river.

A wall of cheers erupted from the pub garden, and Taffy – ever the showman – turned to take a bow.

'Aw,' he said to Dan, between heaving gasps of air, 'isn't that nice – they think I'm pretty.'

As the sun set over Larkford and the tower of the church was illuminated in red and gold, Dan felt his shoulders drop down to their normal position for the first time in weeks. He watched Taffy and Rupert bantering about cricket scores and the likelihood that the Larkford Rugby Club might even take down their nemesis Framley. All felt right with the world.

His conversation with Holly in the graveyard had really got him thinking. About his priorities. About the Model Surgery. About his mindfulness. He'd watched Holly with interest these last few months, as she'd tried to build on the Life Lessons that Elsie had shared with her. It was only when they'd spoken the other day though, that Dan had been able to see the parallels between them – it was all very well going through the motions, ticking the boxes, but with each passing week it got harder. Whether it was mindfulness for his own issues, or positivity for Holly's – this was not something to address in a day and Dan knew, to his cost, that these things only worked if you *actually* used them. Lived by them. Every day. Until it became a part of who you were.

He wondered how Taffy managed to walk his path so effortlessly. He made everything seem easy and his genuine affection and humour drew people to him, just as the smell of baking bread swelled the queue at The Deli every morning. He glanced over to see Taffy's eyes resting on him in concern.

'You okay?' Taffy mouthed across the table.

Dan nodded, distracted for a moment by the sight of poor Percy Lawson, with his wrist in a splint and an angry bruise on his face. A shadow of guilt passed over Dan for their sweepstake at work – it surely wasn't right to have their fun at their patient's expense. It was only a fleeting moment though, as Dan spotted the red BMW motorbike parked diagonally in front of the pub and the leathers that Percy was wearing – obviously his 'little scare' still hadn't been enough to put him off.

'Last one for me and then I should probably call it a night,' said Taffy, as Rupert climbed on to the wall and started to sing. 'Not sure I'm up to this on a school night anymore.'

Dan couldn't help but agree. He didn't need to stay out until the wee small hours to get his jollies – he'd had more fun this evening than he'd had in months, chasing a goose and letting his proverbial hair down. He might even manage a good night's sleep on the crappy bed above the pub tonight.

Jamie and Alice walked across the Market Place towards them, Coco obediently walking to heel and Alice looking delighted. It was incredibly sweet and Dan watched with interest, as Jamie occasionally stopped to interact with the little chocolate dog, even getting down on the verge on his hands and knees at one point.

'That's love, that is,' said Taffy. 'And he's certainly putting in the extra hours with our Alice.'

'And our Grace and our Lucy ...' Dan cut in shrewdly. 'The man is a walking lady-magnet.'

Taffy grinned. 'Well, luckily for us, he seems to have a way with little Coco too. He's certainly putting in the overtime to get her back on track.'

Dan watched as Jamie welcomed an ecstatic Coco into his arms, as they celebrated some dog-training milestone that was invisible to anyone watching. He didn't want to be churlish around Jamie; he was a good bloke. It just didn't help Dan's newly fractured self-esteem to have that much testosterone milling around The Practice three times a week and turning heads.

Marion and the Major stopped by their table on the way out, breaking Dan's train of thought. Spotting the basket of onion rings that had been almost completely demolished, Marion fussed over Dan's health and diet as she always had. 'Ooh and before I forget, Dr Carter,' she said, rummaging in her handbag, 'I found this at the market this morning and I thought to myself, I know who'd appreciate that . . .'

She pulled out a gaudy ceramic fish, carefully wrapped in loo roll, and pressed it into Dan's hand. 'You can add that to your whimsy collection now, Dr Carter.' She looked terribly pleased with herself as she did so and Dan tried hard not to catch Taffy's eye.

It had started out so simply, with each of the two doctors competing to buy each other the most hideous presents – Taffy's gift of a luminous blown-glass fish being the obvious winner. After that, all it had taken was the odd word from Taffy to their patients and suddenly Dan began receiving fish made of wood, wire, glass and pottery – a little thank you here, a birthday gift there.

As Marion wandered away to say good night to a friend, Dan turned to Taffy. 'I blame you for this. How do I tell everyone that I *don't* collect bloody fish?'

Taffy shrugged. 'I hate to say it, mate, but having been in your office lately, I think you need to accept the truth: If you have forty-five fish figurines, then at this point, you probably do.' He ducked the flying onion ring that bounced off his head and began to laugh at Dan's consternation.

'You do realise that this can work both ways?' Dan said, a hint of retribution creeping into his voice.

'Yup,' said Taffy evenly, 'but *you* told everyone I collected Star Wars stuff, and I've been flavour of the month with the twins ever since. Up your game, man.'

Dan looked up, a witty retort freezing on his lips, at the sight of the Major's puce face approaching him. The old boy was clutching at his chest and his words came out in a wheeze, 'I do hate to be a bore, lads, but I rather think I might be having a heart attack.' Even in his obvious distress, he remained courteous in the extreme.

He slumped down beside them and Dan quickly dialled for an ambulance while Taffy checked his vitals. Taffy looked up, confused by all the normal readings, and checked them again. 'Er, Major, tell me again where the pain is?'

Marion had rushed over by this point and her face was ashen. 'Are you getting those pains again, Peregrine?' she said in a no-nonsense tone of voice that seemed oddly unsympathetic given the circumstances. She rummaged once more in her enormous handbag and shook out a tablet into his hand. Before Dan or Taffy could intervene, she'd deposited it into the Major's mouth with instructions to 'chew that'.

She sat back on her heels and gave the doctors a judgemental look. 'I suppose one of you bought him a cider, did you?'

'Oh, don't go on at the lads, Marion. They're good boys,' the Major managed. He sat up a little taller, rotated his shoulder back and let forth the most enormous belch. 'Scuse me,' he said formally.

Marion stood up and glared at Dan and Taffy as the ambulance's sirens could be heard echoing down from the Bath road. 'Honestly, you two – have you never seen our Peregrine after a pint of fizzy cider? Bugger of a heartburn, granted, but it'll take more than a pint of Scrumpy to finish that one off.

Still,' she relented, taking in their stricken expressions, 'better safe than sorry, eh?'

As the paramedics parked up and ran over to give the Major a check-over – just to be sure – Dan and Taffy slipped back into the growing shadows.

'Maybe one more pint?' Taffy suggested, by way of diffusing the awkwardness that had settled over their lovely evening.

Dan just nodded. Marion's capable and firm understanding of her husband had left him feeling oddly unsettled. Holly and Taffy had it. Hattie and Lance had it.

And whilst Dan wasn't really sure what 'it' was; he did know one thing – he and Julia most clearly did not.

And keeping their break-up a secret wasn't allowing either of them to move forward.

Suddenly, it felt like the most pressing thing in his world. Even if it involved the fight that was long overdue and the cross words that were bubbling into his head with alarming regularity, it was time to talk to Julia.

Chapter 30

On the other side of town, Julia stood in the doorway to the Gatehouse in haggard disbelief. Heels swinging from one hand, she steadied herself against the doorframe with the other. Her mother was lying on the sofa, cocooned in Julia's favourite cashmere throw, a dribble of vomit on her chin and the wrought-iron wastepaper basket wedged within arm's reach.

She rubbed her eyes exhaustedly and wondered what her mother's excuse would be this time and, more to the point, how she would try to justify this latest fall off the wagon. After a hellishly long day filming, she just didn't have the emotional reserves that she needed to cope with this. She could only hope that her shame had been limited to these four walls and not the whole town.

She turned, fake smile firmly fixed in place, and waved into the darkness at Quentin's departing headlights. His idea – the whole wining and dining persuasion routine. She couldn't be sure whether it had made any difference to her decision-making process though, as she honestly had no idea what to do for the best. Larkford or London? Fight for Dan or run away? And where did her mother fit in to all of this?

She walked into the sitting room and the combined aroma of whisky, vomit and urine made her heave. A rush of bile hit the back of her throat, all the memories of her childhood rushing in to overwhelm her; the child within her wanting to stamp her foot and shout, 'It's not fair!' She'd worked so hard to build a relationship and a home here, but her screwed-up family seemed determined to contaminate that too.

She stumbled back to the kitchen and filled a glass with Volvic from the fridge, trying not to cry. It was one thing to feel vulnerable, it was quite another to show it. She tore at the cuticles around her nails with her teeth, nervously running scenarios and conversations in her head as she stared out of the kitchen window.

A gentle knock at the back door made her stiffen, hoping her silence might force whoever it was to leave. Instead she heard the sound of a key turning in the lock as Dan's voice called out quietly, 'Only me.'

She flew to the doorway, catching the heavy oak door before it could swing open and reveal the chaos inside. She hovered uncertainly then, her face only inches from Dan's and with no chance to wipe away the streaks of mascara from her tears.

'Oh Jules,' Dan said, with heartfelt sympathy. 'Don't do this. Don't shut yourself away and cry. Please.'

For a moment, she wanted to laugh at his immediate assumption that the tears were for him, for their shared heart-break. She didn't know how to tell him that with everything else going on, their break-up had been stuck firmly in her peripheral vision while other demons shouted louder.

'Can I come in?' he asked politely.

She shook her head. 'I don't think that's a good idea. It's late and we've already said everything there is to say.' She paused, reviewing their last conversation at the launch party. 'You can't carry on, remember. And I don't blame you, Dan. I know I'm not easy.'

He stepped forward and even as Dan's warm arms slid around her waist, her head automatically sought its resting place against his chest. There was nowhere on earth she felt more at peace, but for Julia it still wasn't enough. It wasn't enough to ease the constant hunger in her for more – she didn't honestly know what more meant, but she knew that it wasn't enough.

'You okay?' he said gently.

She shook her head, the softness of his shirt absorbing her tears, yet again, words eluding her.

They stood there in silence for a moment, the warmth of his body slowly filtering through to her. She hadn't realised until that moment that she'd been violently shivering – that hideous uncontrollable reaction you get when you've pranged the car unexpectedly.

She knew Dan was the nominated PTSD sufferer in their relationship, but for the first time, she wondered whether it was something one could have by degrees. This extreme emotional reaction to finding her mother in this state in her home was not normal by any stretch of the imagination. Neither of them spoke, as he slowly took her icy fingers in his warm hands.

There were no questions, no urgent requests as to what on earth had provoked this reaction, although she knew that Dan had every right to do both of those things. He just held her and, in that moment, she wondered whether just maybe she could bring herself to commit to the life he wanted: she didn't yet know, but she was beginning to think perhaps she could at least try.

The sound of retching and vomit splattering on the flag-stone floor wrenched both of them from their reverie. Julia shuddered with repulsed disgust.

She pulled back from Dan, breaking their intimacy and her train of thought. Who was she kidding? She didn't get to have a happy ever after and it was time she grew up and acknowledged that.

'I think you should leave,' she said, her voice entirely devoid of emotion. 'It was nice of you to come and I appreciate that, but I think you should leave.' She pushed at his chest until he took a small pace backwards and she made to close the door.

Dan hesitated for a moment, rebuffed and hurt, and she could understand why.

Her heart was crying out to thank him, reassure him, to have the conversation they both so clearly needed to find closure or even to agree to another chance. Her head, however, had switched into self-preservation mode. She'd done this particular shift too many times before. As the door slammed shut, she let out a tiny sob before the habitual tightening in her face turned her expression into a mask. She reached under the sink for the rubber gloves and the Dettol, poured another glass of water for her mother and walked into the sitting room and away from the man on her doorstep who, for a brief moment, had offered her a different life.

She wondered whether she should just have let him in. Maybe it was better that he saw her reality now, warts and all, before romantic notions got the better of him and he got all misty eyed about bringing another little drunk into the world. Genetics did have a habit of being passed down after all . . .

*

Julia watched her mother fitfully sleep – the hours of being passed out cold had evolved into patchy naps, punctuated by intermittent bouts of vomiting and crying.

She felt cold, despite the blanket around her shoulders and she shivered. The heavy dread had settled in her own stomach at around 3 a.m. and now, with dawn beginning to break outside the windows, she allowed herself a moment of honesty. Silently weeping, she struggled to admit, even to herself, the source of her grief.

It wasn't, as Dan might assume, that she was upset about their break up, or even worried about her mother, perhaps fearful of what would happen next – although all these things were also true. What gnawed at Julia's soul this morning was the hollow, empty feeling that overwhelmed her when she looked at her mother. Sure, there were wisps of emotion around the edges of her consciousness – fear, disgust, defeat – but the tears stemmed from a deeper source. Julia rubbed at her eyes in frustration as she struggled to acknowledge the truth: when she looked at her mother now, there was a blank space where the affection used to be. It was upsetting and liberating in equal measure.

There was no love, no shared emotional bond tying them together. It was all gone. Tested beyond reasonable belief, with no happy memories to call up, to reignite the fire. There were simply decades of abuse and drunkenness and guilt. Dear God, there had been so much guilt, Julia felt as though she might suffocate under its pall. Add together a Catholic education and an alcoholic mother and it was actually a wonder that Julia was able to function on a daily basis at all. The sudden void and exhaustion as all of that left her, made Julia want to crawl into bed and sleep for a year, just to wallow in this nothingness. In itself so cold and horrific, but yet still so much better than what she had been living with before.

She looked down in horror, as a sharp pain bit through her finger, where she had systematically been shredding her cuticles with her teeth as the hours ticked by. She hadn't even been aware that she was doing it, although the metallic taste of blood in her mouth now registered beside the tangy saltiness on her lips.

'He seems like a lovely young man, your Dan,' said Julia's mother out of nowhere, pushing herself up from horizontal and wincing at the jarring pain that was clearly shooting through her temples right now.

'He is,' replied Julia coldly.

Her mother looked shifty, obviously annoyed that her usual cocktail of inveiglement and insincerity was not having its usual guilt-inducing effect.

A sneer lifted one side of her thin, once beautiful, mouth. 'I imagine he'll be in trouble for seeing all your filthy secrets, won't he, Joo?'

Julia shuddered slightly at the nickname and the accuracy of her statement, pulling the blanket tighter around her. Her mother was a professional at this part of the proceedings. Deflecting blame, stirring discord, undermining choices – these were her mother's long-honed weapons of choice. She did her work well.

'You can tell me yourself, or I can fill in the usual blanks, but it might be easier if you just stopped playing games. What happened this time? And I'm not interested in another dose of bullshit.' Julia caught herself before her rant could escalate further.

'Your father called. He's leaving me,' said her mother in the lightest of whispers. 'I don't think I can do this without him.'

The voice was vulnerable, but the gaze was defiant. 'Please help me, Joo. I need someone to help me, if your dad's not going to be around.'

Julia stood up abruptly and dialled her father's mobile number, with little regard to the earliness of the hour. She'd expected it to ring out, as he blearily emerged from sleep, or perhaps to ping straight through to voicemail. She had certainly not been prepared for the automated message that the number dialled was no longer in service. He hadn't just left her mother and all her problems behind. It rather looked as though the ever-patient man from Dorset had left her too.

Coldly immune to the heaving and retching behind her, Julia walked to the back door and pulled it open. The cold air made the raw skin around her fingernails sting with a sudden intensity, paling by comparison with the searing wrench in her chest.

Her life here in Larkford, so carefully crafted and protected, was supposed to have been her salvation. A fresh start. She looked down the driveway into the town below her, the Market Place already starting to come alive with the farmers' market. She imagined the pity that would replace hard-won respect in her patients' eyes . . . Her mind running on, she saw consequence after consequence of letting her mother back into her life on a permanent basis and none of them were good. There was no way that she'd be able to keep all this a secret in a town this small, especially when she had a film crew on her tail for half of every week.

She'd be back to trawling the bars at closing time, looking for her mother to bring her home, or worse, bailing her out yet again. When her mother fell off the wagon, she did tend to take it to extremes. Julia simply wasn't sure that The Kingsley

Arms was ready for a drunken pensioner who thought she was Brigitte Bardot.

How did this work, she wondered.

If parents care for children and provide love and nurturing and support, it only seems fair for the children to step up when the roles are reversed, surely? But what if there was no tit for tat – if the child in question had been abandoned from the very beginning, clothed and fed, but emotionally starved and ignored – what then? Was the familial contract still valid?

She was to all intents and purposes an orphan with living parents, she decided – all the obligations and hassles and none of the benefits.

'He ran off with that blousy Do-Gooder from the town-hall, if you're wondering?' her mother said, when Julia eventually came back in to the kitchen to find warmth.

'Who?' asked Julia distractedly, flicking on the kettle and noticing her mother already had a mug in her hands, having relocated to the kitchen table. A strip of paracetamol lay beside her.

'The woman who worked on reception. Apparently they would have their little getting-to-know-you-chats while I went to that AA meeting your dad insisted I went to. Well, I guess we know his motivation now, don't we? Less of the sober wife, more of a quick feel of the Double D-cups.' She all but spat the last sentence, but the pain in her eyes was too vivid to hide. 'Screw him, eh, Joo? She'd need to be a bloody saint to put up with his moods.' She laughed. 'We'll be alright together, you and me? You won't let your old mum down, not my Julia, eh? You know I wouldn't feel safe on my own.'

'You can't stay here,' Julia said automatically, thinking that if anyone in this scenario had been a saint, it was her dad for the last forty years. Maybe he deserved a bit of happiness in his twilight years, but did he have to shaft his daughter quite so comprehensively in the process?

'Course I can, love.'

'No. You can't, because I don't want you to. There is no place in my life here for you. You have to go home. There's no place here for you.'

Julia's mother paused, almost as though recalibrating her approach. She carried on then, deliberately misunderstanding. 'I won't take up much space and it's not as though I've got a lot of clobber with me. And,' she eyed Julia carefully, before playing her trump hand, 'your beau didn't seem to think it would be a problem, not when he invited me to stay. Maybe I could help? You both work long hours – I could get the food in and cook?'

Now there was a joke if ever she'd heard one – throughout Julia's childhood, the family had mainly existed on Fray Bentos pies, Findus Crispy Pancakes and, if they were lucky, a dented tin of peaches with evaporated milk. Until she was fifteen, Julia hadn't known that stewing meat didn't always come in a can. She doubted whether her mother would know how to sear a tuna steak if her life depended on it, let alone roast a chicken or prepare a salad. She doubted very strongly, whether her mother had ever spent the weekly grocery money on anything other than vodka and fags. 'I think we both know that's a joke,' she managed, 'and Dan has nothing to do with this.' She didn't feel the need to share the fact that he didn't love her anymore; her mother would only take it as an invitation. 'This is about you and me and too little, too late. You don't get to call in your chips now.'

It was like a red rag to a bull and Julia's mother leered forward, with both hands planted aggressively on the kitchen table. 'Oh really? Are we actually going to play *this* game, Miss High and Mighty? You turned out alright, didn't you? Got you to medical school, didn't we, your dad and me? Only to be expected that you'd be an ungrateful little snob, I suppose. But we didn't bring you up to think you were better than us.'

'You didn't bring me up, you dragged me up and then dragged me down,' said Julia with no emotion in her voice, just an echoing tiredness of having had this conversation a million times before. 'Do you have any idea what it was like growing up like I did? Never knowing how each day would end? Scraping you and your vomit off the floor? Never having friends round in case you were on one of your binges? You turning up drunk to the school play and trying to kiss my English teacher at parents' evening? And that's if we put aside the constant put-downs, the screaming, the rage ... I have got the life I have *despite* you, not because of you.' The only hint of emotion came in that final comment, as Julia's voice wobbled slightly. She looked at her mother and it was like looking at a stranger. 'I won't have you here.'

Her mother sipped at her coffee mug slowly, not looking up. 'I don't think you have a choice, Joo-Bear. After all, what would that lovely TV production company think, if they knew their beautiful TV doc was a heartless bitch who abandoned her mother when her good-for-nothing father walked out after forty years of marriage, hmm?' She stood up and drained her mug. 'I think I need a shower and then we can sort out that bed in the study for tonight. The one your lovely chap said was mine for as long as I need it. If I'm moving in for a bit, you can't expect me to stay on the sofa-bed.' She leaned in to Julia and the wine fumes wafted over her face in warm gusts with each word. 'And maybe the apple doesn't fall that far from the tree, eh, Joo? Nice drop of Pinot you've got hidden in the back of the fridge there.' She pushed the empty mug across the table and the dregs of wine in the bottom were clear to see. 'Notice you don't mind a drop of the hard stuff yourself sweetheart.'

Chapter 31

Holly turned to Taffy and pulled a face. 'Good luck.'

He shook her hand. 'You too.'

As one, they leaned forward and pushed open the double doors to The Practice. It was only one hour since Julia's e-mail had popped up in their inboxes, not so much an invitation as an early-morning summons. 'And you have no idea what she wants to talk to us about?' Taffy clarified.

Holly frowned. 'There's so much going on,' she hedged, 'it could be anything.'

They walked through to the doctors' lounge, the whole building eerily quiet at this hour and wondering why they needed a meeting before the start of the working day and what was so urgent it had required them to deliver the twins to Lizzie's house, still dozing in their pyjamas.

The large pine table in the lounge had been scrubbed clean and cleared of all magazines, quizzes and the Rubik's Cube that had been tormenting them all for weeks. Instead there were neatly printed out agendas, six coffees from The Deli and a platter of Danish pastries. Julia sat at the head of the table, with Grace already seated beside her. 'Come in, come in. I'm so glad you could come,' Julia said, on her feet and greeting them as though to a family wedding.

Holly and Taffy exchanged glances. Julia's normally immaculate appearance had clearly taken somewhat of a battering and she now looked an awful lot like Taffy's mad Aunt Ivy. He gave her a look that said, 'See, I told you this meeting was because Julia's finally gone off her rocker.'

Dan pushed open the door behind them and the pad-padding of tiny paws followed him, Alice virtually silent in her ballet pumps. Poor girl, thought Holly, she looked utterly discomfited and Holly's own frustration at Julia's dramatics was in danger of reaching critical mass. Taffy, attuned to her wavelength, hurriedly pressed a coffee into her hand and plonked an apricot Danish on a plate in front of her. 'Never murder a colleague on an empty stomach,' he murmured under his breath and Holly had to swallow hard not to choke with laughter. He gave her knee a squeeze under the table, a kind of Morse code SOS that made her smile.

'You're probably wondering why I asked you all to come?' Julia began.

'Have you been at the Agatha Christie again?' Grace said, unusually irritable. 'I'll save you some time – it was the exhausted Practice Manager in the doctors' lounge with a scalpel – the jury will exonerate her, based on the hours she'd spent on Excel spread-sheets last night and the fact that she's had three hours sleep!'

Everyone around the table was shocked into silence. Grace looked up and saw their faces. 'Oh,' she said. 'Did I say all that out loud?' She appeared to be on the verge of tears and pushed back her chair as though to leave.

Dan, who had been sitting beside her, turned swiftly and took her hand. 'Sit down, Gracie. Let's have this meeting and then we can talk about the overtime that's driving you to distraction.' He handed her his coffee to supplement her own and Holly noticed Julia twitch at the intimacy of the gesture.

'Right,' Julia said. 'I know we've all been juggling our own personal issues a little of late, but I thought it might be time for a little frank conversation? I know what *I* think our biggest challenges are, but let's go around the table and start having an honest dialogue about our concerns, shall we?

'Who'd like to start?' she challenged. Holly deliberately kept her gaze averted, this open platform to have a moan was all well and good, and might conceivably be productive, but she was deeply concerned that once she started, she wouldn't stop.

'Taffy?' Julia said, putting him on the spot, as he'd accidentally managed to catch her eye whilst eyeballing the last *pain aux raisins*.

'Right then,' said Taffy, his Welsh twang incredibly pronounced under pressure. 'Well, I'll kick off by saying that Grace is carrying too heavy a load on the admin front, this Model Surgery bollocks is causing all sorts of nervousness amongst the team, we're very worried about poor little Coco, Quentin is telling all the staff that you're leaving, we've loads of money raised from the Health in the Community launch but no clear plan how to spend it, and you and Dan bickering like teenagers is really starting to piss everybody off.' He paused for breath and looked around the table. 'Did I miss anything?' he drummed his fingers repetitively on the table and Holly had to use all her willpower not to reach out and clamp his hand still.

Silence.

Alice tentatively raised a hand. 'Do I really need to be here, only this seems like it might be a partners' meeting . . .'

Holly couldn't help but agree. It was one thing for the four of them to squabble behind the scenes, it was quite another for poor Alice to be exposed to their petty rivalries and resentments.

Grace cleared her throat. 'Actually, Alice, if I may, I think it's a good idea we both stay. Better to hear things from the horse's mouth, I often find.' She gaped unattractively for a moment. 'Not that I'm calling you a horse, Julia!'

To everyone's intense surprise, Julia burst out laughing. 'This is brilliant. We should have done this months ago. All this crap—' she enunciated the 'p' to perfection and sat back in her chair. 'Okay then, let's start working the issues.

'May I start?' she looked to Dan for his support and Holly knew then what Julia was doing – she was hiding the head-line. 'It's true that Quentin has offered me a job, but it is incredibly unprofessional of him and premature to tell anyone that I intend to accept the position. I would welcome your patience while I decide what to do and I can promise you it will not be a decision I take lightly.'

Holly frowned. Julia was sounding more and more like a politician or TV spokesperson and less and less like herself. She wanted to be cross with her partner for selling out, but instead Holly found herself concerned.

Julia had carried on talking all this time, filling in the details of the job offer and how it would likely affect them all, should she choose to accept it. 'We also wanted to tell you all together, that Dan and I have sadly, but respectfully, chosen to part ways in our personal life, but that we are confident that our friendship means that this will have little impact on our working relationship.'

To be fair, thought Holly, there was very little 'we' involved in that statement, as Dan was looking just as surprised as the others around the table. Taffy turned to stare at her in shock, narrowing his eyes as he realised that, for Holly at least, this was hardly breaking news. 'You knew?' he mouthed at her.

She nodded, hoping that he wouldn't be furious.

He looked incredibly irritated for a fleeting moment, before nodding his approval, presumably grateful that Dan had found somebody he felt able to talk to.

Dan spoke up then. 'We wanted to let the dust settle a little,' he glanced at Julia, 'make sure we were completely happy with our decision, so please forgive us if there was a little delay in sharing the news.' He looked straight at Taffy.

'Well,' said Taffy, trying to lighten the atmosphere, 'at least we've got one or two other things to focus on, rather than whether you two are going to have another lovers' tiff in the stock room.' He grinned at Julia. 'The things I've heard through the air vents to my office! So take note, young Alice, if you and Jamie are looking for a little alone time, there's no such thing as privacy around here!'

'Taffy!' she protested, on the spot and embarrassed. 'Besides, I reckon it's Grace we should be talking to,' Alice deflected, 'Jamie's rather fallen for her chocolate Hobnobs.'

Holly sat back in her chair, drinking her coffee and watching the meeting descend into chaos around her. She would have to have been blind to miss the grumpy expression on Dan's face, but perhaps she was the only one to have noticed when it began.

She looked over at Julia to find her glowering at Grace and quickly realised, maybe not.

'I'd like to talk about the Model Surgery,' Holly interrupted loudly. 'I'd like to talk about the balance of give and take. And actually I'd like to discuss a more proactive approach. If they've never made this nomination before, then I don't believe we have to simply accept their demands or their terms. Obviously,' she cast a glance at Alice, 'we don't want to jeopardise the perks and benefits of the situation and we are already committed, but I think we can all agree that taking time away from our patients, or indeed running our Practice Manager into the ground is hardly a long-term solution.'

'Hear, hear,' said Grace whole-heartedly, before hurriedly shutting her mouth. 'I just meant to say, well, I agree. But I really do want to be your liaison person, so please don't take it away from me altogether.'

Sitting around the table, batting ideas back and forth, with Grace pulling contracts and paperwork like magic from her Big Green Folder, they achieved more in the name of unity than they had in the months before. It was ironic in a way, thought Holly, as she scribbled a few items of note onto her agenda, that it was Julia – the most divisive and opinionated out of all of them– that had been the one to get them around the table.

She couldn't have been more delighted to hear Dan championing some of the concerns she had raised on the bench the other morning. He looked over at her and gave a supportive wink. She sat back, happy for once to let someone else take the lead.

'For what it's worth,' said Taffy, 'if we're going to discuss the local funding for the Health in the Community Scheme, I'd like to make a suggestion. We can control the education and mobile clinic budget, but I think we should set aside a certain amount and let the residents of Larkford nominate a worthy cause, what do you say? Can we take a look at the Big Picture?'

Holly took a deep breath. Every time Taffy uttered the phrase 'Big Picture', she could hear his pompous brother's voice in her head and it felt like nails on a blackboard. He obviously had no idea how often he said it, or how it undermined his credibility in Holly's eyes.

'Strike one for democracy!' said Dan, oblivious. 'As long as it doesn't involve another slave auction. I don't envy Taffy having to spend a day with blousy Betsy Harrington. She'll be wanting to get her money's worth out of you, mate!'

'Living in fear, mate. Living in fear.' said Taffy with feeling. 'Still, she's got six months to call in her docket. Maybe she'll have forgotten by then? Any Alzheimer's in her family? Degenerative diseases?' He looked around the table hopefully.

Julia shook her head. 'So, then, Alice . . .'

Alice looked like a rabbit caught in the headlights for a moment. 'Yes?' she said tentatively.

'What can we do to help with Coco?'

Holly looked up, jolted from her own reflections and caught unawares by the fact that Julia had even noticed there was a problem.

Alice shrugged. 'Bear with us for a bit? I know it must be annoying, but Jamie's doing everything he can, so it might be a case of wait and see?'

Holly leaned forward. 'Don't forget to get that list of names together for me. We can have a look and see if there's a common link? It could be something as simple as undiagnosed diabetes . . .'

Alice nodded gratefully. 'Now that would be great – well, not for them obviously, but for Coco.'

Grace scribbled another note on the points of action plan she had volunteered to type up and circulate. 'Just one thing,' she said, looking from Julia to Dan. 'I know it's not easy, but

I think the rest of the staff would prefer to be told about your, er, new situation, rather than hear it as gossip? Even a round-robin e-mail? The nurses sometimes feel as though they aren't really in the heart of the team and, to be honest, meetings like this might feed in to that?'

Julia looked appalled at the notion, but Dan was clearly not planning on letting her off easily. 'Rock-Paper-Scissors?' he suggested.

Holly stepped outside into the morning sunshine and checked her watch. Her entire body clock had been thrown out of sync by the mad morning rush to get here, but she couldn't deny it had been the most productive hour they had spent on the admin front in weeks. And they had Julia to thank!

Taffy wrapped his arms around her shoulders, the air still carrying a chill until the warmth of the day banished every drop of dew. 'Well, that was a bit surreal. And, you know, even though we've all been joking about it for months, I still can't believe Dan and Julia are really over. They're like Romeo and Juliet, aren't they? All passion and squabbling, but can't be apart?'

Holly turned to face him. 'Nah, they were star-crossed lovers, remember? These two are more Elizabeth Taylor and Richard Burton – can't live with each other—'

'Can't live without each other,' Taffy finished. 'Although I am thinking that, if that's your go-to reference, you might be spending far too much time with Elsie!'

'You're probably right,' Holly agreed, 'but there's just so much to be done over there. Elsie seems to have bewitched this publishing chap into thinking all his Christmases have come at once. And I have to confess, Taffs, some of her photos are – well – they're pretty sensational.' She paused for a moment. 'But actually, even if it all comes to nothing, I still think it's good for her to have a focus, don't you? Rather than lying in bed and dwelling on her health?'

He nodded, obviously torn. 'It's a tricky balance. Medically, the rest might actually do her recovery more good . . .'

'But psychologically?' Holly countered. 'There has to be something for keeping her engaged and sane.'

'Well, I admire the sentiment, but this is Elsie we're talking about,' he teased her.

Holly swatted at him, as Billy, the newspaper delivery boy, performed a perfect skid to a halt beside them on his bike and thrust a bundle of tabloids and broadsheets into Taffy's arms. 'All yours, Dr Jones. And the missus there, looking rather fit in the *Daily Mail*, we all reckon. Plus, you know, Dr Channing in that little skirt – phwoar!' He gave an adolescent chuckle and scooted off on his bike.

Holly and Taffy scrambled amongst the heap of papers to pull out the *Daily Mail* and there it was on the front-page banner. 'The way forward – the Face of the NHS' with a tiny headshot of Julia beside it. Page 14–15 promised further details.

Spreading out the pages on the front wall in the car park, Taffy and Holly were momentarily stunned. A huge picture from the Health in the Community launch party dominated the page – Holly, Taffy and Dan deeply engrossed in conversation, looking friendly, approachable and amused, while Julia hovered uncertainly at the edges, looking rather like the grown-up at the kids' table. The publicity shot from her TV show gave an altogether different perspective on Julia Channing MD though, not least the sheer length and shapeliness of her legs.

The headline was – 'This is The Face of The NHS. And

this is their Model Practice. No bosses, just teamwork. Find out what it means to you and your healthcare.'

'So they went ahead with their PR thing early, then,' said Taffy drily.

As Holly read through the piece under her breath, she couldn't help but think how ironic it was that, on the very day that more than five million Britons were reading all about their 'very modern approach to medicine' and their wonderful teamwork, two of those team members, not to mention the newly anointed Face of The NHS, were inside working out how to tell the team they were finished.

'Right then,' said Taffy, 'we'd better go and spread the glad tidings.'

Grace looked up as they walked in the door, 'The phone's been ringing off the hook. Apparently we're in all the papers this morning!' She clocked the bundle in Taffy's hand. 'As you've already seen.' She stood up and smoothed her hair behind her ears. 'We've got ten minutes until the first patient – gather the troops.'

Within moments they were all assembled back around the kitchen table and Holly felt the first wave of caffeine jitters surge through her tired body – and she still had a full clinic to get through.

'Right then,' said Taffy, taking charge. 'It looks like this story is everywhere. So, in the good news column, the Health in the Community Scheme has had a real shot in the arm and our communist approach to medicine has received mixed reviews.'

'It's not a communist approach – it's teamwork,' said Dan through gritted teeth.

'Not . . .' flourished Taffy,' according to the *Daily Mirror*!'

Dan and Julia were deliberately avoiding each other's gaze,

but they both looked up at that little gem. 'Seriously?' Julia exclaimed. 'I'm a communist now, am I? Perhaps they'd like to do a photo shoot of me in a bikini next to a sodding Trabant next?'

Taffy grinned, seemingly unfazed by the multitude of tensions in the room. 'I wouldn't say that in front of a journalist or a marketing executive, Jules. They might just think it's a brilliant idea.'

Dan slammed his fist on the table. 'Could you stop arsing about and keep your head in the game for just sixty seconds? We have a problem here. Actually a hundred bloody problems here, but let's focus on the ones we can do something about.' He glared at Julia then and she, to her credit, did not bite.

'Let's just remind ourselves too, that whatever may have been going on here for the last few days,' Taffy interrupted sternly, 'this is something we wanted. Publicity we knowingly and actively courted. Raising the profile of the Health in the Community programme? Getting the additional funding as a Model Practice? Starring in a TV show, anyone? Don't go getting all hypocritical because it's caught you on the hop and you don't like your photo, alright?'

He shook the *Telegraph*'s less sensationalised piece at Dan by way of explanation. 'This is fresh from *our* press release, that *we* wrote. You can't ask for more than that. Okay, so the *Sun* seems to think we all live together as a "couple" in a commune, but that's just media hype and people know it.'

Holly leaned forward, rummaging through the decimated papers for the *Sun*. 'Are we really a couple?' she laughed, hoping there was a photo to boot. That level of silliness took all the pressure off, as far as she was concerned.

Taffy and Dan just grinned, their momentary spat already forgotten. Julia was being remarkably quiet.

'It's alright for you to joke, but do you know what happens to people that the media put on a pedestal?' she said eventually, her exhausted and measured tone making all of them stop in their tracks. 'They pull you down, with whatever dirt they can find.'

Holly immediately felt flippant and gauche. Of course Julia's media career would make her see things differently. Holly had just been relieved that their extra funding for new staff now seemed to be confirmed in black and white in a quote from the local Primary Care Trust and it might give them some leverage when it came to negotiating their deal. Well, also that she had her eyes open in the photographs they'd chosen. Take away the threat of further Milo-offspring coming out of the woodwork and she could almost convince herself that she was relatively relaxed about the whole thing.

Dan and Julia glowered at each other and Holly had that awful feeling when you know you're out of the loop on something big. '*Is* there a particular skeleton you're worried about, Jules?' she asked gently, wondering – and not for the first time – whether getting back together with Dan hadn't put the brakes on Julia's personal growth. It had all looked so very promising at one point – and Holly had felt a real connection growing between them. She did not feel that this morning.

Out of nowhere, Julia burst into heaving, sobbing tears. It was so unexpected that they all froze. It was somewhere up there with Kate Middleton jumping on the table and doing the Can-Can, right on the scale of things nobody would have thought possible.

'Errr,' managed Taffy, the sight of female tears enough to throw him into complete disarray. 'Shall I give you guys some space?' he offered, the desperation to be released from the room writ large on his face.

'No, it's fine,' wailed Julia. 'I'll be fine in a second.' The tears continued to flow and Holly began to wonder whether there was about a decade's worth just pent up and waiting for liberation. It seemed like an over-reaction to a slightly dodgy photo.

Dan had cycled through a variety of expressions by the time he decided to just give the girl a hug. Starting at aghast, via overwhelmed, panicked and exhausted, he'd eventually settled on affectionate and supportive. He cradled Julia to his chest and whispered into her hair.

After five incredibly awkward minutes that felt more like fifteen and during which Holly realised she didn't really know Julia half as well as she thought she did, Dan spoke up, 'Guys, I think you need to know what's going on.'

Julia wiped her nose on the immaculate sleeve of her blouse and sniffed. Holly tried hard not to gasp out loud at this ludicrously uncharacteristic display.

Julia's eyes never once left Dan's face as he gently and tactfully filled the others in on Candace's behaviour of late. It was not as though hearing about Julia's mum's taste for alcohol was new news; it was more that the scale of the problem was clearly larger than they had been led to believe. Julia was clever like that – she told people just enough information, so that they thought they knew everything.

In terms of their friendship, Holly decided, it was like dealing with an iceberg, where the vast majority lay unseen beneath the surface. It was not her moment to feel aggrieved, though; it was time that they all rallied around their friend in her hour of need.

Julia looked at them blankly as they offered their support. 'I don't understand. Why would you want to get involved? It's a train wreck.'

'Well, I think,' said Taffy, 'that you and Dan are far too close to the situation. You can't have any objectivity about what she needs medically and until she's ready to look for help then there is a chance that this will make a great story.'

Julia began to sob again. 'What if someone sends a reporter to the Gatehouse looking for me? What if they get pictures of her instead? She'd be utterly mortified, to have her dirty laundry exposed in public.'

Holly and Dan's expressions mirrored each other, both hit by a bump of surprise that, even with everything else going on, it was actually her mother's welfare and sensibilities that were concerning Julia. Holly felt yet another shard of guilt, for expecting Julia's first concerns to be her career and, judging by the look on Dan's face, she wasn't the only one.

Chapter 32

Taffy looked up and smiled as Holly came in. 'Check it out, Holly, the boys made supper.'

'Wow!' she managed, trying not to sound shocked or annoyed. When Taffy had offered to pick up the twins from nursery and make them tea, this was seriously not what she'd had in mind. It looked as though the entire contents of the fridge had been upended on the kitchen table, buttered crusts of bread littered the floor and a bowl of dripping eggshells sat beside the hob.

'They've been great. I hardly had to lift a finger. Come and join in,' Taffy said, indicating the blanket on the sitting room floor where they had decamped to eat; obviously there being no room left on the table. Eric chewed contentedly on a sausage roll, Tom was tucking into a wedge of some kind of gooey frittata and Ben was struggling to get his small mouth around the most enormous club sandwich Holly had ever seen.

It was one thing to ask the boys to start helping around the house a little, maybe even put their pants in the laundry basket, but this scene of devastation hardly counted as 'helpful' at the end of a very long day, by any stretch of her imagination.

'In a minute, I'll just get their bath running—' she said carefully, unconsciously adopting the tone that she used when the twins had frayed her very last nerve and she was still determined to be good-Mummy, calm-Mummy – not exhausted-at-the-end-of-a-bloody-long-day-and-merely-a-wobble-away-from-the-edge Mummy.

'Oh, don't worry, we've already had showers,' Taffy said easily. 'So we could have tea in our PJs, look . . .' He frowned when he noticed Holly's expression. 'The world won't end if we do things in a different order, Holls,' he said quietly, the smallest edge of irritation sharpening his words.

'But—'she began, stopping herself. It apparently didn't seem to occur to Taffy that, by the time the twins had finished their carpet picnic bonanza, they'd require hosing down just to get the sticky off them. She swallowed hard. Taffy had made it perfectly clear how he felt about her arbitrary parenting timetable, teasing her when she talked of 'being late' – 'How can you be late for something when you've just randomly assigned a time for it?' he would remonstrate.

She'd tried so many times to explain that her system had evolved gradually over the last four years out of sheer necessity – as a way of coping with two small, opinionated humans on her own, without sacrificing every ounce of her sleep, self or sanity.

He leaned over and scooped up a can of orangeade with a curly straw in it. 'Come on, Holls,' he said. 'Sit down. We're having fizzy pop to celebrate Ben's achievement.'

Ben looked up at the mention of his name, shoving a large chunk of avocado into his mouth. 'I can count to twenty now.' He looked utterly delighted with himself. 'Twenty things in my sandwich, Mummy.' He waved it at her to demonstrate and the bread flapped alarmingly, scattering a combination of what looked like Pringles and *Hundreds & Thousands* everywhere.

Taffy looked askance at Holly, waiting for her to click into gear, to be the proud cheerleading mummy, to stop staring at the drink in his hand as though it were toxic. 'It's only a small can,' he said, pre-empting any disagreement about sugary drinks before bedtime.

And to think that she'd been fantasising about a glass of wine and a quiet evening all the way home.

She breathed out slowly, trying to let go of her exasperation with Taffy's Peter Pan approach to life – it was certainly a mixed blessing and one that continued to take her by surprise on occasion. 'That's brilliant, Ben. Twenty! That really is A Lot.' She folded her legs beneath her as she sank down on to the blanket, defeated. There was no point fighting her corner this evening – the ship had sailed and the only position left would be as Captain Killjoy. She sipped at the can of lurid orange pop that Ben victoriously thrust into her hand, unable to believe his luck at this unprecedented turn of events.

'And you made all this yourselves? Aren't you clever,' Holly said.

'Taffy watched cricket,' Tom said earnestly. 'It's boring. So now I'm Head Chef!'

Holly raised an eyebrow and looked at Taffy who just smiled and shrugged. 'What? It was on in the background. Besides, with these two in the kitchen, I would only have cramped their style.' He squeezed Holly's knee reassuringly, as the boys divided the grapes between them, each one deliberately counted out for absolute fairness. 'They have to start somewhere. And before you say anything, of course I was there for the hob and the knives, I just let them do the prep work.' He looked almost baffled by Holly's lukewarm reaction to the whole scenario. What had he been expecting, she wondered, smothering a yawn.

'Different isn't wrong, Holls,' he said gently. 'I need to do *my* part *my* way.'

She nodded silently, understanding. 'I know. I do.' She took a sip of the orangeade, pleasantly surprised by the burst of flavour and fizz. 'But does your way have to be so *very* different to mine?' She was aiming for humour, but her question was just a little too close to the mark for either of them to find it amusing.

He shrugged. 'Well, I can still remember the first time I made supper, you know. I was maybe four and Aldwyn was supposed to be in charge, but he couldn't be arsed. So I had milky tea, made with cold water, and Angel Delight, which didn't set. But I felt so grown-up. Like I'd been trusted to do something special. Runny Angel Delight never tasted so good.' He paused to let this sink in. 'But after that I discovered the cheese toasty maker, so from there on in, I was pretty much a culinary god.' He grinned and shuddered. 'The combinations I put in that machine, it's a wonder I didn't get food poisoning—' He stopped abruptly. 'Okay, not helping, but do you see what I mean?'

Holly yawned again and looked around her at the mess, at the sticky puddles, at the delighted expressions on her sons' faces – of course she could see his point, but surely he could see hers as well. There was plenty of time for culinary adventures when they were a bit bigger, less chaotic, less likely to lose a finger on the chopping board. When she wasn't already running on fumes ... She shrugged. 'I'm glad you guys had fun, I am—'

She let the 'but' hover.

She didn't want to be *that* parent.

'Right then,' said Taffy, clambering to his feet and stretching, rattled by her reaction, but obviously making an effort to bite his tongue. 'I might just pop out for a quick run now you're back.'

Holly stilled in disbelief. He wasn't serious? Tired to the point of tears, grateful of course that he'd helped out with the boys, but to leave everything like this? She closed her eyes and took a breath, deliberately calming herself so that her weary disappointment wasn't written all over her face and couldn't be mistaken for ingratitude.

When she opened them again, the boys were on their feet too – Tom holding a bin bag and Ben a whistle. 'Ready, steady, go!' they squealed.

It was wasteful, it was carnage, but the next five minutes of unadulterated leaping around and 'tidying up' were undoubtedly efficient. The floor, the table, the plates all swept clean by tiny grasping hands in competition to get the job done.

Taffy blew one last blast on the whistle. 'Cadets! Wet flannels on my mark!' and to Holly's disbelief the boys lined up beside him to have their hands and faces firmly scrubbed.

She laughed despite herself. It wasn't her way and it vexed her on so many levels, but she had to confess that the twins were in their element.

'What a tidy up!' she said to the boys. 'Good job. Great job, actually. I thought you were going to leave it all for Mummy to do.'

'Don't be silly,' said Tom seriously. 'Tidy Up with Taffy is the best game.'

Taffy tried not to look smug. 'See, different's not always worse. Mess isn't always bad.'

'It's true,' said Tom seriously. 'You cannot make a yummy omelette without breaking eggs. I tried.'

And even Holly had to concede, he might have a point.

Hours later, with two hyperactive little boys finally convinced into bed and an emergency take-away demolished, Holly and Taffy looked at the paperwork spread out on the kitchen table in resignation. So much for the wine/sofa/box-set suggestion.

To be fair, Grace had done them proud today as the press had circled their wagons and the phones had burned white hot. Fielding every enquiry with calm, professional aplomb, Grace had firmly maintained that the medical staff were busy with their patients, doing their job – the very job they were receiving all this attention for – and could not be disturbed. Insisting on a written request for each press enquiry had filtered out the more casual applications and now Taffy and Holly were charged with responding.

Even despite Taffy's complaints, Holly still felt that they had got the better deal. Dan's role this evening had been to escort Julia home and to try and persuade Candace that now was the time for treatment and discretion. Press releases still felt like the easy option.

'Did you actually read all those articles this morning, Taffs?' she asked. 'They are just waiting for us to start squabbling amongst ourselves and fail. Vultures! It's almost as if they can't compute that life can work without a hierarchy. We just have to find a way to be a team on this.'

He shrugged. 'I know, I know, teamwork et cetera, et cetera – we're all making compromises, but—' He stood up abruptly and filled the kettle, almost on autopilot. 'Compromise isn't always good though, is it? Compromise is just another way of saying that nobody gets what they really want.'

The expression on his face was inscrutable and Holly felt an involuntary flicker of unease. 'How do you mean?'

He shrugged. 'Ignore me. It's been a long day.' He sloshed some hot water into a mug and ladled in three spoonfuls of coffee. 'I seem to be wearing so many hats at the moment, I keep forgetting who I'm supposed to be. At work, at home—' He broke off, looking uncomfortable as he registered Holly's expression. 'I don't mind all the hats ... Honestly. It's just—'

Holly polished off the last of the spring rolls, buying herself time to think. She was finding Taffy hard to interpret this evening. Maybe Dan had a point and she had just been asking – and expecting – too much? After all, Taffy wasn't known for his ability to say no to anyone.

'I just don't know how you do it,' he said quietly after a moment. 'You change gears so seamlessly, Holls – doctor, mum, girlfriend – and now media consultant too apparently ... I don't know where to start and I feel like I'm making it up as I go along.'

Holly couldn't help but laugh. 'Oh Taffs,' she said gently, 'we're *all* making it up as we go along.' She swallowed hard, in for a penny, 'It's why I set myself these arbitrary things to work to – bedtimes, mealtimes, walks in the park even if it's raining – otherwise the whole thing just spirals out of my control ...'

'If I think about the detail too much,' Taffy interrupted, 'the tiny jigsaw pieces that all need to fit together to make everything work, it makes me feel—' He waved an arm in a circle in the air and looked at Holly expectantly as though she might have all the answers.

'Dizzy?' she offered.

'No, no – more like, well, drowning?' He phrased it as a question, but Holly knew from the look on his face that it was closer to the truth.

'Okay,' she said slowly, trying to understand, trying not to take it personally or feel hurt. 'That doesn't sound great. Are you feeling that way now?'

He shook his head. 'No, I mean, yes – a little bit.'

He looked so vulnerable in that moment, Holly truly wanted to comfort him. Perhaps this was just his manly equivalent of her spinning plates dream, the one she'd been having ever since the twins were born? He just hadn't had the years to gradually adapt to a total loss of control or spontaneity. But what if it was more than that?

'And the run didn't help?'

He shrugged. 'I just felt bad about leaving you with all the work when I said I'd help.'

Holly took a breath, feeling as though she were walking on eggshells, knowing that they were talking about so much more than handling a few press releases or rustling up nursery tea. 'Sometimes,' she said slowly, 'it's better to say you can't help . . .'

'And leave you in the lurch?' he said sceptically. 'How crap would that be?'

Holly shrugged eloquently. 'I think sometimes, it's better to say no, than to say yes and resent it.' She looked up at him, her face an open book. 'I think that you do so much for me and the boys and The Practice, that it's okay if you can't always muck in. And, honestly, I think that saying yes and then feeling, well, like this—'

'It's worse, isn't it?' Taffy cut in. 'But I *do* want to help. I *do* want to muck in . . . All my efforts though seem to . . . '

Holly noticed his hands slowly unclench. 'I just don't want to be like Milo.'

'Oh Taffs, no, you are nothing like Milo. I can promise you the fact that you're even thinking that, means you're safe on that front.'

Taffy looked up. 'But I got as far as the end of the road and I realised something – all this talk of the Big Picture I've been going on and on and on about? And don't pretend it hasn't been pissing you off, because I've noticed. It's just so I don't have to focus on all the little pieces. There's bloody hundreds of them!'

Holly smiled, trying to soften the intensity of his words. 'Well, that's kind of better in a way – if anything, I thought you were turning in to Aldwyn for a minute there.'

'Oh dear God!' said Taffy with feeling, following her lead. 'And, to be clear on this, Holly, you do know you can't win, don't you? If you're all independent and don't ask for my help with the boys, I think you don't really need me and I'm getting in the way. And if you ask me to step up all the time, I get panicky. Really, seriously overwhelmed. And I know it annoys you when I do things my way. And I can't even moan about it, or I sound like your ex.'

Holly nodded. 'This is new territory for me too, but it all sounds fairly normal to me.'

'Really?' Taffy said incredulously. 'Well, it seems pretty fucked-up to me. And what do you do, when you feel like that?'

Holly thought for a moment. 'I suppose I talk to a friend, or eat a Hobnob or seven, or have a little cry ... Depends on the trigger really. But most days, the drowning feeling is more like a wave I can ride.'

'This too shall pass?' Taffy said aloud, his Catholic

upbringing leaving its mark despite his rampant atheism these days.

'Erm, something like that – more shit-happens, what's next?' She grinned. 'I read that in a parenting book somewhere, but it works in most scenarios. But you know, if your running-like-a-loon plan works too, then let's not fight it. Just because we're both juggling doesn't mean we have to use the same balls.'

'You should embroider that on a pillow,' Taffy said drily.

'Make it part of a "Big Picture"?' Holly countered.

'Touché.' He smiled and the atmosphere between them shifted slightly. 'Holly,' he said, 'I meant it. I don't ever want to be like Milo. I don't ever want to make you feel the way he does. That text . . .' He held up his hands as though words failed him. 'One text. And I've seen you these last few days, how much it's been preying on your mind.'

She nodded, unable to deny it. 'What can I say though? When it comes to Milo, to the divorce, all I want is for it to be over. But I guess it never really will be, will it? Because of the boys.' She sighed, the reality of that statement taking overwhelmed to a whole new level. A lifetime of negotiating with Milo, of managing her reactions to Milo, of comforting her boys when he inevitably let them down.

'Probably not,' Taffy conceded, his voice heavy with unspoken emotion.

Silence stretched out through the kitchen, broken only by Eric's snores from under the table. Holly had absolutely no idea what to say next.

In her lifetime, she'd dealt with strong men, bullying men, controlling men even – but she had no idea how to handle someone who wore their heart on their sleeve and was prepared to tie himself in knots just to avoid a poor comparison.

For all the talk of tight family units building self-esteem, it was actually quite the revelation that underneath the surface, Taffy was just as vulnerable as the next person. And now Holly had to wonder whether she should follow Dan's advice and actually start turning away Taffy's help and support for his own good, before he promised himself into a position of no return.

Chapter 33

'And then I found that if I blow my nose too hard, it actually comes out of my eye!' exclaimed Cassie Holland. She was one of the last patients in an extended morning surgery for Holly and it had been slow-going from the start.

Holly was still doing her best to resist Julia's insistent requests for Quentin and his film crew to shadow her that afternoon. It was becoming increasingly difficult to avoid and it didn't really help that her in-tray was full of yet more press requests that Grace had edited thoroughly until only the important ones remained, but to Holly's mind, there still seemed to be plenty of those.

As her gaze wandered to the clock on the wall, she was quietly counting down the hours until lunch when she had plans, big plans, to make Elsie's first trip to the Stroke Rehabilitation Unit fun.

'And I tried steaming with menthol, Dr Graham, but it didn't seem to make that much difference, to be honest,' Cassie continued.

Holly smiled patiently. 'Cassie, I know you don't like taking antibiotics, but sometimes they're necessary. You have acute sinusitis and we've tried all the other ways to treat this, so you need to listen to me now – take the antibiotics and let's deal with the infection. But you will need to stay out of the sun while you're taking them, okay? The ones I'm prescribing are the best for sinus problems, but they do increase your photosensitivity, so please be sensible.'

Cassie pouted. 'But I'm going on holiday next week.'

Holly took a deep breath, trying not to let her thoughts show on her face, namely that if Cassie had listened to her three weeks ago then it wouldn't be an issue by now. 'Are you going somewhere very hot?'

Cassie shrugged. 'Wales.'

Holly's lips twitched as she fought the urge to laugh. 'Then just pop on some sunscreen and maybe a hat? The weather forecast isn't great for the next few weeks anyway, so I suspect you'll be fine.'

Cassie fidgeted in her seat, never one to surrender even a moment of her allocated slot. 'I'd also like to talk to you about Tarquin. It's one of the struggles with having a gifted child, I know, but can you offer some advice about how to help him adapt to spending time with his less mentally enabled peers? Maybe you could refer him to a child psychologist – you know, so that he can really get the best out of his social interactions?'

Holly nodded, wondering how to tactfully phrase what she really wanted to say: he's not gifted; he's spoiled. Tell him to stop sticking things up his nose to get attention and being unbearably snobby around his 'peers' and he might find things easier. Also, wash his hair more often and stop dressing him up like Little Lord Fauntleroy.

Obviously, she said none of those things out loud. 'Cassie, if you'd like to talk to me about this then do feel free to make another appointment and bring young Tarquin in, but I'm afraid I have a full list this morning and yours was an emergency slot. But I'm sure the antibiotics will sort you out so you can enjoy your holiday.' Holly stood up and opened the door – it was normally enough to provoke even the most recalcitrant of patients to leave, but Cassie was made of sterner stuff and showed no sign of moving.

It wasn't until Dan Carter walked past the door that she reluctantly got to her feet and left, with her prescription in her hand and a displeased expression on her face.

'Dan?' said Holly. 'I don't know quite how to ask this, but what are you wearing?'

He did a little twirl in the corridor, much to Cassie's disgust as she muttered to herself walking back to reception, 'Oh you've got time for silly business, but not for my son . . .'

Dan laid a cautionary hand on Holly's arm as she looked as though she was about to lose her rag. 'Don't let her get to you.'

Holly couldn't help but wonder, looking down at Dan's hand, why he was wearing padded gloves in the middle of summer. 'Dare I even ask?' she said eventually.

Dan's outsized shirt was straining at the seams over what appeared to be a layer of padding and he was walking strangely too. 'It's a fat suit,' he said proudly. 'It's part of a new initiative to raise understanding of our obese patients. The idea is to wear it for a day and see all the challenges they face, that we have no idea about. I've already got stuck in the loo cubicle at The Deli – definitely fattist dimensions there – and I've had three lads call me Fatty at the supermarket. Not only that, but with these sausage fingers I can hardly type.' He looked delighted at his recent discoveries.

'Okay,' said Holly slowly. 'And this is an NHS initiative?' She was mainly confused because it sounded so forward thinking and empathetic – hardly the usual penny-pinching, broad-strokes approach they were used to.

Dan blushed a little then. 'Well, to be honest, it's more something Taffy and I were trying out after we saw them on the Science Channel.'

'You mean it's a bet?' said Holly.

'Not just a bet,' interrupted Taffy as he squeezed his newly upholstered form out of the gents' loo. 'It's raising awareness and understanding, too. And we do seem to have a lot of overweight patients at the moment. You can blame Mrs Darnley, if you like. I saw her last week and to be honest, I didn't even know you could get fungus in that many places!'

Dan shook his head as he grimaced. 'Bit of a shocker that one. But if you were open to a little feedback, Taffs, I've also found that morbidly obese patients much prefer it if you don't keep going on and on about how much they have to eat every day to stay "that fat". And she did mention to me at the weekend that you seemed far more excited about finding her missing TV-remote when swabbing the rash than she was?'

Taffy looked a little bit guilty. 'True – but then also, you have to remember that she's been stuck watching E4 for the last few weeks because she couldn't change channel. I bet she was a little bit excited really, you know, as well as the whole mortified and embarrassed bit?'

'Hmmm. Possibly,' Dan conceded. 'But chances are she'll be back in a week, because there's no way she'll be sticking to a sugar-free diet, is there?'

'It's just madness that we can't refer her across to the Obesity Clinic though, isn't it?' said Holly. 'I mean, the woman is putting her health in grave danger and I'm sure they're better equipped to deal with her.' They all looked ruefully at the broken office chair in the corner.

'She's just not big enough to qualify,' said Dan. 'How mad is that? She just doesn't make the cut.'

Taffy scrunched up his face, his ever-present idealism clashing horribly with reality. 'So we have to let her get even heavier, before we can get her proper targeted help to get thinner.' He sounded despondent for a moment before rallying. 'And so we're doing this. A few days in one of these and we'll really be able to understand Mrs Darnley's challenges and we'll be better doctors for it, I'm sure.'

Holly said nothing, Taffy was highly skilled at self-incrimination. 'And – okay – whoever wears it the longest, wins,' he confessed. 'You don't mind some extra junk in my trunk, do you, Holls?' He came towards her for a cuddle and Holly couldn't help but laugh.

'I have a clinic full of patients waiting and there's press all over town. So, hats off to you both!'

The two men looked at each other, as if this thought hadn't crossed their minds and then dismissed it: vanity was not an issue where these two were concerned. Holly shrugged, frankly just relieved to see Dan smile again. 'Your call.'

'Join us at the pub for some lunch?' offered Taffy.

Holly shook her head. 'Not today – I have plans.'

The two men waddled away from her towards the exit.

'Your round,' Taffy reminded Dan as he pulled open the door.

'Well, you're not exactly svelte, my friend,' countered Dan with a grin.

Holly beeped the horn as she pulled up outside Elsie's house – late, as usual. Grace leapt out of the passenger seat and rang the doorbell, just as Lizzie arrived, out of breath, and clutching a large carrier bag.

'Good to see we're on top of things,' she gasped, her legendary efficiency having been ditched along with the power suits and paycheque. 'Sorry, just nodded off for a moment . . . And then that blasted goose nearly had my ankles on the corner.' It hadn't escaped anyone's notice that, having time on her hands to consider her options, had essentially meant that Lizzie's get-up-and-go had got-up-and-gone. For as exhausting as Lizzie could be when she got revved up, it was still preferable to the lethargy and indecisiveness she'd been exhibiting recently. And every single time Holly tried to ask how the anxiety therapy was going, Lizzie kept cutting her off at the pass. Holly was all for honouring confidentiality in therapy, but she was feeling seriously out of the loop.

Lizzie held her hand to the stitch in her side and tossed the carrier bag through the open passenger door towards Holly.

'Thanks for picking these up. I know it was a bit last minute, but Grant at the print shop was so sweet this morning when I called and I just couldn't resist!' She pulled out the four silver bomber jackets and her face lit up when she saw the legend 'Team Elsie' emblazoned across the back with a large number on each.

Grace grinned as she rang the doorbell yet again, waiting for Elsie to make an appearance. 'Quick, let's put them on!'

'You called?' chirped Elsie, opening the heavy panelled door with surprising force for an ailing octogenarian. Dressed with aplomb in a tailored pair of cashmere jogging bottoms and a linen t-shirt, it was clear she meant business. Grace and Lizzie had just had time to slip into their jackets and the three women did jazz hands in front of Holly's battered Golf, the midday sunlight glinting off the silver lamé. Elsie raised an eyebrow. 'You're all quite, quite mad, you know that?' she said.

She tried to look as though all this silliness was beneath her, but the twinkle in her eye was hard to miss.

'We're your crack support team,' said Holly gleefully. She flung open the boot. 'We have jazzy trainers for the ultimate in hospital gym fashion, we have *Heat* magazine, prosciutto paninis and Gin & Tonic-in-a-can for after – just the one to share – as it's a school day! What do you think?'

'I think,' said Elsie, the smile now hovering closer to her lips as Grace helped her into the Number One jacket, 'that I'm prepared to give you all the benefit of the doubt.' She slid into the passenger seat with a regal air and only leapt fractionally out of her skin when Holly started the engine and the summer soundtrack she'd compiled for this morning blared out across the Market Place – the perky proclamation that they were Walking On Sunshine startling Gerald the goose into a display of honking and scarpering that had them all in pieces as they drove away.

'Good God,' said Grace, as Lizzie, Holly and Elsie sang along at the top of their voices. 'If this is what you three are like when you're sober, what on earth will you be like with a drink inside you?'

'What on *earth* makes you think that we're sober?' cried Elsie happily. 'We have things to celebrate, ladies. Exciting times ahead!'

Holly looked across at Lizzie in confusion. Elsie's unexpectedly exuberant reaction to her first rehabilitation clinic had thrown her a little – perhaps the silver lamé had been de trop and tipped her over the edge?

Elsie caught the look and leaned in. 'I'm going to be immortalised in print, darling! They called just now to offer me a deal. Isn't that wonderful?' She shrugged happily. 'Obviously I'm playing hard to get—'

Lizzie rolled her eyes, her own dreams of becoming a published author mothballed along with all of her other schemes and plans. 'Just take the deal, Elsie. Do you have any idea how hard it is to get a publisher these days?'

Elsie shook her head. 'Not really. I just phoned them up and offered. Is that not how it normally works?' She waited a beat and then winked at Lizzie. 'I know, I know, I'm a very lucky girl and I promise to behave.'

She leaned across and tooted the horn as they drove past a building site, making Holly blush. 'You could start now if you like,' Holly protested under her breath, as she concentrated on weaving through the traffic on the outskirts of Bath.

'They keep talking about this book being my legacy though, darlings. It makes me feel like the sodding Olympics! It really won't stand. Not to mention, they're being incredibly tiresome about publishing dates. I told them it had to go to print *this* year, but they will insist on talking about next year's list and taking some time to build my brand.' Elsie sighed, obviously piqued. 'I shall have to speak up, because I rather think my public know who I am already.' She paused for a moment. 'And let's be honest, who knows how long I've got left?'

There was a sudden silence in the car, the mood instantly punctured. Holly reached across and squeezed her hand. 'There's plenty of time. We do the rehab, we do the diet, we take one day at a time. It really wouldn't be the end of the world if the book came out next year, you know. Please don't let the fear of what might be colour your judgement too much – all your test results are so promising and there's so much we can do to get you back on fighting form—'

'Oh my love, aren't you sweet with the bullshit,' Elsie interrupted, patting her hand, before pointedly placing it back on the steering wheel. 'Now, why don't you concentrate on staying in the right lane? Your driving is probably my number one risk factor for another stroke right now.'

As Elsie did her rehabilitation assessment in a hospital department with walls the colour of rancid brie, the others twiddled their thumbs in the soulless coffee shop. The hospital had clearly tried so hard to lift the mood in the sweeping atrium and a volunteer in a neon tabard was playing Scott Joplin for all she was worth on a grand piano surrounded by glossy green plants. But the fact remained that every single person in the coffee shop was there under sufferance – nobody wanted to be eating cardboard sandwiches and drinking crappy coffee as they waited for news of their loved ones.

Only a new dad, clutching a giant teddy bear and a vast balloon claiming 'It's a boy' brought any amusement to the proceedings, as he dozed off in the queue and the balloon took flight, soaring up to the higher concourse to join a selection of others. 'Happens all the time,' said the bored-looking girl clearing the table next to them.

'You know,' said Grace, 'if Elsie has to come in every week, this is going to be her undoing. She only agreed to come today under sufferance – how's she going to be a month down the line? I reckon the prospect of sitting here would be more damaging than helpful, don't you? We need to keep her spirits up, not depress the hell out of her.'

Holly nodded. 'I did call to see if we could get private sessions on her healthcare policy, but everybody said the same thing – the treatment centre here is second to none and she'd actually be missing out on the quality of the speech therapy by going privately. So—' she held out her hands in dismay. 'Here we are.'

Lizzie frowned. 'Listen to you two – it's not that bad. It's clean and bright and the treatment is apparently great ... so she has to walk through the café of doom to get there – we'll take it in turns to bring her and whisk her past the sobbing relatives.' She paused for a moment. 'I'm being insensitive, aren't I? I mean, you two can't skive off work every time Elsie needs physio, can you?'

Holly caught Grace's eye and they both looked uncomfortable. Like it or not though, it was a factor to take into account.

'Will you let me do this?' Lizzie said quietly. 'I feel like I need something at the moment? I mean, it's all very well being a stay-at-home mum, but with the kids at school in September, I'll just be a stay-at-home, won't I?'

Grace took her hand. 'Don't kid yourself, just because they're at school doesn't mean you won't be busy. It kind of snowballs, as I recall. Soon you'll be up at midnight drying sports kit, baking cupcakes for the bake-sale they forgot to tell you about until bedtime and hemming random nativity costumes.'

Lizzie smiled, grateful for the advice and Holly sat quietly, taking it all in. She had to confess that, in her naïvety, she had also assumed that getting the twins to school would be the beginning of life-getting-easier.

Grace continued and the niggling jealous feeling that Holly had been harbouring towards her began to slowly release its grip. So, Elsie's conversation had been peppered with 'Grace says ...' or 'Grace thinks ...' for the last few weeks. Surely it was actually a blessing for Elsie to have another ally in Larkford. God knows, Holly was finding it hard enough keeping her plates spinning, knowing that Grace was a little more flexible with her commitments and happy to step in to keep Elsie company should be a cause for celebration.

'You're so like Dan,' Grace said. 'Perhaps there's a sequence in your family's DNA that means you have to be on a mission? He's so committed to his Health in the Community Scheme and seems so much happier for having a sense of purpose and something to focus on.'

Lizzie nodded. 'Given the energy and the time, I reckon Dan and I could take over the world, or maybe just Larkford and get things ship-shape in no time.' She looked pale, Holly thought, as she watched her friend talk, her words in complete contrast to her wan body language.

She gathered up their rubbish and grinned, knowing exactly how to get a little colour back into Lizzie's cheeks. 'Retail therapy, anyone? I know it's only a hospital gift shop, but—' She didn't need to say any more. Lizzie was on her feet in an instant.

'Excellent suggestion, Graham. Shall we say a budget of a fiver, most ridiculous purchase wins?'

'So like Dan,' Grace murmured to Holly with a smile, as Lizzie dashed across the main concourse and they trailed in her wake.

Lizzie, as usual, didn't miss a trick. It had been a moment of hesitation, that was all. But as Holly's eyes had fallen on the rack of tiny babygros, still white and pristine on their miniature coat hangers, she'd felt such a tug of longing it must have been written all over her face.

Lizzie's eyes widened in disbelief as she took in the possible implications and stared at Holly's stomach. 'You're not . . . ?'

Holly shook her head. 'No. I'm not!' She laughed nervously, caught on the hop, not only by her friend but also the gamut of emotions assaulting her. 'But would it be so *very* bad if I was? You look as though you've seen a ghost.'

'Well, it would be the ghost of our new-found freedom if you were,' retorted Lizzie with feeling. 'Why on earth would you want to go back *there*?' She talked about it as though it were a dodgy holiday resort they'd endured together. 'We've just got through the hideous bit and now we get to enjoy our families as they grow up. Surely you can't want to go back to leaky boobs and exploding nappies again?'

Holly shrugged, struggling to put how she felt into words. 'It's different for you. You and Will and your kids have got your happy ever after, haven't you?'

Lizzie frowned. 'I think we'll brush over the insensitivity of calling my unfocused search for the Meaning of Life a happy ending and focus on the What The Hell? Is Taffy pressuring you into this?' Lizzie looked genuinely perturbed at the thought. 'Last we spoke, you were grumpy as hell about the world and his wife wanting you to get married again and now we're talking babies . . . What happened to keeping your independence?'

Holly had tried so hard to explain to Lizzie about her reluctance to remarry – obviously she still hadn't succeeded. It had nothing to do with independence – she simply couldn't bring herself to make a commitment that had proven to mean nothing. To her mind, the fact that she and Taffy chose to be together every single day meant so much more than a marriage certificate. And if they chose to have children, so what? Were the children of parents wearing a wedding ring necessarily happier?

She pointedly chose to ignore the little voice in her head that suggested they actually might be. That security might mean more to a child, than her own stance of 'fool me once, shame on you – fool me twice, shame on me'.

'It's nothing really,' she reassured Lizzie. 'I've just been thinking about it. One day. Maybe. Who knows?' Holly didn't know where all this was coming from, she certainly hadn't planned to share any of these thoughts with anyone.

'Let's have a little walk down memory lane then, shall we?' Lizzie said as she caught hold of Holly's hand and pulled her into the adjoining maternity section of the shop, the strangled cries of a tantrumming toddler immediately assaulting them. 'Best contraceptive in the world coming in here.' Lizzie grinned. 'Right. Let's start at the nipple pads and work our way down to those enormous pants.'

Chapter 34

Dan scrolled down the application form on his computer and wished there was more he could do to help.

Candace sat before him, with bloodshot eyes and mascara streaked down her face. She rocked gently in the chair, looking so much older and more fragile than he had ever realised. It was as though the make-up, the hairspray and the forced (and probably fake) bonhomie had been the only things holding her together.

The massive conflict of interest with this particular patient was definitely clouding his judgement – it wasn't something he hadn't experienced before, though. Living in Larkford, every patient was also a neighbour or a friend or, sometimes more uncomfortably, an enemy. But how did you begin to categorise the mother of your ex-girlfriend, who didn't appear to have realised that the 'ex' part was even in play?

'Do you think Julia will find out?' she asked tentatively, raising her gaze to Dan's face, the hope flaring briefly.

'It's a small town,' Dan prevaricated gently. People always talked about addicts having to hit rock bottom, about alcoholism being a 'self-diagnosed disease' and that there was no point forcing them to get help until they were willing to admit they had a problem. The issue Dan had with that perspective, was how many lives were wasted, in a prolonged and public cry for help.

If Candace had wanted to, she could have quietly main-lined a bottle of gin in the privacy of her own home. By choosing The Kingsley Arms as her stage, she had essen-tially – like a teenager on the lam – been asking to be seen.

The fact that she had been seen by the local press was an unfortunate development. The fact that there was now a series of photographs charting her descent into an alcohol-fuelled rant probably more so.

Dan could only be grateful for the fact that he himself had been having an awful morning and had popped over for a swift half at lunchtime. The irony was not lost on him.

He clicked on several menus and sighed. 'There's an amaz-ing facility nearby – one of the best – but they can't take you for a few days. I'm tempted to say let's just wait, because the alternative is a little, shall we say, grittier?' He leaned forward and his heart went out to the woman in front of him – her husband gone, her daughter clearly pushed beyond her toler-ance with this situation. 'I'd normally suggest family support and daily AA meetings and to try and get you into the best facility possible, but I'm not sure that's an option, is it?'

'I'm not sure family support is on the table,' she said. 'I may have burned one or two bridges this week, this month, this year ...'

'I could go with you, to the AA meetings, if you'd like,' Dan offered, wondering why he felt moved to do so. It wasn't as though he was trying to win back Julia's affection.

Even clutching the mug of industrial strength black coffee that Lucy had made for her, Candace was nothing if not astute. 'Now, why on earth would you want to do that?' she asked, her eyes narrowed and her brain sluggishly working it through. 'I'm drunk, not stupid, Dr Carter. Did you think I hadn't noticed your absence? It seems to me, that you two aren't being exactly honest with each other. Are you still in love with my daughter?'

Dan blushed awkwardly, unused to being on the receiving end of the questions in his patient consultations. 'Truthfully? Yes. I think I'll always be a little bit in love with her. But we are not good for each other, Candace. I am not my best self when we're together and I think Julia would say the same.'

'Well, I know that she is not her best self when I'm around – I can tell you that for a fact.' She stared at him appraisingly. 'If we're being candid, then at least tell me this. Is she right? Am I the reason you left?'

Dan mouthed helplessly. What could he possibly say – that Julia's Pavlovian response to her mother's presence had shown him an entirely new side to her personality that scared him senseless? That her ambition and constant desire to prove herself made him flinch? He took a deep breath and managed to compose himself. 'It's been a long time brewing,' he said tactfully.

'Now,' he continued, turning the conversation back to the constructive, 'I'm going to get Jade to draw some bloods and send them off – you might need a little support nutritionally and she's amazing at handling that side of things. And then we'll get you over to Sunnyside – you may not be able to check in for a few days, but if we ask nicely you can join in their daily programme as an outpatient. And, I could be wrong, but I think the support there is exactly what you need.'

'Whatever you say, Dr Carter,' Candace replied, her own ability to decide anything at all seemingly languishing under the bottle of Hendricks, the triple espresso and a desire to turn back the clock. 'But perhaps you could be the one to tell my daughter?'

'I'm so sorry to rope you into this as well,' Dan said under his breath as Julia took a short break from yelling at them to answer an urgent phone call. It was the end of a very long day and they were all keen to get home. 'I may have misjudged the best way to handle all this.'

'You think?' said Holly tiredly.

Dan gave her a sharp look. 'Listen, Graham, I'm still feeling my way through all of this. I tried all the negotiating tricks I used in the Army, but Julia is pretty formidable. I swear some days it would be easier haggling with the Taliban.'

'Dan!' said Holly, a little shocked at the bitterness in his voice.

'What?' he replied defensively. 'You know I love the daft mare to pieces, but my God, has she been hard to live with. It's like she turned into an angry teenager with no rational thought processes the moment her mother turned up. And she wasn't exactly low-maintenance before.'

He stopped himself going further with one glance at Holly's face, knowing he'd overstepped the mark and was in danger of dividing her loyalties. And it wasn't as though he hadn't been warned; Taffy and Holly had both been supportive when he chose to reunite with Julia, but they had both quietly expressed their concern. If there was a Happily Ever After ending to the story, then brilliant. Their concerns had been more focused on, well, this exact scenario, to be precise.

It wasn't just a relationship at stake; this affected everybody's working life too.

'I'd hoped it might be easier if we told her together, more supportive, I guess?' The question mark hung in the air and they both knew that he'd got this one wrong. Rather than feeling that they were both there for her, Julia had lashed out as though they had ganged up on her.

Julia hung up the phone and, to her credit, attempted to compose herself before she re-joined them. 'That was my agent, in case you were wondering. She was keen to know how the tabloids got hold of photographs of my mother comatose in a local bar. The Kingsley Arms, apparently. And apparently,' she spat the word out with a barely suppressed fury, 'a local doctor, friend of the family no less, came and picked her up. Sounding familiar?'

Dan tried to hold his ground with Julia, urging himself not to look away first, but he failed. He did, however, manage to locate his crumbling resolve whilst staring at his boots. For some reason the sight of his sturdy 'desert' boots gave him a little nudge – after all, if he could cope with being an army doctor and the subsequent years of flashbacks, he could cope with a furious ex-girlfriend. Especially when he knew that everything he had done, he had done to help her, with the very best of intentions.

He cleared his throat. 'Let's get this clear, shall we? And then maybe we can let poor Holly out of this hideous conversation that, let's face it, has nothing to do with her.'

Julia flushed and shot Holly a filthy look. 'Well it seems to me that Holly was the one who drove my mother to a rehab facility for an afternoon of therapy and didn't bother to tell me about it. So, yeah, it seems like she might just be involved.'

Dan sighed and ran his hand over the buzz-cut that had recently regrown on his scalp. The haircut, the boots, the feeling of being under siege: all he needed now was exploding IEDs and he'd be having another PTSD relapse rather than dealing with the job in hand.

Fighting the urge to shout, he sat down and splayed his hands in a universal gesture of submission. 'Come and talk to us, Jules. This must be incredibly hard. I did ask Holly to help, yes. But mainly because I hoped she would bring a little objectivity to the problem. Something that you and I both lack at the moment.'

Julia softened slightly, but she still prickled with a static energy that was unnerving at best and a little terrifying at worst. Dan rather wished he hadn't stayed up late last night reading Stephen King.

Dan gave Holly a nudge. 'You get off home, Holls. God knows what Taffy's cooking up for the twins' tea. Unless you want them addicted to scampi, I'd steer him well away from the catering detail.' When Holly looked hesitantly at Julia, Dan stood up and opened the door, making the decision for her. 'Seriously, Holls. I can handle this and any questions Julia has about her mother's care. Thanks for staying, though.' He dropped his voice. 'I'm so sorry for dragging you into this. My mistake.'

Holly looked as though she was about to protest, but after a moment's hesitation, she took Julia's silence as consent and left the room.

Almost immediately after the door closed, Julia let rip and Dan could only hope that everyone else in the building was long gone. As she un-bottled all her fears and frustrations, Dan felt oddly removed.

He was sympathetic, of course – up to a point – although seeing his smart, brittle ex-girlfriend unravel before his very eyes was somewhat disturbing. It was also, he realised, some-how inevitable.

'Why couldn't you just let me handle this myself?' she hissed at him eventually, when none of her other loaded barbs had elicited a response. 'You knew how I felt. I'd told you over and over and over how I felt – but you still welcomed her here – to my home – to Larkford – to my sanctuary. You just threw a grenade into my life and you expect me to believe you were doing it to help?'

Dan was torn. He wanted to defend himself and his choices, to remind her that this situation had taken on a momentum all of its own the minute her father had absconded; but the part of him that still loved her, just wanted to give her a hug and let her cry. Maybe if she'd done a little more crying over the years, he thought, instead of stubbornly papering over the cracks, she wouldn't be on the brink of unravelling now?

'She gave an interview to the press, did you know that? While she was drunk out of her mind at The Kingsley Arms and before you swept in yet again on your sodding white horse. That's why my agent called.'

Dan felt detached as he watched the spittle settle on Julia's bottom lip, her hair deranged and her shift dress crumpled after a long day. The ambiguity must have been written on his face because for the first time, Julia drew breath and there was a flash of genuine fear in her eyes. Did she realise that she'd gone too far, he wondered.

Maybe there really was no such thing as a 'civilised' break-up? Certainly all the hurt and pain seemed to be channelling itself into this conversation: was this the blow-up row that was long overdue? All their unspoken issues seemed to be bubbling to the surface – Candace providing the leverage to open their own personal can of worms.

'When are you going to accept that you can't control everyone around you,' Dan said in that calm, disconnected tone that signified to anyone who knew him that, under the surface, he was seething. 'Your friends, who love you, tried to help your mother, who – let's be frank – was in need of a little support. Is there just a small chance that you're angry with yourself for not being there, or is it just the interruption to your stellar career that's bothering you?'

'There's nothing wrong with ambition, Dan,' Julia spat. 'Maybe you should try it sometime?'

'There is something to be said for an ambition that benefits the greater good, you know, ' Dan retorted. 'The whole community will benefit from my Health in the Community Scheme – and you know what, Jules? That makes me feel pretty good when I go to sleep at night. What do you think about? Ratings figures?'

She glared at him. 'Well, excuse me for not wanting to settle. Some of us can see beyond the edge of the valley, you know.'

'Do you mean settle, or is it settling down that's so terrifying for you?' asked Dan – his anger giving him the courage to address the question that had been niggling him for days.

'I'm not done yet. Can't you see that?' Julia shouted back, all inhibitions discarded. 'I don't want to settle ...' There was a telling flush that gripped her neck as she realised what she'd said.

'Well, I have no desire to be somebody's consolation prize,' Dan said coldly. 'So, I guess we made the right decision. I don't want the kind of relationship where you love me so much you can lash out at me with all your grievances. I'm not your mum. I'm not your dad. And if you stop to think for just a moment, you would recognise that all my intentions were good. Everything I've done was to try and help you.

'I made sure she was safe, I made sure she was taken care of and supported. And yes, I drafted in Holly – your friend – to help me. Whatever you may think of our relationship, and you can hate me if you want to, Jules, you cannot deny the facts. We all love you and we're here to help – no matter how scared or angry or helpless you feel.' He shrugged and for a moment wondered whether he had the strength to deal with this. 'Let's just call it a night. We can work out what to do next in the morning.'

She said nothing. Her face was pale and her teeth worried at her bottom lip, tearing the fragile skin in her distress. 'I can't believe you and Holly got her admitted to the clinic without even talking to me,' she said eventually in a small voice. There was an edge to her tone that made Dan wonder if she was actually more annoyed that he had succeeded where she had failed.

Dan nodded. 'We did. But in the end, it wasn't your choice to make. Your mum knew she'd hit rock bottom the moment she spilled her guts to that journalist. It was your mum who asked me for help, Jules. She knew you were too close to the situation and she probably knew how angry you'd be when you heard what she'd done. There's no easy way to handle this, so Holly and I just went for simplicity. She can have some time there to take advice and consider her options. You can maybe take a break from worrying where she is every minute of the day – seems to me like it might be long overdue.'

'There you go again – telling me what's good for me. Don't you realise that's the worst part of being an alcoholic's daughter? The helplessness – the not knowing what's going to happen next and always, *always,* expecting the worst – that's what gets you. And now, here you are, claiming to be my friend – whatever that means – but still taking away all my choices. Am I supposed to be grateful?'

Dan sighed, exhausted beyond measure and struggling to

keep his cool. 'Well, it wouldn't hurt,' he said flippantly, with a lop-sided smile.

He didn't even see the stapler until it glanced off the side of his forehead and the hot sweet smell of blood filled the air. He lifted his hand as though in a daze and stared at the red stain on his fingers in detached disbelief.

Julia's hands were over her mouth as though she were trying to stifle the words that she had already spoken. Her eyes were filled with horror at what she had done; aghast with herself no doubt for losing control, but also for hurting Dan.

'Well then, I guess it must be true,' said Dan dazedly, 'you always hurt the ones you love.' He picked up a wad of tissues from the desk and pressed them to his temple, pushing away Julia's jerky and disjointed attempts to help.

'Get some help, Jules,' he said coldly, unable to muster even a scrap of affection in his voice. 'Take some time off work. Go visit your mother, visit a therapist. Just get your act together, would you, please. If not for me, then for yourself. And, if you really are as self-loathing as it appears, then maybe just do it for The Practice. Alcoholic mothers raging in the press, we can cope with. Abusive and unstable GPs are a slightly harder sell.'

He stood up, ignoring the swell of nausea that undulated through him. 'And for the avoidance of doubt,' he said as he grabbed another wad of tissues to replace those saturated with his blood, 'you and me? There's no going back. We're done.'

Slumped on the sofa at Taffy and Holly's house, Dan wondered whether he had done the right thing in coming here. It was all he could think of at the time, unwilling to call in external help. On some level, no matter what he'd said, he couldn't bear to see Julia's tantrum splashed all over the tabloids and a First Responder would have been forced to file a report. Instead, losing blood and with a searing headache, he'd blundered through the darkened streets of Larkford, arriving at their front door looking like a train wreck. Thank God, he thought now, that the twins had been in the bath, or he would have frightened the life out of them.

Now, with Taffy having sterilised and sealed the two-inch gash in his hairline with Steri-strips – forehead wounds always bled like the devil – he could finally stop to think. Holly was upstairs reading the twins *The Gruffalo* for the umpteenth time and Taffy was rummaging in the freezer for frozen veg – some to make their supper stretch to another portion and some to stick on Dan's head.

So much for modern management, he thought ruefully. With four equal partners, they had all been so invested in the future and growth of The Practice. They'd joked about how incestuous it was – two couples running a business together. God only knew what they'd been thinking.

Perhaps they'd been caught up in the romance of saving The Practice from closure against all odds, in finding each other amongst the stress and debris? Taffy and Holly had certainly felt like a foregone conclusion to him – their orbits set to collide the moment Milo was removed from the picture. In their haste to find their own happy ending, it looked as though he and Julia had forgotten everything they'd learned the first time round.

Taffy came in with a bag of something orange and two mugs of tea. 'Pureed veg,' he clarified, passing him the frozen block. 'Could be peaches, could be sweet potato. Hard to tell at this point. Although Holly did try and make some apple sauce last week with what turned out to be cauliflower.' He shrugged. 'I suspect she got carried away with the whole

weaning programme, because those lads have been eating
more than me for the last year now, but there's still bags and
bags of pureed shit in that freezer . . .' His voice petered out
despondently.

Dan lifted his mug in thanks and acknowledgement that
Taffy was trying his best to find normality in an incredibly
surreal situation. 'Thanks, mate,' he said simply.

They sat in silence for a moment, sipping at their tea.

'Weird,' said Taffy eventually.

'Yup,' said Dan, slightly moving the brick of orange on his
forehead that appeared to be slowly melting into putty.

'And she actually meant to throw it at you? She wasn't,
I don't know, gesticulating wildly?' Taffy was reaching
for straws, but it wasn't anything that Dan hadn't already
attempted.

Dan shrugged. 'To be fair, she did look pretty shocked.'

'Not surprised,' said Taffy seriously, 'I mean, to manage
to hit your teeny-tiny head from that distance – it must have
been a fluke.'

Dan attempted a scowl and winced. 'Can we leave the piss-
taking until I've stopped bleeding at least?'

'Do you think that she's a bit unhinged, then? Because if
she is a raving loony, we should probably keep her away from
the patients . . . I mean, if she gets one of those whiney women
who think they've got problems because they get stressed
going to Tesco, she might legitimately throw a stapler at them
too . . . Not that I haven't considered it myself from time to
time. That Cassie Holland? Christ – she's enough to make
anyone snap. The last time she was in, I genuinely wanted to
shove cotton wool balls in her mouth just to shut her up . . .'

He rambled on and on and, in a way, it was oddly soothing. By the time the two of them had been through their

own individual lists of Top Five Patients I've Had Murderous Thoughts About, they were both much calmer.

Another cup of tea and a quick check that Dan was showing no obvious signs of concussion and they flicked the TV on. An old episode of Inspector Morse was playing and Dan finally began to relax.

They both jumped out of their seats when Holly came downstairs and flicked the light on. She didn't look or sound very happy and Dan immediately felt guilty for dumping on them. In all honesty though, where else was he going to go?

She sat on the arm of the sofa and took a sip of Taffy's tea. 'Now, since the kids are in bed and the food is burned to a crisp, I guess there's two things we need to discuss: one – who's going out for the take-away and two – what the bloody hell has been going on?'

Chapter 35

Julia sat in her car and shivered. She didn't trust herself to drive until the hammering in her chest had settled. Still in shock at what she'd done, Julia replayed the scene over and over in her mind.

Was it the sheer frustration that had tipped her over the edge, or the very fact that Dan and Holly had succeeded where she had failed? Gaining her mother's trust and getting her to voluntarily ask for help?

It seemed incomprehensible that, after all these years of struggle, her two friends had just swept in and made it happen. What kind of a daughter did that make her?

The summer rain lashed against the window of her car and the smell of wet tarmac filled the air. Her phone vibrated beside her with social media alerts, one after another – all her dirty laundry laid bare for Middle Britain to scrutinise and judge. All those years of work and commitment and always, always keeping her nose clean and now this? Her mother had barely been in Larkford for a fortnight and the scenes of devastation were so much worse than Julia could possibly have imagined.

The bitter taste of disgust made Julia's mouth go dry. She looked across the Market Place and for the first time, she could understand the attraction of sitting in the pub with a glass of wine in her hand. Before she could stop and analyse the feeling, she was striding across to the welcoming lights of The Kingsley Arms.

She'd sabotaged any hope for a friendly post-break-up relationship with Dan, her personal hell was on the internet for all to see and Julia's inner-demons suddenly couldn't give a shit about what anyone else thought. Even as she rummaged in her bag for her purse, she could imagine so easily the enterprising young snapper who could upload a tweet of her this evening, sodden and sozzled – 'Like Mother, Like Daughter?'

'A large glass of white, please, Teddy,' said Julia hoarsely, plucking at the wet clothes that now clung to her body.

'White wine?' he queried, as he'd already got a bottle of Julia's usual tomato juice in his hand.

She nodded, unable to meet his eye and knowing full well that The Kingsley Arms had a thriving following on Twitter and Facebook and that Teddy had, in all likelihood, been here for the hideous drunken photo debacle with her mother.

He poured a large glass and slid it across the polished oak of the bar. 'This one's on the house, okay. Seems like it's medicinal.' His voice was so soft and sympathetic that Julia dared to look up. 'Nobody here is judging, Julia. We've all got families too and God knows, if people judged me by my brother Peter . . . Well, let's just say that he's the success of the family and I'm the poor imitation.'

He poured a packet of Twiglets into a bowl and they munched companionably for a minute or two. It was another sign that Julia was in a bad way, that she didn't even query the volume of carbs and additives she was shovelling into her mouth. She just knew that she wanted to feel – better. She'd regret it later, but when your worst nightmare was laid out in column inches, did it really matter whether her size 8 jeans still fitted to perfection?

The Major and Marion came in from the rain, shaking their soaking umbrella and looking in need of a drink. Grover trotted obediently at the Major's heels, his wiry fur bright with raindrops. He shook violently, showering them all and looking almost delighted with himself as he set off around the bar looking for titbits. They pulled up stools beside Julia without even hesitating, something that Marion certainly would not have done a year ago – a year ago when Julia was still perceived as stand-offish and rude. A year ago, when the Major had been one of the few souls in Larkford to see behind the mask. Since then, the whole community had welcomed this softer, more amenable Julia into their fold – she was good enough for their beloved Dan, ergo she was okay by them. Julia wondered what they would say if they knew what she'd done this evening. From the ill-disguised pity on their faces, they already knew what she'd been doing for the last three decades.

Teddy had their drinks in front of them before they'd even got out of their wet coats. 'Pork scratchings, anyone? Or is this a Twiglets evening?' he asked.

Marion chuckled as she leaned across and snaffled the last handful from the bowl in front of Julia. 'Fill her up, Teddy. And get this one another drink while you're at it. She's a face as long as Livery Street and I'll wager she'd rather have a gin than a hug from me.' Marion gave Julia's taut shoulders a squeeze anyway and Julia did her best not to tense up even more.

Never great with physical contact at the best of times,

she did struggle with the way everyone around here was so touchy feely. And it didn't end there – they all knew each other's business. Even those who didn't share childhood memories of growing up here entered into a weird social contract of sharing the minute they moved in. It was one of the things that had made Julia so unpopular when she first arrived. After all, she'd happily lived in London for years without even knowing her next-door neighbours' names, let alone how 'Our Cathy' was doing with the breastfeeding.

The minute people discovered you were a doctor, they shed all boundaries and inhibitions.

Well, Julia quite liked boundaries and inhibitions; they kept her feeling in control. She took a large mouthful of wine and tried not to gag at the grapey flavour, whose very smell triggered all sorts of memories she would rather forget.

She felt such a failure – and now she couldn't even hit the booze when times got rough. There would be no comfort in the bottom of this wine glass, because every sip just assailed her with hideous childhood memories. She pushed the glass away.

Without missing a beat, Teddy poured a glass of tomato juice and set it down in front of her. 'It's not for everyone, Jules. And I can always add a sneaky shot of vodka to that, if it's oblivion you're craving.'

Marion and The Major supped at their matching pints of Guinness and the general hubbub in the bar around them meant their silence was not uncomfortable. There was no urgency to fill the void with pointless chit-chat and Julia was actually grateful for their company. Whilst the promise of alcohol had summoned her in, it was the warm camaraderie and familiarity that made her stay, chomping quietly on Twiglets and trying not to think.

It was Marion who decided to stop pussy-footing around the obvious first, but she did it in such a gentle and tactful way that Julia almost – almost – felt like hugging her. 'I was thinking that you probably had enough on your hands at the moment, Dr Channing, what with being the Face of the NHS and all, not to mention *everything else*. So we were thinking you might like to stay on at the Gatehouse for a bit, until things . . . well, until things . . . until you're ready?'

'That would be lovely,' Julia said gratefully. The very idea of finding somewhere new to live, whilst juggling work, Dan, her mother and the media beast on her back, was simply too overwhelming to consider.

'We'll shut the main gates too, I think, come in by the back lane instead – should keep those ghastly photographers out of your hair for a bit.' The Major spoke gruffly and didn't even look up from his pint, but he had obviously been giving the matter some serious thought. 'Keep the curtains drawn on the front and you should be alright.'

He went back to feeding Grover bits of Twiglet and giving him the occasional sip of Guinness.

Marion tsked at his matter-of-fact advice and gave Julia's shoulders another squeeze. 'You'll be alright, won't you, love? I mean, at least you know how to handle these media-types and that programme of yours is just charming. So informative. A little set-back like this won't bother you for long will it, not with your lovely Dan to keep you on the straight and narrow?'

Julia couldn't help it. Marion's well-meaning platitudes had hit the mark with such unerring accuracy, it was hard to maintain her fragile composure. She let out a small sob and clapped her hand over her mouth. How would everybody in Larkford react when they found out how hideously she had behaved this evening? Maybe they might have been prepared to cut her some slack about her mother, but pile this on as well? Hurting Darling Dan would have her on Larkford's Most Wanted List in no time.

Marion tried to soothe her. 'There, there, love. It'll be fine. All these newspapers are just tomorrow's fish and chip paper really.'

The Major harrumphed beside her. 'Don't be naïve, Marion. It's all on the Interweb now, isn't it? Chin up though, girlie. Don't let the bastards get you down and all that.'

Even through her own distress, the Major's bluff outlook on life made Julia want to smile. Until she remembered why she was upset and what the Major and Marion would say if they knew. She stood up abruptly. 'Time to call it a night, I think.'

Marion's face was scrumpled in consternation. 'You can't drive home all upset, Dr Channing. Dan would be furious if he thought we'd let you. Join us for a bite of something? We'll have a good rant about the Unfairness of Life, if it makes you feel any better?'

The Major cleared his throat again. 'Maybe we should be having a chat about inviting the bloody media into our lives in the first place though, eh?' His tone was just erring on the nice side of judgemental, but Julia had to concede he had a point.

True, it was social media and the weight of popular opinion that had helped their Save The Practice campaign, but Julia had also gone courting fame and success with her appearances on *Doctor In The House* too. And once they were in ... well, there was no controlling what they found or reported on. Suddenly Reverend Taylor's sermon last week on the hand that giveth also taketh away made a lot more sense – so much sense in fact, that Julia half wondered whether it had been drafted with her in mind.

Feeling like a fraud for accepting their hospitality while her guilty conscience eroded at her sanity, Julia pulled her damp coat back on. Marion stood up and gave her a lung-crushing hug, which Julia tried so hard not to resist.

'Ooh, it's like hugging a grumpy cat, Dr Channing. You should just relax a bit, love. Maybe get yourself a dog – they know how to give a cuddle. Don't you, Grover?' Marion looked around for the little scruffy terrier that was the Major's one true love – she'd long since resigned herself to coming second in his affections. To be fair though, Grover was the sweetest most intelligent little dog ever to walk the streets of Larkford and there really was no contest.

'Grover?' said Marion again, looking around wildly when the little dog failed to appear. They all looked over to the pub door, just checking that nobody had left it open and inadvertently allowed the little chap to wander.

It was the hideous retching sound that caught Julia's attention first. Quiet but gut wrenching, the pitiful sound came from under the long trestle table behind them.

Without thought for her Armani trousers or what she would find, Julia dropped to her knees and there he was. Poor little dog was spasmed on to his knees, making a rattling sound as he dragged in each shallow breath. God knows how long he'd been under there, with all the noise and chaos around him and nobody hearing him struggle. She lay flat on her stomach and gently pulled him towards her.

She wasn't even that fond of dogs, but the sight of him, with his ears flattened on his head and his eyes wide in fear just spoke to a part of Julia's soul that she didn't know she had. She lifted him onto an empty table and began a rapid assessment. She didn't stop to think dog or human, she just treated him as though he were somebody's baby in distress – which in a way of course, he was.

The Major and Marion stood beside her and the pub fell silent as Julia called out what she needed. 'Teddy, I need a torch, some water, olive oil if you have it and do you have any food preparation gloves?' Within moments, he had everything she needed plus a towel from the bar to stop him shivering.

She didn't say that the shivering was more from a shock reaction than the cold, but instead quietly suggested that he phone the Out of Hours vet and call in an emergency. She pulled on the gloves to stop her long fingernails scratching the little dog, who was now floppy in her hands. She lifted his jowls and his gums were the deep purple colour that told her what she needed to know. Moistening her fingers with the olive oil she held his uncomplaining mouth open. 'Marion. Shine the torch down here for me. Teddy, I need tweezers, or a couple of drinks stirrers if you've got them.'

The Major said nothing. Marion trembled and the torch light wobbled, until Julia gently whispered to her, 'You're doing okay, just try and breathe and hold it still. He'll be okay. I'll make sure he's okay.'

With no tweezers to be found, despite Teddy hollering at every woman in the bar to empty their handbags and check, Julia only hoped that her skill with chopsticks would be enough. She held the drink stirrers in one hand and slowly breathed out. She could see the offending Twiglet wedged sideways at the far reaches of Grover's throat and the last thing she wanted to do was to push it down further.

She slid the stirrers in until she could feel them take hold and then slowly, slowly, slowly began to withdraw the blockage from his throat. At the last moment, the little dog convulsed and gagged and threw up all over her shoes. He coughed and heaved and then threw up some more, before giving himself a shake and licking Julia's hand.

In that moment, there was nobody else in the world but herself and that little dog and she scooped him into her arms and sobbed into his fur. The sheer relief from saving him, the sheer bloody hideousness of her day caught up with her and she couldn't stop.

'Aw, Dr Channing,' said Marion. 'And you said you weren't a dog person.'

The very gratitude and affection in her voice made Julia sob even harder. It was only when the Major reached over and rescued Grover that she was able to pull herself together.

'Go easy there, Dr Channing,' he said, his voice all choked. 'It would be a shame to suffocate the poor little bugger when you've only just saved his life.' A fleeting clasp of her hand was filled with gratitude and respect, but his attention was reserved for Grover.

'You daft little sod,' he crooned to his dog. 'I told you all that junk food would be the death of you.'

It took a little while after all the excitement had died down for Julia to slip away. She'd spent the last twenty minutes longing for solitude to get her thoughts in order, but when she finally had it, she couldn't bear the cacophony of voices in her head.

She couldn't begin to place the unfamiliar emotion at first. It niggled at the edge of her consciousness, toying with her emotions. Just then, in the pub, as she'd held Grover's trembling body, there'd been a startling moment of clarity. It was the first time, in a very long time, that she'd done anything without thinking of herself first. And it felt amazing.

Terrifying too, but definitely something she wanted to explore. If only she knew where to start.

It was strange to her how life was all a question of timing. If her mother had come to visit on a different week, without the press lurking around every corner, would things have turned out differently? If she hadn't been feeling so utterly flummoxed just now in her car, would she even have taken Quentin's call?

It was immaterial to analyse that now, she realised, as she pulled up outside Quentin's townhouse in Bath. Parking the car on a double yellow and shoving a 'Doctor on Call' card in the windscreen, the irony of the situation made her wince. She smoothed her hair down and looked up at the sash windows, trying to work out which one was his bedroom and whether she might be seeing this view from the other side tonight.

There was nothing rational about Julia's decision-making this evening; it was almost as though she were wired to self-destruct. Even saving Grover and earning the gratitude of her neighbours had only served to remind her how much she stood to lose. Perhaps it was the easiest way? To go out with a bang?

She checked her phone for messages. Nothing. Even though she had expected that, it still hurt. Surely Holly and Taffy knew what had happened by now?

It wasn't the first time and it wouldn't be the last that Julia questioned the progress she had made in Larkford. True, she had friends and a social life, even a smattering of social skills, now. But was she necessarily any happier than when she had been more self-contained? She certainly felt more vulnerable now, knowing she had so much more to lose. She took a deep breath, wanting to find some solace or distraction from the pain.

Quentin's front door swung open, the light illuminating her car and, as he strode towards her through the rain, Julia couldn't help but think that oblivion in his arms sounded like a very good distraction indeed.

Chapter 36

To say that Holly was pissed off the next morning would be understating her position by an exponentially growing factor. It was one thing to receive a phone call at breakfast time asking you to come in early to see a patient; it was quite another when it was a journalist and photographer awaiting your arrival.

Harry Grant from the Primary Care Trust had been terribly apologetic. 'I can't get hold of Julia and I'm really in a bind here, Holly. Please, just this once, can you do the interview?' He'd muttered something about deadlines and edicts from Derek Landers and then echoed Taffy's misgivings about there being no such thing as a free lunch almost word for word. Their status as a Model Surgery was already eliciting far more interest than they had bargained for. Now buzzwords like 'transparency' and 'accountability' and 'consensus management' were being tossed around in the national press. Having a photograph of Julia looking like a catwalk model had certainly piqued a little interest; that self-same picture twinned with one of her mother on the lash had all but crashed the NHS Twitter feed.

The *Powers That Be* were not happy, sweaty Derek Landers was loving every column inch of their downfall and now

Harry Grant was calling in a favour. His high regard for Holly after her Save The Practice campaign had made her the obvious choice to step into the breach – that and the fact that he had held on to her unlisted home phone number. And it didn't look as though she was going to get much choice in the matter, irrespective of how incredibly uncomfortable it made her feel.

Hence the dress. And the make-up. And the vertiginous heels that were elegant and elongating but eminently impractical. But, no matter how ridiculously overdressed she might be feeling, Holly had to concede that wearing the beautiful Diane von Furstenberg wrap dress for the meeting with Elsie's publisher had made her feel powerful, competent and in control. Exactly the feelings she was lacking today. So, since basically six o'clock that morning, Holly had been repeatedly, and a little maniacally, mumbling under her breath, 'What would Elsie do?'

She'd also been trying not to think about where Julia might have disappeared to, having tried every single phone number she could think of and left a series of increasingly worried messages. Whatever had gone on between Julia and Dan, Julia was her friend too, even if she was no stranger to a little melodrama.

Holly just wanted to know that she was okay and alive somewhere, preferably so she could find her and then kill her for landing her with this media circus.

'Bloody bastard interview,' cursed Holly as she snagged her tights for the second time in as many minutes. In fact, if Taffy hadn't plied her with an emergency bacon sandwich and a strong espresso, Holly couldn't truly have vouched for anyone's safety today.

He looked tired and dishevelled after their abrupt start to

the day, but nevertheless he was making time for her. Again. Making time to drop the twins with Lizzie. Calming her nerves. Making her a priority.

The sudden flush of guilt as she dashed through the streets of Larkford took Holly by surprise – when had she ever done the same for him?

Walking into reception moments later, Holly was immediately gratified to see early-birds Grace and Lucy look impressed at her new polished appearance. Perhaps it had been worth the ridiculous effort after all? 'Will I do as your responsible and refined representative?' she joked, striking a pose and nearly falling over her own feet.

Lucy snorted with laughter appreciatively. 'Well, at least you haven't gone all hoity-toity in that posh frock. I did wonder there for a minute and to be honest, there's only room for one Alpha female in this practice.'

'I'm not an Alpha female,' said Grace, batting the compliment away, before realising that – (a) it wasn't a compliment and (b) it wasn't intended for her.

Holly grinned and balanced her bottom on the edge of Grace's desk, for fear of creasing. 'We obviously know that *you're* the powerhouse here, Gracie, but we're keeping it under the radar in case the NHS try and poach you away with the promise of chocolate on your Hobnobs.'

Grace looked from side to side and pulled open a desk drawer that was stuffed with fancy chocolate biscuits. 'We may have cut back in the doctors' lounge, but the admin team have a secret kitty. We'll cut you in, if you promise to keep it under your hat.'

Holly laughed. 'I still think you should have just rationed the boys – they eat like they're teenagers.'

She took the proffered biscuit and leaned forward to nibble it without getting crumbs on her dress – it rather undid the whole elegant, poised image she was trying to portray. 'Did they say what time they'd be here? My shadows for the day?'

Grace looked up. 'Oh, they're already here, Holly. Doing some vox pops in the car park with the patients. Didn't you get my text?'

Holly nearly choked on her biscuit, as she hurriedly brushed away a few stray crumbs and checked her teeth for give-away chocolate chips. 'How the hell Julia does this every day without going insane, I do not know.' She took a deep breath.

'I am calm, confident and capable,' Holly muttered over and over, just as Elsie had taught her. She pulled open the door and pasted on a smile.

'Harry,' she said, shaking him by the hand, as he apologetically mouthed 'sorry' at her. 'And Derek too, how lovely to see you again. So glad we could make this happen today.' She turned to the journalist who was young and eager and basically Holly's worst nightmare. 'Hi, I'm Holly Graham,' she said. 'Let's pop inside and get you a coffee before we open up and you can tell me what you'd like to see.'

Gary Hynde paused the recording he was making on his iPhone and shook her hand. She fought every instinct in her body not to instantly wipe off the sweat from his limp, clammy palm. 'All in good time, Dr Graham, or Holly? May I call you Holly?'

'Of course,' she managed, trying to be obliging but already prickling at his intimate tone and invasive once-over.

'I've just been having a lovely chat with some of your patients out here. Catch them on the way in, you know.' The unspoken sequitur of 'before you can brief them' hung in the air. Derek Landers said nothing, he just looked smug and Holly knew in that instant that he had been the one to organise this at short notice, hoping to catch them on the hop.

Holly just smiled, having a quick glance around the car park to see whether those patients had been friend or foe. If he'd happened upon one of their Midweek Moaners, they may as well shut up shop and go home now.

Charlotte Lansing tapped Holly smartly on the shoulder, her wicker basket slung over one arm and her quilted jacket looking, as always, in need of a jolly good wash. Her vowels may be perfectly crystal clear and well honed, but the same could not be said for the other residents of Blackleigh Farm – except possibly the horses, who Holly gathered, enjoyed four-star accommodation. 'Don't look so worried, Dr Graham, we've already told them how wonderful you are and that you take fabulously good care of all your ladies.'

She made it sound as though Holly popped round to their afternoon tea parties for individual consultations, like something out of a Jane Austen novel, but Holly still managed to hold on to her smile. We're a modern, forward-thinking practice, she told herself, and Gary can see that for himself in just a minute.

'And of course, Mrs Lansing kindly filled us in about Dr Channing,' Gary said, watching her reaction carefully.

'Wonderful,' said Holly faintly.

'Ooh, Dr Graham,' said Mrs Lansing, unable to restrain herself, 'I heard all about what Dr Channing did last night. I have to admit, I was a little bit shocked – I mean you don't expect it, do you? Not from her, anyway. So I was saying to Mr Hynde, just now, you should never judge a book by its cover should you? Shocking really.'

'Well, yes,' Holly gulped, silently offering a prayer to the universe for a small seizure or collapse of some kind to strike her down at this point – nothing lasting, obviously, and preferably not too painful either, but just enough to make this stop.

'I mean it's a good thing, obviously. We all had her down as a bit starchy, you know.'

'Quite,' said Holly, wondering if she could fake a small heart attack without arousing suspicion. Failing that, could she claim temporary insanity, if she strangled Julia later for putting her in this unbearable position?

'And Mr Hynde here was terribly interested, weren't you?' Mrs Lansing continued as she turned to Holly, 'It's the human angle, isn't it? And he wants to get some photographs too, while it's all fresh in everybody's mind.'

I'll bet he does, thought Holly, wondering how colourful and photogenic Dan's forehead would be this morning. Almost certainly vivid enough to warrant a full-colour spread, she thought.

Mrs Lansing sighed. 'Now if I'd known all this time that Dr Channing was a dog person, I'd probably have liked her a little bit more, you know,' she said confidentially.

Maybe I am actually having a seizure, Holly thought. Maybe this is what it feels like. Either that or her new support tights really were too tight and there was no blood returning to her brain. The conversation around her seemed to make no sense at all and with Gary Hynde's beady eyes watching her every move, it didn't seem like a good idea to admit that she'd been holding her breath for so long, she could no longer feel her fingertips.

'You're not a dog-lover yourself then, Holly? You look spectacularly underwhelmed by your colleague's courageous rescue,' Derek Landers probed.

'Oh, Dr Graham has a beautiful Labradoodle, don't you, Dr Graham? It's a funny story actually . . .' said Charlotte Lansing, finally catching on that all was not well, as she tucked her arm through Derek Landers' and expertly manoeuvred him towards the front door. She cast a concerned glance back in Holly's direction, but prattled on all the way inside.

Harry Grant looked terribly uncomfortable as he dropped back to talk to Holly. 'I'm so sorry about this. I just didn't get much notice . . . I know a heads-up would have been helpful.'

'You could say that,' said Holly distractedly, still trying to eavesdrop on whatever tale Mrs Lansing was spinning.

'Frankly, thank God for Dr Channing's heroics – it's all anyone has been talking about,' he said with an exhausted sigh.

Holly gave him a sideways look. There was nothing about throwing a stapler at Dan's head that would count as heroic in her book and what the hell did that have to do with dogs? So far as Holly could tell, pets were just another weakness as far as Julia was concerned. Jesus – she'd barely been on board with the idea of Alice having an assistance dog at work . . .

'Do you ever feel like everybody knows something that you don't?' Holly asked him.

Harry raised one eyebrow. 'Oh, Holly. I work for the NHS. I feel that way every single day.'

Credit where credit was due, when Gary Hynde had requested a shadow day, he really meant it. Derek had bowed out after the first excruciating half hour, but not before making it known that he was watching their every move. And now Gary was lurking two paces behind Holly every step of her day, almost as though he'd been specifically briefed. It had taken a rather awkward moment when he'd attempted to follow her into the Ladies' for Holly to spell out her terms. 'Gary, it's wonderful having you here and obviously, we want to show you everything, but I think we can both agree that you're taking your brief a little too literally.'

She'd tried to inject enough humour into her voice that he wouldn't take offence, attempting to channel Elsie once again and her ability to manipulate almost anyone to her best advantage. 'I just need a moment . . .' she clarified, realising that her supplicating tone and constant use of her new bête-noire 'just' would not be something that Elsie would even contemplate.

Leaning her head against the cool tile in the bathroom, Holly couldn't believe how exhausting she found this constant scrutiny. Surely nobody on the planet, let alone in the cosy world of Larkford, could bear up to such close inspection? She was beginning to understand how Julia's brittle mood swings might actually be a by-product of her camera-shaped shadow.

Checking her phone and finding no response from Julia at all, she swallowed the awkward realisation that – had it been Lizzie in trouble – she wouldn't have satisfied herself with a few hurried texts and voicemails, she would have been physically knocking on her front door. But between hearing Dan's side of things, dealing with the monsters in Ben's wardrobe all night and then the farce that was her morning . . . Well, there hadn't really been a moment, had there, she justified.

She stepped out into the corridor, full of resolve to cut herself some slack – seeing their working life through Gary's tiny little eyes, was beginning to give her an entirely different perspective. Every single one of the team was diligent and compassionate, prepared to go the extra mile, even when the man-on-the-street would be calling time. This patience, this nurturing side of their characters, always wanting to give

100 per cent, was something she was in danger of taking for granted.

Speaking of which, she watched Taffy parry Gary's intrusive questions with calm authority, as he led him away from whatever emotional meltdown appeared to be taking place in the waiting room. For them, it was a regular part of their working day, but for Gary – on a hair trigger for a 'story' – who knew what he might choose to focus on?

As Taffy easily deflected Gary's none-too-subtle enquiries about Mental Health in their community, Holly watched from a distance. Really watched. And as she took in Taffy's gentle demeanour and his humorous take on Gary's borderline offensive prurience, she caught her breath. Somehow she was carrying an internal divide between her heart and her head.

And she wasn't even sure why any more.

Why did she subtly push him away every time he talked of the future?

Why did the notion of commitment scare her so fundamentally?

It was almost an ingrained habit now, like Eric with the vacuum cleaner – even though he now dwarfed its dragon roar, he was still the frightened puppy wedging himself behind the sofa every time it came out of the cupboard.

If only Holly knew a way for them to outgrow their fears – God knows there was a dearth of support in the women's magazines she occasionally flicked through for advice. According to the popular press, every woman on the planet was clamouring for a wedding ring and only manly men and playboys had issues with commitment!

Her reverie was interrupted by Dan's arrival – late, fully padded in his lifestyle-fat-suit and huffing and puffing his way towards her. Let nobody say he didn't take his bets with Taffy seriously – unfortunately he didn't appear to have received the message that all hilarity must be on hold for the day. And since both Julia and Quentin had been a no-show, it looked as though filming was too.

They should be grateful for small mercies, thought Holly, as Gary's antenna for a story was so easily distracted. One camera at a time was plenty – after all there was only so much smoke and mirrors they could deploy to protect their patients from the intrusion.

A kerfuffle in Alice's consulting room caught her attention, and Holly glanced sharply at the journalist only to see that he was caught up in Dan's story of how his DIY had gone awry. The pointed look Dan was giving her though was all but indecipherable due to the dark and angry bruise above his eyebrow. 'I'm going to take Gary over to The Deli for a coffee, really give him the low down on how things work around here,' Dan said, as subtle as a brick.

'Sure,' she said slowly, 'I'll come over in a bit, but I need to log in at home first.' She could see Gary waiver, clearly wanting to stick to her like bindweed, but she was banking on the fact that mundane domesticity might not be too much of a draw. 'Blinking washing machine on the fritz again – you wouldn't believe how much laundry two small boys can generate.'

Holly smiled to herself as she walked away. If her years with Milo had taught her one thing, it was that tales of laundry, periods and home furnishings were guaranteed to have a soporific effect on the average male, somewhere equivalent to the tipping-beyond-45-degrees that seemed to induce coma-style snoring from every man she'd ever met.

She knocked gently and pushed open the door into Alice's

room, the yapping growing ever louder, to find Coco circling madly around Jenny Lyle's legs. Alice was on her knees trying to calm the little dog, but Coco was most insistent, refusing to leave Jenny and yapping so pitifully, it was almost as though she were desperate to be understood.

'Call Jamie, Holly. Would you?' Alice asked sadly, knowing all too well what this latest episode might mean. 'Would you tell him it's happened again?'

Holly nodded. 'Silly question though, Jenny? You're not here for diabetes testing, are you?'

Jenny shook her head. 'No.'

Holly saw Alice's shoulders slump still further and wondered whether she'd been having similar thoughts. Perhaps, surrounded by all these ailing people, Coco was no longer content with just helping one of them?

Thank God Gary Hyndes hadn't been here to witness this, though – it was hardly playing in to the polished professional image they were desperate to portray.

And that said it all: desperate. Desperate for funding. Desperate for security. Desperate to please. At no point had anybody seemingly stopped to think whether they were also desperate to do a good job. With the lunatics now running the asylum, were they really a model surgery, or just an experiment that was failing?

The sense of responsibility on this front seemed to weigh heavier on Holly's shoulders than for the others. They were focused on patient care and rightly so, but Holly knew only too well that it took more than five excellent doctors to run an excellent practice and there was only so much that Grace could do on her own to keep them sailing straight. They needed a senior partner – an experienced practitioner – to chart their course and look at the bigger picture. And truth

be told, Holly didn't think that any of them were up to the
job at the moment.

'Collaborative management, my arse,' she mumbled as she
scrolled through her contacts for the Diabetes Dog Trainer
and Jamie promised to be there as quickly as possible.

Taffy was leaning in her doorway as she hung up. 'I gather
we're going to The Deli for lunch with Nancy Drew,' he said.

'I don't see how we can, to be honest, not with all of this
going on.' She threw her hands up in the air in defeat. 'And
I can't get hold of Julia at all. I have to confess I'm starting
to get worried.'

'Are you serious?' Taffy asked, his voice tight. 'I can't
believe that you're thinking about Julia at a time like this.
The Practice – possibly – I mean, how can we function in
our ridiculous top-heavy way, if two of the partners are
fighting? But seriously, Holly, our friend has a two-inch
gash to his forehead. There's press circling like vultures and
a mental spaniel in the hallway. And you? You're worrying
about bloody Julia!'

The outburst was so blunt, so uncharacteristic of Taffy's
laissez-faire attitude to life that Holly almost wondered for
a moment whether she was so tense she was hallucinating.

Neither of them spoke for a moment as the atmosphere
in the room began to cloy with the intensity of unspoken
emotions.

'They're both our friends, Taffy,' Holly ventured. 'Dan *and*
Julia. And they're both having a horrible time. Julia possibly
more so, if you sat down to make a list.'

'And you can bet she bloody well has,' muttered Taffy.

Holly scowled, disappointed that, at the very first hurdle,
Taffy seemed so ready to throw Julia under the bus.

Okay, so the whole stapler-throwing incident hadn't exactly cast Julia in the best of lights, but Holly could almost understand the frustration and anger that had driven her to it. If only Julia wasn't such an over-achiever – even her over-arm throw hit target. Nobody would have been half as stressed if the bloody stapler had cracked Dan on the shin or broken a vase.

'Julia is our partner and our friend. It's not up to us to take sides,' Holly insisted. 'Plus, surely you can see how alone she must be feeling right now? Dan's here with us. Her mum's at the clinic. Who else does she have?'

Taffy blew out a long slow breath. 'This is probably why they tell you not to put all your eggs in one basket, right? Work friends, home friends, boyfriend? If they happen to overlap . . .'

'They overlap for all of us though,' she reminded him. 'Just remember that.'

He sighed wearily. 'Go on then, send the mad psycho a text.' He caught sight of the look on Holly's face and held up his hands. 'Too soon to joke?'

'Definitely,' she replied, already tapping out yet another message to Julia. She looked up to find Taffy staring at her with an odd expression on his face. 'What?'

He shrugged. 'You always look out for everyone, don't you? I mean, I could only see Dan as the injured party in all this – plus, you know, freaking out about work. And then you start seeing both sides of it . . .' He paused by the doorway, his expression inscrutable. 'Damn it, Holly – you really do know how to make a man feel incredibly shallow.'

Chapter 37

Dan looked up and the exhaustion was clear for everyone to see. 'Jesus – your face looks like cheap steak,' said Taffy with his traditional delicacy, as he came into the doctors' lounge later that afternoon. 'Hope you didn't let that sad little journo see you looking like that?'

Dan quickly put his finger to his lips and jerked his head sideways, watching in amusement as Taffy spun around, fully expecting to see Gary Hynde and his omnipresent iPhone recording every word he said.

'Oh yes, very funny,' Taffy grumbled as he slumped down into the seat beside Dan. 'But seriously for a minute, what the hell did you say about your head? It's not as though you can comb your hair over the cut now, is it? Not to mention that on a ratio basis, that cut must comprise, what, forty per cent of your bonce?'

Dan rolled his eyes and then promptly wished he hadn't. His headache had been growing gradually worse through-out the day, to the point where he'd given himself a quick concussion once-over after lunch. It probably wasn't terribly effective shining a torch in one's own eyes and checking for reactions in a mirror, but had he let on to the others how hor-rific he was feeling, then two things would have happened:

one, they would have sent him home and two, they would almost certainly have resented Julia that little bit more. And he wasn't sure quite why, but he was pretty confident that Julia had enough demons to battle all on her own, without him adding to the mix.

'Told him it was a bit of DIY gone awry,' he said, belatedly replying to Taffy's question. 'He didn't bat an eyelid.'

'Hmm,' said Taffy, clearly unconvinced. 'Well, let's hope so. Whatever stunt Julia pulled off with the Major's dog last night has clearly got her in Larkford's good books. There's three boxes of chocolates in reception for her.' He looked sheepish for a moment. 'Okay, there are now two boxes of chocolates in reception for her . . .'

Dan grinned, Taffy's voracious appetite being a wonder to them all. How he kept so incredibly fit whilst eating so much crap was an indictment of medical science.

'I think she's with Quentin,' said Dan quietly, apropos of nothing. 'Or should I say "Quinn".'

'Figures,' said Taffy quietly. 'It would give her the illusion of control to be the first to move on.'

Dan gave him a sideways look. 'Have you finished *Marketing for Dummies* and moved on to Psychology? And yes, I did see the marketing book in your bathroom so don't deny it. Therapy for Beginners not so much.'

Taffy took a sip of his Coke, his only concession to day-time drinking being that it must include as much sugar and caffeine as humanly possible. 'She's not at home. I checked. Holly guilted me into it, so don't tell her I went.' He sounded properly riled.

'Trouble in Paradise?' Dan asked.

Taffy shrugged. 'If there is, it'll be your fault. It's a thing, you know – I read it in *Cosmo*. It's called the Ripple Effect.'

'*Cosmo?*'

Taffy looked embarrassed for a moment. 'Actually, it might have been *Heat*. Either way – when one couple splits up, their friends often do too – and you have to admit that we've been more like a foursome than a couple for ages . . . Well – I worry – that's all. Not to mention, I seem to be doing my part by acting like an absolute dickhead every opportunity I get.'

Dan nodded. 'I get it, but unless you're planning on sleeping with Quentin too, I reckon you're probably safe.' He sighed. 'I went round to Julia's first thing. Hence . . . you know . . . Quentin.'

'You'll be okay, though,' said Taffy seriously. 'You've done all this once before.'

Dan's expression was bleak. 'Is that why I feel like this, then? Like we did all the pain and recrimination the first time around and this time the only thing hurting is my pride? Learn from my mistakes, Taffy, don't rush what you have with Holly and ruin it. Julia always made it clear that her career was her priority, but I suppose I thought that would change once we had a solid relationship to build on.'

Taffy frowned in thought. 'Couldn't rush her even if I wanted to – she knows her own mind, does Holly. But, I don't think it's like that with us, to be honest. We both want to be together, build a home together. I think.' He shrugged. 'She just prefers having me as her illicit live-in-lover, rather than her husband. It's hardly a make-your-family-proud type scenario, is it?'

'You're arguing about semantics then really, aren't you?' Dan replied despondently, unaware that Taffy had been just as much in need of reassurance in sharing that particular confidence. 'Whereas with me and Jules – it's as though we just want different things out of life to make us feel fulfilled. So you're right, I've got some thinking to do, because it's almost as though we learned nothing the second time around.'

There was an awkward pause as both men suddenly realised how intimate their conversation had become.

Taffy stepped into the breach. 'To be honest, I just meant you'd done this break-up once so you'd probably be a bit pissed off and in need of a revenge shag, but your way works too.'

Dan couldn't help but smile. 'You're a dickhead.'

'Wanker.'

'Arse-face,' Dan responded, almost lovingly. He clapped a hand on Taffy's shoulder and looked self-conscious. 'Can I tell you a secret?'

Taffy looked left and right, only partially joking, as he scoped out the doctors' lounge for journalists.

'There's somebody else I like. Have started to like . . . Well, it's a bit weird actually, because I've known her for ages, but it's like I never really *saw* her before, you know.'

'Like totally, Tiffany,' Taffy replied in an appalling American accent, slurping his can of Coke through a straw like a teenage girl. When he realised Dan wasn't kidding about, he stopped dead. 'Oh. Okay. Lindy?'

Dan shook his head. 'If I've been thinking about somebody else while I was still with Julia, was I actually the one cheating?'

'Do you *want* to have been the one cheating?' Taffy asked, trying to work out if this was a self-defence mechanism against Julia's apparent leap into Quentin's bed.

'To be honest, mate, right now, I don't whether I want a shit or a haircut.'

Taffy laughed. 'Then let me make this simple for you, mate – you have no hair left to cut.' He stood up and shoved his hands in his pockets. 'Come on – it's a gorgeous evening and we've done our bit for the lame and the ailing, I reckon. Let's go to the pub and have a game of snooker. Take your mind off things.'

Dan rose to his feet, trying to ignore the mild wave of nausea that overcame him. 'Since when did The Kingsley Arms have a snooker table?'

Taffy shepherded him out of the door and they ambled towards the Market Place and commandeered a table outside. Drinks duly ordered, Dan utterly bemused, Taffy filled him in on the rules. 'So you need to see a red car, then you get to go for your colours. Remember "You Go Brown Before Potting Black".'

Dan blinked twice. 'Am I having auditory hallucinations?'

Taffy laughed. 'Yellow, green, brown, blue, pink, black? You remember the snooker mnemonic. Just pot the balls in order. I'll break, shall I?' He looked around the Market Place and within moments, the traffic lights changed and the cars began streaming past, 'Red car, yellow car, red . . . Argh. No greens. Your go.'

Dan shook his head. 'Where on earth did you find this game, Taffs? It's a bit off-piste even for us.'

'Chief Inspector Grant told me about it the other week. They used to play it when they were doing spot checks for MOTs or speeding – to stop them getting bored. Did you never wonder why you got pulled over so often when you had that little red Audi? Well, now you know. Car snooker.'

'Mentalist. Besides, I thought you had another wheeze going on with Jason – there was lots of shouting and laughing when I joined you the other night.'

Taffy looked a bit embarrassed. 'You wouldn't like that game, though, Dan. Trust me.' Under Dan's questioning gaze,

Taffy buckled immediately. 'Drink along with *Doctor In The House*. Every time Julia grimaces, drink. Every time she says "basically", drink. Every time she ...'

'I get the premise, Taffs. And you're right, I'm not sure that one's for me.' The traffic lights changed again. 'Red, yellow car, red, green car, red lorry?'

Taffy shook his head. '*Car* snooker, Dan. Just cars. Otherwise it would get ridiculous.'

Dan laughed for the first time, as the hustle and bustle of the end of the day began to mellow in the pub garden. 'Yup, because *that's* what would make it ridiculous.'

Dan swallowed a couple of paracetamol with a sip of cider and rubbed the back of his neck. Taffy was phoning home to check that Holly was back from seeing Elsie and that he wasn't needed for Twin Watch. Dan couldn't help wondering whether he himself would ever be so amenable. As Dan watched Cassie Holland corral Tarquin-the-Terrible away from the newsagent's, he realised that his own emotions had finally settled on that front.

It wasn't Julia's lack of maternal urges that had been their undoing, he realised now, it was the fact that he was ready to settle down and she wasn't. She still had so much to prove – to herself and to the world at large – and now Dan had a better understanding of her upbringing and her motivations, he could kind of understand why.

He slipped another handful of popcorn down to Gerald the goose, who pecked at it delicately from Dan's palm. It was oddly satisfying having been adopted by a goose, Dan decided, even if he did get odd looks whenever Gerald spotted him in the Market Place and zeroed in on him with rather terrifying focus. But Gerald was most definitely his own master, taking his treats before making his retreat. 'You're only in this for the popcorn, aren't you, mate?' said Dan, as Gerald bustled his way through the busy pub garden, belly full, and back towards the river bank.

Dan watched Jamie the dog trainer, walking loops through the town with Alice and Coco. They went in and out of shops as they were all shutting up for the night, criss-crossing the Market Place, as if seeking out maximum distractions. Thankfully Coco seemed to be happily doing her job and the relief on Alice's face was clear to see. Maybe he should get a dog, Dan wondered. At least then, somebody would always be pleased to see him and it was probably more sociably acceptable than a goose.

He watched, in horrified slow motion, as Percy Lawson revved the engine of his motorbike to attract attention and then inadvertently powered it into a large hedge by the pub. He emerged moments later unscathed, as though it were the most natural way in the world to park his bike. But then, based on the row of large holes in said hedge, perhaps it was a daily event. Dan made a mental note to talk to him about private health insurance and drank his pint in peace, just a tiny bit disappointed not to have crossed off another square on the Injury Bingo card that Jason had so sweetly devised for them all.

Jamie and Alice wound up inevitably at The Kingsley Arms, just as Grace had finished locking up The Practice for the night and was walking through the Market Place on her way home. Dan noticed instantly that Jamie's attention was no longer on Coco.

'Grace?' Jamie called. 'Come and have a drink? We're just road-testing Coco in different environments.'

Grace tucked her newly trimmed hair behind her ear and

changed course to join them. Jamie, bless him, was quick off the mark to help Grace with all her shopping bags. 'What can I get you?' he asked, before Dan had even formulated the thought.

Thank God Taffy was still on the phone, Dan realised, or one look at the piqued expression on his face would rather give the game away. He pointedly said nothing as Jamie and Grace chattered away happily about the pros and cons of fruit in Pimm's. By the time Jamie went in to order, Grace was blushing prettily and there was a sparkle in her eyes that Dan hadn't seen before.

'You're in demand,' he said to Grace, aiming for light and breezy, but ending up sounding childishly churlish.

She looked a little taken aback. 'I could say the same about you.' She nodded her head to the left where a neighbouring table was packed with the training group from the Larkford Harriers, including Lindy Grey, whose gaze was firmly fixed on Dan.

He smiled tightly at Lindy and turned back to Grace. 'And this Jamie chap – is he a good egg?' There was a loaded tension in their conversation that had never been there before and a confusion in Grace's eyes that, in all probability, mirrored his own.

It was as though the ground beneath their friendship had subtly shifted and neither of them had been expecting it.

'I hear you've been having a tricky few days,' Grace ventured, deftly folding his empty crisp packet into a perfect triangle, corners all tucked in, neat and perfectly designed. Dan took a gulp of his cider as he realised that the same might apply to the fold-er, as to the fold-ed.

'Probably long overdue,' he hedged.

Grace leaned over and squeezed his hand. 'If everyone

Penny Parkes

around here is taking the time to consider their priorities, maybe this will turn out to be a good opportunity for a little reflection yourself?' There was nothing flirtatious in her tone, she wasn't trying to comfort him and come on to him at the same time, the way some girls did. From the expression in her eyes, Dan could see that Grace had only one agenda – for him to be happy. For a moment, with the summer sun glancing off the buildings behind her, the resemblance to Elsie was uncanny. Not so much in looks, as the calm certainty that suffused her.

He was about to reply when Alice – lovely, sweet, relieved Alice – wandered into the conversation with both feet, completely oblivious to any undercurrents and shattering the intensity in a moment. 'Isn't Jamie wonderful?' she breathed, sounding so much younger than she normally did. More her actual age in fact, rather than her emotional age, which seemed to be somewhere in her mid-fifties. 'He's being so good with Coco and he's so sensitive to my feelings about the whole thing – I mean, I really thought for a moment there that Coco might need to . . .' She petered out and sat down beside Grace. 'He's so lovely too, had you noticed?'

Dan frowned. 'Everybody in the Somerset postcode has noticed, Alice. The question is, does he give this much personal attention to all his clients, or is there is a little something in Larkford that keeps him coming back?'

Alice blushed prettily. 'Oh no – he's terribly professional.' A slightly dreamy look replaced her usual efficient gaze. 'Shame, really.' She pulled herself together quickly, looking embarrassed. 'Besides, who really has time for a relationship these days.'

'Three pints of lager, a packet of crisps and a fruit-based drink for the ladies,' Jamie joked as he plonked a tray down in the middle of the table, rather undermining Alice's notion of him as a sweet sensitive soul.

He passed Alice her drink with a wink, which to be fair, didn't look terribly professional. The lingering smile he saved for Grace though seemed, to Dan at least, to be in a different league. It was all that he could do to muster a thank you for his pint and not flinch from the matey slap on the shoulder that Jamie delivered as he sat down between them.

Before Dan could work out how to get the maelstrom of his irrational feelings under control and begin to make polite conversation, Jamie's attention was caught up with Coco, who had started to exhibit some of her new, unsettled behaviour.

'What's the matter with you, Muttley?' asked Taffy affectionately, as he returned to the table. 'Stop being daft or we'll have to retire you to a farm in the country.'

'Taffy!' cried Alice, clapping her hands over Coco's ears. 'They wouldn't put her down just because she can't function as an assistance dog anymore.'

Taffy sipped at his drink, raising his glass to Jamie in thanks. 'I didn't think they would. I just thought she might like to spend some time at my folks' place, run in the fields, let off steam, do what spaniels do best. You know – doggy stress relief?' He sounded a little perplexed at Alice's distress.

Grace leaned in to him and quietly explained the euphemism, as his eyes widened in disbelief. 'Well that confirms it, you English are mad.'

'I'm Scottish,' said Alice immediately.

'Potato, Potah-to,' said Taffy with a wink, knowing just how much it would wind her up. It had also made her smile though and they could all see that that was progress.

Coco circled at her feet again, pulling at the lead and

distracted. 'Is she after the crisps at the next table?' Grace
wondered.

'Maybe she just prefers cheese and onion,' Alice said, more
in hope than in humour.

'Let her off the lead a minute, Alice, would you,' Jamie
said. 'I'll stay with her, I just want to see what she does.'

Predictably, Coco was off the minute she got the chance,
over to the neighbouring table and yapping. She sounded
almost in distress but the athletes there just leaned down and
scooped her up for a cuddle, even as her little body wriggled
frantically. She ended up in Lindy's arms and she stood up to
bring her back to their table.

'I think you might have lost something,' Lindy said, even
as Coco burrowed against her arm and whined pitifully. She
released the squirming bundle into Jamie's outstretched arms
and leaned against the edge of the table next to Dan. 'A little
bird told me that there was trouble in Paradise?'

'Really?' said Dan nonchalantly. 'I don't think I got that
memo.'

Lindy smiled and gently stroked his arm. 'Well, you know
where I am. If you need distraction.' She leaned in and kissed
him slowly on the lips before walking away with a swing of
her hips.

Dan could feel the heat in his cheeks but didn't dare look
up. He knew perfectly well how Grace felt about these girls
and their 'hook ups' – God knows, she'd been vocal enough
about them in the past. He didn't think he could bear to see
the disappointment on her face that Dan might fall into that
category too.

When he did dare to raise his eyes, it wasn't the expression
on Grace's face that shocked him, it was to see Julia hovering in the gateway and looking stunned. Lindy was Julia's

Kryptonite – her constant presence and offers of 'availability' had made Julia incredibly nervous and insecure when they'd first got back together. How did it look now, that the minute they had parted ways, Dan was smooching with her in public – or so it would seem.

He made to stand up, to go to her and explain, but a car door slammed and Quentin strode into view before he could. The way his arm slid around Julia's waist and the way he possessively held her close told Dan everything he needed to know about where Julia had spent last night.

As the chaos of the pub garden on a summer's evening ebbed and flowed around them, it felt for a moment as though they were the only two people in the world – the connection between Julia and Dan across the garden almost tangible. But there was no anger there anymore; it was merely a sad acknowledgement that their time together was over.

Even as Quentin leaned in and kissed Julia's cheek, her eyes held an apology that Dan chose to accept. He shrugged and smiled ruefully and in that moment, it seemed as though they were closer than ever, through being apart.

Chapter 38

'Morning, Holly,' said Julia. 'I got you a coffee from The Deli to say sorry for being such a bitch the other day. Hattie said this was your favourite – I hope that's okay?' She handed Holly a tall skinny cappuccino with extra foam and extra chocolate sprinkles – the extra chocolate sprinkles being her not-so-secret vice.

On hearing the news from Taffy that Julia and Quentin had spent the night together, before the blood on Dan's forehead was even dry, Holly had been all but braced for fireworks. Walking into The Practice to find Dan and Julia happily chatting to each other about the Health in the Community website had therefore completely thrown her.

'Dan and I have been talking and I appreciate that you both had my best interests at heart when it came to my mother, even if I wasn't great at showing that. I'm so sorry,' Julia said.

Holly's gaze flickered towards Dan to check whether he too was finding this whole scenario to be a bit surreal, but Julia beat her to the chase. 'I've already apologised to Dan for the whole stapler-lobbing catastrophe and we've agreed to keep our relationship strictly professional from now on. I hope that won't make you and Taffy uncomfortable?'

Gratitude? Apologies? Consideration? Dear Lord – what had happened to Julia overnight and was it contagious?

Dan righted Holly's coffee, as it listed towards tipping point in her hand. 'There's no need to look quite so shocked, Holly. Julia and I were always going to find a way through this.'

'I know, I know,' covered Holly quickly. The images of the blood on Dan's forehead and the fury in Julia's expression were all too vivid still in her mind though – she couldn't help but wonder how these two had evolved so quickly, when she herself was still processing their outburst, even as a bystander.

But this morning, she had to confess that the body language between them was easy and convivial – the most relaxed Holly had seen them in weeks.

Quentin and his camera crew came barrelling through the front door and Holly immediately noticed the spark of awkwardness between Dan and Julia that seemed to flare and extinguish itself just as quickly. A micro-reaction that made a whole lot more sense of the situation. She nodded slowly. 'Okay then. Well, you two kids have fun and Julia, thank you for the coffee. It was a lovely thought and God knows I could use the caffeine this morning.'

Being the face of The Practice, albeit temporarily, had been exhausting and confusing in equal measure for Holly. She was delighted to see Julia back, of course, but there had been something seductive about being her own advocate for how she believed their unique approach to medicine could really make a difference on a larger scale. True, she'd spent an awful lot of time talking about their Health in the Community Scheme, but it had been illuminating to realise that was where her passion actually lay. There was a ripple effect here, as the endorsement brought focus and momentum to their little project. In fact, Holly realised, she didn't have half as big an issue with being The Practice's spokesperson if she got to do it on her own terms, in her own words, in her own way. She was sorely tempted to do the next interview in her own clothes too, looking how she normally did – scruffy and exhausted but caring, professional and committed – until she realised with a jolt, that now Julia was back, there probably wouldn't be a next time.

She quietly excused herself, uncomfortable in the extreme at the surreal conversation developing in front of her as Dan, Julia and Quentin began discussing the morning's filming with exaggerated politeness and deference.

Sitting down at her desk moments later, with the door firmly closed and a smattering of foam on her upper lip as she sipped her coffee, Holly began to consider whether she'd maybe hit the brie too hard last night and this whole scenario was simply a vivid Technicolor dream? As her gaze fell on to the pile of post on her desk, she was forced to re-evaluate: the postal stamp of Milo's solicitor adorned a large white envelope sitting on top. In her experience so far, good news never came in a large envelope where the legal profession was involved.

And where Milo was concerned these days, he didn't so much haunt her dreams, as hold star billing in her nightmares. His single text had been enough to throw her off balance completely. No matter that the likelihood of him turning up on her doorstep was slim, involving altogether too much effort on his part, she still found herself flinching every time the doorbell rang. She was clearly kidding herself to think she had found her balance on that front.

What was it Elsie said? If you're still thinking about someone, or talking about someone, then chances are you still care about them – if only Holly could work out why that might be the case. Were these shadows and vestiges of emotion always going to be there, she wondered, simply because he was the twins' father? Because if anyone had asked her a week ago whether she was over Milo, she would have answered with a resounding 'yes' – now though, thoroughly rattled, she wished she could be so sure.

Checking the clock, she laid a hand on the envelope and tried to run scenarios in her head. Uppermost in her mind was the fear that he was following through on his earlier threat to re-open the issue of Access where the twins were concerned and that their own legal advice to leave well alone had been misjudged. Best-case scenario, he was holding out his grubby paw for yet more money. When it came to the narcissistic workings of her ex-husband's mind, Holly was only too familiar with his self-serving notions of what was fair and reasonable.

After all, there was faint chance that the contents of the envelope would take her any closer to the closure and freedom she craved.

Like a child playing Hide and Seek, she jerkily pulled open her desk drawer and thrust the envelope inside – out of sight, out of mind. She knew perfectly well that hiding her head in the sand was not what Elsie had meant when she encouraged Holly to pick her battles. For this morning though, Holly's inner-child had other ideas. Whatever the contents of the letter, they could wait for a few hours at least.

Midway through the morning and valiantly trying to ignore the white envelope lurking like an unexploded bomb, Holly was counting down the hours until her break. She could only hope that Taffy's abrupt start to the day – when the twins had decided to use his car keys as the prize in an elaborate treasure hunt scenario before the sun had even risen – hadn't soured his mood irreparably.

Holly felt a prickle of unease as she even thought about it – playing at Happy Families was one thing; taking on a custody battle would be quite another proposition. For all Taffy's good points, and God knows there were plenty, only Holly really got to see the other side of him. The side that liked to rationalise and understand every choice and motivation, the side that was *always* in a hurry to reach a satisfactory conclusion, irrespective of the number of steps he might skip in the process. The side that got so easily frustrated when life got complicated. But, in Holly's experience anyway, life *was* complicated and Taffy's insistence on always choosing the path of least resistance didn't really seem like a long-term strategy.

Holly pulled her attention back to the job in hand and scrolled through the various screens of notes, trying to get a clearer picture of this patient's medical history, trying desperately hard not to look shocked. This was one of the downfalls of being a GP in a small community – what you didn't already know via the grapevine, you could find out with a few clicks of the mouse. Lindy Grey fidgeted on the chair beside Holly's desk and pulled the sleeves of her training top down over her hands.

'You've gone awfully quiet, Dr Graham,' she said tentatively. 'I'm guessing there's a lot on that screen that you didn't know about me?'

Holly swivelled her chair around and made sure that she had her features properly arranged before she spoke. 'Let's talk about the letter from the screening centre first, shall we? Then we can look at some factors that might be contributory in all of this.' She reached out and took Lindy's hand. 'And for the record, you did exactly the right thing coming to me with this. I suspect you and Dr Carter have a little too much history to make that an entirely objective conversation.'

Lindy nodded. 'I keep thinking I've brought this on myself, Dr Graham. You can be blunt with me – I'm better with blunt. All the hooking up, the abortions ... That's why my smear test came back as abnormal, isn't it?'

Holly swallowed hard; it was all very well Lindy asking her to be forthright and not edit her opinions, but there was also the small matter of sensitivity to be considered. 'Well,' she said slowly, 'there is a known link between the HPV virus and cervical cancer, of course, and the more partners one has – especially from an early age – will increase the likelihood of carrying that virus. But, Lindy, let's be clear, I also have patients with cervical cancer who have only had one sexual partner in their entire lives and I see women with multiple partners in perfect health.' She paused, trying to formulate what she was trying to communicate. 'It's a bit like drinking – the message we're trying to convey is to enjoy everything in moderation and be sensible. Knowing about safe sex and practising safe sex are two rather different things. But, Lindy, this lab report will only give us a snapshot at the moment. The presence of abnormal cells, even pre-cancerous cells, doesn't automatically mean you have cervical cancer.'

'Would be a fairly karmic diagnosis though, Dr Graham, wouldn't it? I had my first abortion when I was fifteen – that has to make a difference, doesn't it?'

Holly watched her patient's expression carefully; Lindy's usual bravado was replaced today by an unfamiliar tension that Holly recognised only too well. There was something about the word 'pre-cancerous' that made even the most confident of souls question everything they thought they knew. And right now, Lindy was clearly beginning to question a few of the more reckless choices she had been making for the last decade or so.

'Don't get ahead of yourself,' cautioned Holly. 'There's a long way to go yet and it looks like they've already initiated a referral for you. Lindy, I won't lie – whatever further exams they need to do won't be comfortable, but they will hopefully put your mind at rest. The odds are that you might need a little procedure called cryotherapy where they essentially freeze away the dodgy cells, but the team there will talk you through every step of the treatment and they are used to people feeling nervous and frightened – it's a perfectly natural response.'

Lindy shrugged. 'Thank you for seeing me on such short notice, Dr Graham. When I opened that letter this morning . . . Well, it completely threw me, to be honest.' Her face furrowed in concentration. 'Maybe I'll look back on this and see it as a Wake Up Call? Who knows . . .' She went to stand up, the letter clutched tightly in her hand, crumpling around her white fingers. 'Is this like with STDs then, Dr Graham? Do I have to make the *Phone Call Of Shame* to every man I've ever been with?'

As Holly talked Lindy through the stages of HPV and who might potentially be affected, the colour rose from Lindy's neck to her face. When she looked up at Holly, there were tears welling in her eyes. She gave a strangled laugh. 'Well, I don't think I'm going to be terribly popular for a bit, am I? Plus, you know, I might need to upgrade my call plan.'

Holly saw Lindy to the door and she couldn't help but worry about the young woman's coping skills – it was one thing to be completely gung-ho about sexual freedom, but if there was one thing she had seen time and time again as a doctor, it was so often the women who paid the price.

*

As the door swung open, Holly could see there was a small gathering in the reception area and it didn't take a genius to figure out why. It was true that whenever Jamie the dog trainer arrived in Larkford, he seemed to gain an instant entourage. Not showy, just ridiculously handsome and incredibly genuine – the local female population seemed to be highly tuned to his presence.

Lindy gave Holly a watery smile. 'Seems the dog whisperer has got his own little fan club going.'

'All the more so, since he only seems to have eyes for one particular brunette,' agreed Holly. Jamie's easy-going non-chalance only seemed to add to his appeal and Holly had noticed that despite the attention, his focus was firmly rooted where it should be – with Coco.

Right now, he was working with Alice to persuade Coco that all the distractions in the communal areas just weren't that interesting. He talked to the little spaniel constantly – a reassuring hum of words that kept her calm and focused. Alice walked beside them, the hope on her face almost palpable.

She smiled at Holly and Lindy as they walked in. 'She's doing so much better, Holly. Look, Jamie's been teaching her how to tune out all the distractions.'

Jamie smiled in greeting but carried on murmuring to Coco, but something had shifted. Coco whined and began scuffling backwards, pulling on the lead in Jamie's hand. She circled and whimpered and eventually gave a tug for freedom before hustling over to greet Holly and Lindy.

Jamie's face was a picture of disappointment, but it was nothing to the flash of despair that filled Alice's eyes. She wordlessly picked up Coco's lead and kindly led her back to the office. Jamie laid a hand on Holly's arm as he followed. 'Don't give up on her just yet, will you?'

Holly wasn't sure whether he meant Coco or Alice, but her answer would still be the same – The Practice was a team and they all looked out for each other. At least, Holly temporised, that was the theory.

Grace beckoned Holly through into the office and picked up some papers from the printer. She was looking distinctly more polished of late and Holly could see extra little touches that suggested Elsie was up to her old tricks again. Holly had to swallow a moment of unaccountable envy at this revelation and force herself to focus on the positives of Grace's decision to carve a bigger role for herself here at The Practice, with her unexpected internet dexterity and calm media savvy.

'I've printed out a list of patients from Alice. The ones where Coco has acted strangely – she said you'd asked for it?' Grace handed over a sheaf of notes. 'Are you thinking they might have undiagnosed diabetes?' she asked with interest.

'Something like that,' replied Holly.

'It's fascinating, isn't it? How their little minds and noses work? I was reading up on it last night after talking to Jamie at the pub. I knew they had more smell sensors than us – but 300 million? That's like smelling in High Definition!' Grace seemed enthralled by the notion. 'I wonder what else they're capable of?'

'To be honest, I'm just following a weird hunch right now, so don't make a big thing of this list with Alice, will you? I feel like she has enough to keep her focused at the moment. But I tell you what would be helpful – do you have a mobile number for Jamie? I have a few little off-the-record queries.'

Grace quietly pulled her mobile from her pocket. She tapped at the screen a few times and looked up without meeting Holly's eye. 'I've sent it over to your phone,' she said.

'Oh, not you two as well,' came a grumpy voice from the

doorway, as Dan ambled into the office. 'Anyone would think Jamie Yardley is the first good-looking bloke ever to walk through these doors.'

'Aw, but you know we love you the best though, don't you?' teased Holly in reply, as though he were a puppy in need of attention.

Dan couldn't help but smile, as Holly held out a Penguin in her palm like a doggy treat. 'Well, it wouldn't kill you to say it once in a while, is all I'm saying.' He unwrapped the Penguin and devoured it in three bites.

'Jesus,' said Holly. 'I reckon Eric has better table manners than that.'

Dan shrugged. 'I'm just hungry. Turns out sleeping in a crappy bed above the pub works up quite the appetite.' He stretched as though the mere memory gave him neck ache. 'I seriously need to sort out some proper accommodation.'

Holly nodded. 'Well, if you're nice to Grace, maybe she'll loan you her spare room while the boys are away?'

'Oh no,' flustered Grace uncharacteristically, 'I don't think that would be a good idea at all.'

There was an incredibly awkward lull in the conversation until Dan rallied, 'You're absolutely right there, Gracie. I'd be an awful flat mate, forever finishing off the Shreddies and hogging the shower before work.'

Grace looked up for the first time, her expression earnest and her words rushed. 'I didn't mean that at all, Dan. I'm sure you'll make someone a lovely housemate. I just meant that . . . well, when you're getting over a loss, sometimes it's nice to have some space to yourself, isn't it?'

Dan pulled her into his side in a gentle half-hug. 'I'm sorry, Gracie, that was insensitive of me. Of course you still need your space after Roy and everything.'

Grace looked up at him with wide grey eyes and Holly almost felt as though she were intruding simply by standing there. 'Oh, I didn't mean me, Dan. A break-up can be like a mini bereavement after all. Like I said last night, you'll be wanting a little time and space to work out what you want from life, won't you?'

Holly quietly slipped away then, one look at Dan's face suggesting that he already had a few ideas on that front. Holly didn't know whether to be delighted or concerned that his primary focus right now seemed to be Grace. She did make a mental note though, to pop into Julia's office and put away her stapler, along with any other potential missiles – just in case.

Chapter 39

Julia pulled down the sleeves of her cashmere jumper as the summer evening chill made her shiver. Quite why she'd foregone supper with Quentin in the new Michelin-starred restaurant in Bath for *this* was anybody's guess. If she were a betting woman, she might say it had something to do with trying to ease her conscience: she felt bad about Dan, she felt bad about her mother and, if she were being completely honest, she felt bad about Quentin too. She hadn't deliberately tried to mislead him; he just seemed to assume that the moment she'd succumbed to his advances in the bedroom, then by extension, it meant she was going to accept his job offer too. Partners in every sense of the word. Only Julia had no intention of doing so.

She didn't want to leap straight from one incestuous work/life conflict into another. And Quentin was no Dan Carter – he wouldn't cut her as much leeway as Dan had always done. Dan had truly loved her – foibles and all. For Quentin, she was merely his *amour du jour*.

She swallowed down the rush of sourness in her mouth, as she walked through the Market Place, with her mother talking nineteen to the dozen beside her. It was hardly the mother-daughter outing that every little girl dreamed of, but at this moment in time, it felt like the very least she could do. If only she could concentrate on the job in hand.

'You're making a huge mistake, you know,' said Candace, the twilit streets of Larkford giving her face more definition and shade than usual – a sense of seniority and gravitas that was normally missing – and Julia had to concede that, when it came to Dan Carter, her mother may actually have a valid point.

Candace though, never knowingly ventured far from her usual self-oriented train of thought and clearly hadn't given her daughter's break-up a second thought. 'You're pushing me away and you *say* you don't need me, but I'm *it*, Joo – I'm your family. Just me, with your dad gone God-knows-where.'

Julia frowned, wrenching her thoughts away from her own relationship carnage to at least try to consider Candace's point of view.

'Nobody's pushing you away, Mum,' she said tiredly, ignoring the little voice in the back of her mind that told her she was bending the truth in favour of trying to have a proper conversation with her mum. 'I just needed you to appreciate that I have worked really hard to build my own life here. My own identity. And my friends ... well, my friends here feel like family too.' She blushed a little as she said that, realising even as she spoke, that she had managed to articulate what she'd been feeling for a while now. She could only hope that her mother would understand.

'Pht,' exhaled her mother with feeling, dampening the small flicker of optimism that Julia had been clinging on to. Compassion and understanding had never been high on Candace's agenda. The classic narcissist, her world – as she conceived it – began and ended with herself. 'They'll be like family when it suits them, Joo, you'll see – for the parties and the triumphs. Mark my words, you won't see them for dust when you've a crisis in the middle of the night.'

Julia stopped walking and Candace crossly ground to a halt ahead of her. 'What?' Candace sulked, turning around grudgingly.

Julia shook her head, trying to formulate her thoughts. 'The middle of the night . . .' she repeated slowly.

A sly smile spread across Candace's heavily made-up face. 'I know it's hard, darling,' she said, in a saccharine tone of voice, 'but you have to recognise that. They won't be there for you when you need them.'

Julia took a deep breath and looked her mother squarely in the eye. 'But then, to be fair, Mum, neither are you.'

Candace wavered for a moment then. Surrendering her moral high-ground made her sway precariously. She opened her mouth as though she were about to unleash a retort, but then slowly closed it again. 'We're going to be late,' she managed eventually, marching off towards the church alone and disappearing into the back room that housed Larkford's support groups.

Julia's gaze fell upon the much-annotated poster in the foyer and she couldn't help but smile at the various addendums.

Monday – Alcoholics Anonymous (including, but not limited to, drugs (recreational), drugs (prescription), sex, food & shopping)

'I don't know about you,' said Marion Waverly, appearing silently at Julia's side, 'but that sounds like my perfect night out!' She took a Sharpie out of her handbag and laboriously added the words 'Netflix & Box-sets' to the poster before giving Julia a wink and going inside.

Julia tried not to speculate what Marion Waverly might be sharing with the group and wondered, not for the first time, whether accompanying her mother tonight had been such a good idea. She felt as though her resolve was skittering out of her control, nervousness always making her uncomfortable and putting her humour on a hair trigger. The last thing she needed was to get a fit of inappropriate laughter in there, as she had at Uncle Jim's funeral. She loitered by the main entrance, reading down the list of support groups that probably told her more about the darker side of living in Larkford than she really wanted or needed to know at this point.

**Tuesday – 'Knit & Natter' & Phobia support
Wednesday – Al Anon & Family counselling
Thursday – Prayer group & bereavement support
Friday – Problem Parenting /
Wine tasting (alternate weeks)**

By the time she got as far as Friday she was holding herself together by a thread. The way Reverend Taylor had paired up the groups had her in stitches. She'd love to be a fly on the wall on a Friday night when they got the schedule in a muddle – on the other hand, she reflected, perhaps a night away from the kids with a nice Chablis in hand, might prove more effective at handling stressful parenting situations than sitting around sharing toddler horror stories.

The door beside her was yanked open forcefully. 'Well?' demanded her mother. 'Are you coming to be supportive or not?'

It was all Julia could do not to stare. The little hall at the back of Larkford church was packed and the 'anonymous' appellation was clearly in name only, as it would probably be quicker to count the number of families who weren't represented by at least one member. Everybody here knew everybody else and Julia was forcibly struck by the secrets they all held and knowingly entrusted to one another. There was none of the judgement that she had anticipated, only quiet nods of greetings and the occasional supportive smile.

She quietly took her seat beside her mother, who preened slightly at being one of the newbies on the block, the group leader singling her out for welcome. Julia stared determinedly at her feet as the people around her began to speak: sharing, over-sharing sometimes ... She was stunned to hear the openness and vulnerability in the room. There were none of the awkward confessions and hesitations that she heard in her consulting rooms and here, she was nobody's GP – she was Julia, daughter of an alcoholic, and therefore every bit as damaged and in need of help as all the supportive relatives around her.

As Marion got to her feet and spoke with feeling about her obsession with scratch cards, it was easy to see the manifold ways in which addictions of all shapes and sizes had insidiously wormed their way throughout their community. Marion speaking candidly about having to endure temptation right there in front of her in the Spar shop all day every day, painted an entirely different picture of craving to the debauched, drunken exploits of her mother. But when Julia raised her eyes, summoning the courage, she saw the exact expression of anguish on Marion's face that her mother wore when the urge to drink was tormenting her.

For the first time, Julia felt a small part of her unfurl and began to tentatively acknowledge that this 'problem', this addiction – it really was nothing personal. Candace

Channing drank because her inner demons compelled her to – apportioning blame in any direction was a fruitless enterprise.

After the fifth 'share' Julia had stopped pretending not to listen. After the sixth, she was unashamedly hanging on every word – every story carried a resonance, a familiarity, that she could no longer ignore. As a sweet, funny girl, of barely twenty years old – an alcoholic child of alcoholic parents – spoke eloquently of her constant search for external validation, Julia felt the ever-present tightness in her chest loosen just a notch.

She leaned forward, elbows on her knees, oblivious to any attention she might be drawing. The urge to stand up and shout, 'Me too. That happened to me too and I know how you feel' was almost overwhelming.

As the girl sat down to quiet murmurs of support, Julia leaned across to her mother. 'The external validation thing?' she whispered. 'Don't you think it sounds like me? It makes so much sense – don't you agree?'

Candace said nothing, the sideways look she gave confirming two things for Julia – one, it was not okay to 'chat' during the shares, and two, checking for approval from other people about whether you might have issues with external validation might be considered confirmation in itself.

As Julia lay in bed that night, the sound of her mother's ragged snoring echoing through the Gatehouse, the bed around her had never felt so empty. She wanted Dan. She wanted his calming presence and wry, affectionate understanding of what he had originally called her foibles and, towards the end, her 'quirks'.

She couldn't deny that she was proud of her mother

for going back to the AA meetings – although she could objectively see how having an understanding and captive audience might ultimately have an addictive quality all of its own. But she had looked around that room – at teachers and farmers and teenagers alike – and seen that they were united in a common goal. They all wanted to regain control of their lives, rather than surrendering to their various urges and addictions.

It was the first time that Julia had considered that there was a place for her in that room too. Not just as the supportive daughter, but as someone who had spent their entire life reacting: reacting to opinion, to stress, to other people's desires for her. And when she'd reached for balance, had she not over-compensated? The pendulum swinging wildly back towards compulsive and controlling behaviour?

She swallowed hard. It was no wonder Dan had left. Living with Julia must have been like trying to keep your balance on a constantly shifting surface. She spread her fingers across the cold sheets on his side of the bed experimentally, waiting for the familiar shaft of pain through her chest. It never arrived.

Instead, the words from the meeting scrolled through her mind: Lord, grant me the serenity to accept the things I cannot change, the courage to change the things I can and the wisdom to know the difference.

As her fingers tightened on the edge of Dan's pillow, she felt the knot in her chest loosen another small notch. It had felt so good to apologise to Holly yesterday – at least, if one put aside the bone-gnawing discomfort that she had experienced at the time. It had been the right thing to do though, and the expression on Holly's face had almost made the embarrassment worth it.

Julia rolled over, initially as though to escape the feeling, but then surrendering to it, in all its awkwardness, and daring to consider where else in her life the same might apply.

She buried her head into the pillow, the aroma of Dan's aftershave still lingering despite changing the sheets. He'd done the right thing by her so many times, she realised. He'd stood by her in the last few weeks when she could tell that his heart was no longer in the relationship – not wanting to leave her high and dry, to cope with Candace alone. The realisation was overwhelming. Everyone around them must have seen it – but she'd been oblivious, pushing him further and further away.

Maybe Holly wasn't the only person to whom she owed amends?

She just wanted to go to sleep at night, knowing she'd done the right thing; to look in the mirror and not flinch from her own gaze. She just –

She screwed her face up into the pillow, Holly's joking words in the doctors' lounge popping into her head. How many times today had she used the word 'just' to qualify or soften her requests, her explanations, her excuses ... It was never a word you would hear from Quentin, or even Dan or Taffy. When exactly had the sneaky *shoulds* gained a partner in crime?

So, she thought, as she pummelled her pillow into submission, if we're going to do this, then let's do it properly. Over half an hour later, Julia was still murmuring her way through her mental stocktake. The number of people to whom she owed an apology was longer than she had even considered – not always for big stuff, but for the first time she could see clearly that sometimes the little indifferences actually cast a longer shadow.

The meeting this evening had been a life-changing

revelation – all she needed now was the courage to see it through – on her own, without anybody telling her she was doing the right thing. She couldn't help but wonder whether her constant search for validation and approval might be a harder addiction to break than her go-to habit of instant judgement.

Whatever she might think of her mother for her 'weaknesses', in that moment it was clear to Julia that she was really in no position to judge – if anything, she'd been incredibly lucky that her own particular affliction was more socially acceptable. Having said that, it still had the potential to be equally damaging to her relationships, as she'd so recently been reminded.

In fact, as Julia went through her list of amends one more time, as her eyelids grew heavy with exhaustion and the sky outside her bedroom window grew pink with the haze of morning mist, she kept returning to the same notion time and time again. Was it actually possible that the person whom she had slighted and ignored the most – dismissing their ideals and wishes at every turn – was actually herself?

'Lord, grant me the serenity to accept the things I cannot change, the courage to change the things I can and the wisdom to know the difference,' she murmured under her breath, as she finally succumbed to sleep.

Chapter 40

Holly watched as Taffy read the documents once again, checking that there wasn't something they'd overlooked. He glanced up at Holly. 'I don't understand.'

'Me neither,' Holly replied, glad that they'd waited until they got home to open the envelope. Her hands clenched around her mug of tea as though it were the only thing keeping her functioning. 'He must have his own reasons.'

'Oh, I'm sure he does,' Taffy said with feeling. 'And it's not as though there are any substantial marital assets to split, are there?'

They both looked around the tiny kitchen of the rented terraced house that Holly had called home for the last two years. Putting aside her beloved Golf, Milo's pretentious Saab and more books than was reasonable, this whole divorce should have been signed and sealed months ago. Only Milo's reluctance to commit to anything without a fight had slowed the process down – that and his erratic disregard to the interim Access Agreement that he had fought for and then ignored. Holly couldn't actually remember the last time Milo had seen his sons and, if you discounted that weird text threatening a visit, he had shown little inclination to change that.

If only Milo didn't still have the ability to throw her

life into a tailspin every time he raised his head, Holly was convinced she would be able to move on more easily. It hadn't escaped her notice though, that the only person who could change that reaction was Holly herself.

And that was where she hit the stumbling block every time. She'd realised lately that going through the motions of recovery was absolutely not the same as working through the *emotions* of recovery at all. Yet that's what she'd been doing. Every time she was mistrustful of somebody else's motives, she slipped into autopilot – being reactive, not proactive.

Holly took a mouthful of tea and spluttered when she realised it was stone cold – she'd lost track of how long they had been staring at the divorce papers, all neatly signed by Milo and awaiting her own signature.

'But why would he suddenly relent? It's not as though he wants to make my life easier, is it?' Holly asked, with little expectation of an answer – they were both too stunned. 'He seemed to be out for as much money and heartache as he could muster five minutes ago.'

'Did he ever really want custody, do you think, or was it just a power play?' Taffy murmured.

Holly spread the pages out on the kitchen table again, grateful that the twins were fast asleep, exhausted after a lengthy game of chasing Eric around the house and dressing him up. Eric himself was still sporting a Bath rugby shirt, which he inexplicably refused to part with, and was fast asleep on Holly's feet. The house was quiet – free of distractions – but still Holly's mind refused to engage.

'We should go through these, line by line.' she suggested in the end, her radar for suspicious motives pinging like a nuclear sub.

Taffy pushed his chair back suddenly and stood up, as

though he had no immediate control over the urge to move and the sheer effort of restraint was visible on his face. Holly frowned and returned to focus on the documents in front of her; she couldn't deal with Taffy's physical agitation right now. She was about to suggest he shake it off and let her concentrate, when he spoke and it became clear that he was actually trying to choose his words with such care, it was that which was making him stumble.

'Don't let him do this, Holly. Please don't let him dictate the terms. You have to stand up and fight.'

Holly stared, completely thrown by the coiled emotion in his every staccato sentence. 'Why?' she said tiredly. 'Why does this have to be a fight? Surely you understand that I just want this to be over. Finished.'

'But at what cost?' asked Taffy in frustration.

Holly gasped, blindsided. 'I can't believe you're thinking about the money!'

'I am not thinking about the sodding money!' Taffy shouted, stunning even himself with his own vehemence. Weeks of biting his tongue had only served to pent up his emotions on this particular topic. He sat down again and took her hand. 'I'm thinking about the boys. That their dad is willing to just give up on them. What kind of message does that send?'

Holly sighed. 'Probably a similar message to upping and leaving in the first place? I can't *force* him to be a father to them, Taffy.' She looked up at him, her eyes filled with tears. 'I'm not that naïve.'

It was true. It didn't matter that the waves of emotion surrounding this divorce still took her by surprise at the strangest of times, but when she wept now, she didn't weep for Milo, or her marriage, or her mistakes – she wept for her loss of innocence – her absolute sense of certainty that the world would just keep turning until the happy endings settled into place.

These days, Holly knew better – she knew that an ill-chosen phrase or a choice in a moment of anger could cause ripples of collateral damage. And every choice Milo had been making for the last few years had been with one goal in mind – his own happiness and his own successes.

She couldn't force Milo to be a father to his children.

She couldn't make him behave like the man she'd known him to be at the beginning.

But on some level she still desperately wanted him to, if only to prove that she hadn't been entirely mistaken in her original estimation of him, in believing him to be so much more.

She sighed and took Taffy's hand in hers. It was touching how protective he was about the boys, but did he really have the full picture? And what was she trying to prove? The Milo she had first fallen in love with, before his ego crept out and insidiously sequestered his soul, would have cared about his sons and been invested in their future. She just needed to be sure that *that* Milo was long gone before she closed the door for good.

But however worthy her desire to rebuild the twins' relationship with their father, rather than this absolute rejection, Holly couldn't even begin to envisage how that conversation might go. She could remember all too vividly the helplessness of trying to have a rational conversation with an irrational person, caught in Milo's web of controlling behaviour.

'Let me explain,' Holly said softly, as she leaned her head against Taffy's shoulder, relieved to finally have the opportunity to discuss this.

*

Hours later, the papers still unsigned and halfway down a
bottle of rosé, a loud knock at the door made them both jump
and Eric leapt to his feet, barrelling through the hall in his
Bath shirt like a rugby forward. 'Coo-ee,' cried Elsie through
the letterbox. 'It's only me!'

Taffy opened the door and Elsie marched into the kitchen.
'Dear Lord, who died?' she said tactlessly, throwing herself
into a chair. She gently pushed Eric aside as he took rather a
liking to her leg and propped her feet up out of harm's way.
She topped up Taffy's glass of wine and then appropriated it
for herself without even missing a beat. 'If you'd told me how
wonderful steroids were, Holly, I'd have been on board with
this anti-inflammatory business much sooner you know. I've
been full of beans for hours . . .'

Holly managed to smile despite herself – there was something almost contagious about Elsie's good mood that Holly
was only too willing to embrace this evening. Hours of stressful back and forth had achieved nothing and the very relief of
a distraction was almost intoxicating. 'Your consultant sent me
an e-mail earlier. He said you had the whole neurology suite
joining in a sing-along at one point. And he's pleased with your
progress, so don't get too used to your steroid high; it's only
a temporary trial to see if it helps with some of the swelling.'
She paused for a moment. 'I wish you'd let me go with you.'

'Pish tosh, you've got better things to do with your time.
Besides, I like to have a little wallow about the unfairness of
life and how bad things happen to good people while I'm
there – it takes my mind off seeing all the me-in-a-few-years'-
time patients. Such a thrill to look forward to. Becoming a
dribbling, piddling liability.'

'Elsie . . .' interrupted Taffy warningly.

She scowled at him. 'Okay, maybe not *everyone's* the

poster-patient for utter dependency, but do let a girl have a little artistic licence, why don't you?' She shoved Eric away again. 'What the hell is going on with this dog?'

Holly and Taffy exchanged glances. 'He appears to be going through a little phase,' said Holly delicately. Elsie smirked and looked over at Taffy for clarification.

'He's shagging anything that isn't nailed down, okay? And actually, sometimes, things that are.' Taffy reached out and summoned Eric away from the sofa cushions with a click of his tongue. 'Lizzie has decreed it's time for him to visit the V-E-T but I'm trying to persuade her out of it.'

'Well,' said Holly matter-of-factly, 'I think it's high time he had a little snip or there'll be mini Erics running all round Larkford in no time. At least, once he figures out what it's all about.'

Taffy squirmed and crossed his legs uncomfortably. 'How can you be so cold? This is his manhood you're discussing. Dan and I think you two need to be more patient while he works through his issues.'

'And half the canine population in Larkford,' Holly remonstrated. 'Poor Coco's thinking of taking out a restraining order and I've washed Winnie the Pooh three times this week!' At the very thought, Holly couldn't maintain her poise and snorted with laughter.

Elsie chortled contentedly. 'Glad to see nothing's really changed around here then. I rather miss a bit of chaos.'

'Well, you've come to the right place then,' Taffy said, the fatigue of the last few hours laced into his every syllable.

'Don't knock it, until you've tried the alternative,' said Elsie with feeling. 'A calm, restful home is just another way of saying boring and lonely. Why do you think I've come round here this evening?'

Taffy fetched Elsie some apple juice before she could sneak another sip of wine. 'I assumed it was because you were high on steroids and looking for mischief?'

Elsie twinkled at him contentedly. 'I knew I liked you.' She drew him down to her level and kissed him on the cheek, making him blush.

Holly scowled. 'What are you two whispering about? You look very suspicious over there.'

Elsie smiled as though butter wouldn't melt. 'Just telling Taffy that I was on his side, when it comes to protecting young Eric's crown jewels. You never know when he might need them.'

Holly nodded but she wasn't convinced.

Elsie, her lack of boundaries now almost legendary, leaned forward and picked up Holly's divorce papers. She'd barely scanned the first two lines when she looked up sharply. 'What's the little shit up to now?'

'Elsie,' protested Holly, unwilling to be drawn back on to the farcical merry-go-round of debate.

'Well,' said Elsie, 'I call it as I see it. Holding up the divorce for months and suddenly he's all peachy keen?' She rootled in her enormous vintage Birkin bag and incongruously pulled out her shiny new MacBook. Within moments she was typing away furiously. Elsie's MacBook may have been a recent acquisition, but she'd wasted no time in mastering the basics. This last may have been almost entirely due to Ewan from the local computer store who popped round to give her one-to-one tuition and the fact that Ewan looked almost exactly like a young Sean Connery.

'Erm, Elsie?' interrupted Holly after a moment, having waited in vain for Elsie to explain herself. There was a hint of the feverish in Elsie's activity this evening that even her prescription cocktail could not explain. Elsie held up a hand, flashing Taffy a glance as she did so.

'Give me a moment, darling girl . . . Can't rush genius, you know . . . That Grace is a dark horse – she's taught me all sorts of tricks on the social meed-yah.' In a final flurry of typing, during which time Holly had unloaded the dishwasher and made yet another pot of tea, Elsie ground to a halt.

When Holly turned around, there seemed to be an unspoken conversation going on across the kitchen table and Taffy's eyes were fixed on Elsie with an odd intensity.

'What?' Holly said eloquently, plonking down the steaming pot on the kitchen table and barely missing a Play Doh model of a diplodocus.

Elsie slowly turned the screen of her wafer-thin laptop until Holly could see it.

'Twitter?' she asked in confusion. 'You've lost me.'

Elsie clicked on a link and the screen blossomed into an American trade publication. 'You can't keep secrets these days, Holly. Not without *somebody* knowing about them . . .'

Holly's eyes darted back and forth across the screen. Firstly trying to work out who @LoveBunny64 might be and also why they were so keen to help Elsie at a moment's notice.

'Twitter's wonderful for casting a net,' Elsie was saying to Taffy as Holly continued to read. 'You can just ask a question and throw it out there.'

Holly sat back in her chair and poured some tea as though on autopilot. 'So Milo's making a movie, is he? And a fortune into the bargain.' She sipped at the tea and her unfocused gaze seemed to reach beyond the windows of her tiny kitchen for a moment.

Elsie leaned forward. 'There's no way he pulled together a deal like this overnight, you know. These things take ages.'

She typed a few words quickly and hit 'send' with as much force as a pissed-off Octogenarian could muster. 'That horrid text was just designed to scare you senseless, so you'd be ripe and willing to sign these the minute they arrived.'

Taffy nodded. 'Typical Milo, trying to coerce you into playing by his agenda. Holly, let's get some advice – please? These papers may look like the Holy Grail, giving you full and uncontested custody of the boys, but you'd be missing out on a huge financial settlement too. After all, he wrote that bloody book while he was married to you and it looks like he's signed the film rights away before the divorce is finalised . . .'

Holly nodded silently, trying to marshal her thoughts. But if anything, this latest turn of events crystallised her thinking in a way that Taffy would probably never understand. If there was one thing more dangerous than a narcissistic Milo out to cause her pain, it was that self-same person with resources behind him. She read the website again and then re-read the terms of the divorce, as laid out by Milo's solicitor. There was a reasonable stipend for the boys' living expenses – something she'd earlier been pleasantly surprised to see – but nothing else financial on the table. He did, however, relinquish all custody of Ben and Tom. It was a bold manoeuvre, certainly.

Holly looked up to find Taffy and Elsie both watching her carefully, as though they were worried that a sudden move might startle her.

'We can take him to the cleaners now, darling,' Elsie said firmly.

Holly shook her head. She picked up one of Ben's marker pens. 'I don't think so. If you think about it, I've already got the only settlement that really matters. If I'm going to get divorced, I'd rather like to do it on my own terms,' she said slowly, straightening the papers in front of her and pausing to check with Taffy. 'Do you think I'm mad?'

Taffy nodded. 'Honestly? Yes.' He leaned forward and kissed her on the cheek. 'But I suppose I shouldn't have expected anything else.'

'But, but, but . . .' spluttered Elsie as she realised what Holly was about to do. 'You can't just give up on all that money,' she protested. 'Think of what you could do with it? School fees? A house? Holly, please, don't do anything rash.'

Holly hesitated for a moment, but only to put their minds at rest. The big blue marker pen was still firmly clasped in her hand. 'But none of that means anything if Ben and Tom are being shuttled back and forth under some transatlantic Access Agreement, having their little personalities bent out of shape. It's just too high a price to pay. And this way, I can be in control – full custody – flexible, but on my terms.' She paused. 'Besides, we're not doing so badly on our own you know. It's enough. It's more than enough.'

It was hard to tell whether Elsie's tears were as a result of Holly's impassioned speech or whether it was the thought of throwing all that money away. She sat back in her chair and sighed. 'Go on, then. Do the deed and I'll be your witness. Terribly bad taste to have your live-in-lover sign one's divorce papers.' She paused and gave a flicker of a smile. 'Apparently.'

The room was silent as Holly scrawled her signature across the papers in triplicate. As she finished, she let out a little sigh and Elsie was quick to respond.

'We can just burn them and start again if you've got Divorcee's Remorse?'

Holly shook her head and wiped her eyes with the back of her hand. 'It's finally over. It's done. I'm free at last.' She looked up at Taffy with tears shimmering on her lashes and gave him a lingering kiss. 'Don't go getting any ideas though, will you?' she said with a cheeky smile.

Taffy looked disquieted for a moment, as though comforting his girlfriend over the end of her marriage was a step too far in his quest to be a sensitive soul, or perhaps he was just jolted by her immediate reflex to ask him to stand down. Elsie on the other hand looked completely at ease – after all, she'd been through this process a few times herself and knew what was coming next.

Holly's smile of sheer relief and joy gradually emerged and she stood up. 'Well, if this isn't an excuse for celebration, I don't know what is!' she declared. She rummaged around in the fridge and emerged looking bemused with a very smart bottle of bubbly in her hands. 'I don't remember buying this. Taffs, is this yours?'

Taffy laughed. 'I bought it for a special occasion. You know – just in case. I think this kind of fits the bill . . .' He reached over to the dresser and pulled down three champagne flutes, but Holly ignored them and grabbed three tumblers from the cupboard. Taffy couldn't be sure, but he thought he'd last seen them full of Nutella.

'Not those, Taffy,' Holly said, pushing the flutes to one-side. 'They were a wedding present. In fact . . . Elsie, will you help me do the honours?'

Elsie was on her feet in a moment. 'On three?' she queried, before Taffy had even cottoned on to what they were up to.

The sound of glasses breaking in the sink had a wonderful clarity and chime to it. 'The Liberty Bell!' declared Elsie. 'And we can add another toast to our list.' She picked up her tumbler of fizz and though her hand may have trembled slightly as she downed the bubbles – against doctor's orders, of course – there was a feeling around the kitchen table that the evening had been the start of something special. 'To new beginnings and the future. Long may it last!'

'I'm so glad you're feeling a little better . . .' Holly ventured as she tucked Elsie up in the spare room later that night, the long day having finally caught up with her as her pharmaceutical high had worn off.

'I'm so glad you walked away from the money actually,' countered Elsie. 'Life really is too short, you know.' She sat up abruptly. 'There it is – the name of my book – we'll call it *Life's Too Short*.'

'I like it,' said Holly simply. 'It kind of resonates.'

Elsie snuggled down under the Bob the Builder duvet cover and caught hold of Holly's hand. 'With me too, darling girl. With me too.'

'Thank you for tonight, Elsie. I mean it. Without you, I would never have known the full story, would I?'

'Seems I'm the golden goose today,' said Elsie with a tired smile.

'Fairy Godmother, more like,' Holly teased her, switching out the bedside light.

'Bippety Boppity Fucking Boo,' rang Elsie's reply drily in the darkness. 'You don't hear much about her, do you, once Cinderella gets her man? Superfluous to requirements . . .'

'And that's why fairy tales are crap,' interjected Holly. 'Because in this version the Fairy Godmother becomes an honorary granny and far too loved and special to ignore.'

'Oof,' replied Elsie. 'Easy on the treacle, darling. Let's just be grateful that we both get to start over.' She paused and Holly quietly stood up to leave. 'If we're going to be brave, Holly, let's jump in with both feet, yes?'

Holly smiled. 'I was thinking I might.'

Elsie drifted off to sleep. 'Lovely bubbles tonight, Holly. Your Taffy has excellent taste.'

My Taffy, mused Holly, as she locked up for the night and checked in on the twins. Suddenly those two words held a world of possibilities.

Chapter 41

Dropping the twins off at pre-school by 8 a.m. was always a challenge, but knowing that they had to be there punctually the next morning had obviously been tempting fate a little too far. One disassembled alarm clock (Ben), one tantrum over the need to wash (Tom) and one slightly unexpected grump over the choice of morning breakfast cereal (Elsie) meant that they were all running late before the day even began. Despite all this though, Holly couldn't stop singing to herself. She'd plastered on extra postage, just to make sure, and sent off her signed divorce papers with a deep breath and a spring in her step. The relief was greater than she'd even dared hope, even if it did come with an oddly bitter aftertaste that she couldn't quite identify – like winning by default.

Even a nervous Mrs Harlow, on the warpath before the Ofsted inspector arrived, wasn't enough to throw her off her stride.

Holly crouched down and tucked Tom's shirt into his shorts. The odds of it staying there were slim to none, but at least Holly felt that she was making the effort. She kissed them both gently on the cheek, Ben's little soft hand resting on her neck as she did so. 'You will be good today, won't you? Because you see that man with the clipboard? Well, he's

very important and you want him to see that you're both very
helpful and kind.'

Tom sighed crossly. 'Home's more fun. This is just boring.'
He said the last part so loudly that it echoed around the
courtyard and Holly could see the vein pulsing menacingly in
Mrs Harlow's forehead. As her doctor, Holly wanted to question how this might affect her blood pressure; as a working
mother, she thought it was about time that Mrs Harlow knew
the true meaning of the word stress. Holly kissed the boys
again and ushered them towards the cloakroom, wondering
how to confirm her own suspicions that their recent bad
behaviour was merely a symptom of the lack of supervision
and stimulation they were receiving at pre-school.

As she turned to leave, trying to avoid Mrs Harlow's glare,
the Ofsted inspector materialised at her elbow and Holly
managed a smile. 'Sorry about that.'

'No problem. I'm Richard Holder by the way.' He held out
his hand to shake. 'I'd like to talk to you about the Gifted
and Talented programme here. Your boys' test scores alone
indicate it's worth us having a chat.'

As Holly dashed through reception, late again and barely
pausing to wave hello, she couldn't stop thinking about what
Mr Holder had said: exceptional scores . . . high IQ . . . Gifted
and Talented programme . . . All these words ran through
her mind and made her wonder how she could possibly have
missed it. Not to mention how Mrs Harlow could have omit-
ted to tell her. She thought about her recurring dream of all
the spinning plates and tried not to read anything into the fact
that, last night, she had dropped every single one. Another
parenting triumph.

She smiled though, as she remembered the inspector's

spot-on joke that you could always identify the parents of a G-and-T child, because they needed a stiff G&T every evening to cope with their child's constant questioning and inquisitive cross-examination. By that token, having twins, Holly thought she must be due a double at least.

The morning went downhill from there frankly, and by the time Holly had dealt with an infected toe-nail, a coil removal that did not go to plan and at least three patients sobbing in front of her, Holly felt like joining in. The sun was shining outside her window and the closest she would get to being outside today would be walking home via Marion's for an emergency Chicken Kiev, since she'd clearly forgotten to get supper out of the freezer before she left.

Taffy poked his head around the door. 'Listen, I'm finishing early to head down and do the health and safety assessment for the Rugby Club. Do you think Mrs Harlow would breathe actual fire if I scooped up the twins afterwards and took them for a swim – it's such a beautiful day, it's a bit criminal for us all to be cooped up inside.'

Holly nodded. 'I was just thinking the same thing. Are you going down to the River Club? I could swing by on the way home if you think you might still be there?'

Taffy left the room whistling and Holly tried not to feel envious. Surely she should be grateful that there was someone else looking out for the boys too? The words of the Ofsted inspector clashed in her mind with the shattering of plates from her dream – she only hoped she hadn't been too hasty in turning down the chance to go after Milo's filthy lucre. Would Mr Holder be suggesting all sorts of expensive courses to keep them fully engaged and on the straight and narrow?

*

After a succession of patients clearly designed to torment and exhaust her, all Holly could think about was getting home.

The recent feeling that she was 'on call' in her home life, as well as in her professional life, had begun to take its toll: Elsie, the twins, solicitors ... They were all pulling on her time and attention in ways she hadn't foreseen. Even Lizzie was getting the short-end of the straw these days and their new text-based relationship wasn't half as fulfilling as their sitting-in-the-pub-with-a-Pimm's version. She didn't feel as though any one of them were getting her undivided attention at the moment – God knows, Taffy seemed to be getting more quality time with her boys than she did and Lizzie was now unwilling to relinquish her temporary role as Elsie's Hospital Companion. She didn't even have time to stress about this Model Surgery farce or indeed little Coco. She slammed her desk drawer shut with annoyance, frustrated at how short-changed she was feeling when there were so many things to be grateful for.

Moments later, Dan was standing in Holly's doorway, car keys grasped in his hand and Holly had that awful sensation when you stand up too quickly and the world seemed to kaleidoscope around her. Her thoughts rearranged them-selves like a game of Tetris, slotting into place in a different formation.

'Holly, darling, we need to go to the hospital. Ben's there already, on his way into X-ray and Taffy's with him. They think he's swallowed a battery.'

All the way into Bath, Holly was mentally running check-lists in her head. It didn't seem to matter that the nurse in the ICU had been fulsome in her praise on the phone just now, as Dan flicked on his hazard warning lights and wove through the traffic on the outskirts of the city, his knuckles white on the steering wheel. His skill in tactical driving was obviously yet another remnant of army life that he'd never forgotten.

Apparently Taffy's quick thinking might have made 'all the difference' to Ben's chances of recovery, yet that made no difference to the overwhelming sensation of guilt Holly felt for not being there. Holly didn't even want to think about what that might mean. When it came to these tiny coin-sized batteries, one could only hope that he'd swallowed it properly. Lodging in his oesophagus would be the worst-case scenario, causing a blockage, or corrosive leakage, or even a fistula. A little knowledge on this front for Holly was a dangerous thing, as her imagination ran riot through the possibilities.

They hurtled to the entrance of the hospital in record time and Holly ran. As she buzzed the door of the Emergency Care Unit, she could feel her breath coming short and fast, her fingertips tingling as she struggled against the urge to hyperventilate. The moment of waiting before the doors swung open to admit her giving her just enough time to find a semblance of balance – she was here to support Ben, not frighten the life out of him.

The first face she saw was Taffy's, stricken and pale. The sight hit her like a body-blow to the chest. 'Is he . . . ?' she managed.

Taffy engulfed her shaking body in his arms, talking calmly and slowly as he did so. 'He's okay and they've got the X-rays done, although he was all over the place and they had to sedate him a little. We've worked out it was a Lithium cell, which is obviously the best possible option from a poisoning perspective and they've given him some oral antacids in case it will reduce corrosion of the cell, plus a low-dose metoclopramide to encourage the gastric-emptying. They're really on top of this, Holly – you can breathe now, honestly.' He drew her towards a curtained-off bay. 'Come and see for yourself.'

Nothing had quite prepared her though, for the sight of her little boy, ashen and sleepy, with monitors bleeping. She took his little hand in hers and whispered to him over and over that she was here now. He opened his eyes sleepily and looked as though he was about to cry. 'Sorry, Mummy,' he said, before dozing off again.

She swallowed down the tears of relief and murmured sweet nothings and reassurances into his ear. There was nothing to be sorry for. They could deal with recriminations and analysis later. At that thought she turned to Taffy. 'What happened?' she whispered.

Taffy pulled over a chair for her, sensing that there was no way she'd be relinquishing her hold on Ben's hand anytime soon.

'I got there just after lunch and, you were right, Mrs Harlow was rather sniffy about me taking the boys out early. Said that Ben had been making a fuss all morning, saying he was bored, being a nuisance. Stupid, stupid woman,' he cursed, side-tracked in his narrative by his obvious disdain for Mrs Harlow's lack of attention. 'Anyway, she gave him some old toys to take apart; thought it would keep him quiet, apparently.' He shrugged. 'I don't know why, but it put me on guard as soon as she said that. And then when we got to the car, Ben kept rubbing at his chest, coughing a bit. It was all so, well, weird really. You know Ben doesn't make a fuss about nothing, does he? I mean if it were Tom . . .'

He swallowed hard to collect himself, but Holly was

listening to every word, even if her eyes had not once left Ben's face. She felt incredibly lucky that Taffy knew her boys well enough – knew which one was the brave soldier and which one could moan and whine about the slightest paper cut. She nodded.

'Well, I got them to the car and told them we were going swimming at the River Club and – well – nothing. And you know how Ben loves the river?'

Taffy glossed over the moment when he'd pulled the Land Rover to one side and given Ben a thorough once over. Nothing specific to tip him off, just a lacklustre little boy with a headache and a sore chest. He didn't mention the internal dialogue he'd fought over – knowing that the advice he'd give his patients to go home, keep a close eye and rest up, suddenly didn't feel proactive enough for the little boy in his care.

'You're going to think I'm mad, Holly, but I thought I'd drive into Bath – call it a Sixth Sense, if you like. Worst-case scenario, he has a little nap in the car and we go out for ice cream. I just wanted to be near the hospital, you know, just in case.'

Holly turned to look at him properly then, at the hollowed expression of fear in his eyes. How could she have thought that she would have caught this sooner? He'd basically brought Ben here on nothing but a gut-feeling.

'It wasn't until we were parking up here that Ben started talking about the toys and the funny shiny button. And then I knew.'

Holly's eyes filled with tears. 'Well then, he's a very lucky boy. Thank you, Taffy.' The words didn't seem enough somehow, but they were all Holly could spare, seeing Ben so fragile. She looked around. 'Where's Tom?'

Taffy nodded his head towards the nurses' station, where

Tom was tucked up in a swivelling chair, happily playing Candy Crush on Taffy's phone. 'He's had a snack and all the nurses at his beck and call – he's pretty much unfazed by the whole thing, as far as I can tell.'

For the first time Holly noticed the sticker on Taffy's breast pocket, marking him out as visiting staff. 'What's with the . . .?' she asked.

He shrugged. 'I'm not technically family, so they were worried about letting me back here. The boys, of course, had other ideas and it seemed like the easiest solution in the end.' He wrapped his arms around Holly's shoulders as she remained by Ben's bedside trying to let this tsunami of news sink in. Tom had waved happily across the room, when he looked up and saw his mum, before returning to his screen – the treat of being given unfettered access to video games seemingly more interesting than the dramas unfolding around him.

The medical staff were clearly stretched pretty thin, as they dashed between the various bays in the ICU. The fact that Ben now seemingly had his own personal medical team, meant that they were focusing their attention elsewhere for now. After all, his meds were all rigged up, further X-rays monitoring the progress of the battery through his digestive system were pending and now it was basically a waiting game.

The on-call paediatrician stopped by their bay to update them on his proposed treatment protocol. Holly blinked hard and tried to concentrate – for Christ's sake they were talking about her son's prognosis here – this was her field. Why in hell was her concentration slipping through her fingers like jelly? She blinked again, only hearing every third or fourth word. Is this what it felt like to be the helpless parent? A pair of strong arms guided her away from the bed and into a chair. Taffy crouched down beside her. 'Holly? Are you okay?'

She shook her head and her voice trembled as she tried to explain. Perhaps it was delayed shock, she wondered, or perhaps this was how it always felt – as the parent.

Taffy sized up the situation in a heartbeat. 'Right now, you have one job, okay? You sit beside Ben and talk to him and stroke his hair and tell him you love him. Dan's going to drop Tom at Lizzie's for the night and I can do the hands-on stuff and keep an eye on test results and the like. You're just here for moral support. You're the parent today, Holly, not the doctor.'

'Thank you,' she managed, still stunned that all her years of medical training somehow hadn't prepared her for this. She had never been more grateful for Taffy's reassuring calmness in a crisis.

As the afternoon turned into night and the lab results came back, they were able to tailor Ben's treatment to the specific battery and its position in his digestive system. Dan had driven Tom back to Larkford and left Taffy and Holly at Ben's bedside. The Ward Sister had finally won her battle to keep 'this circus' out of her domain and Holly was relieved that surgery was no longer being discussed as an option.

Holly held Ben's hand as he slept and Taffy continued to play medical envoy. The slow rhythmic drip of the IV was almost like Chinese water torture, as Holly's eyes flickered back and forth across her son's sleeping body and the monitors beside him. Whether for better or worse, if there were any changes, she wanted to be the first to see them.

As three o'clock rolled around, the ICU staff seemed to go from one resuscitation to another. It really was the graveyard hour. Holly felt Taffy's gaze on her and looked up. 'What would have happened if he'd stayed at nursery this afternoon?' she asked.

Taffy said nothing for a moment. 'It didn't happen, though. So don't torture yourself. Plus, you know, Ben's a professional – if he's going to swallow a battery, he's going to swallow it well – none of this pesky obstruction business for him.'

Holly nodded, logically understanding the wisdom of those words, but emotionally unable to leave the train of thought. 'If you hadn't noticed, if you hadn't been so attentive . . .' She reached out for his hand. 'And I don't think you're mad, by the way. I live my life by the commandment of Just in Case.'

He smiled gently. 'It didn't seem like there was a downside to being extra careful where this little chap was concerned. It was weird though – kind of like a sixth sense . . .'

Holly nodded. 'I thought it was just a Mum thing. Maybe dads can get it too.'

Taffy nodded, unable to speak for a moment. 'I like that.'

'I'm so sorry,' she said. 'I can't believe they wouldn't let you in here with him.' She stroked the wisp of hair back from Ben's face and sighed. 'We should sort something out, when he's better, sign a form or something.'

There was a moment's silence. 'Well there's something else we could do. I mean, I know this isn't the time, or the place, or the way I'd imagined it, but Holly . . .'

A monitor to their right began beeping loudly and Ben's eyelids flickered. They both leapt to their feet, instinctively primed for action.

When Ben opened his eyes and looked straight at Holly, it was as though she could finally breathe again. 'Hi, Mum,' he said in a tired, reedy voice. 'I'm really hungry.'

Holly swallowed a sob. 'Of course you are, Monkey,' she managed, laughter and tears making her voice wobble. 'You slept right through supper.' She clasped his hand tightly and tried not to cry.

'Mum?' Ben said, sounding more than a little annoyed. 'Can you stop squeezing my hand now?'

Chapter 42

Grace clicked on 'print' and leaned back in her chair as the room filled with the aroma of warm paper and fresh ink. It was quickly becoming one of her favourite smells, as it had come to signify yet another task ticked off her ever-expanding list. With Holly out of commission for the last few days, as she took care of young Ben, it would be all hands on deck yet again, but the sheer relief of knowing that the little lad was on the mend made that seem like an irrelevance. Her mobile vibrated on the desk beside her and Jamie's name flashed up on the screen. She was going to have to do something about that, she thought. Not that she wasn't flattered, but it was all a little too Mrs Robinson for her taste – he was a sweet lad, she thought, but didn't that just say it all?

She didn't want a 'sweet lad'; she wanted what Lucy always referred to as a 'Manly Man'. In fact, she'd been half tempted to sign up for a dating website dedicated to people who liked men in uniform, until she realised it wasn't the actual uniforms that floated her boat, it was more the sense of confidence and competence that made her knees go weak.

'Hi, Jamie,' she said, attempting to keep her voice strictly professional. She may be picky, but she wasn't dead.

'I'm coming over to try some new training protocols with

Alice later,' he said, the line slightly crackling as he was obviously off in a field somewhere with one of his other charges. 'Good boy!' he said effusively, confirming her suspicions. 'And, well, I wondered if you might like a drink?'

'Me, or the dog?' Grace clarified, surprised at the flirtatious humour that had crept into her tone. She quickly moved to cover. 'It's a lovely thought, Jamie, but I'm afraid I already have plans for dinner with a . . . with a friend.' How on earth did one even begin to describe the powerhouse that was Elsie Townsend?

Unwittingly though, she had hit upon the antidote to young Jamie's affections. 'Oh!' he said. 'Oh, I see. No problem. I'll just – well, I'll see you. That is, when I see you.' His confident demeanour had been instantly deflated by the very thought that there might be somebody else on the scene and Grace immediately knew she'd done the right thing. She needed someone with a bit of stamina and backbone – somebody who might enjoy a bit of healthy banter and challenging conversation.

As though her thoughts had summoned him, Dan Carter walked into her office, sat down on the end of her desk and pinched her last Jaffa Cake. 'Morning, Gracie. Thought you might like to know they've discharged Ben and Holly's taking him home. So we can all breathe again.' He paused and smiled, the weight almost noticeably lifting from his shoulders. 'You're looking fabulously efficient there with that pencil behind your ear.'

Before she could remove it, he reached forward and tucked her swinging bob back behind it. 'That's better. You'd better watch out, or all the patients will be having Naughty Librarian fantasies . . .' He looked stunned then, Grace thought, as though he could hardly believe the words coming

out of his mouth, but unlike Jamie, he surrendered to his faux
pas and fell about laughing. 'I'm absolutely sure that's the look
you were going for when you got up this morning, wasn't it?'

Grace smiled and shooed him off her desk. 'Clear off and
do some work,' she said, and there it was again – that flirtatious tone that hadn't been heard for two decades, but now
twice in one morning! 'Seriously, unless you would just love
to come and help me and Julia sort through the donations
and charitable status application forms, then I'd find myself
a patient. Stat!'

'Naughty librarian, naughty nurse . . .' debated Dan as he
left the room with a backwards glance, his face suffused with
laughter. 'Naughty secretary,' he said, almost out of earshot.

'I can still hear you, you know!' called Grace, wondering
whether it still counted as sexual harassment in the workplace,
if it actually made your day.

As Grace bundled into Julia's office, with an armful of ring
binders and a pen between her teeth, she was perfectly aware
that she was hardly looking her finest, yet somehow Dan's
comments had managed to make her forget the slightly ageing
shift dress she was wearing and the fact that she had been
forced to buy some glasses from the supermarket yesterday,
just for the magnification of all these sodding spread-sheets.

'Ah, the worker bee approaches her queen,' proclaimed
Quentin, pretentious wanker that he was, but Grace was
nonetheless grateful when he made a show of gallantly pulling
out a chair for her to gladly deposit all her work.

She pushed the tortoiseshell glasses on top of her head,
and flipped through the pages of her spiralbound notebook
to where she had scribbled the 'agenda' for their hurriedly
scheduled meeting. She looked up and was surprised to see

that Quentin had returned to perching his pin-striped bottom on Julia's desk, for all the world as though he owned the place.

Grace shifted uncomfortably on her feet as he leaned in and kissed Julia lingeringly on the lips. 'Get finished up and come over to mine, yeah? The bed's definitely too big without you, baby.'

It was small comfort that Julia looked just as mortified as Grace felt.

'Shall we agree never to mention this?' Julia said quietly, after Quentin had made a rather swash-buckling exit.

'No problem,' said Grace vehemently, wishing she could erase the vision of a grown-man blowing a kiss from the doorway quite so easily. 'Fight Club rules.'

'What?' said Julia shortly. 'What does that even mean?'

Grace shrugged, unfazed by her ire. 'Doesn't matter – it's a line from a movie.'

Julia frowned. 'You and Dan should get together and quote stuff at each other – he seems to have something for almost every occasion.' She sighed. 'Maybe that's why I never really understood what he was saying? I should really watch a movie occasionally.'

Grace spread out the folders in front of her, desperate to change the subject. 'Ooh and I've got your post,' she said, rummaging through the pile. 'I had to sign for this one. International delivery, so it might be something interesting?'

Julia shrugged. 'Probably just another invitation to speak at some tin-pot medical conference in Switzerland, where you end up paying for your own travel and hope that at least a dozen delegates turn up, who don't also happen to be presenting a paper.' She spoke as though this kind of invitation happened all the time.

Grace passed the letter across the desk and the expression

on Julia's face indicated that she too had instantly clocked the logo on the envelope.

Slowly, almost as though she had forgotten Grace was even there, Julia picked up the letter. The laurel wreath and the familiar image of mother and child seemed to have rendered her speechless.

Grace waited for her to say something, or even open the envelope. After a few moments had passed, she couldn't sit by any longer. 'Do you want me to give you a minute?'

Julia looked up, her eyes shining with an almost evangelical brightness. 'It's from Unicef,' she said needlessly. 'Unicef are writing to me.' She spoke in the tone of voice, as though for them to even acknowledge her very existence, was an achievement beyond measure.

'Open it then,' encouraged Grace, bemused by her hesitation.

Julia held the envelope in her hand, her thumb running almost unconsciously over the logo. 'It's probably just a fund-raising circular,' she said quietly. She looked up at Grace and it was the first time that Grace had seen the person behind the façade, the vulnerable Julia.

'But nobody else got one,' Grace said reassuringly. 'And I'm not sure that they're in the habit of organising a couri-ered delivery for just anyone.' If it was anybody else at The Practice, Grace knew just what to provide: a hug, some space, a coffee, a willing ear. But with Julia this morning, Grace was in new territory, for this was not the fire-breathing Alpha female they were so accustomed to. Indeed, there was some-thing so fragile in the hopeful look in Julia's eyes that Grace barely dared move for fear of startling her.

Julia exhaled slowly, as though the anticipation of some-thing special might yet prove more rewarding than whatever reality was inside – easier, in fact, just to savour a moment heavy with possibilities.

Julia slowly slid her fingernail under the flap at the top of the envelope and a single piece of paper slipped out. Grace discreetly averted her gaze, giving Julia a moment of privacy, even as she was desperate to leap up and read over her shoulder.

To her immense surprise, when she did look up, it was to see Julia's beautiful brown eyes filled with tears and duly magnified to Disney Princess proportions. Incapable of speech, she merely handed Grace the letter – an endorsement of trust that was unheard of in this particular office.

Grace quickly skimmed its contents, her attention held for a moment by the strap line across the headed paper – *For Every Child in Danger*. Well, she thought, perhaps Julia could identify only too well with that emotion, with Candace as a mother? Although obviously, the scale of their first-world difficulties probably paled into insignificance compared to what Unicef handled.

Her eyes leapt from paragraph to paragraph, only occasionally looking up for Julia's approval to continue reading what turned out to be a very personal letter. Praising Julia's ability to connect with the public on screen and her professional manner in medicine, it was obvious that they held her in the highest regard. As it turned out, the quiet-spoken, intellectual man Julia had seen as a guest patient only last week, had gone promptly back to work and recommended her for this role. Ambassador for Immunisation. What a title . . . What a role . . . What a difference she could make . . . And it was hers. All Julia apparently had to do, was say yes.

Grace experienced a moment's guilt that she and the team hadn't appreciated Julia's skillset enough while she was here – reading this letter, it was obvious that not everyone was looking for a lollipop and a hug from their doctor. It was an absolute endorsement of Julia's professional, if occasionally removed style of practising medicine that they were offering her – and only her – this coveted position.

'This is amazing,' said Grace quietly, having almost blushed herself, after reading on through yet more fulsome praise to the end of the letter. 'What will you do?'

Julia just looked completely overwhelmed, as she carefully and lovingly folded the letter back into its distinctive envelope. It was quite remarkable to watch her transformation, as the reality of her over-sharing suddenly hit home. Even though to everybody else here, it would just be called sharing, thought Grace.

'Can I ask you not to tell anyone about this, Grace? I'd really appreciate a few days just to take it all in,' Julia said.

'Goes without saying,' said Grace, opening a ring binder in front of her. 'We can just carry on as though nothing happened.' She looked up and risked a grin. 'Although then, you would have to navigate Her Majesty's Revenue & Customs website with me to sort out all this Gift Aid business? I'm not convinced I'm qualified.'

Julia nodded. 'I know what you mean,' she said ambiguously.

Keeping a secret, thought Grace, was so much harder than she remembered. All day, her attention had been wandering back to Julia's job offer and the possible ramifications for The Practice. Even now, sitting at Elsie's counter top and popping ice-cubes into a jug for some virgin cocktails, she was still distracted. It had been one thing to consider that Julia's filming commitments might pull her out of the surgery with increasing regularity, but the idea that she might pack up and emigrate was a whole different ball game.

'Do you know,' said Elsie sniffily, 'I feel like I've been talking to myself for the last five minutes. What on earth is going on with you this evening, Gracie? Didn't you realise that I only invited you over to have somebody to moan to?' She flashed her trademark enigmatic smile, as though she was joking – they both knew she wasn't really. With Holly caught up nursing Ben back to health and Lizzie's own particular brand of care-giving being a little exhausting, Elsie had called on Grace for a pick-me-up.

'Sorry,' said Grace quickly, before Elsie could start interrogating her, 'I was just—'

Elsie faked a yawn, fanning her hand in front of her mouth. '*Et tu*, Gracie? Since when did you lot do so much "justifying" yourselves? Kick it to the kerb, would you please. We'll take baby steps with you, because I know you're nice – we'll build up to saying what you actually mean so you don't get whiplash!'

Elsie held out her glass for the Raspberry Blush, or whatever today's concoction was called. 'But right now, I need to talk to you about Holly. All this business with the hospital and the divorce – I want to do something constructive to help. Sitting around feeling old and useless is not terribly satisfying, to be honest. Imagine that.'

Grace nodded. 'Well, I'll gladly join forces with you, if you'd like.' They all knew only too well what a dynamo Elsie Townsend on a mission could be and Grace was under orders to keep her calm and comfortable. That didn't mean she couldn't still have a life though, Grace reasoned. 'What did you have in mind? God knows we're missing Holly enough at work, but I daren't think how hard she's finding all this.'

Elsie frowned, her features uncharacteristically sombre. 'You will look after her for me, won't you? When I finally quit the stage?'

'Oh Elsie,' Grace chided. 'I can absolutely make you that promise, if it helps, but I have a feeling you'll be outliving me at this rate. All your latest tests came back as top notch – A★ in fact – model patient.'

'Too good to be worm fodder just yet then?' Elsie clarified. 'That *is* good news. I have so much superior meddling left in me, you see. All you girls . . . women, I mean,' she corrected herself, rolling her eyes at the political correctness she was expected to employ in her later years. 'I worry about you so. Holly's finally on the right track – if you ignore her flagrant disregard for the value of money – but it's as though I've only just taken her stabilisers off and she could veer off course at any point. Lovely Lizzie is driving me to distraction with her well-meaning, but dear God, utterly exhausting Quest For The Meaning of Life and you—'

Elsie leaned forward and clasped Grace's hands in her own. 'I see so much of myself in you, Grace. And I wish *you* could see that it's okay to let others in to boost your happiness. You've become so incredibly balanced and self-sufficient, I worry that you might not let anyone into your life again, in case they disturb the status quo you've worked so hard for.'

Grace squeezed Elsie's fingers. 'I haven't cloistered myself away, Elsie. I'm out every night, you know,' she offered as reassurance.

Elsie waved her hand dismissively. 'At yoga, or meditation, or swimming at the River Club – it's hardly living the high life, is it?'

Grace grinned. 'Makes me happy though. Little goals, minor milestones – like swimming the River Race when I never thought I could, and perfecting my headstands . . .' She subconsciously patted at the bob that had made that possible. 'I'm all about what my body can *do* these days, rather than what I weigh, or what I look like – it's been kind of liberating actually.'

Elsie snorted. 'Oh the irony!'

Grace's confused expression made her laugh harder. Elsie slid off the kitchen stool and pulled Grace into the hall. 'Look at you! You're gorgeous! Now don't tell me you hadn't actually realised the allure of the girl-who-didn't-give-a-stuff?'

Grace looked flustered, taking in her image in Elsie's floor-length antique mirror. Seriously, who had time for navel-gazing and self-scrutiny these days? What she saw there pleased and frightened her in equal measure – clear skin, glowing eyes, a figure she would have killed for as a teenager – how was it possible that she was looking the best she ever had, when her best years were already behind her?

Elsie leaned in and kissed her cheek. 'You are a beautiful woman, Grace, inside and out. Don't be afraid to embrace those that can see it too?'

Grace blushed instantly, her thoughts filled with the gentle attentions of Jamie, and Dan, and the lovely guy at the baker's who had taken to adding 'a little something extra' to her bag every time she went in.

'You're in your prime, darling girl. You wander around, thinking you're over the hill, but you haven't even got to the top yet – climb on up, darling – the view is sensational!' Elsie waggled her eyebrows as though to reinforce the salacious undertones.

'But I—' began Grace.

'No buts,' Elsie interrupted, 'unless of course you mean—'

'Oh dear God,' implored Grace, feeling incredibly

uncomfortable with this line of conversation. 'I can't do filthy jokes about bottoms without at least a gin and tonic!'

Elsie harrumphed. 'Well, it's not me who locked the liquor cabinet! And God knows I needed the gin earlier.'

Grace guided her back into the kitchen and refilled her glass of Raspberry Blush. 'We could do some yoga together, if that would help?'

Elsie just looked bemused. 'I *honestly* do not see how that would help.' She held out her hand and for the first time, Grace noticed the empty ring finger where Elsie's antique diamond ring normally took pride of place. 'I lost my ring—' she sighed deeply. 'And you just *know* it's the carer, don't you? At least that's what Panorama would have us believe. And I was about to fire Sarah – who by the way is an angel and a Godsend, but thank God I didn't!' She paused for dramatic effect and looked at Grace expectantly.

'Because she hadn't taken it?' Grace offered.

'Exactly! Mortifying! But I've lost so much bloody weight being old and decrepit that it just kept slipping off my finger, you see ... So that's why I needed the gin,' she finished matter-of-factly.

Grace nodded sympathetically. 'I see what you mean. All terribly stressful, but gin isn't always the answer. We could try meditation to calm your thoughts ...'

'Oh no, I've found it already,' interrupted Elsie again, infuriating to the last. 'It was in the herb garden all along.' She pulled a very muddy, clearly very expensive diamond ring out of her pocket and dropped it on the kitchen counter, where it spun around like a top on the polished granite. 'Oh Grace, do try to keep up – we need gin for the ring.'

Grace looked sceptical. 'Because it's had such a tricky week?'

Elsie burst out laughing. 'Because it's filthy and gin makes diamonds shine. How could you not know that? But I think that settles it actually.'

Grace could feel herself losing the plot a little at the sheer number of abrupt turns this conversation was taking. 'Settles what?' she managed.

'Well, I can't go anywhere, can I? You all need me too much. I shall just have to cheat the Grim Reaper for a few years longer until I've got you all settled. Now, did you decide who was worthy of your affections in the end? Are we going for an inter-office romance or are we dabbling with being a cougar? Go on, go on, any first step will be hard, but we'll have your stabilisers off in no time, too.'

'I don't remember mentioning either of those options actually, Elsie,' Grace replied faintly.

Elsie looked smug. 'No, I don't believe you did.' She refilled her glass and looked Grace squarely in the eye. 'But you need to make a decision because you'll be needing a "plus one" at my party.'

'I will?' Grace said, grateful for a moment for Elsie's new range of virgin cocktails. At least she could have more than one without getting utterly squiffy, embarrassing herself and agreeing to God-knows-what.

'Indeed,' replied Elsie gleefully. 'There's altogether too much doom and gloom in Larkford at the moment, so I've decided to throw a launch party for my book!'

'The book that isn't published yet?' Grace clarified.

Elsie shook her head. 'Oh dear God – what's the matter with everybody. Are you so against a little gratuitous fun? You sound just like my publicist! So the *actual* book may not exist just yet, but the ink is dry on my contract and I read somewhere that it's important to celebrate every milestone as an author. And I want *you* to help me organise it.'

'Okay then,' Grace acquiesced instantly, firstly because it was sometimes easier just to give in to Elsie's schemes and plans, and secondly because a party in Larkford sounded like exactly what they all needed after the last few weeks.

'It needs to be a garden party,' Elsie said. 'My poor gardener Brian has been slaving away all summer and nobody has been able to appreciate his hydrangeas. It's almost criminal. And we'll need cocktails and mini food and candles – Grace, are you even writing this down? There's an awful lot to do!'

Grace pulled a diary from her handbag and flicked through the pages. 'We should probably think about setting a date first.'

Elsie shook her head. 'Oh, but I have. And I've booked the most delightful photographer. Next Friday gives you plenty of time to organise the rest, doesn't it? I mean, it's only drinks for a few hundred people ...' She clapped her hands together excitedly, completely missing the stunned expression on Grace's face. 'It's going to be so much fun!'

Chapter 43

'I come bearing yet another casserole, if you're not sick to death of them already, some rather stunning flapjacks and a cunning plan,' said Hattie, standing on Holly's doorstep looking incredibly pleased with herself. Her own small twins were fast asleep but she didn't bat an eyelid as Tom and Ben swarmed out to greet them, immediately fascinated by the enormous double buggy and its clever mechanisms and gadgets.

'That's so thoughtful,' said Holly, hurriedly pulling her unwashed hair back into a bobble and wishing that today was the day she'd actually managed to get dressed. The house was in chaos around her, but Holly couldn't seem to muster the energy to care. 'I'll get some more coffee on.'

Her fridge was full of casseroles, her window sills laden with flowers and she hadn't quite realised how many Meccano sets were available these days: it seemed that half of Larkford had the same idea – to stop Ben taking things apart and encourage him to build his own. The support and generosity of her friends and neighbours had been almost overwhelming, but still Holly felt oddly removed from it all.

It was over a week now since Ben had been sent home from hospital with a clean bill of health and the simple instruction for him to take it steady for a bit. And it was fair to say that Holly and Taffy were struggling to come to an easy under-standing of what that actually meant.

Holly's interpretation had been to wrap Ben in proverbial cotton wool and focus her attention almost exclusively on him. Taffy had returned to work, Tom had welcomed the opportunity to spend hours playing in the sandpit at home, but still Holly could not bring herself to take the next logical step.

Even with Ben bouncing around the kitchen with his brother, there was a wealth of medical knowledge running through her mind like a ticker-tape. Relapses, complications, close-calls . . . Her mind was a veritable button box of what-ifs and maybes – all of them negative. On some level she knew she might be over-reacting, but on every other, the guilt was overwhelming; the curse of the working mother, it clouded her every decision at the moment.

She pushed the window open and a warm breeze feathered through the room, smelling of hot grass and summer flowers, with a hint of warm tarmac. A tiny taste of the world outside. For the first time all week, with Hattie babbling away at her kitchen table, it didn't seem quite so unbelievably daunting.

'Well, you're away with the pixies this morning, Holly,' Hattie said, as Ben lost interest in the buggy and turned back to the Lego set that Dan had delivered in person. It had been a transparent ploy to discover when Holly might be coming back to work and she flushed a little to think of her response.

'Oh, Hatts, I'm turning into a total fruit-cake this week. Poor Dan came by with that Lego for Ben and I practically bit his head off for suggesting I should try and get things back to normal – which we both knew was code for get myself back to work . . . I told him he wouldn't understand because he wasn't a parent. The look on his face, oh, it was awful.'

Hattie nodded. 'You do have a point, though. I'm not sure anybody can understand the fear and responsibility and juggling that goes on inside a mother's mind unless they've actually been there.'

Holly managed half a smile. 'He has a point though, doesn't he?' She watched as Ben bounded around the sitting room without a care in the world. 'Ben's clearly better. I just can't bear the thought of him being out of my sight. Not to mention all the issues I know are waiting for me at work. I'm being a complete ostrich about the whole thing.'

Hattie leaned forward. 'Listen, Holly, you know I'm the first person to say put your family first because nothing else really matters – I mean, when Lance was ill, I literally could not bring myself to give a fuck about anything else . . .'

'Hattie!' said Holly, a little shocked.

'Well, call it like it is. But Ben is fine now and I imagine Mrs pole-up-yer-bum Harlow has had the fear of God drummed into her?'

Holly nodded. 'She's been suspended, actually. She came round here to apologise, but it was so obvious she didn't want to do it.' The light came back into Holly's eyes a little as she told Hattie about the look on Mrs Harlow's face when she'd seen the big white envelope on the kitchen table with the solicitors' postal stamp on it. 'And I didn't feel particularly inclined to tell her it was my divorce papers. Let her stew on her stubborn, negligent crappery.'

'Is that even a word?' Hattie asked.

'Probably not, but it should be,' said Holly with feeling. 'The way she's handled the boys has been nothing short of appalling. I've heard all about their Key Stage assessments and the lovely Ofsted man said it's perfectly normal for children to get troublesome when they're under-stimulated. He reckons that Ben's health problems last year just mean that he got pigeon-holed. When he felt better and the pair of them were egging each other on, the staff just saw it as bad behaviour.'

'I guess you can see how that might happen,' Hattie said, ever the voice of reason. 'But we both know that Mrs Harlow wouldn't have stepped an inch out of her way to help them. This battery business is the final straw really.' She stopped for a moment. 'Look I don't want to sound like this is a sales pitch, but I popped round with a suggestion that might help. You know Lance and I have been talking about expanding our business at The Deli? Well, what I didn't tell you was that we're turning the building next door into a crèche. I've got my Early Years registration and we were hoping that some of the freelance mummies around here might find the odd session with us more do-able than a full on commitment at Pinetrees. And it's not like there's any other choice around here, is there?'

Holly felt a lump in her throat, as if all her worries about the boys returning to Pinetrees were bundled together with knowing that, in order to return to work, she didn't really have an option. She'd kept Tom home every day this week as well, even once she'd heard about Mrs Harlow's suspension, simply wanting to have him home safe with her. 'Are you suggesting ... ?'

Hattie nodded. 'It's not officially open yet, but I could have my twins and your two for the next month or so, and then they'll be off to school. You can get back to work and get your own life a little more balanced, without the constant worry of what might be happening with them.' She smiled. 'And I can promise you that under-stimulation will not be a problem. We seem to have toys and puzzles and books coming out of our ears.'

'Are you serious?' Holly said, dumbfounded that the solution she'd been searching for could actually be so simple.

'Absolutely. We can start gradually, or all at once . . . You tell me.' Hattie grinned. 'And just for once, I get to help you out, after everything you've done for me.'

'I don't know what to say,' Holly managed. 'It would be wonderful. Thank you, Hattie. Seriously. I've been so stuck . . .' She didn't need to elaborate for Hattie, for if anyone in Larkford understood, it was her. She would surely identify with all those hours in the darkest part of the night, sitting at Ben's bedside, only giving Holly more time to dwell on what might have been – holding his hand, marvelling at his beautiful face, the snuffling noises he made in his sleep. This whole situation could have ended so differently, but for Taffy's quick thinking.

'I know,' said Hattie gently, as though reading her mind. 'I do. But when you get to the part where the worst bit is over, it takes a while to sink in, doesn't it? I felt like I was poised for the next drama for months after Lance . . .'

'It's true,' Holly nodded. 'I just keep thinking – what next?'

It didn't take long to find out. Holly stared at the screen on her iPhone later that day, as it skittered across the coffee table, rebounding off crayons, Lego bricks and an optimistically laden fruit bowl. She clasped her now empty, still warm, coffee mug to her chest and tried to ignore the automatic wave of discomfort that seeing Milo's caller ID had triggered within a single breath.

She felt an uncomfortable tightening in her chest that drew her breathing into an escalating swirl and yet her hands still stubbornly refused to move. Decline the call – it was one flick of a finger and she could have peace again, she thought.

That was the thing about smartphones and gadgets – you were never out of reach, never truly able to relax. A single ping of a text or an unwelcome e-mail and the course of a day or an evening could be thrown with one intrusive message. And God knows, she had enough experience of that of late.

The very thought brought her up short – compared to the acidic horror of the phone call about Ben, this was child's play. A week later and everything was relative now: he was home and he was safe and that was all that really mattered. This empowering perspective was like taking off an ill-fitting bra at the end of the day: a sudden release of the band around her chest and the ability to fully inhale for the first time in what felt like forever.

'Hello, Milo,' she said calmly, picking up the phone moments before the voicemail kicked in. 'You took your time.'

There was a pause at the end of the line, a transatlantic crackle of static that barely disguised the surprised intake of breath at her detached tone. Whatever Milo had been expecting, it wasn't that. 'How is he?' Milo said.

Thank God the twins were super-glued to a Pixar double bill when Milo had finally deigned to make contact, Holly thought, trying not to second guess Milo's motivations in actually picking up the phone. Better late than never, she supposed.

'He's on the mend,' she replied, feeling no need to elaborate for the moment, unable to quash her anger that it had taken him so long to respond to her message about Ben's accident.

He breathed out in a whoosh, as though he'd been holding

his breath all week. The cynic in Holly wasn't buying it though. It took all her reserve to patiently wait him out.

'And you?' he said, the intimacy in his voice so entirely misplaced as to be almost bizarre. 'How are *you* coping? I mean, the timing of this . . .' He stopped dead, changing tack abruptly. 'I can't believe you signed those papers, Holly.'

'What was I supposed to do with them?' she asked, standing up from the sofa and walking through to the kitchen. She was grateful that Hattie's visit had given her a much-needed boost of energy and resolve.

'I thought you'd call me,' he said, hardly sounding like himself at all. 'I honestly thought you'd call me and yell at me and tell me I was making a huge mistake. That they needed their dad in their lives. They're my boys, Holly. You let me walk away, and now—'

She flinched against the barrage of his words, his uncharacteristic anxiety making her feel all the more in control. 'I didn't *let* you do anything, Milo. You created this situation and I'm truly sorry if you don't like the consequences, but—'

'I can't believe you signed them,' he said again.

Holly checked that the twins were still engrossed in their movie and slipped into the laundry room. How ironic, she thought, to have returned to the very scene of so many of their disagreements. 'Stop saying that. Just stop. It makes you sound disingenuous or, possibly ignorant, and if there's one thing you're not it's ignorant, Milo. So come on, let's start how we mean to go on.' Her tone was deliberately measured and open, and Holly found that the longer she spoke, the more her confidence was growing, the anger morphing into quiet resolve. 'The boys are happy here, Milo, and I presume you're happy with this film deal thing you've got going on?'

'You know about that?' He sounded genuinely surprised. 'And you signed anyway?'

'I know about that,' she answered simply. 'And no, I don't want your money. I do want my kids to be happy though, and now we're actually talking, we could discuss how we're going to do this.'

'It's already done. Apparently,' Milo replied, his tone laden with resentment.

Holly slowly exhaled, forcing herself to breathe. It was all very well spending hours thinking about how she would like to handle their future interactions, to talk of leading not following, but their twisted dynamic had been set in stone for so long, Holly felt genuinely unnerved by the task ahead of her. It was no small ask, but it was yet another thing that had been eating away at her dawn hours all week at Ben's bedside.

This was no time to be passive. This was no time to let Milo dictate the terms of their un-married relationship, the way he had domineered her as his wife. Even taking into account his discombobulating and mercurial mood swings, it was never going to be easy to rewrite the very tenets of their relationship – she knew that. But here and now, she actually had an opportunity to give it a try and she was damned if she was going to pass that up.

She slipped up onto the worktop and let her legs swing down. 'It's true. That was the end of our marriage, but it was also the beginning of the rest of our lives, our boys' lives. And assuming there's still a part of you that can look beyond what *you* need and see that they have needs too, I'll do what I can to keep a relationship going between you. Not custody. I think we both know that's not the answer, but – well, something, at least.' The relief from saying it aloud was almost tangible.

It was the right thing to do; the bitter after-taste from signing those papers gone in a moment.

'I love them,' he said simply in reply.

'I know you do, in your own way,' Holly said unbowed. 'But you need to *show* them that too ... Thinking it, thinking about them? Assuming they know? It just isn't enough, Milo.'

'But I try—' he made to interrupt, but Holly was having none of it.

'No,' she said. 'No, you don't. Not really. For God's sake, Milo, you offered up their custody as a negotiating tool. Your go-to instinct was to give them up to save yourself some money! So, let's at least be sensible here. You have burned an awful lot of bridges and it's great that you've picked up the phone, but this? This is where the effort part has to kick in.'

There was silence at the end of the phone and Holly began to wonder whether he'd hung up halfway through her impassioned speech.

'I don't know what to do,' he said eventually, quietly. 'Do you remember, Holly, how it used to be between us? It was good, wasn't it? When they were babies and we used to sit up with them at night and plan their futures together?'

'I remember,' she said softly, braced for a wave of hurt and anger. And then stopped.

Nothing. She felt nothing for him, except possibly pity. Maybe there really was only so far that he could push her, before whatever tangible bond that remained had simply frayed away and given out. The sense of freedom was almost palpable and it made the next step somehow easier.

However lousy a husband Milo had been, and however *she* felt about him, Holly still firmly believed that he would regret not being the father he had always claimed he wanted to be. She owed it to her boys to at least keep this door unlocked – not gaping open with two-way toxic traffic – but even the notion of *possibility* was so powerful to a child ... She didn't believe it was fair to deny them that.

'Look, Milo. This doesn't have to be difficult. I know you have a whole new life over there, but if you want your children to know you love them, that you value them, then you have to tell them that with everything you *do* – they don't have to be your number one priority, but they have to be up there somewhere north of your job or your car.'

'I know that,' he said. 'I do. It's just—' His voice had taken on a slightly petulant quality and Holly allowed her expectations to settle somewhere around basement level. There was only so much that she could do, after all, before ultimately the relationship he had with his sons would be the one he deserved.

'Think about it,' she suggested. 'I'm not going to force this. But if you want to talk to them, to Skype, to come over and visit them even, the door is open.' For a brief moment, she pressed one hand to her chest, where it suddenly felt as though a bubble of acid were eroding at her hard-won determination and resilience. The very idea of inviting him over might be madness, but she had to try, even if only to salve her own conscience. 'Don't make me a fool, Milo – it may be over between us – but don't make me a fool for having believed in you in the first place,' she said tightly.

'You don't like me very much, do you?' he said after a moment's hesitation.

'I don't have to like you, Milo, that's the beauty of divorce, but you are father to our beautiful boys – we just have to work out where to go from here.'

'I miss you, Holly,' he said, his despondency now almost audible down the phone line. 'When I heard about Ben, it was all I could do not to jump on the next plane to be with you.' The switch back to intimacy was too much, felt too contrived and invasive, as though he were still trying to manipulate her and Holly felt her hackles rise. She'd gone out on a limb for this man, with this offer, and still she felt as though he was trying to control her.

'What exactly do you want from me?' said Holly.

'I want you to like me again,' he whispered.

'And I just can't give you that,' she said, sharing her moment of clarity with brutal honesty. She paused as the thought occurred to her, 'Maybe we could work towards respect, but you are going to have to *earn* it.'

'I'm trying, Holly. Please believe me – I just – you seem so different, I don't know what you need.'

'What the boys need,' she corrected him firmly. 'I'm good, actually.'

And for the first time in a long time, she meant it.

Chapter 44

Julia slipped the Unicef letter from its envelope again. It had become something of a ritual. As she scanned the words, the telephone call that had followed replayed in her mind. It was so beguiling, to be courted like this – not for her looks or her figure, but for what she personally could bring to the table. For her own particular experiences and how they had shaped her view of the world.

In a way, it was the kind of courtship that Julia had always secretly dreamed of. She could acknowledge now, that as a perfectionist with validation issues, it had been all too easy in the past to be influenced by other people's opinions of her and how they 'saw' her. It was becoming increasingly clear though, that superficial motivations led to superficial relationships. Was it actually okay to wish for more?

For the first time in months, Julia felt the hairs at the back of her neck prickle with new possibilities, as she ran her thumb over the embossed Unicef logo for the umpteenth time, the sensation of the raised circles speaking to her on an almost visceral level. It was as though Julia's subconscious had a mind of its own – so to speak.

She had become so adept at pushing her instincts aside, it

had become second nature to apply logic over emotion. Take away the logic and she was lost.

Could she really dare to take such a huge step and choose her own personal fulfilment over all the commitments and responsibilities that currently filled her time? Even if that meant facing the inevitable criticism of selfishness head on?

She paused then to consider the source of that little gem. Was it actually selfish at all, or just the echoes of her mother's voice over the years, every time Julia made a decision that didn't suit Candace's personal agenda?

Julia closed her eyes and tried to imagine a future for herself, where doing 'the right thing' meant putting *herself* first – blatantly and unapologetically, without caring what it looked like to the world. How long had 'the right thing' meant appeasing other people's needs, not her own, she wondered.

It made her head spin just to consider the logistics of what she was actually considering. Dan, The Practice, her mother, Quentin . . . The list of responsibilities went on, and she could recognise that, whatever the outcome, there would be a pall of guilt overshadowing this decision.

Perhaps she simply didn't have the emotional software that Holly did, she thought, as she slipped the letter neatly away. Popping in to visit last night had been a huge mistake. Watching her friend and colleague willingly putting every aspect of her life on hold to care for her son had been an unwelcome demonstration of selfless dedication.

And if she were honest with herself for just a moment, Julia knew that wasn't something she herself could realistically do without resenting every moment. Maybe she really was just wired differently, she thought, unable to connect on an intimate level but so totally engaged by the prospect of a broader circle of influence.

Watching Holly and Taffy dealing so adeptly with the twins had felt like reaching for a word or a name that remained stubbornly out of reach. She knew what she was supposed to be experiencing at a time like this – the emotions had names and descriptions; they just didn't correlate with anything she was currently feeling.

Tucked away in her favourite corner of the doctors' lounge, Julia sipped at her vibrant purple smoothie, and tried not to be annoyed when Alice Walker sat down beside her to chat.

Alice looked awkwardly around the room. 'I know this is probably going to sound incredibly callous, but do you have any idea when Holly might be back at work?'

Julia shrugged, deftly sliding the letter into her handbag. 'Indefinite leave was mentioned.'

Alice nodded, her neck flushed and red. 'So, it could be ages? I mean, obviously we all hope Ben makes a full and speedy recovery, but in all likelihood . . . ?'

'Ages,' nodded Julia, intrigued to see the normally kind-hearted Alice having what appeared to be her first moral dilemma. Julia didn't want to feel secretly pleased at this apparent weakness in Alice's otherwise flawless personality, but she couldn't deny it was oddly satisfying.

Alice sat back in the armchair and sighed. 'Holly was help-ing me with Coco, you see. The trainer – Jamie – you might have seen him? Well, he seems to be running out of options and Holly mentioned that she'd had a few thoughts . . .' She ground to a halt and looked embarrassed. 'You probably think I'm a heartless witch for thinking about Coco, when Ben's been so poorly.'

Julia shook her head, thrown by the echoes of her own internal struggle. 'Coco is your priority; Ben is Holly's. I don't think there's a right or wrong to it. We all have our own issues to deal with.'

'Do you really mean it?' asked Alice, a hint of insecurity making her all the more likeable in Julia's eyes.

'I do. But then anyone around here will tell you that I have my priorities all wrong – I'd be the person putting work first every time. All that deathbed malarkey – I'd be the person thanking my lucky stars that all my patient notes and tax returns were up to date.' Julia managed a strangled laugh. Clearly the stress had got to her more than she had realised over the last few days.

Alice laughed too, a little uncomfortably. 'I so need to get Coco back on track, it's colouring my judgement of everything. Thank God we're crazy busy here covering shifts or I'd be going quite mad. It's almost a relief to have something else to think about . . .' She clapped her hand over her mouth. 'I didn't mean it quite like that!'

Julia smiled and stood up. 'I don't mind how you meant it, Alice. Honestly. We're all just doing the best we can.'

As she walked through to her consulting rooms, Julia replayed that sentence in her head. There was that dis-connect again, that she couldn't quite put her finger on. Was she, in all honesty, doing the best she could? Being the best she could be? Julia opened the file for her clinic and ran her eyes down the list of patients awaiting her attention, the thought that she was trying to bend herself around like a pretzel to fit into somebody else's idea of 'the best she could be' wedged firmly in the back of her mind.

Clearly, going to that AA meeting with her mother had had more of an impact than she realised. That bloody Serenity

Prayer was still whistling around inside her head like a wasp in a jar. *Accept the things I cannot change, courage to change the things I can ... And the wisdom to know the difference.* 'Well if I knew that, I wouldn't have an issue, now would I?' she muttered, wondering when and how she might actually find some clarity herself.

After a morning of filtering her thoughts, being compassionate, and generally finding it hard to muster the enthusiasm for yet another asthmatic who forgot to take their inhaler, an athlete who refused to rest an injury and an obese gentleman who had come in with pizza sauce still dribbled on his chin, Julia felt she could do with a little serenity about now.

Her wish was clearly not about to be granted, she thought, as Quentin bundled into her office as if he owned the place. 'Morning, Gorgeous. Where were you last night?'

Julia felt that trickle of unease again – the one she'd been dodging for the last few days. She had known deep down that her relationship with Dan was on the rocks and, with the benefit of hindsight, there were easier, less cowardly ways for her to have ended things. She wasn't even sure what had persuaded her into Quentin's bed, other than a longing to feel desirable and in control when it felt like the whole world was against her.

He stroked her hair back from her eyes and she did her best not to flinch away. Dan had known how uncomfortable she was with any public display of affection and yet here was Quentin, throwing away his hipster cool just because they'd slept together.

'Don't do those Bambi eyes on me, Angel ...' he leaned in and kissed her slowly, the trickle of unease fast becoming a tsunami as his beard scratched at her skin. Where had he picked up his bedroom lingo anyway – was '70s porn the go-to setting for the hipster generation?

She pushed her chair back suddenly. 'Not here, Quinn.'

He frowned. 'It's a little bit late to start playing hard to get, Princess. One little letter from Unicef does not make you the next Mother Teresa, you know.'

She tried not to rise, to replay the lovely sentiments expressed in the letter in her head instead, blocking out Quentin, who was busy making dismissive jokes about how rubbish she would be when it came to helping children, since she didn't especially appear to like them very much.

Julia didn't even bother to tell him to stop; he clearly thought this whole invitation was hilarious.

Why bother correcting Quentin in his assumption that she didn't like children very much? Everyone around here had jumped to pretty much the same conclusion. How were they to know that the apple-cheeked, bright-eyed children in Larkford made her intensely uncomfortable simply *because* their lives were so damned easy? In all her time at The Practice, the only children she'd felt anything for had been the sorry, bedraggled ones from the Pickwick Estate – a place that brought the meaning of 'sinkhole' to entirely new depths.

'Come on,' said Quentin, narked that he hadn't been able to provoke a reaction, 'let's photocopy that and stick it on the noticeboard for a laugh. After all, it's not as though you're going to accept it, is it? We could even tweet about it! Hashtag fail. I mean – can you imagine?' He stopped then and stared at her, unnerved by her absolute composure. 'You're not *seriously* considering this are you?'

Julia said nothing, just looked at the man in front of her,

almost as though he were a stranger. How had this man invei-
gled his way into being one of her responsibilities, when all
she was to him was a punchline?

'It's an amazing opportunity,' said Julia quietly.

'It's an amazing cock-up, is what it is,' he said, even as the
laughter slowly dried in his voice. 'You do know you'd be
utterly out of your depth with this? You'd have to get your
pretty little hands dirty for a start.'

She couldn't blame him for thinking that. After all, wasn't
that exactly the persona she had chosen to embody? If she'd
been dishonest in how she portrayed herself, was it really fair
to hold him accountable?

This sudden epiphany that getting her hands dirty might
be exactly what she needed wasn't Quentin's fault. Having
spent her entire adult life sanitising every aspect of her world,
from her bathtub to her relationships to her work, the idea of
a peck of dirt was suddenly incredibly appealing. And maybe
in the dirt, she thought, there might even be room for a little
spontaneity and growth. Sterile, after all, had more than one
meaning.

'Oh Quinn,' she said, 'we really need to talk.'

His face coloured instantly. 'You have to be kidding me?'

She shook her head. The very idea that she had even considered turning down this opportunity for Quentin and his
primetime show about first-world problems seemed almost
laughable in that moment. She'd foolishly made him a priority in her life, when all she'd been to him was an option.
'I'm sorry.'

'I don't believe you are,' he said, his tone cold and measured. 'I think you've been stringing me along. And all this
Ambassador bollocks? Well, we both know that's not who
you really are.'

'But maybe it's who I could be,' Julia offered.

'I won't wait for you,' he said bluntly. 'You're not the only blonde in a doctor's coat, you know.' He paused, waiting for a reaction, clearly infuriated at finding none and switching up a gear. 'I'm going to make this show with you or without you, Julia. It's your decision, but you have to know that you are completely replaceable.'

To his intense surprise, she nodded and a smile lit up her face. 'And I think I'm looking for something, or maybe somebody, where that's not the case.' She leaned in and kissed his cheek. 'Bye, Quinn. And good luck.'

She left the room in a daze, replaying her own words in her head. True, she had dared to hope that Quentin and his show could fill the Dan-shaped hole in her life, but she'd been wrong. All this time looking outwards, when the answers had been there all along, if only she'd been brave enough to look.

She wasn't cut out for television shows and media parties with Quentin. Or for that matter, domesticity, babies and country-living with Dan.

The idea of helping other children thrilled her far more than the notion of having her own. Rather than focusing on the petty weaknesses in her messy, disjointed life, she could actually use all the skills she'd painstakingly acquired to bring relief to others. And maybe, at last, she would be able to sleep at night.

Her mind flew to Dan for a second, to the look on his face if she said yes to this. Would he be proud, she wondered? And then gave herself a shake. If she were going to do this, really do it and take a leap of faith, she could only do it with the best of intentions. Her own.

And who knew, maybe on some level, a little altruism in her life might give her a taste of the serenity she'd been hearing so much about. She couldn't change who she was, but maybe she *could* make a difference to these children's lives. On her own terms.

One of Elsie's favourite platitudes popped into her mind. 'Sometimes when things are falling apart, they might really be falling into place.' The first time she'd heard it, she'd dismissed it instantly. This time, it actually made sense.

In for a penny, Julia sat down on a chair beside her mother and looked around at the Sunnyside rehab facility. It had been an impulsive decision to come here during her break and she was embarrassed to admit that this was the only time she'd seen the true delights of the Visitors' Room. She had managed to make sure that her previous visits had been taken as uncomfortable strolls through the grounds. The heavy wooden armchairs were bolted to the ground in small clusters and even the paintings on the walls were screwed firmly into place. The number pad at the door, not to mention having her handbag frisked, had all added to the surreal sense of her mother being here against her will, when in reality, for the first time that Julia could ever remember, this was actually her mother's choice.

She reached out and straightened her mother's cardigan, as close to an affectionate gesture as she could manage right now. It had seemed such a good idea, after talking to Quinn, to get all her tricky conversations handled in one fell swoop, while her confidence and conviction were still burning strong. She hadn't foreseen the quenching effect of so much beige paint on her momentum.

'So stop twitching and tell me what you came here to say,' said Candace bluntly. 'You certainly didn't come here to make small talk about the soft furnishings,' she said, having obviously noticed Julia's eyes roaming about the depressing room. No matter how many cute kittens on branches were encouraging her to 'Hang in there', there was no escaping the sense of the institutional about the place.

Julia was about to protest when a sharp look from her mother stopped her. She may well be an adult now, but some behaviours were programmed from childhood and Julia knew better than to defy that particular expression on her mother's face. 'I've been offered a job,' she said. 'It's a bit, well, it's a bit of a change in direction for me, but I think it might be good. A good thing.' She hated the hesitation that had crept into her voice, no longer sure of how to 'sell' the idea.

'Off to London then, is it?' Candace said, not looking vaguely surprised.

Julia opened her handbag and pulled out the leaflet that had accompanied the letter from Unicef. She passed it to her mother wordlessly, allowing the images to speak for themselves.

Candace said nothing, as she quietly read the leaflet from cover to cover. Julia waited patiently, quashing every urge to interject.

Candace nodded to herself as she read, before passing the leaflet back to Julia and looking at her properly for the first time since she'd arrived. 'Well, it's a slightly longer commute,' she said, aiming for humour, but the tremor in her voice giving her concerns away. 'What does your Dan have to say about this?'

Julia twisted her fingers together in her lap to stop herself ripping at the cuticles. 'He's not my Dan anymore, so I guess it doesn't really matter what he thinks.'

Candace sipped at her can of Coke, her craving for sweet things seemingly out of control since she'd stopped drinking.

Julia resisted the urge yet again, to talk to her about the vast quantities of Haribo her mother had been mainlining on every visit. One thing at a time. They could deal with the sugar addiction later.

'So what's stopping you?' asked Candace astutely. 'If you want this job, you should take it. What's making you hesitate?'

Julia reached out and took her mother's fragile hand in her own, trying not to be hurt by Candace's instinctive reaction to pull away. 'Well, nothing really, except . . . Well, you.'

Her mother's laughter was so unexpected as to jar in the stultifying atmosphere of this place. Julia pulled her own hand away then, the concept of détente suddenly feeling like a lost cause.

'Is that really so awful?' she said coldly. 'That I might want to spend a little time with my mother? I was quite looking forward to building a relationship with you, now you're not two-thirds down a bottle of gin by lunchtime!' Even as the hurtful words spilled out of Julia's mouth, she knew she was going too far, but was somehow unable to stop.

'You always were a prickly child,' her mother said without emotion.

Julia stood up. 'I can't imagine why.' She pulled her handbag over her shoulder and looked down at her mother, seemingly smaller and frailer than she had remembered. The soothing voice of the counsellor at the AA meeting was in her head again, even as her temper rose. Julia hadn't realised how much of what the woman had said seemed to have really resonated with her. 'I can't feel badly enough to change the past,' Julia muttered to herself as she stalked towards the door, all her earlier serenity and enthusiasm exhausted, 'but I can have a say in my future.'

She felt a peculiar lightness behind her eyes, rather proud of herself for having come to that conclusion on her own. But as she looked out of the windows at the town of Larkford nestled in the valley below, she realised it was a false pride really – ironically, it was the very security of Larkford that had given her the strength to turn her back on it. Knowing it would always be there for her, had finally given her the confidence to spread her wings.

She stopped dead – was that how some people felt when they left home for the first time? Brave and bold, but cushioned by love and support? It had to be better than the stay-or-go-but-don't-come-back she'd been issued with, as she packed for university all those years ago and that part of her was anticipating reliving today.

She turned back towards her mother, knowing that if she were heading overseas, this might yet be their last goodbye.

'Sit down, Joo Bear,' Candace said gently, an unfamiliar compassion in her voice. 'You can't go striding out of the room every time we disagree. And I can't go sneaking off to the pub. So, you and I? We need to find a different way to communicate.' She patted the seat beside her. 'Now, sit your skinny arse down and tell me all about this job.' Candace's smile wobbled a little then, showing the effort it was taking to reach out to her daughter. 'You deserve to be happy, darling – someone in this family should be. Statistically.'

Statistics Julia could handle; it was all these pesky emotions that everyone insisted on having that made her feel so incredibly uncomfortable.

She took a breath, knowing that how she handled the next few moments could dictate the relationship with her mother from here on.

'I'd love to tell you about it. This is something really

special, Mum.' she said, sitting back down, her conviction making her vulnerable. 'There's so much I can bring to this project, you see. And I think it will make me happy. Really happy.'

Chapter 45

'Ah, I see we're using the humble legume as contraception again,' said Taffy, as he unceremoniously plonked two pints of cider on the table and sat down opposite Dan, who was mainlining peanuts from a bowl – its very presence enough for the delectable Lindy Grey to give him a very wide berth. Dan knew he would be easy-pickings tonight, should Lindy decide to turn on the charm. It seemed so much easier to snaffle some extra peanuts instead.

The whole of the pub garden was humming with the gentle laughter and conversation of a warm summer's evening, but Dan couldn't concentrate on any of it. He wasn't entirely sure that he was supposed to be consuming the draft pages of Elsie's biography with the fervour normally reserved for a teenage boy and a copy of *Razzle*, but there was something in her story that seemed to be speaking directly to him. The title said it all really – *Life's Too Short* – and all the anecdotes were laced with Elsie's trademark wit and observation. It was as though, with the benefit of hindsight, she could see all life's motivations and machinations for what they really were. He could understand now why Holly had pressed it into his hands like contraband, making him promise to 'really, *really* read it'.

He pushed the well-thumbed manuscript back into his bag and took a long sip of his cider.

'No Gracie this evening? I thought she said she was coming out for a quick one?' Taffy asked.

Dan shook his head. 'Nope. She's having a spontaneous picnic with Jamie the Wonder-boy down by the river.' He looked as glum about this development as he sounded.

'Right,' said Taffy, a little bemused. 'Why?'

'That's what I said,' Dan replied. 'It's not exactly an obvious pairing, is it now?'

'And?' Taffy stole a handful of nuts from Dan's stash.

'"Because he asked," apparently. She was a bit weird about it, to be honest. Not that he's not a good guy.' Dan looked suddenly morose. He knew deep down that actually Jamie was a kind, honest man – the kind of man you would choose for one of your friends. Objectively, he could even acknowledge that Jamie was rather easy on the eye and his love for his work made him the perfect candidate for the attentions of every female in Larkford. The fact that he only seemed to have eyes for Grace (well, and Coco) was annoying and unnerving. It made Dan feel as though he'd missed the boat, even though he had to confess that he had no intention of trying to catch the boat in the first place.

'Oh Eeyore,' said Taffy. 'Did you think she was going to sit around for ever, just in case you decided to make a move?'

'What?' Dan spluttered, choking so hard on a peanut that his eyes watered. 'Don't talk rubbish. I've only just come out of a relationship . . .'

'Okay,' said Taffy easily. 'If you say so. But if I were to play the hypotheticals, then I'd say this.' He paused for a moment to collect his thoughts, taking longer than was strictly necessary when he saw how fidgety it was making Dan. He waited until Dan was on the verge of launching a peanut volley in his direction and then grinned. 'Julia's already moved on. By all accounts, on and on. So maybe you could do with a little *carpe diem*-ing yourself. And I'd have to be blind not to see the way you've been looking at Grace recently.'

Dan sighed. 'I'm not really up to seizing anything at the moment, not even Grace, sadly. I think Elsie might be more what I need.'

Taffy looked stunned and took a long draught of cider to recover himself. 'Crikey. Ok-aay. Well, whatever floats your boat, I suppose. I just never had you down as a granny-chaser ... A chubby-chaser, maybe ...' He scrumpled up his face in thought.

Dan couldn't help himself, the laughter bubbled up in his throat. 'Not like that, you big perv. I'm not going to hit on a fragile old lady for my jollies! I just meant this ...' He pulled the manuscript back out of his bag and thrust it into Taffy's hands. 'It makes you think, that's all.'

He watched as Taffy flicked through the pages, stopping now and again to read a passage that caught his eye. For Dan, Elsie's prose had forced him to reflect on what it was that *he* needed from life. Bizarrely, the thought that had sprung immediately to mind wasn't the happy marriage and 2.4 children he had always imagined it would be. He wanted more.

His place in the world had to have value, he realised – not necessarily just to a special someone, but in his contribution to life in general. He wanted to feel that life in Larkford would be better for his patients because of the contribution that *he* had made. The Health in the Community Scheme was a good place to start, he thought. But was it enough to really make a difference?

It was becoming a familiar refrain and he wondered when he might actually sit up and take notice.

'Whatever Elsie has been teaching the girls, I want some too,' Taffy said eventually, his brow furrowed in concentration. Condensation ran down the sides of his ice-cold cider, creating a small puddle that edged ever closer to the discarded pages he had already skimmed through. 'Some of this is genius.'

Dan nodded over towards the Major, who was getting Grover to balance crisps on his nose for applause. 'Our role models aren't quite so inspiring, are they?'

Taffy looked left and right, like a character in a cheap spy movie, tapping the stack of papers in front of him. 'Maybe we could get Elsie rigged up with a live radio feed. Have you read all of this? No wonder she always seems to give the most ridiculously on-point advice.'

Dan laughed. 'We should try it at her swanky party. It would be just perfect. We'll get her one of those little *Mission Impossible* earpieces and it could be like Cyrano de Bergerac. She'd like that.' He gave Taffy a sideways glance, 'We could have code names. You could be – ooh I don't know – Meirion maybe?'

Taffy sighed and held up his hands in defeat. 'So, she told you then? I suppose it really was too much to ask to keep that one under her hat.'

'What?' said Dan completely lost.

'Holly. I trusted Holly with that one.' He tucked his hands under his legs and frowned. 'I do wonder if we'll ever be on the same page.'

'Well, I don't know what you're going on about, but, my little Meirion, that was just my way of saying your mum called earlier. She wants to talk to you about Christmas.'

'Christmas?' Taffy said, a full range of emotions scudding across his face. 'Oh, for Christ's sake, it's August!' He sipped at his pint and Dan couldn't quite decipher the look of relief on his face.

'Oh my God,' Dan said. 'Merry Christmas – oh, are we going to have fun with that one!'

Taffy lobbed a peanut at him in response and they sat in companionable silence for a moment. And then, 'Storm warning,' muttered Taffy urgently under his breath, suddenly finding something incredibly fascinating on his beer mat.

'Mild turbulence or Full F5?' Dan queried, deliberately not looking up, their shared love of the film Twister serving them well.

Taffy stood up. 'Hard to say, but now incoming fast at 3 o'clock. I'll be at the bar when you need me, okay?'

'Wish me luck,' Dan said quietly, as Julia weaved her way towards them through the pub garden with a determined expression on her face.

Taffy punched Dan hard on the shoulder in lieu of formulating the words he seemed unable to say.

'Me too, mate,' said Dan quietly, squeezing Taffy's arm in reply. 'Me too.'

'You're a hard man to find today,' said Julia as she slipped into the seat opposite him and delicately pushed Taffy's empty pint glass to one side. 'And I know you're probably busy, but I'd love it if we could talk?'

Dan looked up in surprise – there was nothing confrontational in her tone, or even in her expression. On the contrary, she looked almost ... well, peaceful. 'Of course,' he said automatically and then stopped. The rules of engagement had changed and he was no longer sure of his role here: boyfriend, ex, friend, colleague?

To her credit, Julia noted his discomfort and moved to reassure him. 'I know it's been uncomfortable since we broke up and I wanted to say how sorry I am. About the things I said, the way I behaved.'

Dan froze, completely blind-sided by this uncharacteristic outpouring.

'I seem to have been making some really bad choices recently and I know I've been hurting the people I care about. So I wanted to apologise. For the stapler, for Quentin, for being such an ungrateful shrew when anyone could see you were only trying to help with Mum.'

Dan tried not to show how utterly stunned he felt, especially at hearing her refer to Candace as 'Mum'. 'You don't need to apologise, Julia. Honestly. We can all see you've had an awful lot to deal with,' he said gently.

'Oh, but I do,' she said fervently. 'I need to apologise. I can't leave Larkford knowing how badly I've behaved when everyone has been nothing but welcoming and supportive to me the whole time I've been here.'

Dan nodded. 'London calling?'

'Nope,' said Julia with a certain satisfaction. 'Geneva. I'm going to work for Unicef, Dan, can you believe it?' The smile that lit up her face said it all and Dan put aside the momentary quiver of disappointment that it hadn't been him that could make her shine with such enthusiasm and contentment.

'I'm so pleased for you, Jules. Genuinely. I mean – obviously it won't be the same here without you . . .' he grinned. 'I mean, it might even be safe now to venture into the stationery cupboard without a helmet.' It felt good to be able to tease her again, to have found a footing that worked for them – even if one foot was about to be in another country – but then, he realised, maybe that was the key?

'Tell me about this job, then?' he said, with genuine interest.

Julia looked perplexed. 'But I'm making amends.' She said it as though she had a mental check-list of all the things she needed to get off her chest. Dan wondered for a moment whether, being Julia, she actually did. 'I need to explain how bad I've been feeling about us – the way it ended – how awful it must have been to see me with Quinn like that . . . And so soon.'

Dan reached out and took her hand. 'But you've already apologised.'

'Not enough,' said Julia persistently, 'I don't think you realise how—'

'Look,' interrupted Dan. 'I'm a bloke. You've said sorry. I don't need a whole self-flagellation routine to convince me of your remorse. Did you mean to hurt me with that stapler?'

'No!' she exhaled. 'I just—'

'Did you deliberately flaunt your relationship with Quentin to hurt me?'

She hesitated. 'Maybe a tiny bit?'

Dan laughed out loud. 'See? We're good. A little bit of honesty goes a very long way with me, Jules, you know that. Now – do I get to hear what's so special about Switzerland? Except cuckoo clocks and chocolate, of course.'

As Dan listened to Julia's impassioned description of her new job, it all made so much sense. He couldn't quite believe they hadn't worked it out before. He had always just assumed that Julia didn't have a charitable bone in her body – he hadn't foreseen that the expression 'charity begins at home' meant something rather different for her – all her empathy, all her altruism, had been funnelled into Candace Channing. There really hadn't been so much as a drop left to donate elsewhere. But with Candace seeking treatment – finally – and the scales of responsibility dropping from her eyes, Julia was finally able to fulfil her own potential.

In fact, thought Dan, although becoming an Ambassador for Unicef hardly seemed like the logical step for someone whose interest in children only began once they hit senior school, as he listened to her heartfelt explanations, the logic for using her media skills for a greater cause just somehow made sense.

This wasn't so much a job for Julia, as a calling.

'Don't you see?' Julia carried on. 'If I can give one child a better childhood than I had, then it's all been worthwhile, hasn't it? Maybe they'll grow up to do something remarkable and I can know I had a hand in that.' She paused. 'It's what I've been looking for all along, without even realising it.'

Dan sighed; he had never thought that he would ever be counting on Julia for inspiration on this front. 'I think it sounds perfect,' he said.

Her eyes shone. 'Do you? Do you really?' She stopped then, as though trying not to laugh. 'Jesus, I really have a problem with external validation, did you know that?'

Dan grinned and reached out to shake her hand. 'All the best people do, so join the club.' He leaned in. 'I'm always incredibly suspicious of people with inner-confidence and unshakeable self-esteem.' He gave a mock shudder.

She narrowed her eyes and looked at him, really looked at him and Dan felt as though his soul were laid bare. 'Do you know,' she said slowly, 'I don't think we're so very different, you and me. And if you didn't have this all-consuming love for this barmy one-horse town, I'd be asking you to come with me, make a difference, be the "best of the best".'

'You watched Top Gun!' Dan exclaimed in delight. If only *this* Julia had been the one he had been living with, he couldn't help wondering whether they would have stayed the course.

She grinned. 'Talk to me Goose ...'

Dan frantically shh-ed her. 'Just don't mention the G-word! I'm quite convinced that Gerald knows when we're talking about him.' He looked around, checking the coast was clear and he wasn't about to have a 25-pound bird descending on them for twiglets and attention.

'What about you though, Dan?' Julia said, shaking her head at his antics. 'Have you worked out what you're going to do next? Do you think you might ramp up the Health in the Community Scheme now you've got a bit more funding and one less GP to pay?'

Dan frowned. 'Well, there is one thing I've been thinking about, but I'm not sure it's even practical, let alone possible.'

'Sod practical,' Julia said with feeling. 'We only get one shot at this, yes? And I think we've both been compromising for other people for far too long.'

Dan hesitated. He loved talking to Julia, appreciating her analytical brain and her ability to see things in black and white, but he wasn't sure it was appropriate now. He looked at her, all the old feelings tumbling through him, but somehow righting themselves in a different configuration that just felt ... better.

'I really would like to be Senior Partner,' he said. 'And if that won't work for whatever reason, then I think Holly has a point – part of being a grown-up is accepting our limitations and being mature about how we handle them. We should think about getting somebody else in who has more experience, particularly on the management side of things. We can't carry on as we are.'

'Crikey,' said Julia, clearly taken aback. 'And what about the Model Surgery whatnot.'

Dan shook his head. 'Not sure. If we changed our "collaborative structure" we'll probably lose the funding, which means losing Alice ... That's why I'm a bit stumped.'

Julia nodded. 'And this role you envision. Do you need a sign on your door, or a pay rise?'

'Nope. Just an identity and the feeling that one person is steering the ship with an end-goal in mind and following through on making it happen. I think it's for the best: for the patients and the long term.'

'That's exactly what Holly's been saying for weeks,' Julia said quietly.

'Well, don't let on that she got there faster than we did, will you, or we'll never hear the end of it.'

'I'm so proud of what we've achieved here though, Dan, aren't you? And it has been a team effort, to keep The Practice open – I suppose that's why on one level, it makes sense that it stays a team endeavour. But here's the thing – if you're going to commit to spending your working life here, your whole life here, then isn't it also okay to ask for what *you* need? And whether you like it or not, Dan, country GP isn't going to tick all your career boxes for long. You need a challenge – a role where you can make stuff happen.'

'I'm not leaving,' Dan said, a flare of indignation in his voice.

'Calm down, I wasn't suggesting that you should. I just think it's okay for you to mould the role to suit *you*, to keep *you* professionally engaged and satisfied. At least until you can distract yourself with a gaggle of mini-Carters to drag around to rugby and ballet and swimming and ...'

Dan gave her a look and she quickly shut up. 'But seriously,

where's the harm in taking a private vote, awarding you seniority internally and then shutting up about it?'

'Wouldn't that be fraudulent?' Dan said.

'Oh. It might be actually. But you know who might have
the answer?'

'Holly?' Dan said with a sigh. 'You know, I'm never going
to hear the end of this.' He drained his cider glass. 'Look, do
you fancy a drink? You can tell me more about Geneva and
we can work out how to persuade Holly to be our new media
spokesperson?'

'Cut her some slack, you know she hates the limelight.
And this whole poisonous battery entrée? It's really knocked
her confidence.' Julia paused, biting on her lip as she frowned
in thought. 'You know, if you could find an issue that she
felt really, really strongly about, she might not take as much
persuading as you think.'

She stood up and smoothed down her immaculate linen
trousers, jumping slightly as Gerald-the-goose materialised
beside her with a plaintive 'honk'.

'You're leaving?' Dan said. 'I thought we were going to
have a drink and hatch a plan?' He felt oddly bereft, not
knowing when he was going to see her again.

Julia leaned in and kissed him on the forehead, just shy
of where the stapler had landed. 'Take care, Dan. And you
don't need me for this.' She stepped out of reach of Gerald's
inquisitive bill. 'You've already got your wingman.'

Chapter 46

Taffy plonked his bag on the kitchen table and braced for impact from two excitable small boys. 'Well, I bumped into your Aunty Lizzie in the Market Place,' he told them, 'and she just found out that she might be looking after a puppy for a little while. How cool is that? And then,' he crouched down on the floor so that he could talk to the boys eye-to-eye, 'this little puppy is going to go off to school, just like you, so he can become a working dog like Coco.' The boys were suitably impressed for all of two seconds before they scooted back off towards the towering heap of Meccano.

'Really?' Holly looked up from scraping Play Doh off the kitchen table.

Taffy nodded as he straightened up. 'I have to say, Holly, she looked happier than I've seen her in ages. Jamie had somebody drop out at the last minute and he thought of Lizzie. She's going to be a puppy walker, if all goes well. Maybe all she needs is something to focus her energies on? Although, I have to tell you that poor little Coco went bonkers at work again today, so this assistance dog business isn't exactly fool-proof.'

Holly felt the very first stirrings of professional interest she'd had all week, as though sorting out her childcare arrangements had allowed a different part of her brain to re-engage, as though a fog had lifted. 'Which patient were you seeing?'

Taffy frowned. 'Poor Lindy Grey had some bad news about her cervical procedure. Looks like it might be cancer, but they've caught it early. She was desperate to see you actually – could hardly send her in to Dan with that one.'

Holly leaned back against the kitchen worktop, her mind slipping back into methodical analysis, glad of a challenge that didn't involve equal allocation of raspberries or Nerf bullets. 'And Coco went nuts?'

'Completely. It was awful timing though actually, because Harry Grant was there, giving Derek Landers a full guided tour and Quentin was having a strop with Julia about his London project. Speaking of which—' He looked up at the enormous station clock that dominated the wall above the oven, 'any chance we can persuade the boys into bed a little early? There's quite a lot we need to talk about. There's only so many balls I can keep in the air at work without dropping them all.' He ran his hand around the back of his neck and Holly realised how exhausted and drained Taffy looked.

He basically looked how she had been feeling for the last few days and the guilt washed over her. She wasn't the only one who'd been worrying and juggling and trying to find a path forward – Taffy had too – the only difference being, that she hadn't been there to hold his hand.

It was over an hour until the boys were due to hit the hay, but the expression on his face convinced Holly that it was one of those occasions when emergency measures were justified. She glanced over her shoulder to check the twins were still engrossed in their Meccano and leaned forward to fiddle with the small cog behind the clock, whizzing the hands forward an hour. She held her finger to her lips as Taffy was about to speak.

'Oh my goodness!' she exclaimed loudly for the twins' benefit. 'Look how late it is! Tom, Ben, chip chop. Doesn't time fly when we're building Meccano.'

The boys were thankfully nothing if not suggestible and they both ambled over, Ben even squeezing out a yawn. 'Can we have a really long story, Mummy?'

Holly crouched down and scooped him into her arms. 'How about, as a very special treat because you've both been so good today, you could listen to one of your Roald Dahl CDs. In bed!'

She'd obviously hit upon the magic words, because both boys were up the stairs before she could say any more, squabbling admittedly over whether to listen to *George's Marvellous Medicine* or *The Witches*. 'Back in a sec,' said Holly. 'Get the kettle on and you can tell me everything.'

The sheer relief on Taffy's face that she was even prepared to engage in a conversation about work said it all.

When Holly came back downstairs a few minutes later, it was to find Taffy almost asleep on the kitchen table, his head on his arms and a pile of paperwork spilling over in front of him.

Just persuading the boys into their pyjamas had given her a moment to think and she was pleasantly surprised to find that she was actually able to focus for the first time in days. Strike that, she thought, she actively *wanted* to focus on something outside these four walls. She flicked off the boiling kettle and filled two mugs, gently making just enough noise to rouse Taffy.

'That was quick,' he said sleepily. 'I had no idea you could be so devious, Holly Graham.' He said it with a smile, an almost impressed smile. 'Which is handy actually. In light of today's events.'

He sat up and yawned, marshalling the paperwork in front of him. 'We need to talk about Julia,' he said.

Holly nodded. 'God, yes – we do. And this is actually happening, is it, this Unicef thing? I half wondered if I'd imagined the whole conversation after she phoned.'

He nodded. 'It's taken us all a bit by surprise. But honestly, she's so over the moon about it, it's hard to be churlish. And she wants to keep it quiet for a while, but there are decisions that have to be made and you should be involved in that.'

Holly nodded. Today was turning into the perfect storm of momentous events. She glanced over at the large canvas propped against the wall that Elsie had delivered earlier that day, the large lilac letters looping across the creamy background:

'Love many, trust few, but always paddle your own canoe.'

She had been mildly relieved at the time that Elsie hadn't been tempted to send her a real canoe, but the words resonated all the same. It was time that she stepped back in and picked up her proverbial paddle.

'Tell me what you need,' she said simply.

It was amazing, thought Holly only an hour later, how much she could achieve when she put her mind to it. Checking over the partnership agreements and the report that Grace had hurriedly compiled about the financial consequences of Julia's departure was one thing; making long-term decisions about who would pick up her work-load was another. Who knew Julia was quietly instrumental in so many areas?

Taffy paused, chomping on yet another packet of crisps in

lieu of breaking for supper. 'So, what do you think? I know it's not ideal, but how do you feel about heading up the Model Surgery business? Being our spokesperson? Grace will do the admin, but we need a face – and let's be honest, yours is far more approachable and credible than mine or Dan's.'

Holly frowned at the very thought of being a spokesperson for something she didn't really believe in. Even the very suggestion had the hallmark of Harry Grant all over it. 'There's no rush though, is there?' she prevaricated.

'Ah, well,' said Taffy awkwardly. 'That's the other thing.' He didn't meet her eye as he outlined the interview that Julia had already set up with Edgar Herring, renowned for being one of the most astute and analytical journalists in the medical field. 'All the prep work has been done and Grace and Julia both firmly believe we can stand up to scrutiny, it's just that, with Julia leaving—'

'Please don't say you're expecting me to do it!' Holly exclaimed, even as her logical brain ran through the options and alighted on the self-same solution.

Taffy looked up at her. 'Harry Grant is convinced you're the man for the job. And I could take the day off, look after the boys?'

'What?' said Holly, distracted by the very thought of being quizzed about their unorthodox partnership arrangements and equally disconcerted by the small thrill of excitement she felt at being back in the game. His words finally registered and she looked up and smiled. 'I knew there was something I wanted to tell you.'

As she filled him in on Hattie's visit and the prospect of having a child-minder who wasn't a complete and utter liability, she watched his whole demeanour relax. It was all very well the two of them struggling by, but sometimes raising kids really did take a village and it was just wonderful to have someone else on their team.

'Not only that,' she said, unable to disguise the satisfaction in her voice, 'but I spoke to Milo earlier.'

Taffy blinked. 'Seriously? He called?' He narrowed his eyes, waiting for the bombshell.

'He called,' confirmed Holly, 'and I got to say everything I've been wanting to say for weeks, years actually. It was—'she struggled to find the word, 'incredibly cathartic. And a lot cheaper than therapy!'

'Did he actually listen?' Taffy asked, knowing only too well how much Holly had been thinking about this mythical conversation of late, even though Taffy himself had been convinced it would probably never happen.

'I have no idea,' said Holly calmly. 'But I'm not sure that's important, is it? He's going to do what he's going to do – but at least I got to have my say. And he's gone away to think about it. I'm not exactly optimistic that anything will change for the boys, but at least I know I did the right thing and I can stop feeling guilty about it.'

'Okay then,' Taffy said, still clearly braced for more. 'And he didn't try to manipulate you?'

Holly laughed. 'Oh, I wouldn't say that, but that is *so* much easier to ignore when you simply don't care what he thinks of you. Who knew?'

Taffy's gaze softened as she spoke with ease and simplicity, clearly unfazed by this momentous achievement with the added benefit of hindsight.

'I am so incredibly proud of you,' he said, leaning forward to kiss her on the forehead.

For a moment there was a certain tension in the air and Holly half wondered whether Taffy was about to pick up where he left off in the hospital, but the compassion in his eyes was a dead giveaway that he was still basically in care-and-sympathy-mode. She could only hope that her withdrawal these last few days hadn't given him time to reconsider his role in their dysfunctional little family.

Holly considered for a moment how they had managed to change gears quite so completely. She didn't want to be Taffy's patient, or his responsibility, she realised. She wanted to be the object of his lust and affection. Pulling the sleeves of her jumper down over her hands, she caught sight of her reflection in the oven door. Perhaps, she thought, getting back on her feet would have to start with baby steps. Like shampoo, or sleep.

Or simply getting back to work and doing this interview.

She might not have Julia's flair for media relations, but Holly knew she had something else to bring to the party – her absolute conviction in her ability to make the best of every opportunity that presented itself.

Not only that, she thought happily, but this week, at least, she seemed to be on a roll.

Holly smoothed down the soft grey fabric of her dress over her hips and looked at herself objectively in the mirror. Only two days ago she'd been firmly committed to her pyjamas and the very thought of what she was about to do would have seemed impossible. It was probably better that she hadn't had much notice, as it had given her less time to stew and tie herself up in knots. It was a baptism of fire and Holly was determined to rise to the challenge. And this was just the challenge she needed – no matter how daunting – the catalyst required to kick-start herself back into action. It was about time.

'You know you're going to be amazing at this, don't

you?' said Taffy reassuringly. 'If you can cope with Twenty Questions from Ben before coffee, then this will be a walk in the park.'

Holly scowled, completely unconvinced. The nerves were definitely getting the better of her. She'd been thrown completely in at the deep end with this interview and they all knew it. Sink or swim. No matter how supportive the other partners had been, how lovely Lizzie, Grace and Elsie had been in rallying around to have her looking her best, there was still a nest of pythons squirming in her stomach. 'What happens if I throw up on this guy? Do you think he would judge me?'

'Looking like that? Nah, I think in that dress and those heels, Holly, he'd probably just call it adorable.' Taffy grinned, teasing her with the kind of deliberately sexist humour that always riled her up and distracted her from the issue at hand. 'Come on, relax. You know your stuff and you have a plan. Just stay away from words like "collaborative" and stick with "contemporary and innovative" – just like you said. You said you wanted to do this your way and this is your moment, Holly.' He swallowed hard for a minute. 'And besides, whatever this journalist might say, just because Dan has expressed a desire to be Senior Partner and Julia has expressed a desire to be almost anywhere other than here, it doesn't change the fact that we are doing a bloody good job.'

Holly nodded. 'Patient satisfaction is up, referrals and waiting times are improved – all round happy bunnies – got it.' She paused and smoothed her newly coiffured hair-do. 'Do you think they'll do the photos first, before I get all red-faced and fidgety in the interview?'

'We can but ask,' Taffy said calmly. 'He seems like a good guy on the phone. Just because he's the country's top medical journalist, doesn't mean he's not human. Just make sure your skirt isn't still tucked in your knickers when you meet him.'

'What?' yelped Holly in panic, reaching around the back of her perfectly smooth skirt. 'You little . . .' She burst out laughing, nerves and excitement getting the better of her.

Taffy pulled her into a hug. 'There now, what's the worst that can happen?'

Holly pulled back and looked at him. 'I can give you twenty-seven scenarios right off the bat, actually. I can't believe I'm doing this on my first day back! It's madness.'

She'd tried very hard not to feel hurt this morning as both twins had skipped into Hattie's beautiful crèche with barely a backwards glance. One look at the basket of intricate wooden puzzles and their mother was all but irrelevant.

Holly took a deep breath, reminding herself of all the reasons she'd soldiered on being a working mum while they were small – money, yes, but also a sense of her own identity. It was something worth remembering every now and again, and if Julia was brave enough to say 'fuck it' and follow her heart, then maybe it was time that Holly did too.

She was perfectly happy to let Dan take on a senior role in administration, but she was damned if she was going to give up her place at the helm; when it came to steering The Practice into the twenty-first century, she intended to be right there, helping to choose the direction.

And so what if their collaborative style of management needed a little tweaking? They were still the most forward-thinking and innovate practice she knew and, for all his bluster and interference, Derek Landers knew it too. Why else would he have sicced this journalist on them at short notice? Elsie wasn't the only one who could use a Google search engine around here and Holly took comfort in knowing that Derek and Edgar Herring were old school chums. To Holly's mind, it meant the team had to be doing something right, to get Derek-the-Walrus that worried.

Besides, even if her own personal reservations were all completely sound, they were also best kept private, as a springboard to fine-tuning an otherwise inspirational 'big picture'.

She checked her watch and saw that she had a few moments to spare. 'Taffy? Thank you for being so understanding – I know I haven't been easy to live with the last few weeks.'

He raised an eyebrow. 'Is that what we're calling it?' He smiled. 'It was quite a revelation to watch your tantrum last night, you know. I'm beginning to see where the twins get their stubborn streak from.'

'It was *not* a tantrum,' she protested, trying not to laugh, because they both knew that had been exactly what it was. The idea of an interview with Edgar Herring was one thing, knowing that the future of their standing as a Model Surgery depended on it, was quite something else. Dan had been gently persuasive, Julia had been oddly keen to hand over the media mantle and Taffy had been calm and convincing – they had all agreed, she was the person to get this done. Late last night though, nerves had set in – sometime around the fifth attempt to blow dry her hair into submission.

Taffy squeezed her hand. 'It was actually quite fun seeing you with a bit of fire in your eyes. I've missed that. We all know what you've been dealing with recently – the only person who doesn't think you're being amazing is you. Dan and I agreed, we'd have been sobbing into a pint glass days ago.'

'It's not the end of the world if we lose our funding though, is it, Taffs? I mean with Julia leaving, we can still afford to keep Alice on, can't we?'

She'd realised at roughly 3 a.m., that her loyalty to her workmates and their shared vision of medicine trumped almost every other criteria for The Practice. Obviously she wanted to be honest and open and completely above reproach – but that didn't mean she needed to wash their dirty linen in public, and every new system required a little modification at first, didn't it?

That's when Holly had known what she needed to do – but if she was going to pick up the gauntlet that had been thrown into her lap, she was going to do it *her* way. No compromises with the truth and, finally, some authenticity in her life that extended beyond the theoretical.

Chapter 47

An hour later, Holly stood in reception, twisting her fingers together until they turned white.

She'd just had Hattie on the phone, with a pitifully sobbing Ben in her arms. Today of all days, his precious Winnie the Pooh had gone missing. She'd offered as many soothing platitudes as she could to Ben and then a flurry of apologies to Hattie. No teddy bear at the crèche would suffice though, and she could hear her little boy working himself up into proper, snot-bubbling histrionics. 'Oh, Ben.' She couldn't help thinking she'd been tempting fate when she'd earlier bemoaned the very idea of feeling irrelevant. 'Mummy has to do a big chat at work and then I'll find Winnie, okay?'

She'd got off the phone feeling properly unsettled and choked up. Hearing one of her boys so upset had a hard line wired to her emotions.

Taffy had checked his watch. 'Then it's decision time, Holls. I can be here to hold your hand or I can look for the errant bear, but I can't do both.'

She'd only hesitated for a moment. 'I'll be fine here. At least my skirt's not tucked in my knickers, anyway. Can you ring Hattie too? Maybe just knowing that you're on the case might calm him down?'

She'd known it was the right choice straight away, but that didn't mean that the nerves weren't getting the better of her as she waited for the arrival of her ~~interrogator~~ interviewer.

'Shouldn't he be here by now?' she asked Lucy, who was fresh off the phone, having manfully wrangled one of their regular no-shows into line.

Lucy shrugged. 'He'll be here when he's here. Listen, I've had a few messages for you from Jamie the dog guy, if you want to take a minute. He said it was urgent and that he had that information you requested. He and Grace have been up since six getting it all together and Grace says she's on the case with everything you discussed. All very cryptic.'

Holly just nodded and took the message slips. 'Okay, but let me know the minute Mr Herring arrives?' At least having lovely Jamie to talk to would take her mind off her impending moment in the spotlight.

So, Holly realised, as she finally got to shake hands with Edgar Herring, she should remind herself never to make assumptions based on fear or ignorance. The mental picture she'd been building of Mr Herring overnight had him tall, foreboding and out to cause destruction – in other words, the journalistic equivalent of budget-slasher Landers. The genial gentleman in a cardigan now standing before her had a twinkle in his eye, a notepad in his hand and Holly would bet good money there were Werther's Originals lurking in his pockets.

'It's an absolute pleasure to meet you, Dr Graham. I'm so glad you were able to join me and I'm thrilled to hear your little lad is on the mend.'

Holly was so touched by his interest in Ben and his amiable demeanour that she immediately softened. They chatted casually on the way through to her office, talking about ways to improve the safety of children's toys. Holly gave herself a little nudge that maybe this was his sly journalistic way of getting her to let her guard down, but his interest seemed so sincere. Either way, she thought, keep it together, Graham.

'I don't suppose we could grab a cup of coffee and chat in your common room, could we?' asked Mr Herring politely. 'I'm not great with tiny rooms at the best of times and of late, I've developed quite an aversion to the doctor's lair.' He managed a little laugh, but Holly was only too familiar with the issue.

'I'm sorry to hear that,' she said. 'It happens to a lot of patients actually, when they've had some bad news health-wise. That is, I mean to say . . .' She stalled, her go-to setting for compassion making her overstep the mark. 'I'm so sorry, Mr Herring, that was entirely inappropriate.'

'Call me Edgar,' he said with a smile. 'And to be honest, you're not too far off the mark. Now, let's get some coffee on the go and we can have a nice little chat about this Model Surgery business.'

Give him his due, Holly couldn't help feeling that the vast majority of her interview had taken place while they rootled around for milk and sugar and attempted to unearth an uncompromised packet of biscuits. She was only grateful that the rest of the team were busily occupied elsewhere – she wasn't to know that Grace was standing sentinel in the hallway, ushering everybody away.

'So then, talk to me about this collaborative management style I've been hearing so much about? I take it you're not all actually communists, or indeed polygamists?' He chortled to himself at his own little joke.

'There have been a few rather odd interpretations of our

work, haven't there?' said Holly. 'But in truth, all you need to know about The Practice is that we like to keep an open mind – our approach is very contemporary, true – we like to focus as much on health education and prevention, as we do on treatment and awareness. Our Health in the Community Scheme embodies that really – we work *with* our community to improve their health, rather than only being there to pick up the pieces, as it were.'

'And you really don't have any seniority between you?'

'Well,' Holly said carefully, 'obviously Dan Carter has been here the longest and so there is a certain level of local experience that he brings to the table. Taffy Jones is our go-to guy for all sports injuries. I tend to be the one who might get called in for any emotional or reproductive issues . . .'

'And Dr Channing? You didn't mention her. Is that because she's too busy with her camera crew?' Edgar interrupted.

'Julia Channing is a first-rate physician and her commitment to spreading awareness through her TV show has been a huge success. We each have our strengths, you see, Edgar. And because we're not bound by a strict hierarchy, we have the opportunity to play to those strengths.' She paused and took a sip of coffee. 'But to be honest, Edgar, none of these ideals would be possible without the phenomenal support we get from our administrative and nursing staff. We really are all working towards the same goal – a healthier, and by extension, a happier Larkford.'

She took a deep breath then, hoping against hope that she'd said enough.

'So you never squabble? Disagree about fund allocations? Nothing ever gets missed because you all think somebody else has ticked that box?' Edgar pressed.

Holly smiled. 'Well, we did have a tremendous to-do about

chocolate biscuits, but I think we've resolved that now. On the bigger picture issues, we're very good at being adaptable. Obviously, sometimes we need to review how something is working – for example, we're hoping that Dr Carter will have a much bigger role in liaising with our wonderful Practice Manager in the future. When they put their heads together, things do tend to run more smoothly.' Holly tried not to blush as she answered. To her own ears, she sounded evasive, but Edgar Herring clearly had a different headline in mind.

'So they have a close personal relationship too, do they?'

'We're all very good friends,' Holly dodged, feeling a trickle of cold sweat down the back of her neck – she wasn't prepared to go into the details of their complicated love lives on the record. 'You see, in Larkford . . .' she began, as the door swung open and Alice Walker wandered in, Coco at her heels.

'Oh sorry, Holly. Am I interrupting?' she said nervously.

Holly could have kissed her. 'No, no. Grab a coffee – it's fine. And then come and say hello to Mr Herring.'

'How lovely to meet you, Mr Herring, I'm Dr Alice Walker – the new recruit.' She wandered over and shook his hand, while Coco finished her traditional sweep of the kitchen floor looking for a stray Hobnob.

'And who's this little chap? Unusual to see a dog in a medical setting,' Edgar said to Holly, just as Coco trotted over, close enough for her little red jacket to be legible. 'Oh, I see. How wonderful. And he belongs to you, does he, Dr Walker?'

'She does yes,' said Alice, with just the same ease and generosity as she had at her first meeting with Holly. They were soon talking nineteen to the dozen about diabetes detection and leaps forward in its management. It was only as Coco started to whimper that Edgar Herring smoothly turned the conversation towards slightly more contentious ground. 'So, Dr Walker, do be blunt. What's it like having a whole team of bosses – do you sometimes wonder whether you're coming or going?'

'No, not really . . .' Alice began. 'Oh Coco, do settle down.'

Mr Herring's glance flickered towards the fidgety little dog, but he carried on undeterred, 'I bet it gets tricky with all the personal relationships too though, doesn't it? Too many cooks and all that? Tell me, is it difficult knowing that there's no real structure in place if things go wrong?'

Alice looked completely flustered. 'I'm sorry, could you say that first question again, I didn't quite catch it.'

Mr Herring flicked open his notebook. 'Well, in simple terms, I'm asking you whether you think this Model Surgery nomination is a bit of a farce?' He said it so sweetly, so gently, it took a moment for both Holly and Alice to realise that this was no cuddly Grandpa – Edgar Herring was a top-notch journalist and his nose was telling him that there was a story here that needed to be told.

Coco sat back on her haunches and yapped, before circling around Edgar's legs.

'I don't think it's a farce at all,' said Alice firmly, in that no-nonsense Scottish voice she saved for patients who wouldn't listen. 'We like to look at the big picture here, Mr Herring, and as is often the case, the more pairs of eyes, the better. Our Health in the Community Scheme has received a huge amount of praise.'

'Yes, yes,' said Edgar, flapping his hand, eyes gleaming as he moved in for the kill, 'but I want to hear all about this contemporary management style – all very innovative – but does it *actually* work?'

Holly silently handed him the print-out of their latest

patient satisfaction survey. She would bet the contents of her pension fund that he hadn't seen one as positive as that in a while.

Holly looked up and caught Alice's eye. Alice gave a nod and Holly breathed a sigh of relief. Holly's Plan B had all been so rushed this morning that she'd had no way of knowing whether Jamie and Alice would have had time to talk during her interview. Thank God for Grace, her right-hand behind the scenes, pulling it all together.

Coco yapped again, almost as if on cue.

'And of course, the innovation at The Practice doesn't just end with our management style, or our health education programme,' said Holly. 'Coco here is one of the first dogs in the UK to have spontaneously acquired the most wonderful skill. She's going to be receiving additional training through the assistance dogs' programme, but she'll be doing most of that here and in the hospitals nearby.'

Holly looked up to see the pride glowing on Alice's face.

Just because Coco had been able to see beyond the limitations of her original role, it didn't mean she was broken. Holly knew only too well that, as a grown-up, one tended to see how the world worked and think that was the only way. But her children and Coco clearly knew otherwise – take off the limitations and then you start to see what's possible. Coco wasn't broken, she had merely succeeded in achieving what the humans here were aiming for and evolved to the next level of care.

'Coco is able to detect abnormal cells with her nose,' Holly said slowly. 'She can smell cancer.'

Edgar looked up, his face a picture of amazement. 'But she's trained for diabetes?'

'That's right,' said Alice, 'but since she's been here at The

Practice, she also alerts when a patient has cancer cells. We don't know yet whether that's all cancers, but we're hopeful that we can hone this incredible skill.'

Holly carried on. 'So far, Coco has spontaneously alerted for cervical and prostate cancer, melanoma and breast cancer.'

'And pancreatic,' said Edgar quietly, swallowing hard. 'I only found out last week.'

'Oh no,' said Holly, her growing antagonism towards him instantly disintegrating. After all, he was only doing his job and, indeed, asking all the questions she herself would have asked too.

'Can't be helped,' he said. 'But there's my story.' He leaned down and stroked Coco's ears and she instantly relaxed, as though her message had been heard.

Edgar Herring looked up at Holly. 'Look, we both know that there are enough holes in this Model Surgery nomination to drive an ambulance through, but I can't fault your intentions. Innovation, compassion, education. It's what we should all be striving for, if we didn't have to jump through hoops for funding. And God knows, if you've got Derek Landers on your case, he won't give up without a fight but, to be frank, I don't really appreciate being used as a pawn in his personal vendetta. So for now, let me write about Coco and the wonderful team I've met here and you lot can figure out your relationships and management style in your own time.'

'That sounds just wonderful,' said Holly, as Coco leapt onto Edgar's lap and even her waterproof mascara struggled to keep up.

She wiped her eyes with one of Taffy's ironed handkerchiefs and a slow smile spread across her face. She could get used to this feeling of empowerment. Not so much 'fake it till you make it' she realised, as complete belief in herself and her abilities, to the point where they became a reality. And she knew now with absolute clarity what she had to do next.

Holly was still feeling flushed with nerves and relief by the time Taffy appeared at The Practice, looking incredibly pleased with himself and with Eric trotting beside him. 'Mission accomplished! One bear located and reunited with tearful owner. Tearful owner now happy as a pig in muck.'

'But how ... ?' Holly managed, knowing full well that a Winnie the Pooh Search could easily be a day-long operation, due to Ben's penchant for tucking him away 'somewhere safe'.

Taffy leaned down and scruffed the top of Eric's downy head. 'Well, I have to confess, I did have a little help. I got Eric to sniff Ben's pyjamas and then took him all around the house saying, "seek him out".' He was obviously terribly proud of this stroke of inspiration.

Holly threw her arms around his neck and hugged him hard. 'Thank you. That was genius. I couldn't bear to think of Ben crying all morning on his first day at Hattie's.' She dropped her voice to a whisper, 'I was worried she'd send him back to Pinetrees if he was a nuisance.'

Taffy shook his head. 'Hattie's made of sterner stuff. When I got there, they were baking gingerbread biscuits and the only way you could tell Ben had been having a little snivel were the track marks in the flour on his face. They're fine though, honestly. Although I have had to promise Eric a pint, to say thank you.'

Holly laughed. 'Well, he might prefer a bone, but the thought was there.' She leaned into his side as they made their way back to the doctors' lounge. 'So aren't you going to ask me how it went?' she said, unable to conceal the smile on her face.

'Priorities, Graham. First the kids, then the dog, then me ...' He leaned down and stole a kiss. 'And then we can talk about work. Having said that, your poker face really does need a little work.'

Holly shrugged, totally unfazed that she'd given the game away. 'It was brilliant. I did everything we talked about. Change the focus, change the story. And Coco was amazing. I feel ghastly even thinking it, but it was just perfect that he had cancer too. And he seemed to love the Health in the Community Scheme – that was the real game-changer.'

She was still gushing about the interview by the time they'd made coffee and grabbed a belated breakfast. Sitting back in the big squishy sofa, with Eric on her feet, Holly was able to feel properly proud of what they'd achieved this morning. There had been no need for lies or obfuscation – she'd been able to let the work at The Practice speak for itself. A Model Surgery, some might say, although not necessarily for the reasons decreed by the NHS.

Alice and Jamie walked in together, with Coco trotting neatly between them. In a funny way, the little spaniel looked utterly serene for once, as though she could finally relax now her humans had belatedly cottoned on to what she'd been trying to tell them. Alice took off her little red jacket and Coco immediately made a beeline for Taffy, sitting firmly on his foot and looking at him imploringly.

'Jesus!' said Taffy in alarm. 'Does that mean I've got cancer?'

'No, you muppet. It means you're eating a bacon sandwich.' Holly reached across and tore off a tiny bit of bacon. Coco delicately nibbled it from her fingers and wagged her tail.

Eric's mournful *woo-oo-oo* had them all in stitches. 'You can have a bit too, for saving Winnie,' Taffy said in a silly voice, handing over a sizeable chunk. Eric though, merely laid it on the floor between him and Coco so that they could share.

'Bloody hell,' said Jamie. 'No offence, but I think the dogs around here are more evolved than the people.'

As Coco and Eric curled up together contentedly, Eric's tail beat a slow tattoo against Holly's leg. She smiled at Taffy. 'Thank God for that. Finally. They're in love.'

With a completely straight face, he tore off another chunk of his sandwich and handed it to her. 'Well, if that's how we do things now . . .'

Holly laughed but pinched the tasty morsel nevertheless. 'I don't need bacon. It was going off on a mad jaunt to find the bear that did it for me.'

'What?' Taffy replied, clearly thrown. 'So, not the whole life-saving, quick-thinking, rushing Ben to hospital? Or the most excellent skill-set in knackering two small boys on a Sunday morning? Or,' he leaned in closer, seeking clarification, 'my masterful skills in the bedroom?'

Holly blushed but shook her head. 'Nope. Definitely the sniffer dog approach to family drama. What can I say, I'm easy to please, but infinitely harder to understand.'

Taffy said nothing, utterly baffled.

Julia stopped in the doorway and watched them laughing together. Her evening dress for Elsie's party was ready and draped over her arm and congratulations were poised on her lips. Word was spreading throughout Larkford, as indeed it always would, and already several little baskets of dog biscuits had been delivered to Coco at The Practice and Alice's clinics were fully booked for days. Apparently the idea of getting a 'check-up' from Coco was infinitely more appealing than any intrusive tests or examinations. Julia could easily imagine why, and that empathy alone surprised her – maybe she was finally coming around to the fact that science and emotion weren't such strange bedfellows after all?

Quentin had been in reception grilling Jamie about access and trying to convince him into a special documentary, before Edgar Herring had even left the building. Jamie, however, had been absolute in his response; this was a work in progress and nobody would be relying on a diagnosis from his canine consultant until due process had been addressed.

It had been a further revelation to Julia that she'd wanted to quietly cheer Jamie on from the sidelines, detached in a way she couldn't have foreseen from Quentin's scheming and machinations.

She stepped back out of view now, as the volume and celebrations rose in the doctors' lounge. She didn't need to worry – Holly would be there to keep Jamie on track, and Alice, and maybe one day even Taffy.

She smiled to herself, as she took another step away from the merriment. They had each other and, as long as they remembered that, they wouldn't be short of support.

A warm hand on her waist stopped her short. 'You weren't planning on just slipping away were you, Channing?' said Dan softly. He knew her so well, it was barely a question.

She shrugged, the silk of her evening dress slithering from her arm with the movement. Dan caught it easily. 'I always did love you in this dress.'

Their silence said more than any words ever could. Together, the dress between them, it was a tangible reminder of everything they had loved and lost.

'I thought I might just—'said Julia, unable to finish her sentence, the pain of leaving etched on her face, but the anticipation of her new beginning making her eyes shine.

Dan leaned in and kissed her on the cheek. 'Safe travels, Jules. I'll pass on your goodbyes.' He let go of the dress and, for just a moment, Julia hesitated. Goodbye seemed so final.

'Exciting times ahead,' she managed, nodding towards the others. 'For all of us.'

'I'm so proud of what you're doing, you do know that, don't you?' said Dan quietly, uncertainly – as though he had no idea how this sentiment might be received.

For Julia, the validation was enough – just enough for her to breathe. 'I do,' she said gratefully, as she squeezed his hand for the last time and walked away without looking back.

If she looked back, even for a moment, she was afraid she'd forget ever to look forward.

Chapter 48

There was a brightness and levity in the very atmosphere of Larkford that evening. There wasn't a cloud in the sky and the scent of honeysuckle danced on the evening breeze. 'Trust Elsie to organise the most perfect evening for her party. Although I dare say that even the weather wouldn't dare defy her wishes,' said Holly as they walked across the Market Place towards her house, still buoyant from her earlier success.

Holly slipped the strap of her one and only 'posh frock' back onto her shoulder and smiled at the sight of her three 'boys' all dressed up to the nines. Taffy had even been persuaded to put on a suit and she had to confess that the sight of him looking so dashing had her pulse racing in a most disconcerting fashion. She took the twins' hands and gave them a little squeeze, praying they would be on their best behaviour tonight.

Elsie's huge, glossy front door had been thrown open and the great and the good of the community were turning up on her doorstep in their summer finery. Before they could even adjust to the sight of Elsie's garden dressed to impress, an over-zealous photographer stepped into their path and snapped away, the flash peppering Holly's vision with fireworks and spackles of shadow.

'Bloody hell,' said Taffy under his breath. 'It's like a garden party at Buckingham Palace.'

And he had a point, thought Holly, although going by the conjuror on the patio, the lanterns swaying in the light evening breeze and the uniformed waiters passing around cocktails, perhaps the theme was more royalty of the Hollywood variety.

Eric took it all in his stride, trotting obediently at Holly's heels, looking like the cat that got the cream, although Holly knew he'd be disgusted at the very comparison. The notion of bringing dogs and children to such a swish event seemed like madness to Holly, but Elsie had insisted. And when Elsie insisted, there was little point in arguing.

'You're here!' cried Elsie, spotting them amongst the throng. 'Oh, my darling girl, I hear you were an absolute wonder with that journalist chappie. I'm so, *so* proud.' She kissed Holly deftly on each cheek, leaving a small smudge of Chanel Rouge Allure and then deftly brushing it away with her thumb. 'And you both look so stunning. Ozney, Ozney darling – do come and take a few photos of me with my family.'

She gave Holly a mischievous wink. 'What? We've all been thinking it for months.'

As the twins posed miraculously beside Holly and Taffy, with Elsie tucked in beside them and Eric sitting at their feet, the evening sun cast gentle shadows and the light was just flawless. 'Now *that's* a shot for the mantelpiece if ever I saw one,' said Elsie happily.

'I'll be saying a few little words before everyone gets squiffy by the way, so don't send the boys upstairs too soon. I want to mention you all in dispatches.' Elsie threw up her hands in glee and a selection of diamond bracelets slithered down her slender arms. 'Now, Holly, I'm banking on you to ply me with ginger ale and the odd aspirin. I want to party like there's no tomorrow, understood?'

'Understood,' Holly managed, still wobbly with emotion from the 'family' photo. As they made their way through the crowd of friends, patients, and colleagues, Holly and Taffy barely made it two yards without somebody saying well done on the interview. In Larkford it seemed, nobody actually needed to read a newspaper to know everybody else's business. It was something Holly had struggled to get used to when she first moved here, but now she couldn't imagine it any other way. It wasn't just nosiness, as she'd first assumed; it was very much a desire to feel connected and supported.

Lizzie lurched into view with an incredibly excitable Labrador puppy on a lead. Her usual stylish layers had been replaced by a neat quilted gilet and a clip-on bag of doggie treats. The beaming smile on her face more than made up for the lack of sartorial elegance. 'Meet Roger,' she said in delight. 'I'm in charge of socialising him.' She sounded euphoric and her ever-tolerant husband Will stood beside her, looking frankly relieved to have his wife back on sparkling form.

'And when they said socialising,' Holly teased, 'did they actually mean champagne and canapés?'

Lizzie shrugged. 'Probably not, but then any assistance dog living around here, needs to get used to the high life.'

'Quite right,' interrupted Reverend Taylor, wandering over to stroke Roger's ears. Her own little terrier, Dibley, had been banished from all public events, due to his propensity to mate or mutilate, but Eric and Coco were happily frolicking on Elsie's perfectly manicured lawn with a Frisbee. 'I should have socialised Dibley a little bit more and then he wouldn't be quite so keen to be the centre of attention.' She gave Taffy a nudge. 'Speaking of which, you can't hide forever, young man.'

Blousy Betsy Harrington made her way across the grass towards them, her red patent heels sticking in the soft lawn with every pace. 'Cooeee, Dr Jones?'

Holly tried not to laugh as Taffy visibly shrank back beside her. Winning the Duck Race was obviously a case of 'be careful what you wish for'.

'Betsy!' said Reverend Taylor. 'Have you come to claim your prize?'

'I have indeed,' said Betsy. 'I'm in *desperate* need of some help with my herbaceous borders.' She gave Taffy a slow wink as she walked away with a flirty little wave, which just left him utterly confused, as though this might be yet another filthy euphemism that had passed him by.

'Oh no, Dr Jones, rest easy,' said Reverend Taylor, spotting his expression. 'She really is a very keen gardener and has rather a thing for older gentlemen. Much older. Positively geriatric.'

'I just don't understand women at all, do I?' said Taffy, wandering off grumpily in search of cider and predictable, uncomplicated male company.

It was almost shocking how quickly the party descended into well-lubricated chaos. Dan, Jamie and Taffy had soon abandoned their ties and jackets and were entertaining children and dogs alike with their well-honed circus skills. What Jamie Yardley couldn't do with a set of juggling balls, didn't look worth knowing.

Grace pressed another glass of fizz into Holly's hand.

'They're just big kids really,' she said. 'It's good to see them letting off steam.'

Holly couldn't agree more – the last few weeks seemed to have placed a strain on all of them.

'Jamie's rather lovely, isn't he?' said Holly, watching Grace's reaction carefully and wondering whether he was the reason that Grace's eyes were firmly fixed on the entertainment.

Grace nodded, noncommittally. 'He's a sweet lad. And I keep telling young Alice – there's nothing wrong with mixing business with a little pleasure, so long as you're both on the same song-sheet.'

'Alice and Jamie?' Holly clarified.

Grace smiled. 'Well, not yet – but give it a little time . . .'

Holly didn't dare say any more. There was more chemistry in Elsie's garden this evening than *A Midsummer Night's Dream*. Holly could only hope that she didn't end up as Bottom.

Little tiny tea-light lanterns decked the garden and apple trees and there were strains of Mozart wafting through the French doors. The waves of laughter and conversation billowed around her, as her children giggled and shrieked at their games. Holly breathed deeply, the aroma of sweet peas never far away in Elsie's garden.

'And what about you?' Holly asked, deliberately leaving her question open.

Grace shrugged easily. 'I'm okay. I'm just following my feet at the moment – I want to see where they take me.'

It was such an obscure, hippy-dippy thing for super-organised Grace to say, that Holly wondered if perhaps she'd been overdoing the down-faced dog of late.

'Heads up!' called Dan loudly across the garden, as the Frisbee hurtled towards them on an unstoppable trajectory. Grace barely missed a beat, seamlessly passing Holly her champagne flute with one hand and stepping forward, once, twice, three times, to catch it neatly before it could obliterate the buffet table. Balanced on one foot, over-reaching, Grace froze, just as Dan skidded to a halt beside her.

Catching her around the waist, they both paused for a moment, as though to regain their equilibrium. 'You're making a habit of saving the day at the moment, Gracie,' Dan said quietly, his hands still circling her, even as they now stood face to face, both feet firmly on the ground. Grace's reach had been so instinctive, she looked almost surprised to find herself standing there, her eyes widening as she registered their sudden intimacy.

Dan reached forward and brushed a small lock of hair away from her face, his eyes never once leaving hers. 'Where would I be without you?' he asked. He leaned in slowly and kissed her gently on the cheek, oblivious to the murmurings of interest and speculation rippling through the guests around them. Grace's lips parted involuntarily, as Dan looked longingly at her mouth. This was no kiss between friends; the atmosphere between them was suddenly charged with an emotional electricity.

A wolf-whistle from the Major shattered the moment, even as Marion took him to task for being so insensitive. Within seconds, it was as though it had never even happened, the boys sweeping Dan and the Frisbee back into the game, his gaze repeatedly seeking out Grace.

'Did I . . . I mean, was that . . . ?' managed Grace, with an almost wistful expression, as Holly returned her champagne flute and she downed it in one.

'Well,' said Holly, unable to suppress the enormous smile on her face. 'You did say you wanted to see where your feet would take you . . .'

Grace looked across the garden, her focus on Dan absolute. 'I did, didn't I?' she said slowly.

'Are you having a lovely time, darlings?' asked Elsie exuberantly, completely missing the mood as she materialised at their side.

Holly leaned down and kissed her papery cheek. 'It's perfect,' she said simply. 'A perfect way to celebrate, well, everything really. Best pre-launch pre-advance party, ever.'

Elsie stood between them, tucking her frail arms through theirs. 'Thank you for giving me a kick up the derrière, Holly. I had forgotten how special each and every day could be, given the right motivation.' Elsie rested her head on Holly's shoulder, as they watched Taffy dive for the Frisbee and stand up covered in grass stains, to much cheering.

'Promise me, you two, you won't let stubbornness and fear ruin *your* happy endings,' Elsie said quietly, a note of challenge to her voice. Standing side by side, arms interlocked, there was no reading the expression on her face, but Holly stiffened almost imperceptibly.

'Oh, for goodness' sake,' chided Elsie at her reaction. 'If it doesn't work out, you can always get divorced!' she added flippantly.

Holly felt a burning flare of anger at the very idea. 'I could *never* leave Taffy,' she said with such vehemence, that she surprised even herself, not to mention Grace and Elsie.

Elsie said nothing, but as Holly turned to confront her, she just looked quietly smug. 'Well then, you've got your answer haven't you, my darling. It's time to stop fannying around.' Grace stepped tactfully away, waving her empty glass as an excuse, still looking thoughtful and distracted.

Holly wobbled for a moment then, Elsie's comments unwittingly echoing the circles her mind had been chasing all afternoon. 'I think it might be too late,' she whispered, as the other guests ebbed and flowed around them. 'I've dodged this conversation so many times with him, Elsie. I think he's actually given up on me.' She frowned as Roger the puppy broke free of his lead and dived into the game with gusto. 'Unless you felt like giving him a nudge?' she said hopefully.

'Oh, Holly! Have I taught you nothing? You're not a Disney princess waiting to be rescued – you know what you want now, ask him for it!'

Holly watched Lizzie join in the fray, as Roger paraded round the garden with Elsie's prize delphiniums in his mouth. 'You mean *I* should propose to *him*?' she whispered dubiously.

Elsie just smiled enigmatically and leaned in to kiss her, squeezing her arms gently as she did so, before walking off without a word.

What was the point in having a bossy mentor, if they didn't tell you what to do when it really mattered, wondered Holly crossly.

She sipped quietly at her flute of champagne, relieved to be on the periphery for a moment, as Roger bounded through the garden upending chairs and drinks as he bounced joyfully around the lawn with half the guests in hot pursuit.

Her heart gave a heavy flip at the idea that, amongst all the recent chaos, she somehow hadn't made time to let Taffy know how important he was to her happiness. Strike that, she thought, in a moment of champagne-fuelled feistiness, as she drained her glass – crucial was probably more like it.

As though he could sense her gaze, Taffy looked up and smiled, taking an unfortunate Frisbee to the chest as he did so. Distraction was never really an option when playing with the boys.

*

Holly had to admit it; Elsie could throw a party like no other. The waves of gentle laughter ebbed and flowed amongst the summer blooms and there was an almost surreal quality to the evening, as though real life had been suspended for a few hours, simply so they could all enjoy each other's company.

As Dan escorted Elsie to a chaise-longue under the willow tree and she continued to entertain and delight her guests, Lizzie pulled on Holly's sleeve. 'I'm going to take Roger home before he can eat the rest of the buffet,' she said, still grinning and completely unfazed that her golden puppy was now covered in streaks of beetroot. 'Fancy a walk with Eric in the morning?'

Holly smiled and pulled her friend into an enormous hug, cheered beyond measure by this small sign of a return to normality. 'I would love that,' she said with feeling.

Lizzie just rolled her eyes at the disproportionate emotion and pinched Holly's glass. 'Enough of that for you this evening, madam. Can't have you behaving recklessly, now can we? That's my job. Night night.'

Holly watched her walk away, Will's arm thrown lovingly around Lizzie's shoulders as Roger boinged between their legs. Unaccountably, Holly felt the prickle of tears in her eyes and she had to swallow hard. Looking around Elsie's garden, everyone she loved was here – old and young, kids, dogs and chaos aplenty. This was her true home and, she realised, there was actually only one thing missing.

Dodging an errant Frisbee, she walked across to Taffy. 'Can I borrow you for a moment,' she said.

Inside the house there was a sudden hush, as the noise and the heat of the evening outside was left behind. The other-worldly sensation remained though, as Holly walked along the flagstone hall, the echoing retort of her heels as unusual as the swish of silk against her legs. Tiny dust motes hung suspended in shafts of sunlight and yet more sweet peas released their perfume into the air.

She stopped for a moment, trembling slightly, but unable to conceal the dancing delight in her eyes at what she was about to do. 'Come here you,' she said, taking Taffy's hand gently, 'there's something I want to ask you.'

A volley of shouts and laughter rang out in the house, as Jason chased Lucy past them in the hallway, threatening her with full retribution for daring to ruffle his perfect hair. There was no mistaking the flirtation between them and Holly and Taffy were forced to step back and press themselves against the wall.

Taffy curled his fingers through Holly's. 'Let's pop in here,' he said, a private smile nudging at his lips.

He gently pushed open the door to Elsie's favourite sitting room and Holly's breath caught in her throat. A vast silver bowl of ice supported a magnum of champagne, two glasses and a small bowl of Orange Clubs. She couldn't help but laugh – there were only two people in Larkford that this could possibly be destined for.

'Surprise,' he said quietly, watching and waiting for her reaction.

Seeing his nerves only strengthened her resolve. There really was no time like the present to start living and loving the life she truly wanted.

As the door swung closed behind him, Taffy spoke, warmth and affection layered into his every word, 'Actually, there was something I wanted to ask you too.'

In his outstretched hand was a small antique box and nestling inside was an exquisite diamond ring. A very special diamond ring, that Holly recognised instantly. Her eyes filled with tears, as he dropped to one knee. 'But I was going to ask you . . .' she managed.

'Let me?' Taffy said seriously. 'Please?'

It was one thing to lead, not follow, thought Holly in that moment, but somehow this made more sense. Taffy asking made sense. Even if only to reassure this gorgeous, wonderful man that the anxious look on his face was completely unwarranted.

'I know we said we'd wait,' said Taffy, 'but I have important things to say. The first and most crucial of which, is that I love you, Holly.'

'I love you too,' said Holly, earning herself a stern gaze.

'For the love of God, Graham, would you just be quiet for a moment and let a man propose?'

She pressed a trembling hand to her lips to cover the smile that was in danger of breaking into laughter. All the things she had wanted to tell Taffy when she asked him this very question would apparently have to wait. Maybe sometimes it was okay to wait her turn.

'As I was saying,' Taffy said, knowing only too well that his window of opportunity was small, but determined to say his piece. 'I love you. I love Tom and Ben and Eric and Elsie and your mad best friend. I love everything about our life together, except for one thing.' He took her hand in his. 'I would very much like to be a husband and a father and spend all my days with you. Officially. I'd rather like to stand up and tell the world . . . if that's what you want too?'

Holly nodded, for once in her life, completely lost for words. This was so unprecedented that Taffy actually looked worried for a moment. 'Is that a yes?'

'Yes,' Holly whispered, as Taffy slipped Elsie's beautiful heirloom ring on to her finger.

He leaned in to answer the question before she could ask

it, 'And in case you're wondering why Elsie's vintage corker is currently decorating your finger, I can only say that she wouldn't take no for an answer once she knew what I was saving up for.'

Holly glanced at the ring, entranced for a moment as the diamonds threw a scatter of sunbeams against the wall. It was perfect.

'I love it,' she said simply. 'I love you.'

He smiled and kissed her with a longing and intimacy, that made Holly think of honeymoons and crisp white sheets, before folding her into his arms.

Taking a moment in each other's silence, she allowed herself to embrace the truth – he wasn't just her love, Taffy Jones was The Love – the one she wanted to spend the rest of her life with, to build a family with.

For Holly, family was not about blood, but about choices.

And she chose Taffy, with all her heart.

When she looked into Taffy's eyes, she saw her future there. There would be love and fun and undoubtedly chaos, but they would handle it together.

There was a hammering on the door and the scuffling of small feet on the flagstones outside. 'Did he do it yet?' shouted Ben in excitement.

'Did you say yes?' interrupted Tom, his voice high with eagerness.

Holly burst out laughing, the tears of joy streaming down her face. 'You told them?'

Taffy shook his head. 'God, no,' he replied seriously, kissing her lightly, 'I asked them.'

'Well, thank goodness they said yes too then,' she replied, with a playful smile, as she stood up to welcome them in, and the celebrations could really begin.

Acknowledgements

This book is brought to you by The Dream Team at Simon & Schuster – I simply cannot thank them enough for their warmth, guidance and friendship:

Jo Dickinson – thank you for loving Larkford as much as I do and helping me refine and polish the mad world in my head. Sara-Jade Virtue and Jess Barratt – thank you for your endless enthusiasm in spreading the word and making it such fun. Emma Capron – thank God you're so organised, or this book would still be pages of proofs adorned by my coffee rings! Laura Hough, Dominic Brendon, Sal Wilks, Louise Blakemore and Joe Roche – I owe you many cocktails for always going the extra mile, and for always making me smile.

My wonderful agent Cathryn Summerhayes has made the 'business' of writing an absolute pleasure and I'm over the moon to have become part of the Curtis Brown family. May there be many adventures ahead . . .

And, although my first book *Out Of Practice* was widely available, there have to be a few special mentions to those who outdid themselves in supporting my debut: John Weeks and his team at Cirencester Waterstones have kept me in caffeine, books and moral support all year and I am so grateful; and Pete Selby of Sainsbury's deserves a huge thank you for championing both my work and my cocktail consumption.

Katie Fforde, Nikki Owen, Caroline Sanderson, Jo Thomas and AJ Pearce – our lunches and coffees have been a source of so much fun, but also support, as I find my path in this wonderful world of publishing. I owe you gin! Always.

Likewise, without the kindness and support of the RNA, the world of Larkford would still be bumbling around in my head and I thank you for all the fabulous work you do and the welcoming sense of community from your members.

Percy Lawson – you have now been immortalised in print and I hope you like your character! Thank you so much for bidding at Natalie's Blue Belle Ball, raising money for hospice care and also giving me the opportunity to have some fun with your name into the bargain.

There are two special Emmas in my life who deserve a mention, both of whom make me laugh like a drain and were both inspirational in writing this book, whether advising on how assistance dogs are trained, sharing funny anecdotes or simply making me smile when the words weren't flowing. Thank you both – you're fabulous!

Lastly, but by no means least, the endless tolerance of Mr P, my children and The Ginger Ninja is not to be understated. I'm perfectly aware that living with a writer can't be easy – the constant flutter of Post-its, the far away expression that means I'm not really listening, the distracted scribbling of an idea not to be forgotten… Thank you for your endless patience and support – know that I love you madly and couldn't undertake this crazy journey without you.

Px

BANYAN TREE
· VABBINFARU ·

WIN A HOLIDAY OF A LIFETIME AT BANYAN TREE VABBINFARU IN THE MALDIVES!

Included in the prize:

- A seven night stay at Banyan Tree Vabbinfaru in a Beachfront Pool villa for two people

- Full board basis, incl. soft drinks, excl. alcohol

- Return transfers from Male to Banyan Tree Vabbinfaru

- Two × return economy flights from London to Male up to a value of £700 per person

- Trip to be taken between 1 November 2017 and 30 April 2018 Blackout dates include 27 December 2017 – 5 January 2018